Abroad

The Hellum and Neal Series in LGBTQIA+ Literature

BOOK ONE

Liz Jacobs

The Hellum & Neal Series in LGBTQIA+ Literature
Brain Mill Press | Green Bay, Wisc.

Published in the United States by Brain Mill Press.
Print ISBN 978-1-942083-62-7
EPUB ISBN 978-1-942083-65-8
MOBI ISBN 978-1-942083-63-4
PDF ISBN 978-1-942083-64-1

Cover art by Megan J. Smith.
Cover design by Ampersand Book Covers.

www.brainmillpress.com

To all my fellow immigrant kids

Nick stared out the plane window, knowing he was being abominably rude and still unable to help himself.

"So, tell me a bit about your family. Why didn't you go to Israel instead of the States?"

Nick shut his eyes and leaned back in his seat. *Because none of your business? Because why are we even talking right now? Because screw this, that's why?*

By the time he looked at his motherly neighbor lady, he hoped his smile was more polite. "Didn't make the cut, I suppose."

She pursed her lips. "Well, that's a shame. It's important, you know, for your people to head to the homeland, so to speak. I've always been a big advocate."

Yeah, Nick had picked up on that. His luck that he'd be stuck next to a surprise "Jews, go to your island" lady, which had sort of derailed his plan of spending the whole flight sleeping or playing mindless games on his phone. He either needed to be unconscious or putting together jigsaw puzzles, or he would vibrate right off his seat.

"Yeah, well," he said, unsure how to respond to something seemingly well-meaning wrapped in blatant anti-Semitic rhetoric. *Of course* his parents had tried for Israel first— that's what Russian Jews *did*. Applied for interviews, began to study Hebrew under the cover of darkness, told their curious children that those were Chinese textbooks. Got denied, all three times. Eventually gave up and, on a lark, threw their lot in with those clamoring to get out at all, even if it meant America.

"Well, you should obviously do Birthright," the woman said.

Nick wished he could remember her name, but he'd been sort of running on autopilot when she'd sat down next to him, and while he remembered giving *his* name, he couldn't recall her introduction. She was just Unexpectedly Anti-Semitic Missionary Woman now.

And Nick was probably Unexpectedly Rude Russian-Jewish Boy in Need of Saving.

Knowing that he would probably never see her again and being up thousands of feet in the air gave him the perverse courage to be honest, even if it meant opening up another door he'd rather remained shut. "I've thought about it, but it doesn't seem to be for me."

As expected, she was shocked. *Shocked.* "Why not?" Her eyes grew genuinely huge, and her mouth did a turning-down thing that reminded him sharply of his mom. "You're only, what, eighteen? Nineteen?"

"Twenty," he supplied automatically.

"Plenty of time, and you'd get to know where your people come from. I advocate this on all my missions. Such an important part of your heritage."

Nick was tired. Tired and wired, actually, so he wanted to pick at this like a child. He had nothing to prove, but he couldn't help himself. "My people came from Poland," he told her. "And Ukraine."

"You know what I mean, honey," she said, smiling and undeterred. "But it's okay, you've got time."

Nick gave up. "Sure." He stretched a little, bumping his knees against the tray table, then lifted it out of the way, secured it with the little latch. It felt greasy on his skin. He wiped his thumb on his jeans. Then he crossed his arms over his chest and lay back as far as the seat would allow, compounding the rudeness. If he were on the ground, he would probably be cringing at his behavior.

The recycled air of the plane was cold and dry on his face. He wanted to shut off the AC knob, but he didn't want to move again and disturb the silence that finally descended between him and his neighbor.

He fell asleep with his knees digging holes in the plastic seat in front of him.

✛

All around him, movement. Overhead luggage compartments thumped as they were relieved of their overstuffed contents, phones chimed and came back to life, and *sorry's* and *excuse me's* echoed all around. Tension and urgency after being suspended in the air for seven hours.

"Now, here, let me write down my name and email, all right?" his neighbor lady said. She had a little notebook in her hands, and he watched her scribble everything down. His first instinct was to politely refuse, but the better part of valor would be to take the piece of paper quietly, which he did.

"Don't hesitate to contact me, all right? I know you've never been to London, and I worry about you," she said as he pocketed her info. "I'm here for a month, so let's have tea, okay? I know Russians love their tea as much as these Brits."

She was simply full of fun stereotypes. Though, Nick really did love tea. For a moment he even resented that fact.

"I will, thank you," he lied, smiling. He tugged his overstuffed backpack from under the seat and shouldered it.

"And don't just live on Cup Noodles or whatever it is you young people exist on. You're scrawny as it is."

Nick's smile felt brittle, but at last she was turning around and joining the line down the aisle. He guiltily eyed her giant bag. Did she need help negotiating it off the plane or at the airport? Although, with his own giant suitcase waiting for him on the other side, he probably wouldn't have been much help, anyway.

He rubbed a hand over his face and felt along his jaw. He wondered what his hair looked like and if he was the only one getting off the plane reeking of exhaustion.

He was up next, so he scooted himself awkwardly over three seats and let an old man and his granddaughter out before lining up behind. Flight attendants said good-bye in a British accent to everyone who walked past them while Nick kept a firm hold on his backpack straps and eyed the trash left by the other passengers. Magazines, cookie wrappers, headphones. He was marched past the curtained-off area where the other half lived, with individual podlike beds and glasses that had clearly been filled with complimentary alcohol before being abandoned. Emptying planes always reminded him of disaster movies for some reason.

Then he was off the plane and on British soil.

Gray walls vaulted toward the ceiling and ended with glass at the top, sharp corners, all very monotone and quiet. Every sign looked foreign, despite being in English. Though he shuffled behind all the other passengers, Nick's perception of the corridor was a dreamlike emptiness.

The pouch his mom had given him for his passport and boarding passes was damp in his hand. He'd checked its contents three times on the plane, then zipped it up in the backpack, then taken it out again because he thought he'd forget where he'd stuffed it.

He was being ridiculous. Here was a grown-ass man, scared of traveling by himself.

Last time he'd made a transatlantic flight, he'd been ten, his hand gripped firmly by his mom, and JFK had been in utter chaos. He thought it might have been under partial construction at the time. He remembered colorful balloons with hearts on them greeting someone at the gates. He remembered the four-hour wait at border control, standing behind a pregnant woman who'd been on their flight, and his mom leading her to the bathrooms as she sniffled and blew her nose into Nick's dad's handkerchief. She couldn't have been older than he was now.

He felt like he might jitter out of his skin.

He took out his phone with sweaty hands. He couldn't afford to keep himself on his mom's plan, so this was strictly for Wi-Fi and emergencies. He'd need to figure out a more permanent solution soon, but he couldn't think about that now or he'd—yeah. Not thinking about anything but the customs line and keeping track of his passport.

When his phone woke up, it was on Ann Arbor time. It was still the middle of the night.

Heathrow kindly offered him forty-five minutes of complementary Wi-Fi if he watched an ad, which he did dutifully while yawning. The Wi-Fi chugged slowly, but he could at least send his mom and sister an email telling them he'd landed and then check his bank account, just in case.

Every now and then he'd shove his backpack forward as the line shuffled ahead.

Forty-five minutes later he was handing his passport and boarding pass to a tired-looking customs lady who asked him—in a British accent; someday he'd probably get used to that, but not today—if he was here on business or pleasure. She eyed him pretty heavily. It took him a moment to figure out why before he remembered the *born in* field in his passport.

So many reminders today.

"School." Belatedly, he handed her the customs slip he'd filled out on the plane.

"And where are you staying?"

Sharp eyes softened by a practiced casual voice. Nick swallowed, wondering what would happen if she decided for whatever reason he wasn't trustworthy. "In a dorm." Right. He cleared his throat and gave her the actual address. "Ma'am."

"Do you have your return flight information, Mr. Melnikov?"

Nick was blessed with an obsessive-compulsive mother. After some fumbling in his backpack—*Take these on the plane with you in case your luggage gets lost. And take a toothbrush, too. Oh, and Pepto. Na vsiakiy sluchay*—he managed to tug out his flight reservation printout. Scary customs lady took it from him wordlessly.

"Welcome to London, Mr. Melnikov," she told him eventually, after stamping the shit out of his passport. "Next, please!"

Suddenly released, he gathered up all the papers she'd thrust at him and legged it out of there before she could take it back.

+

The rest of the journey, he was at once aware of everything he had to do and completely separate from it. It felt like when dawn intruded on his all-nighters, illuminating the papers strewn around and his laptop groaning under the weight of all the tabs and Word documents. He had written those words, but he couldn't quite remember *how*.

When he emerged from underground, his arms were ready to fall off. He had packed for a nine-month stay, but even so, the weight of his belongings felt excessive.

He pulled out a map. Embarrassing, but necessary. London surrounded him on all sides, but he couldn't appreciate that fact yet. Pulling himself out of the way of jostling locals, he stared at it.

After several accidental detours and backward walks, it began to make sense. He desperately needed to pee, and to sleep, and to stop feeling like he was driving the wrong way down a one-way street. It took him an embarrassingly long time to stop looking for street signs on the actual street instead of the buildings.

His dorm appearing around the corner—clearly labeled and everything—was such a relief, he nearly burst into tears. Putting his bags down on the floor once he'd wrestled them through the heavy glass doors was a satisfaction previously unknown to mankind.

What was even better, however, was seeing the smiling girl wearing a lanyard and holding an iPad, greeting the incomers.

"Heya!" she said. *British accent. British accent!* "Are you here to check in?"

Numb, Nick nodded. "Yeah, uh, hi." It had been a while since he had to worry about how out of place and wrong his accent sounded. "Do you need my last name or proof of anything? I was told to just come here and—"

"Sure, yeah—you're one of our twenty international students, I believe," she said, looking down at her iPad while Nick felt the creeping of his blush begin somewhere in the vicinity of his chest. He waited until she looked back up to give her his name, and then spell it out after she gave him an apologetic, sheepish grin. "Melnikov, sure...Oh, there you are. Nikolay?"

"Nick," he said, then stuck his hands into his pockets.

"That's a cool name, where's that from?"

She was pretty, Nick noticed. Wide gray eyes, dimples on her cheeks, a dusting of freckles across her nose. He might not have noticed her on the street, but standing here, having a conversation, her simple features sort of forced him to look twice.

"Russian."

"Oh!" She looked back down. "It says here you're coming from Ann Arbor in Michigan..."

"Yep," he confirmed, nodding. He resigned himself to having this conversation several dozen more times in the near future. "We immigrated. A while back."

"Oh, cool." She smiled at him, and then he watched as she clearly remembered why he was there in the first place. While she fished through the tote on her shoulder, he stood there with bags at his feet and let her speech roll over him like a warm wave. "Right, so...This is your key," she said, handing it over, "and these are the instructions on the Wi-Fi and such. If you log into the system, it'll take you through the steps of all of that. You can create your email from there, too—it's all automatic, so you don't have to go to IT or anything." She paused. "Oh, but you can, if you're having trouble with it or whatever."

He accepted the key and the instructions with what was possibly excessive gratitude, but he wasn't really operating on all cylinders anymore. Then he heaved his backpack onto his shoulders and took hold of his suitcase.

"The lifts are just down there." She pointed toward the back. "And oh! I've been ordered on pain of death to tell you all that there's an international student mixer tomorrow night in the blue room of the Student Union. At seven." She smiled, clutching her iPad to her chest. "There's a campus map in the instructions. Welcome to London, yeah?"

Nick smiled back, exceptionally aware of how unshaven and dirty he was, and thanked her again. Then he trudged toward the elevators. *Lifts.*

Right.

The only thing he had any presence of mind to do before falling onto the empty bed was set his alarm to go off in three hours and take out his contacts. Then he balled up his hoodie under his head, which smelled like plane seats, draped a coat over himself he'd extracted from his suitcase, and passed out.

+

He woke up slowly. He should have been focusing on how much his neck hurt because he didn't have a pillow yet, and how he could not even begin to assemble all the crap he'd need just to live like a normal human, and how overwhelmingly huge London seemed now that he was inside it. But he wondered instead what Lena was doing now, and what time it was in Ann Arbor, and whether or not she hated him as much as she'd seemed to, hissing over the phone for him to stop being a whiny dick and just let her get on with her life.

They'd planned on staying together, but a month before leaving Nick had ended it. She'd been pissed. She didn't want to stay friends, she didn't want him to call, she didn't want him to write. She blocked him on Facebook.

Selfishly, for a while, Nick missed her like a sore wound. A week after the breakup, he'd begun to doubt himself. He'd begun to forget, in the way that bodies had of forgetting pain as soon as it dissipated, how being together had suffocated him, like a yoke pulled too tight. Awake at three in the morning, he would think, *maybe if I tried harder, tried more, maybe if I could remember what brought us together in the first place.* He'd think this, and he'd call up her number on his phone the next day, and then he'd stuff it back into his pocket.

Because she was right—once he'd decided it was over, there was no going back. He'd called before he left just to say good-bye. She hadn't liked that.

He blinked and looked around, taking in the details of the room that he'd missed earlier.

It was tiny—cell-like—but it had one distinction few American dorms had: it was a single. It even had its own bathroom. A desk, a set of shelves, and a wardrobe spanned one wall, with the bed barely two feet across from them. A window connected both sides in the small space, and an old-school radiator rattled below. It was utilitarian, drab, and all his own.

He stretched and luxuriated in the secure knowledge that absolutely nobody could walk in on him once he was inside with the door closed.

Then, slowly and laboriously, all thoughts of home pushed firmly to the side, he began the process of unpacking and figuring out his life for the next nine months.

It was possible that Dex should never have agreed to work International Night. But Izzy had looked at him with puppy-dog eyes after Alex had scarpered on her, and Dex could only ever resist her for so long.

Bugger Izzy. Now he was hugging the wall, looking like an utter bellend, while Izzy flittered to and fro, making sure everyone was having an appropriately sociable time. The problem was, Izzy always thought she needed help, when in reality she was capable of doing three people's jobs with zero effort, which was precisely why Alex had bailed on her and Dex was currently going out of his mind with boredom. International Night clearly ran itself. He was meant to be doing stuff like handing out flyers, which Izzy had already done, and making sure people had been provided with name tags, which Izzy had already done, and double-checking that there were enough waters, sodas, and biscuits. Which Izzy had already done.

So now he was stood like a lump in a corner, hands crossed over his chest, scowling at everyone who was busy mingling and chatting each other up, because clearly, International Night really just stood for "an opportune event for pulling each other during emotionally vulnerable times so everybody could regret their choices come morning." At least, that's what it was looking like to Dex. Izzy had taken this project on because of the Italian boy she'd befriended and had a fantastic fuck-fest with last year, but Dex had never had need of this event, so had never been.

He watched a blond guy make a series of inept moves towards a long-haired Asian girl who was not looking terribly impressed with his game. It was entertaining, quickly boring. Two Americans were chatting and gesticulating with crisps and cups of soda. They were boring, too.

He sighed, then fished out his phone. God, he had another two hours to go, at least. Maybe he could claim to have a headache. But Izzy'd see right through him.

"Don't even think about it."

Dex jumped, then glared at where she'd slunk up to him along the wall. "I feel like an idiot, you don't even need me here." He scowled when she grinned at him. "You just enjoy torturing me."

"Bollocks." She was still grinning. His face began to betray him, and his scowl fell off. Izzy stuck a carrot in her mouth and bit it off with a loud snap. "You"—she pointed at him with the bit of it left in her hand—"are just a killjoy. Also, you need to get out more. Enough of being a recluse, I'm tired of watching your pathetic face."

Oh, good, the scowl was firmly back on. "I am not pathetic."

But Izzy was no longer even looking at him. Her gaze turned somewhere beyond Dex, and she got that *face* on her. The face that clearly transmitted the fact that she'd just spotted a bit of dick she'd like to climb.

"Ooooh, dishy dish, two o'clock," she breathed.

Despite himself, Dex turned to where she was looking. The guy was slumped, much like Dex, against a wall, watching the action but removed. Like he was there, but not really there to *be* there. Dex could sympathise. What Dex couldn't understand was why Izzy, of all people, had noticed him.

He looked so...regular. Cute, sure, but nothing like the tall, brooding guys she loved to whip into shape. He was white.

Average height. Dex was pretty sure he had several inches on him. He had a mop of rather crazy light brown curls that weren't really trendy or anything. A hipster, at a stretch, and that wasn't a compliment. And he was skinny, too. So very much not Izzy's type. Nor Dex's, for that matter.

But...Dex watched as the guy took out his own phone, looked down at it, sighed, then folded his arms behind himself and bounced against the wall, chewing his lip. He had nice full lips, as far as Dex could tell. And there was something strangely magnetic about him. He had a pretty profile.

And then he turned towards them, and they made eye contact, and Dex panicked and turned immediately away like the most conspicuous idiot ever.

The guy had *really* beautiful eyes. The second their gazes locked Dex had felt weird and weirdly stupid, because even just one look sort of did stuff to his insides. The guy's eyes were grey and enormous, and they seared through him like an iron poker. What sort of nonsense was he even thinking? *Jesus.*

He became aware of stinging pain before he realized Izzy was slapping his arm with her hand. "Ohhh," she breathed. "He's not for me! Go chat him up! I bet he's Italian and all kinds of intense."

Dex caught her hand in his. "We talked about this," he muttered. "No slapping and no begging or I'm out of here."

"Right, sorry." She didn't look remotely sorry. "It's just look how *adorable*, oh my God."

Dex refused to look. "Then *you* go after him."

"Nope, he's a total poof, just look at him," she said.

Once again, Dex refused to indulge her. "You literally have no idea that's the case. Your gaydar's never functioned properly."

She gave him a withering look. "Did you not see how he looked at you?"

"That's not even a valid mode of enquiry, it was one tiny second."

"An *intense* tiny second."

He gave her a look of his own, then pushed her away. "Haven't you got a thing to do? Go and run your little mixer."

"Tosser," she laughed, then finally, *finally*, whirled away. He loved her, but she could be exhausting.

Dex tried not to indulge himself. He took out his phone, checked his messages. Just one, from Mum, asking him how he was doing. Then, before he knew it, he was looking back at the guy with the hair and the eyes.

Dex had never really gone for tiny white dudes before.

The guy was still stood against the wall, not talking to anyone, which was weird, since this was meant to be a socialisation ritual. He was wearing skinnies, black Chucks, and a soft-looking blue shirt, the sleeves rolled up. Izzy could eat him up and spit him out, and he'd probably thank her for it. Dex was not into boys who looked like a stiff breeze could knock them over.

But he was also not looking away.

Shit. Right.

This was stupid. Dex looked back down at his phone, sent off a quick reply to Mum, then flipped over to Izzy's number, texted her to fuck off and that he'd see her at home, *luv u bye*, then slunk off.

+

He was flipping between ITV and Channel 4 while drinking orange squash in just his pants when Izzy got home. Jonny had fallen asleep on the sofa earlier and after some time of poking Dex's thigh with his toes had gone up to bed. Thursday night as usual.

"Dickhead," she greeted, throwing her keys in the bowl under the mirror and her hat off to somewhere on the floor where it landed with a soft whoosh. "You're on my list," she threw over her shoulder on her way to the kitchen.

"I'm on it every other week!" he reminded her, then decided to settle on an *8 out of 10 Cats* repeat against his better judgement.

Once she was back in the living room with her Corona, Izzy slithered her way into her usual spot between Dex and the sofa arm, which was obnoxious as always, because her elbows poked him in the side and also *accidentally* knocked the remote out of his hands.

"What are we watching?"

"Jimmy Carr's stupid face." Dex shifted to give her more room as she laid her head on his shoulder, squishing his dreads in the process.

"Goody. Where's Jonny?"

"Fell asleep on me."

"Ha. Where's Nat?"

"With Alex."

"The tosser."

"Yes." He petted her ginger curls. "But International Night runs itself."

"It so does not," she grumbled, then grabbed the remote back and flipped over to BBC Two. *BBC at War*, the guide told them. "Ohhh, yay."

Dex switched the channel immediately. "Fuck off, I was here first. Anyway, how did it go?"

"What?"

"The mixer." He shifted.

"Oh, that." He felt her shrug against his shoulder. "Ran itself."

He gave her his best side-eye as she giggled.

"It was a resounding success," she finally pronounced.

"So, dull and pointless."

"Not *totally* dull and pointless." She paused. Dex took another sip of his squash. "Some French boy got off with an American in the corner. That was kind of fun."

"What, did everyone watch?"

"I was keeping an eye on the situation," she said haughtily. "She was way too pretty for him, anyway. Texan, I think."

"*Howdy*, cowboy," Dex said, with what he believed to be a pretty good twang, but Izzy made a disgusted noise at it.

"Your American accent is atrocious and embarrassing, please stop trying."

"Your *face* is atrocious and embarrassing."

"Shut the fuck up." She settled more firmly against him, nudging him in the spleen. "Who's on, anyway?"

Dex squinted at the telly. "Well, that's Mel Gied-whatever over there, I think."

"My once and future wife," Izzy said dreamily, and then promptly fell asleep on his shoulder.

What he enjoyed about living with these arseholes was that nobody actually minded it when he drank squash half-dressed on the shared sofa. And he didn't mind that they were arseholes.

+

Term began not with a bang but with a whimper, as far as Dex was concerned. Year three modules were no joke, and now came the time Dex had been vaguely dreading: research project. He had waffled between doing that or the investigative project, had gone back and forth on it with his advisor and with Alex, who had largely listened to him and then told him to go with his gut. He wound up deciding that he was more into doing his own lab work and experimenting than going over someone else's research and thus tying himself firmly to the unknown.

18

Of course, he would be lucky if he got out of the lab to eat and sleep and piss.

"Why am I doing this?" he asked, trudging next to Alex to his second lecture of the day.

"Because the world needs your brain," Alex said in the tone of a wearied man who'd said these things before. He then threw his cigarette on the ground, stomped it out, picked it up, and proceeded to chuck it into the nearest bin. One fluid movement. "Also, we're all idiots, why does anyone do anything?"

"You should've done a philosophy course, man."

Alex had been Dex's first friend at uni, back when he was just a young innocent queer nerd who wanted to study molecules and shag half of London all in one go. Alex had also been Dex's first uni crush, being tall, dark, and everything handsome, but his unfortunate and staunch heterosexuality had taken care of that diversion pretty fast.

"But then who would cure cancer?" Alex grinned and ran up the hall steps. "C'mon, lover, membrane proteins await."

Dex threw him the two-finger salute and trotted in after him, but secretly he felt a sort of bubbling anticipation in his belly. He fucking loved this shit.

Later, he was getting ready for a truly wild night of bedroom, laptop, research, and lager when Natali knocked, didn't wait for an answer, and slunk in.

"What the bloody hell are you doing?" she asked, gasping and looking at him with wide eyes.

Dex raised an eyebrow. "Please don't tell me that in year three you still don't know what revising looks like."

She gave him an eyebrow of her own and swept her fringe off her face. This hairstyle was new. Izzy's doing, of course. It looked pretty awesome—longer on top, drooping over one eye, buzzed on the sides and back. If Dex knew Nat, it would be dyed green in a day or two. She never could settle into her natural dark brown. "It's the first day of classes, you wanker."

She grabbed his wallet from the dresser and shoved it into her own back pocket easy as you like. "But it's the first night of our last year at uni, and we are going down to the pub to mourn-slash-celebrate." She tucked her fingers into her pockets and stared him down.

He wasn't sure why he was pretending that he didn't want to go out. Obviously he did. He could probably ignore that scratching of guilt for not immediately deciding on a research topic for a night, right?

"Fine." He closed his laptop.

"Good." She grinned, her cheeks dimpled in that Natali way. She slipped his wallet back out and chucked it at him. "Let's go."

He bumped her shoulder on the way out the door a bit more firmly than usual, she retaliated even harder, and then they both nearly tripped while Jonny watched them impassively from the bottom of the stairs, swinging his key ring around. "Ready, are you?"

Natali picked herself up and threw an arm around Dex. "Steph, Alex, and Izzy are meeting us there. Oh!" She turned to Dex. "Iz says she's got a special surprise for you! What d'you think that's all about?"

Dex stopped in his tracks and looked at her. "A surprise? For me?"

Natali nodded, looking curious.

"Oh, bollocks," was all Dex could say.

3

Nick had managed to find a pillow and a comforter—well, a *duvet*, with a cover—and even a set of sheets. He was pretty proud. He'd been spectacularly out of it that first day. But he had walked into a store and trudged up and down the aisles until he found bedding, and even managed not to fuck up the pin-and-chip thing at checkout.

And now he had a bed he could actually sleep in, a brand-spanking-new student ID, a set of classes to attend, and it was all very confusing, but he was okay with that.

Because he was in London.

Now that it had been three days and he was no longer a zombie dragging a giant suitcase behind him with a dead arm, he could appreciate that fact. The city wasn't exactly what he'd been expecting, he supposed. Maybe he just hadn't found the parts of it that would meet his expectations. Then again, if your expectations were more or less created by watching British romantic comedies with your mother and sister, he supposed those would be difficult to live up to. No Colin Firth, for one. The streets seemed both narrower than he'd expected and wider in scope. It was more pedestrian and more wondrous than he could ever have predicted.

It was weird, the things he found fascinating. Like how the windows opened outward instead of up and down like in Ann Arbor. The stores carried brands he'd never seen before, and the milk was packaged differently from home. He'd had to figure out his food situation, so he'd walked into the nearest Tesco and probably looked like a complete idiot, just staring at all the stuff that was new to him. It wasn't as if he'd never seen butter before. But it came in tubs here, and some of it was actually Irish, and he had grinned as he grabbed it. Then he'd gone searching for anything else he might reasonably be able to cook for himself, which largely consisted of eggs (which weren't in the refrigerator section, he noted), cheese, bread, and various cold cuts.

It was a loose definition of "cook."

He'd spent a while perusing the juice section, attempting to figure out what the hell Ribena could be, and then he'd bought out half of the chocolate section and all the Earl Grey he could carry.

Then he'd gone back to the dorm and investigated the kitchen situation, at which point he'd realized he would need, like, cooking implements.

He'd even figured out his phone solution, and now had access to data and voice that wouldn't cost him an arm and a leg. His mom called once every day, as she woke up.

Now he sat on the bed and dialed Zoya's number.

"Bratishka, wazzzuuuuuuuuup!"

God, she was embarrassing.

It was sort of easier for them to speak in English nowadays, even though she had been older than him when they left. Whenever Mom caught them at it, she'd give them her most disappointed look over the rim of her glasses and they'd immediately switch, but she wasn't here, so after Nick's initial "privet," they went straight to English.

"Have you acquired life necessities yet?" Her familiar accent set him at ease. He could hear other voices in the background. She was always surrounded by people. It had been like that back in Moscow, and it was the same now in

Ann Arbor. Nick had never understood her ability to simply walk into any social situation and stay afloat.

Even when they'd started American school, she'd been fine. It was Nick who'd fallen apart.

"I have everything a growing boy might need," he told her. "I even bought a frying pan."

"You have no idea how to cook. Like, literally, you've never cooked a single thing in your life."

"Hey, I can learn. I learn things." He thought about it. "I've made you eggs before."

"Mmm-hmm, 'kay. Well, just don't starve. Have you had fish and chips yet? What about haddock? Trifle? Scones? Oooh, a nice *spotted dick*?"

She was on a roll of amusing herself, so Nick let her tire herself out, then said, "I bought Irish butter, does that count?"

"Why is Irish butter so adorable?"

"It *is*, right?" Nick laughed, feeling weirdly light.

She giggled, then went quiet for a bit. "Hey, uh, I wasn't sure if I should tell you, but I ran into Lenka yesterday."

"Oh." Nick looked down. His left sock was getting a hole straight through the big toe.

"Yeah, she actually stopped to talk to me. Said...to say hi." A clearing of a throat. "To you."

Nick shrugged, then realized she wouldn't see him. "Thanks."

"Yeah. Maybe she thought it was safe now you're out of the country." She sounded tentative, like she wasn't sure if she was allowed to make jokes yet or not.

Nick kept picking at his sock.

"Sorry, I just thought maybe you should know," she rushed on. "Eto nichego?"

"Nichego, Zoykin."

"You know," she said after a while, the voices in the background receding. "You never really said what happened there…I mean, one minute everything seems fine, and then I get back from California and you've broken up…"

"I…" He sighed. Words refused to get past his throat. "Can we not…right now?"

She huffed out a breath, but he knew it wasn't really annoyance. "Fine. It's all right. I'll get it out of you eventually."

"That's fine. Eventually's fine." It wasn't. She would never get it out of him.

"Good."

"Fine."

"Shut the hell up." She laughed, sounding just a tad too forced. "Anyway, sorry. What else you got for me? Meet any cool people yet?"

Nick sucked in his lower lip as he thought. "Sort of…a couple. I dunno."

"You don't know what, if they're people?"

"Shut up. No, just…I went to this international night, I guess, for those who are, you know…"

"I am guessing international."

"Right, so I went and left pretty quickly." He waited to see if she'd say anything, but she was just listening, so he went on. "But there were a few people I talked to." One was a guy from LA who hadn't held Nick's interest in any way, then an Italian boy named Antonio who made every head turn as he walked by. Nick couldn't tell if Antonio had noticed this himself, but he'd had that glow about him. The sort of glow that marked someone out as a higher class of human than the rest. Nick didn't talk to him for long. It had been loud, and Antonio's accent had been hard for Nick to catch in the din. The entire time Nick talked to him, he'd had this sneaking suspicion that he was being indulged. Nick hated being indulged.

And then there'd been the English girl who seemed to be the one running everything. She'd been wearing a floppy black hat that should have looked stupid but didn't on her, and she'd come up to Nick and completely caught him off guard by asking for his number and texting him before he could say, "No, thank you." Not that he would have said no, necessarily, but it had felt a bit like being railroaded by a very pretty, full-figured redheaded train in a short black dress.

Or something.

Anyway, he had a text from her on his phone to meet her at the union tonight at eight. Nick had no idea why.

"Aaaaand?"

"And what? It's been three days, give me a break."

"God, you're difficult." Nick heard Jake's voice calling her name. "Hang on, it's Nick," she called back. "Sorry. We're going to brunch, and waffles wait for no man or whatever."

"Jake does love his waffles." Nick sort of wanted to get off the phone and felt a bit bad about it.

"He can wait. Anyway, what else should I ask you?"

She always said this. It was a family habit, and if he took the time to think about it, which he sometimes did, Nick realized that it was a truly weird way of asking someone about their life.

He shrugged. "Nothing more, honestly. Just settling in."

"Hmm. All right." She sounded dubious, but like she was conceding the point. "I'll call in a few days. Maybe we can Skype, too? I'm going over to Mom's on Sunday."

Nick agreed on a time, and then he sat on his bed and considered the insane notion of going out with people he'd never even had a single conversation with.

+

"Oh good, you came!"

Nick was incredibly grateful that in her railroading, the girl had saved her number on his phone with her name—Izzy— and he didn't have to use awkward maneuvers to get it out of her. He felt furiously self-conscious in a way he hadn't in ages. His eyes had been itchy with allergies all day, so he'd been forced to wear his glasses, and while he'd kind of made an effort with the rest of his outfit, it was also close to what he'd worn the other night. Like a uniform. He probably looked like a total dweeb, but a lifetime of dweebdom had at least instilled in him a certain ability to move on after the first five minutes of feeling awkward and stupid.

"Um, thanks for the invite," he said, and instantly felt ridiculous again. He smiled to cover it up. He had no idea where they were even going, or why.

"My pleasure!" She beamed at him in return and then nearly gave him a heart attack by grabbing his arm and hooking her hand in his elbow like she'd been doing it all her life. She turned them decidedly away from the Student Union and toward the street. "You looked like a cool dude, and I love meeting new people. So, Nick, right?"

"Uh, right." *Cool? Nick?*

"Whereabouts in America are you from?"

"Michigan," Nick supplied as they power-walked down the street. Maybe it was because she had long legs and was wearing four-inch heels, but Nick was barely keeping up.

"Ohhh, don't know that I know much about Michigan. What cities does it have that I might've heard of?"

Nick thought about it. "Detroit, probably."

Izzy made a knowing "ooooh" sound.

"But I'm from Ann Arbor. It's nice, I guess…Small. Ish. College town." He sounded like a tool. "The state looks like a mitten." Even worse.

Beside him, Izzy giggled. She leaned so close against him as she did it that her hair tickled his cheek. A tiny bit of panic shivered through him. "A mitten? For real?"

Nick shoved the panic down and forced himself to smile, looking at her a bit sideways. "Yeah, I can show you. It's stupid. Just a locals thing." He held up his hand in front of them to demonstrate. "That's what the state sort of looks like."

"That's both ridiculous and endearing." She led the two of them down the street past all the places Nick had already seen but was only now starting to get used to. He'd come from *that* corner on his first day, and he'd walked down *that* side street in search of a grocery store. London was slowly solidifying around him.

She made him nervous. He never did well with people who were so in control of their lives. He could barely tie his own shoes, metaphorically speaking.

"Well, we're here," she declared. They'd walked up to a place called the King's Arms. It had a red door and flowers overflowing from pots hung above the windows. Giddiness swelled up in Nick despite the nerves. *A pub!* He was going to have his first pub experience. He braced himself. "All right, c'mon," Izzy said as she ushered them swiftly through the door.

Inside was dim and decidedly warm. Nick felt itchy all over as his eyes adjusted, but he barely had any time to think before Izzy was grabbing his hand and leading him toward a back booth already filled with people. They all turned as Izzy and Nick approached and erupted into various greetings. Nick had to scramble to keep his glasses on his nose because he was so sweaty they'd slid down.

Jesus, this was a lot of people, and it was a lot of people all at once. He gave a vague hand wave, only just stopping himself from hiding behind Izzy. She towered over him. He could have easily done it.

"Right, everyone, this is Nick! Nick's an international student, he's American, and I wanted him to be our friend. Nick, this is everyone!"

Again, Nick gave a small hand lift and smiled, unable to force his tongue to even say hi. Zoya once told him, *If you smile, even if you don't feel like smiling, you'll feel better. Try it*, and then made him stand there in the middle of a school event and smile until he felt less shaky. It sort of helped then, and it was sort of helping now. He scanned the faces around him as Izzy talked.

"So, this is Natali." She pointed to an Indian girl with a punk sort of haircut. She was thin and what his mom referred to as *angular*, with her pronounced shoulders and collarbones. She wore a ribbed tank top under a flannel shirt and had gauges in her ears along with a bullring piercing in her nose. Nick nearly cowed beneath her intense and curious gaze but managed to hold it more or less steadily.

"Over there is Alex." Alex was a black guy with short-cropped hair and the sort of face that you don't expect to see on a human being in person, pretty much ever. Nick theoretically knew that models and actors and such were actual people who existed in the world and were photographed and walked among peons like Nick, but *Jesus*. He got a hold of himself and gave Alex what he hoped was just a regular, friendly sort of nod.

"This is Steph." Izzy pointed to the girl sitting next to Alex. Nick almost jumped—it was the girl who'd greeted him at the dorm on his first day. How had he not noticed her until now?

She gave him a happy grin over her beer glass. "Hiya, mate. Good to see you again."

"This grumpy dude here is called Dex." Nick half-smiled and gave an aborted hand wave and realized he recognized this boy, too. He'd been at International Night, and when Nick had caught a brief glimpse of him, he'd been looking at Nick.

At the time, he hadn't had enough time to process it before the boy looked away, and now he was sort of starting to wish he'd look away again. If Natali and Alex intimidated him, Dex made Nick feel like he shouldn't be there at all. Nick made every effort not to bolt, and just barely stood his ground. For a brief second, he wanted nothing more than to be back on his bed watching *Downton Abbey*. He pulled himself together.

Grumpy, maybe, but—pretty. Dex was black, too, his face framed by neat dreads, all dark except for the occasional green, blue, and purple. Wide brown eyes watched Nick from under intense eyebrows. It was hard to imagine his full, chiseled mouth relaxed into a smile. Nick broke eye contact and looked at Izzy again, because at least she wasn't making him feel like he was intruding on what had been a perfectly nice time up until now.

"And, finally, this is Jonny," she said breezily, pointing to a blond boy with the kind of face it was hard to picture looking unhappy. He was leaned back in the booth, one arm slung across the back of it, holding a beer in the other hand.

"Hey, there," he said. His voice was sweet and slow like molasses, and Nick liked him immediately.

"Hey." He nodded and vowed to just ignore Grumpy Dex as much as he could.

Nick might not have been a people person, precisely, but Izzy had invited him, and he didn't want to let her down.

"Right." Izzy clapped her hands. "Nat, shove over and let Nick sit, and I'll go get us drinks. Nick, what do you fancy? Lager, ale, cider? Wine, something stronger?"

Nick's mind went blank. Somehow, in all this time, he hadn't even considered he'd have to make a convincingly informed choice of drink. He wasn't twenty-one, and outside of family gatherings and an occasional beer with Lena, he barely drank. He would have rather gnawed his hand off than admit it, though, so he just said, "Oh, lager is fine," and hoped that whatever that was, he'd be able to choke it down.

"Cool." She grinned, then bounded off toward the bar.

Which left Nick alone to sit down among five strangers. He clasped his hands between his knees and smiled at the table in general, hoping the conversation would happen around him and allow him to melt into the booth a bit. It was crowded, and he was pressed up against Natali in a way that was a bit too intimate for a first meeting, but she didn't seem to mind, so Nick willed himself to relax. Deep breaths. He felt his face getting warm but tried to ignore that, too.

"So, Nick, how did you meet Izzy? Was it International Night?" Steph asked.

"Yep." Nick nodded, giving her another smile. He really wanted that drink now.

"Cool." She smiled back.

"And where are you from, exactly?"

This came from Natali, and Nick had to tilt his head at an awkward angle to respond. He gave her the short story. "Michigan."

"Nick's also Russian," Steph supplied from across the table, and everyone turned toward her. "Aren't you?" she said in an encouraging sort of way.

"How the hell do you know?" Alex asked, while Nick felt the uncomfortable pressure in his belly, that familiar bracing for questions.

"I checked him into his hall." Steph shrugged. "He's got a Russian first name. Well, and last, too."

"Go on," Natali prompted, nudging Nick with her shoulder, and he ducked his head, wrinkling his nose. "What is it? Does it have a million syllables, like Dostoevsky or summat?"

"C'mon, give the people what they want." Alex grinned, and Nick couldn't help smiling back at him.

"All right, it's Nikolay. Melnikov."

Nick could never decide if "the people" wanted the full, authentic experience, so his accent always landed somewhere in between. Not Russian, not really American. Just an in-betweenie sort of place where it sounded neither. Sounded fake.

"Ohhh, cool. But you haven't got an accent? I mean, not a Russian one, I don't think," Alex said.

Nick ventured a glance across everyone at the table. They were all watching him with what looked to be genuine interest. All apart from Dex, who was busy scratching at a spot at the table with the sort of intensity usually reserved for people who were paid to clean those tables for a living.

Nick shrugged. "It's been ten years. I guess I got lucky. They say that if you're immersed in a language before you're twelve, you won't have an accent." He paused and shrugged again. "I was ten. My sister was fourteen, so she has a bit of one, still."

"Wow," Steph said, watching him with her face propped on her hand. "Ten years old—what was that like?"

"Um, weird, I guess?"

"Fuck's sake, he just got here and we're already pestering him for his deepest stories?"

Nick's gaze flew to Dex, who was now staring into his own drink like it had personally offended him. Everyone else was staring at Dex.

"Oh, I'm sorry!" Steph's gaze skittered between them, looking genuinely distressed. Nick felt just a little bad for her, but Dex had kind of saved him, however unwittingly. "I should have thought...Sorry."

"It's totally fine." Nick glanced over at Dex, and this time their gazes caught. Dex was the first to look away, taking a deep gulp of his drink. Nick looked back at Steph, who still appeared a bit embarrassed. "Really, don't worry about it. It's probably the most interesting thing about me."

"*Pffft*, right." She sent a small grin his way before taking a sip of her drink. "Oh, hey, what are you studying, by the way?"

Nick pushed his glasses back up his nose. His armpits itched. "Um, history."

Steph looked on the verge of asking more, but then a giant glass of amber beer appeared under Nick's face. "All right, there we are." Izzy dragged a chair over and placed herself next to Nick. "Now, what have I missed?"

"Steph asked too many questions." Steph shot Alex a dirty look, which looked sort of funny on her friendly face.

"And Nick is Russian," Natali offered. Since she was smiling at him, he decided not to take offense and smiled back. What a whole lot of smiling he was doing. He took an exploratory sip of his drink.

Hmm. Not bad. Only a little bitter aftertaste.

"Are you really?" Izzy asked. "How cool is that? So much cooler than just being boring old American."

Nick snorted and wound up with beer foam under his nose. He wiped it away hastily and laughed despite himself.

"Izzy!" Steph sounded scandalized, but she was laughing, too.

"What? It's true—Russia's so much more mysterious than America."

Nick was still laughing. "That's one word for it."

Izzy grinned over at him. "At least it's got a history, right?"

"True," he agreed. "That it does."

Izzy clinked glasses with him and took a long pull. Nick followed suit.

$$+$$

The rest of the night Nick spent listening and drinking and asking the occasional question, especially once the beer in his glass began to disappear.

He was warm and a little sleepy in a way he hadn't felt in a while. After the third time Izzy sent Dex what looked to be a mock glare after Dex had made some smart-ass comment, Nick took a sip of beer, leaned back in the booth, and asked, bold as hell, "How did you guys all meet?"

"Oh, I know, I got this!" Natali bounced beside him, honest-to-God hand raised in the air. She brushed her bangs from her eyes and said, "Well, these two"—she pointed at Alex and Dex with her Corona—"met in their ubernerd lectures. Biochem majors, can you believe this shit?"

Alex and Dex instantly gave them identical winning smiles. Nick flushed for no good reason.

"Right, and Dex lived in halls with this harlot." Natali reached around Nick to poke at Izzy, who just stuck her tongue out at her. "They met when Dex was attempting to make an American-style grilled cheese sandwich on the hob and nearly set the kitchen on fire."

"It was so not even close to being on fire," Dex protested like someone tired of pointing it out.

"Excuse me, it actually went up in *flame*?" Izzy said, flicking a coaster across the table. She turned to Nick. "There was a perfectly usable toastie maker right there, too."

Dex went on like she hadn't spoken. "It was a contained grilled-cheese flame that barely even triggered the smoke alarm."

"But it *did*, actually, trigger it," Natali corrected. "Anyway, Izzy had apparently just wandered into the kitchen in her bra and pants—"

"Oi!"

"Excuse me, in her teeny tiny pajamas," Natali continued. "And Dex wound up burning his eyebrows off." She paused. "From what I understand."

When all eyes turned to Dex, he was looking at the ceiling, calmly sipping his drink. His initial bout of grumpiness was hard not to take personally, because as soon as Nick was no longer the center of attention, Dex visibly relaxed. Nick had at first thought it was hard to imagine those stern lips ever smiling, but he knew better now. Dex smiled easily. It dimpled his cheeks and made him look boyish, younger than the rest of them.

The thing was, Nick had a problem with staring. Zoya had pointed it out to him enough times that he'd more or less learned to curb the impulse, but it was hard with so many new people around. They all seemed so easy around each other, so familiar together, that Nick felt himself relaxing alongside them, which led to him studying each of them, one by one.

He tried not to study Dex as much as the others for fear of the grumpy dude returning, but when Dex smiled it was hard to look away.

Now, with everyone else watching Dex, too, Nick had implicit permission. He also had a question he couldn't contain. "You burned your *eyebrows*?"

Dex sighed and frowned as he looked down. "No."

"Dexter," Izzy said tonelessly beside Nick.

"Ugh, fine." He threw Nick a dubious sort of look. "Yes, I singed my eyebrows a bit. Was just startled, is all."

"It was epic, man," Alex cut in, laughing. "He shows up at the lab looking like he'd already experimented a bit too much, and it hadn't even been anything but fucking *cheese*." Alex was shaking with laughter, infecting everyone at the table with it. Nick felt almost euphoric, giggling alongside the others. "A grilled cheese sandwich and a half-naked Izzy were a deadly combination, apparently."

"I hate you," Dex said, but even Nick couldn't perceive any real heat behind it. "Anyway, Izzy and Nat met at some get-together or other, and Steph and Jonny we picked up—"

"Right here in this pub!" Jonny interrupted, lifting his glass. "Steph was determined to make friends despite being a shy young thing."

"Was not," Steph mumbled, pink-cheeked. Watching her gave Nick a similar feeling to walking through his own front door. She put Nick at ease. He smiled at her when she caught him staring, and she smiled back. "I mean, I *was*, but whatever, this was two years ago."

"Shyness is not a character flaw, babe," Natali said. "Anyway, Jonny and Steph met at freshers week stuff, and Jonny took her under his wing, being older and wiser than the rest of us because…well, blah blah, and then we came across them both, and blah blah friendship blah." She gave Nick a smile and finished off her Corona in the next go.

"I mean, it's not like we're a cult. We do know other people," Izzy offered. "I meet people all the time." She pointed to Nick with her glass.

"Izzy likes to pick up strays," Dex added, and just like that, Nick's newly found euphoria popped like a balloon. He hoped his expression hadn't changed, but he knew better. He'd been called an open book by Zoya enough times.

"What the hell?" Natali protested. Nick looked down at his drink, wondering how to extricate himself to get another. He'd never gone up to a bar before in his life. And he didn't even know what he was drinking.

"What?" Dex asked, then said, "Oh. Oh, shit. Sorry, Nick. That wasn't—sorry."

Nick glanced up at him. For some reason, hearing Dex say his name startled Nick, and he shrugged in an attempt to cover it up. Dex actually did look apologetic.

"Oh, it's fine, I didn't even..." He seized the moment. "I was just gonna get another drink, actually. Um..." He steeled himself. "Can I get anyone else anything?"

"Ohhh, yes, please!" Steph raised her glass. "It's the Stella. Cheers, mate."

Nick nodded, repeating *Stella* in his head, and waited for Izzy to move her chair so he could get out.

"Can you grab me another Corona?" Natali asked, and Nick gave her a nod, as well. Right. Three drinks. He could do three drinks.

"Oh, and a cider here," Alex piped up, finishing his glass off in one gulp. Nick got a little mesmerized by the movement of his Adam's apple, then panicked. Four drinks. Okay. He could fight his way through the crowded pub with four drinks. His fingers were reasonably long and grabby.

"I'll come up with you," Izzy said decisively and grabbed his arm like she had earlier. "These lazy tossers," she muttered. Nick tried not to look too relieved.

Once they managed to get through the throngs of drinkers, Izzy bellied up to the bar like she was paid to do it. All Nick could do was stand back and wonder at her ability to pull attention toward herself like she was lit by a spotlight. He noticed that the bartender all but flew over to where she was waiting, much to the annoyance of the dude who'd been craning his neck in an attempt to get attention.

"What'll it be, Iz?" the bartender asked, leaning his elbows on the bar and giving her a crooked smile.

Of course he knew her. Nick hid a smile behind his hand while Izzy rattled off the drink orders. Nick remembered to grab his wallet just in time, shoving his card at the bartender. Who didn't spare him a glance, fair enough. Standing next to Izzy was like a sparrow attempting to upstage a peacock.

"Don't mind Dex, by the way," Izzy said while they waited for drinks to be poured. "It's not you."

Nick shrugged, looking down at the smooth surface of the bar. "It's fine." His face was hot. There was a lot of humanity around him.

"Well, it's *not* fine, him being a bit of a tosser, but he isn't always like that." When Nick looked up at her, she was biting the inside of her cheek like she was holding something back. Not for the first time, Nick wondered about those two. He wondered just what was sticking in Dex's craw, and he especially wondered, with an uncomfortable, clawing-at-his-belly feeling, why Izzy had invited Nick out in the first place.

"Well, everyone else is really nice," Nick offered.

"Oh, no," Izzy smiled, shaking her hair back. "They're also tossers, they're just much cheerier about it. Oh, goody, here we go!" Three glasses and a Corona appeared beside them.

All in all, Nick was pretty proud of himself for not even spilling any beer as he slithered his way between people and set the glasses down on the table without any disasters.

"Cheers, mate," Alex said, grabbing his and Steph's drinks while Nick handed Natali her Corona.

Then he sat back down, took a long gulp of his own beer, and decided to ask no more questions.

It wasn't that Izzy was furious with Dex, exactly, but she was righteously annoyed. And worried. It was some sort of a combination of the two, and she had tried giving him space to sort himself out, but it was about time he stopped acting like a stroppy toddler and owned up to his crap. She marched up to his room, only stumbling on the last step a tiny bit, and slunk in without a knock.

He looked like he'd needed the distraction in any case, because he definitely had one of his incomprehensible textbooks open next to him, along with his laptop and a glazed sort of look on his face.

"You're definitely going to regret that last glass of wine," he told her once she tucked her head up against his shoulder, dislodging his laptop in the process. He shut the laptop and moved it out of the way. Izzy snuggled closer.

"Am not," she said once she was comfier. She never regretted any glasses of wine. Or, well. Most, anyway. Neither did Dex, for that matter. She decided on a sideways approach. "Why aren't you celebrating with us?"

"Thought we'd already done that," he responded in a superior tone that really bloody grated on her.

"There's always more celebrating to do, what the hell are you, forty?" She gathered herself, cleared her throat, and decided sideways approaches were for wimps. "So why were you such a shithead to Nick earlier?"

"Was not," he mumbled. Izzy could have slapped him. "Why did you spring him on us like that?" This time she *did* smack him. He knew. She knew he knew.

"I didn't bloody spring him on anybody, I brought a new friend along. This isn't precisely unprecedented." The last glass of wine had made a sort of a mess out of that sentence, but at least she'd got the point across. She looked him in the eye. "Dexter, seriously. You were a massive dickhead, and I seriously worry about you."

He looked up at the ceiling. "I'm sorry. I'll apologise."

"Yes, you will, but that's not actually my point." She shifted, making sure to knee him in the shins at least once. She loved him to death, but sometimes she just wanted to throttle him. "Look, you've been a brooding pain in the arse, and while I understand a broken heart, it's been literally months. You have got to go out and fuck someone before your balls explode from disuse."

"Nice." He pushed himself away. He looked like a storm cloud. She wanted to hug him immediately, but she really needed him to hear her out first. She was about to open her mouth when he said, "Is that how it works in your world?"

She felt it like a kick in the gut. She pursed her lips to stop them trembling, then got a hold of herself. "Slut-shaming me won't work. And it's fucking disingenuous at best."

"Ohh, big words," he said, and after a flare of bright-red anger, Izzy felt the exhaustion hit her all at once. It had been a long day, and her final year of uni was promising to be terrifying. In this moment, all she wanted was to go to sleep. Best to just get it done with.

"Fine. Fuck right off," she said. "The point is, you're being a stupid arsehole, and even Alex is getting sick of your shit, so pull yourself together, talk to me, or to any of us, or you can just sit in your room until you're a shriveled fucking raisin, but don't pretend like everything is fine, because it's clearly not."

She shoved her way up off the bed and a moment later slammed the door behind her. She staggered the three steps to her own door and slammed that behind her, too, for good measure.

Fucking bastard.

Rich of him to suddenly, what, start having a problem with her having sex? As if they hadn't gone on the pull together countless times and then told each other all about it the following morning in minute detail. It was, she thought as she stripped her dress off, a strange thing to do, probably, but this was Dex.

She stomped towards her bed and fought with her bra clasp. Releasing her tits felt like heaven.

But really, nothing was weird with Dex, not since that first encounter in the kitchen when he'd nearly set himself on fire. For a few moments, she wondered if she'd just met the love of her life—she'd looked at him and her entire body had done a sort of *ping!*—but then, of course: gay. So totally gay. Which was totally fine, obviously, and anyway, they'd probably have made an awful couple.

But he was her best friend, and he'd been acting like a shithead for far too long. A stroppy, grumpy shithead who needed to sort himself out before he alienated everyone. She had tried to say her piece and been rebuffed, so now it was up to bloody him.

She threw on her loosest T-shirt and reached for her phone as she plopped down on the bed. She snapped a picture of her toes tangled in the duvet cover and uploaded it to Instagram with a sleep-face emoji and a filter that covered up the fact that she hadn't painted her toenails in far too long.

She was just about to turn off her lamp and fall into unconsciousness when there was a light knock on her door.

She braced herself for Dex, but it was Natali who peeked her head in.

"Hey, mate, you all right? Heard some shouty words up here."

Izzy shrugged and flung her phone away from her. "Dex is being a stroppy bastard." She wasn't going to go into details, and she most definitely was not going to let Dex make her feel bad for having a cracking sex life. Or making friends.

"Oh, is it Tuesday?" Natali grinned and flopped down onto the foot of Izzy's bed. "What'd he do now?"

"Dunno, said some shitty stuff. Like how I'd apparently sprung Nick on you all." She stared off into the middle distance, and a bother of a thought slowly made its way into her brain. "Nat," she said slowly. "Am I overly controlling or, like...obnoxious?"

"Wha–?"

"I mean, like, I know that I sort of tend to, dunno, act first, think later, but is that necessarily a *bad* thing?" She thought of how she'd railroaded Mum into letting her apply for a film course despite Mum insisting she go for something sensible, like teaching or dentistry or whatever. She hadn't even listened to Mum's arguments, not really. She wanted to study film, so that was what she was obviously going to do. But what if it really was a stupid decision?

"Babe. What'd that stroppy arsehole say? I'll fuck him up."

"He didn't, not—"

"Because that's bullshit, all right? You're not overly controlling, and you didn't spring anyone on anyone, you just invited a boy out with us to celebrate." She must have seen something in Izzy's expression, because she squinted, tilted her head, and said, "I mean, not to question it or anything, but why *did* you bring Nick with you? Just curious, mind."

Izzy gave her a look, but she knew that Nat would get there eventually. "I...he was sweet. And awkward. And he looked like he needed some friends in his life."

"Hmm." Natali was watching her with half a smile on her face. "And it wouldn't be because you've mentioned, you know, once or twice, attempting to shake Dex out of it by dangling new boys in front of him, would it?"

Izzy tried for an evasion. "How'd you know I didn't bring him there for me?"

Nat raised her perfect eyebrow.

"Ugh, fine, *maybe*."

Nat's laugh always sounded like a cackle. "I bloody knew it! No wonder he was in a strop. Not, mind you, that he's ever allowed to make you feel like shit. But, like. He's just not ready, mate."

Izzy slumped down sideways. "Ugh. I know, all right? But I thought—I dunno. He wouldn't stop looking at him at International Night, I thought—maybe."

"Give him time."

"I know," she grumbled.

"But he really was a right dickhead tonight."

"I *know*."

"And you're not a controlling anything, all right? Don't let him take his crap out on you."

Izzy sniffed, suddenly close to tears. She shifted until she was staring at the ceiling so Nat wouldn't notice. "I know."

"Aw, babe. C'mere."

Of course she noticed. Izzy squeezed her eyes shut. "I'm just drunk and tired and emotional. Ignore me, please."

"Nah."

Natali plopped down next to her until they were staring at the same yellow blob on the ceiling from where the Nat had lost a fight with a humidifier last winter. "You're a good egg among some truly rotten pieces of crap. So don't go off the deep end."

"That's...quite a compliment." The thing of it was, for Natali, that was downright effusive. Izzy felt warm inside, a little gooey, and maybe just a little less tired but definitely more weepy. She sniffed. "I'm glad you think I'm not a rotten egg." In the beginning, she'd always felt far too uncool for Natali. It was sort of funny to think about that now.

"Yep. I think there are maybe, like, six of you in total around these parts."

"Which parts?"

"I'm thinking…Mile End. No, wait, London. No, no, wait. How about this entire bloody island?"

Izzy must have been just a little mad, because the next moment she was giggling as she gazed up at the yellow blob, and Natali was grabbing her hand and twisting their fingers together.

"So, yeah. Stop crying."

"Yes, ma'am." She sniffed.

"I'll fuck you up."

Izzy giggled into Natali's bony shoulder and decided that Dex could solve his own problems if he was going to be a bastard about it.

When she finally did settle in to sleep, hours later, she had a text from him.

Sorry I'm a bastard. I'll try harder to be better.

"Yeah, well, I bloody hope so," she muttered, then turned over. He could stew until morning for a text back.

+

She ended up accepting his apology in person, whilst weak with need for caffeine, waiting for the coffee to brew faster. It wasn't like she hadn't been planning on doing it anyway. Having anybody be upset with her set her teeth on edge, and this was Dex.

Funny, when they'd first met, he had seemed so cool. Maybe it was his gorgeousness, because frankly, he wasn't all that cool. Well, he was, but now he was Izzy's best mate, and that took the edge off his cool a bit, made him just, like. Real.

The point was, Izzy hated tension, and she especially hated tension when it came to her housemates. You could smell it in the air whenever anyone was in a strop with someone else. Even if it didn't involve her, it *involved* her. It rubbed her nerves raw, made everything feel wrong and off-kilter.

So when she heard Dex shuffle into the kitchen—she knew his shuffle—she didn't even turn around before saying, "I forgive you, you ninny."

He breathed out loudly behind her. "Thanks." Pause. "Sorry."

She shrugged. She did still have a point to make. "I could be shagging half of London, it would still be total shit to call me a slag."

"I know." She wasn't looking at him, but she still thought he sounded like he'd hung his head in shame. Good. "I'm sorry."

"Yeah, so, like, don't be an arsehole like that again."

"'Kay."

"'Kay."

He reached the counter, and they stood side by side waiting for the coffee to be ready. She glanced at him sideways. "I'm sorry, too."

"For what?"

"Dunno, just, like." She wasn't quite ready to admit that he knew her well enough to see every ulterior motive a mile away. "Stuff."

He huffed out a laugh. "Sure."

"You still need to apologise to Nick."

She felt him tense just a bit. "Yeah," he said after a moment. "When I see him next."

He probably thought it wouldn't be anytime soon, but the truth was, Izzy really had liked Nick. Or maybe *liked* was the wrong word. He seemed lovely, if terribly closed off and almost too shy to bear. She had wanted to spend more time with him and see if she couldn't shake him out of his shell a bit. She felt only slightly like Cher in *Clueless*. It wasn't as if she didn't already have her share of "projects," but Nick clearly had some stories to tell. She wanted to hear them.

He was also totally adorable. She never claimed *not* to be shallow, in some respects.

+

Kat ran up to her just as she was about to step into the classroom. "Hola, lover!"

Izzy rolled her eyes out of habit. Kat was weirdly sort of like if you combined Luna Lovegood and Sue Perkins and rolled them both around in a speedball. Not, like, visually, but in essence. She had an aura of the absurdly hilarious, the dreamy, and the totally fucking off her rocker. Izzy adored her but could only take her in small doses. "Hiya," she greeted.

"Did you see what that twat said about female writers?"

"Which twat?"

"Johannes, obviously. On the forum?"

Oh, right. Izzy kept forgetting to go to their module forum. Or, truthfully, ignoring it. She kept ignoring the module forum, largely because it was like immersing yourself in a YouTube comments section. Kat, on the other hand, loved getting her righteous rage on and would gleefully report the low-lights on a regular basis. Izzy pulled her bag farther up her shoulder. "Oh god, what now?"

Kat, leading them to a far-from-the-door place at the massive table, recounted all the ways in which Johannes shit all over women writers. "Well, obviously, there is no interest in the film world in what women have to say—we all know they largely just want to talk about how all men are pigs and worthless, when men have contributed the most to the fabric of our society, blah blah blah, oh, and also that they should, you know, try it out—by *it* he means scriptwriting, you understand—on material that's more their speed, like, soaps and crap. Or, obviously, romantic comedies, but everybody knows that."

She had barely come up for air and was holding her palm out for a high five, which Izzy indulged her in before flopping down into her chair.

"Not, I might add, that soaps aren't art in and of themselves," Kat went on, dropping her massive messenger bag on the table. "That's me saying that, by the way, not me telling you what Johannes said. Oh, hey, *Johannes*."

Izzy twisted around in time to see the devil himself walk through the door and give Kat the dirtiest look imaginable.

Izzy had actually met him her first week at uni, being in the same course, and he'd even seemed cute at first. Plus, he'd been totally into her, something she hadn't quite been used to at the time. But the shine wore off once she had an actual conversation with him. Now he just seemed like a waste of a good face and rather tremendous body.

Still, she felt herself flushing the tiniest bit while Kat just blew her gum at him and sprawled farther in her seat, legs akimbo, no trace of shame. Amazing. Izzy reminded herself this was *Johannes*, for fuck's sake, and shoved her embarrassment down. While Kat was booting up her ancient Dell, Izzy got out her notebook and placed her phone in her lap where she could check on it every now and then. Fifteen people had liked her feet picture from last night, which was nice. Her aunt had texted, too, a picture of her garden with an uncomfortable number of aubergine emojis. Izzy could never actually bring herself to tell her that aubergines were not to be used as originally intended and that aubergines had, in fact, lost all meaning.

"You should come out dancing with me and my mates," Kat said, blowing another bubble casually in Izzy's direction.

"Ooooh, when?"

"Saturday night, in Vauxhall. Ladies' night." She wiggled her eyebrows. "If you know what I mean."

Damn. "Shit, I've got plans already. Is this a one-time offer?"

"For you, my lovely Girl on Fire?" God, Kat loved teasing the hell out of Izzy. Izzy assumed it was because it was safe but was absurdly flattered every time anyway. It was nice to be wanted by someone as discerning as Kat. "Join us anytime."

Izzy blew her a kiss as the classroom began to fill up with people and their tutor walked in, all weirdo hair and slightly panicked expression. "Done."

Over the weekend, Nick braved the bus system and went exploring.

He was good at maps. He had looked at one of London the night before, then again the next morning, studying it in bed on his dusty laptop, scrolling back and forth to figure out what was realistic for the day. He considered his options. Then he planned out a route.

He felt like the most obvious of tourists, his nose practically pressed up against the front of the bus, seated on the second level of a double-decker. But he was alone, and he would never see the people around him ever again, and he was mesmerized. For years he'd been studying British history, reading books set in London, devouring every bit of culture he could from his quiet Ann Arbor bedroom. The bustle of London around him now was all-consuming.

He drank it in. He scanned every storefront, took in every road name that was so very different from those back home. So many roundabouts. Cars zipping down the wrong side of the street. Everywhere he looked were people living their everyday, normal lives while he peered down from his perch and marveled at how tired and ordinary they seemed. And he was sitting there, bursting with barely contained joy.

What a strange mixture of new and old it all was. Glass skyscrapers rose over the dulled brick-and-mortar buildings that had managed to survive the Blitz. Stately homes bordered monstrosities Nick would have sneered at in Michigan but made his heart pitter-patter because they were here, in London. He knew it made no sense, but with every turn of the bus, every new corner and street, he felt his connection to the city strengthen, as if shooting out from his fingers, his toes, his every joint and bone. Bricks and pavement and anonymous faces all joined until Nick felt like he was allowed to breathe this air, was allowed to be here, *here*, for the next few months at least, and take in all it was willing to give him.

He hopped off the bus before he had planned to and let his legs take him wherever they wanted to go. He walked and walked and walked until he no longer knew where he was, and then he let CityMapper get him home, exhausted and hungry, but something else, too. He groped for what the feeling was, and was just a little shocked to discover it was happiness. Just there, pure and simple. He walked back to his dorm, and with every street he discovered, he wondered to himself what sort of history lay beneath it, as if he could scrape off the layers of stories one by one, like turning the pages of an illustrated book.

He was almost in his room when he got a text alert.

Hosting a brunch tomoz at 11, u should come!

Izzy. She'd texted over the address, as well. Nick frowned at his phone while fumbling with his keys, then continued to frown at it as he got through the door and toed off his shoes, feet and legs whining.

He hadn't actually considered that they'd want to see him again. And this soon, too. Somehow, between the awkward introductions to the awkward drink getting to the more awkward good-byes, Nick had sort of expected the whole thing to go precisely nowhere.

Maybe they just hadn't noticed. Maybe if he never saw them again, he would leave them with a more or less good impression of himself. *Oh, that Nick—wasn't so bad. Never came back, though. That's a bit strange.*

The thing was, he just didn't get it. Why him? It confused him, this sudden attention. He'd had friends before, but they'd mostly been, well, awkward nerds, like him. As a kid with no language in Michigan, it was all he could do to make it home from school every day, and after that, he could never exile that kid from his mind. He might always *be* that kid.

He looked at his phone, checked the time. Sucked in his lower lip, worried at it.

I got invited to brunch by some people at their house, he texted his sister.

Are you asking for permission or a kick in the ass?

He laughed despite himself and texted back. *Probably both.*

Later, he made himself go to the kitchen to put together something resembling a dinner. The kitchen came with a weird little sandwich maker. Nick had picked up on the fact that this was a regular sort of appliance for England, but he still considered it to be a bit of a miracle. He made himself a cheese, bacon, and tomato toasted sandwich, going through the motions familiarly enough. His legs felt a bit like jelly from his massive exploration session.

He was still getting used to the little differences around him. The electric plugs were gigantic, for one. They were different from even the Russian ones, which his hands could still remember the feel of—the simple smooth round prongs, cool to the touch. The stove had a strange little compartment right under the cooktop where you could grill shit like bacon. The bacon itself was different—meatier, less fat on it. All of these differences he memorized like plans of attack. Maybe if he learned these things quicker, absorbed them, he would become just another Londoner, disappear into its corners, get taken in by its tide, no longer a stranger.

For now, he would make his toasted sandwiches and drink his tea, consider going to Izzy's brunch, and pretend like he was just any normal person who could speak to others without worrying about them discovering his true awkward, uncertain self.

You should go, Kol'ka. And you should tell me all about it. <3

Nick wasn't sure he'd know where to start.

He shuffled back to his room with his plate and cup and settled in to watch *Persuasion*.

"Yay! You made it!" Izzy exclaimed while Natali bodily ushered Nick through the door and toward what he assumed to be the living room. He had stood at their door for a good five minutes before ringing the bell, sweating through his nerves. He'd fretted over whether or not to bring anything—he had decided on yes. He'd brought some muffins—and then he'd fretted over whether or not this was the right house at all. It was a narrow brick building in a row of narrow brick buildings, slightly dilapidated but somehow comfortable with it. It wasn't directly on campus, and that was strange, realizing he was in his first actual English house. Or flat. Not for the first time, he felt like a kid in the presence of adults who'd started figuring out their own lives. Moving in together. Paying rent. Paying bills. He was like a ten-year-old peeking through their windows.

"Nick's here!" Natali announced. "Get him a drink, I've got to get back to the hob."

Izzy had already disappeared down the hall, so Nick was left to wave hello to all assembled on his own. They turned out to be everyone from the other night and then some. Nick swallowed as he scanned the room.

"Bloody mary?" Steph asked, hopping up from her perch on the couch arm. Nick agreed readily enough, giving her a hopeful smile. "Back in a tic," she told him and waved him over, presumably to take her place on the abandoned spot of the couch.

"Good to see you again, Mate," Alex said in between what looked to be two separate conversations with three separate people. He patted the couch arm again. Apparently it was a popular spot. "Glad you made it. Izzy makes a gorgeous fry-up."

"Cool." Nick wondered what a fry-up entailed as he perched awkwardly next to him. Steph had made it look easy. He'd rather have sat on the floor. Was that impolite? "How are you?"

"I'm good, mate. Here, let me introduce you." Alex turned to the girls he'd been talking to. "These are Natali's baby dykes."

"Oi!" The nearest one glowered. She had blue hair. "We've got names. And, like, personalities of our own and shit."

"Although I do like the sound of being Natali's baby dyke." This girl had short, almost military-style hair, which made her pixie face look even more fairylike. Nick found her absolutely adorable.

"See, that's my point," Alex told them in a reasonable tone of voice. "If I were a cute lesbian, Natali's side is where I'd want to be all the time." The pixie shrugged, smiling. "Anyway, this is Beth." The blue hair. "This is Chloe." The pixie. "This guy here is Niall." He pointed to a dark-haired boy who was busy slurping a bloody mary from a straw. "And that's his mate Lance." Lance had a mop of crazy brown hair that probably hadn't seen a brush since the third grade or thereabouts and a bit of a dreamy expression on his face. Nick nodded at them, settling himself a lit more firmly on the couch arm. It felt weird to be allowed to sit on it. His mom had always yelled at him and Zoyka for doing it; it was practically taboo. Nick allowed himself to enjoy his own private rebellion.

"And you remember Dex," Alex continued right as Dex walked through the door. Nick's pulse sped up despite himself. He really wanted that bloody mary now. Instead, he gave Dex a bit of a nervous wave, and Dex tipped his chin at him in acknowledgement. He looked different from the other night. For one, much less grumpy. He also looked pretty sleep-tousled, even though Nick would have been hard-pressed to say in what way, exactly. He just looked relaxed.

Dex yawned and stretched, and Nick's gaze zeroed in on where his T-shirt rode up and revealed a neat belly button surrounded by shadowy abs. Dex's hips peeked out from above his basketball shorts. Nick looked away. He could never understand how some people were made. He was so awkward, with skinny limbs and ribs under unremarkable, pasty skin covered in too many birthmarks. Dex's body looked effortless, like the air shifted around it specifically to accommodate all that it contained. Maybe it was a touch of grace. Grace had always made Nick feel nervous and out of place.

"Hiya," Dex said. "D'you want a drink?"

That was some whiplash from the other night. Nick licked his lips before saying, "Steph is on it. Thanks, though."

Dex nodded. He found a spot on the floor by the TV set and seemingly forgot Nick was even there. Nick's heart rate lowered. He gathered his courage and applied himself to the social obligation of conversation.

"So, you're the American boy! Natali had mentioned you," Chloe the Pixie said, clearly abandoning whatever conversation they'd all been having before Nick's arrival.

Nick's neck prickled. "I guess that's me," he smiled.

"Mi...nnesota? Is that a state?" she asked.

Nick laughed. "That *is* a state. I'm from Michigan, though."

"Oh," she grinned. "Soz, I guess. You lot have got too many fucking states."

"This is true." Like Steph, she seemed to put him at ease. It was easy to look at her smile and not attempt to search for whatever judgments might be lying beneath.

"Ask him for his full name," Alex said. "It's wicked. He's Russian."

"Ohhh, are you?" Chloe's eyes all but lit up.

Nick nodded just as Steph walked through the door with what was presumably his drink. He'd once seen his mom order a bloody mary on an airplane. She barely drank, only a glass of wine for toasts on special occasions. The look he had given her made her laugh, and she'd said, *I've wanted to try this ever since seeing it in a movie. Don't look at me like that. I can be unpredictable.* She hadn't let him try it, though. He'd been fourteen.

Now he took his legal drink with thanks and looked into its tomatoy depths. "It's Nikolay, actually."

"Not Nicholas?"

He shook his head, finally taking a sip. He'd been expecting the vodka, but the pepper swiftly traveling up his sinuses was a surprise. He coughed like the amateur he was.

"Izzy makes them strong." Steph grinned. She sat comfortably next to Dex. "So how come you never changed your name? I've met a few people who have."

Nick's mom had. She'd officially become Katherine when their citizenship came through, the last traces of Ekaterina Markovna, of his father's Katen'ka, left for the family to mull over. But Nick had refused. He bit his lip and attempted to line up a way of explaining that didn't sound precious and pretentious. "It's the last thing that I got to keep, I guess. Besides my last name. It was what I'd been called my whole life, so why should I change it at seventeen, you know?" That was when they'd gotten their citizenships.

When he looked back up, even Lance was watching him. Nick shrugged to take the weight off their scrutiny.

"That totally makes sense," Chloe said. "I dunno that I'd want to change it."

"My mom wanted me to," Nick went on without meaning to. "Like, you know. People don't really know how to pronounce it always." And it's like a mark, *foreign.* "It's a constant thing in school and stuff, too, I guess, but..." He shrugged again, took a cautious sip of his drink. "It's me, so."

Chloe reached out and slapped Nick's knee. "I like you. We're keeping you."

Nick hid his face in his glass.

A fry-up was basically a gigantic brunch made up of things Nick hadn't really considered to be part of brunch before. His plate was loaded with eggs, beans, cooked mushrooms, buttered toast, and fried tomatoes. He was fairly certain he'd never actually had cooked tomatoes that weren't pasta-sauce-based. He balanced it all on one knee and ate slowly, careful to take bites when no one could watch him.

The bloody mary had been pretty strong, and when he'd gone into the kitchen, prodded by Chloe at his back, Izzy had taken one look at Nick's nearly drained glass and said, "Want another?"

Nick had said, "Not yet."

Still, the food and drink had calmed him. Now he lounged safely on the floor, propped up by the couch and someone's feet. He was fairly certain they were Chloe's. The room was overcrowded, filled with chatter. Sunlight spilled over the walls and the lucky few who had managed to crowd around a small dining table: Natali, Izzy, Dex. Nick wondered if those who lived in the flat got the table dibs.

"Ugh, I can't believe it's our final year," someone said.

"I can't believe I've got to go to lectures so fucking early." This was crazy-haired Lance. "Bloody fascists."

"Oh, for fuck's sake."

Nick giggled at Natali's eye roll. Lance, when Nick looked at him, seemed unaffected. He shrugged, a bit of egg on a fork frozen halfway to his mouth, and said, "I call it as I see it."

"Lance here believes that unless you're a hardcore, like, Marxist Communist, you're a fascist. This, by the way, means most of us," Alex said. "Just so you know, Nick. This is who you're aligning yourself with here. Getting up on time for lecture? Injustice to the cause."

Nick laughed and tipped his head against the couch, watching Lance, who shrugged again. "So, you think Communism is the way to go?" Nick asked.

"Yeah, man, I'm dead serious. Power to the people, you know?" He made a sort of fist-in-the-air gesture. "I mean, have you seen what's been going on lately?"

Nick had, but he just couldn't take him seriously. Response after response chased each other in his mind, but he didn't think he could reasonably get away with any of them, so he kept his mouth shut. How much power did Lance think people under Communism had, exactly? Had he ever lived outside the UK? When Nick glanced away from Lance, his gaze caught Dex's, and for a fraction of a second Dex's lips twitched and his eyes crinkled at the corners, zeroed in on Nick's. A dimple appeared on one cheek. And then, just like that, he was back to neutral, and Nick was looking away, his stomach clenching around the food and the bloody mary. Was he drunk? He didn't think so. But maybe. Did he want another drink?

One of Natali's baby lesbians solved that problem for him by going around and taking everyone's glasses for refills. Natali and Izzy both graciously offered to help her out, and Nick took the opportunity to find the bathroom.

He probably *was* slightly buzzed, because he petted the cold tap, then the hot, then frowned at himself for being weird and caught his own gaze in the mirror. He didn't *look* like he was completely out of it. He turned his head this way and that, touching a spot on his jaw he'd missed shaving this morning. He definitely needed a haircut. He was starting to look like pictures of his father from the seventies. The curls were out of control.

When he finally came out of the bathroom, he caught sight of Izzy and Dex in the kitchen and froze, unable to look away.

They looked so *close*. Intimate, really. Dex had his arms wrapped around Izzy from behind, and he was murmuring something to her Nick couldn't hear. Izzy laughed. Then Nick watched as she leaned back and planted a quick kiss on Dex's cheek. Nick ducked his head and quickly moved the hell away. He shouldn't have seen that.

More and more, he was beginning to think Dex's instant dislike of him was Izzy-related. It twisted Nick's stomach into knots to think it, because he had it all wrong, Dex had it all *wrong*, Nick wouldn't...he wasn't. He wasn't interested.

His spot by the couch was waiting for him, and as soon as he plopped down, Chloe the Pixie presented him with another bloody mary, which he took gratefully.

"Anyway, who's up for it?" Jonny asked.

Nick took an ill-advised giant gulp of his drink, and it burned on the way down. Maybe he *was* a bit drunk. He wiped his mouth on his sleeve, hoping no one had noticed.

"What about you, Nick, are you in?"

Nick twisted around to look at Alex, which brought on another warm flush, because Alex was just ridiculously good-looking. Staring at him was like staring at the sun. It was probably safer to look through sunglasses, dim his shine a little.

"Uh, sorry—in for what?"

"Oh, nineties night, there's a thing on at a club in Shoreditch. Next weekend. You in?"

He said *weekend* with an emphasis on *end,* and Nick got a little stuck playing it on a loop in his head. His accent sounded nice. Then the question caught up with him. *Wait.*

"Oh, uh..." *Say yes,* said a voice in his head. It sounded like Zoyka. *Say yes, they're waiting!* That sounded more like his own voice. Nick blinked. "Um, s-sure? That sounds..." Was it going to be expensive? He'd been skimping on a lot of things to make sure he didn't run out of money before the semester's end. A club night sounded expensive.

Also insane.

Him, at a club? With, like, music and people and presumably dancing? International night had been enough. No, fuck it, he wasn't going. He wasn't going, and he'd invent some sort of an excuse.

"Brilliant!" Alex grinned, showing all white teeth, staring down at him.

Nick's heart sank. Oh God.

+

It wasn't like the door was barred, but Nick felt it impolite to leave before helping with cleanup, and nobody was getting up to actually start doing it. The crowd dispersed a bit. Lance and Niall left, so did Beth, the blue-haired baby lesbian. There was enough room for Nick to curl up on one side of the couch with his feet up, which he did happily, because he'd finished that second drink. No one was asking him any questions, so he was content enough just to listen.

Alex and Jonny were arguing about something so deeply sciencey, Nick couldn't have followed the conversation stone-cold sober. Steph and Chloe were making plans for a library date, it sounded like. Dex and Izzy were lounging against the wall, simply listening, just like Nick. Every now and then,

Dex piped up to correct something so incomprehensible to Nick, he wondered if it was even in English.

"Nick, so you're studying history, right?" Izzy asked, and Nick took a little bit to wake up from his food and drink coma before the anxiety set in. He nodded. "Ohh, what sort?"

"British history, actually."

"Oh, cool! Is that why you came here?"

Why did it feel so strange to admit to this to actual British people? It wasn't like they were really going to start throwing rotten vegetables his way. Probably. "Yeah. I mean, I've always been really interested in it, and I read a ton of British lit when I was a kid, so it just sort of became a thing, I guess."

"Cool."

Dex was watching Nick, and Nick watched him back, unable to figure out what was behind the look. It wasn't hostile—maybe because Izzy was currently safely next to him—but it wasn't all open and normal like everyone else. Dex was probably judging him for being a stupid American with pretensions toward becoming a British historian. Maybe he *would* throw rotten vegetables at Nick if it were socially acceptable.

Well, fuck him. Nick wasn't good at much, but he was good at school.

"Yeah, I guess I got it from my mom. The interest in British lit, I mean."

"Is she a historian, too?"

"Nah, she's a chemist." He liked that she said *too*. "But she has a lot of hobbies." They were a family of nerds.

Later, Natali got up decisively and said, "All right, babes. This has been ace, but I've got to read for lecture and you all need to clear out."

Nick was immediately shooting up off the couch to help clean up, only a little wobbly on his feet.

Natali loaded his arms up with plates. "I'll be right behind you, just bung those in the sink for now."

Nick followed her orders, careful to step around the doorway and not suffer a repeat of the one and only time he'd bussed tables at a country club. He'd been holding a full tray of dirty dishes, about to swing through the kitchen door, when someone swung through on the other side. He hadn't been asked back once the mess was cleared.

He looked around the kitchen. It was small but nice, sunny. All the cabinets were white, like an Ikea showroom, and it took him way too long to find the fridge. It was covered in the same stuff the cabinets were made of. Weird.

Natali found him with his arms half buried in soapsuds, zoning out on washing dishes.

"Oh, bless you, you can leave those, you know," she said, but didn't attempt to stop him. Natali leaned a hip against the counter right next to him and watched him work, dish towel at the ready. "Dex usually does this part, so he'll be happy."

Oh.

"He and Iz have got this whole brunch thing down to a science, it's wild," Natali went on, inadvertently stepping right into a line of questioning Nick was feeling reckless enough to start up.

"Have they been together long?" He handed her a plate, unable to meet her eyes.

"What, Dex and Izzy?" Natali froze with the plate in her hand. "Oh, Christ, no."

Nick looked up at her, startled.

"One of them's way too queer for the other one," Natali said as she dried.

Oh. Izzy was—

Natali rolled her eyes. "Dex, babe. Queer as a daisy." She watched him take this in. "What? You didn't realize?"

Nick slowly shook his head. Maybe he was too drunk for washing dishes—he hadn't picked that one plate back up in what felt like years. Logically, it had probably been seconds.

"You're adorable." Drying dishes and smiling at him, Natali was so much less intimidating than her appearance had first suggested. Nick dared to meet her gaze. "They're best friends is all. I mean, who knows, if Dex was straight, they'd probably be married by now." Nick caught an edge in her voice, something raspy and sharp.

Why *was* Dex acting like such a weirdo toward him, if not for Izzy? What the fuck had Nick done to deserve it?

6

Dex couldn't stop thinking about Nick, and it was driving him bonkers.

The problem was twofold. The first part was that he had been meaning to apologise to Nick at the brunch for having been a massive dickhead and had found zero opportunity to do so. He had, however, found plenty to *go on* being a massive dickhead. Dex was, in fact, beginning to suspect that he simply *was* a massive dickhead.

Izzy was probably right. Dex seriously needed to get off with someone sooner rather than later. His own hand wasn't cutting it these days.

Regardless, he still owed Nick an apology.

The second part of the problem was worse. Dex was intensely attracted to Nick, against all of his better judgment. That was the last thing Dex needed, and it was the last thing he had expected.

Dex's ex had been the epitome of what he found attractive. Tall, built, dark, handsome. Killer smile. Fit as all get out. Strong.

Nick was the opposite. All but the killer smile, if Dex were honest, but even that was different. He was just so very small. Well, Dex supposed he was average height for a bloke, but he was skinny enough that he *looked* small. He had giant hair and uneven teeth.

He wasn't handsome. He was *pretty*. Pouty mouth, with these strange grooves in the corners that made him look impish at all times. Like he held a mystery inside him he wasn't too keen on sharing. And then his fucking eyes. Dex had been fairly exhausted at brunch, sort of out of it, and also worrying about getting a chance to apologise to Nick. He just kept getting distracted by Nick's ridiculous blue eyes. Maybe they were grey, he couldn't quite tell. They were large, framed by long lashes, and the defined inner corners turned down and made him look like a fox. Another mystery.

Dex rubbed his eyes and refocused on his computer. The last thing he wanted to do was uncover anybody's mysteries. He was too busy uncovering the mysteries of how he was going to get all of this work into one bloody school year whilst working and presumably eating and sleeping and possibly seeing his friends every now and then. Maybe even seeing his family more than once in a blue moon.

He was also going to the club and getting off with the first boy he saw, even if he was a pretentious Shoreditch hipster with a topknot. Hipsters gave hand jobs, too.

He shut his laptop decisively. It was time to go to the Arms, anyway.

He pulled on his requisite uniform of white T-shirt and black trousers, checked himself out in the bathroom—skin looked clear, for once—and set off.

On the way, he calculated how many shifts at the pub he could possibly pick up to cover the rent and have some play money leftover. Nat's uncle gave them a sizable break on the rent, but Dex had just had to splurge on a new laptop after his old one bit it spectacularly, and he was still feeling the effects of the hole burnt into his bank account.

He would probably be all right, but you could never be too careful. Mum had wanted to pay for it when he'd mentioned it, but Dex just felt sort of weird about accepting their money with Albert still in school and needing all the sorts of crap fourteen-year-olds needed. In the end, they went half and half, but it was still sort of more than Dex could afford. God bless Mum, though.

The problem with Nick, too, was what a socially awkward dude he was. Dex couldn't have been the only one to see it. The only time Nick looked remotely comfortable was with a drink in him. *That* boded well, Dex thought, rolling his eyes.

He shook his head. No thoughts of boys who weren't going to help him get off. He had work to do.

He was absolutely bored out of his mind the first hour and completely slammed the rest of the shift, especially since Nicola had had to leave him on his own and go home to vomit through a stomach bug. Once the post-work crowd filtered in, they never stopped, even on a fucking Wednesday. But it kept him from worrying about too many things at once.

After he'd served a rumpled-looking young guy in a sagging business suit, Dex looked up and saw Jonny sidle up to the bar.

"Hey, man!" Dex was already pulling out a pint glass and tipping it under the Stella spout. "Thought you were going to be out with Niall and Lance?"

Jonny rolled his eyes and dropped a tenner on the bar. "Ended up bailing on me. Something about Niall needing Lance's help with a project. Anyway, Steph's meeting me here now."

"That's a better end of the deal." Dex slid over Jonny's drink before grabbing the tenner. Jonny was giving him a look. "Sorry."

"Look, I know they're a bit Tweedle Dee and Tweedle Dum, but they're mates, you know? They mean well. Like, Lance is actually really sweet if you bother to get to know him."

Dex sighed and ran a hand over his locs. "Shit. I know. I'm sorry. Have I been a massive dickhead to *everyone* the last few months?"

Jonny, to give him all the credit in the world, did not laugh at him outright. "Define *massive* and *last few months*?"

Oh God. Dex put his head on his arms and groaned. "That bad?"

"C'mon, mate, up, you're working." Jonny patted Dex's locs.

Dex lifted his head with a sigh. "Really, how bad?"

"I mean, you've not exactly been yourself, but I've been chucking it up to evil Michael's doings."

"He wasn't evil," Dex said automatically. "Maybe he was."

"Talk about a massive dickhead." Jonny cocked a meaningful eyebrow, then relaxed. "Look, you've been grumpy as fuck, and is it hard to be around? Sometimes. But you've never exactly been Mr. Sunshine, and it's not like you've been tearing into everyone or being, like, mean. You've just been, dunno. Less patient or something."

"I think I need to put an end to my ascetic sexless existence," Dex said. "I mean, Izzy's right."

"Nah, man. I mean, Izzy is not all wrong, but I think what you actually need is to get your heart sorted."

Jonny was such good people, Dex thought. Sometimes he'd forget Jonny was older than the rest of them, but every now and then those extra years of wisdom would show themselves and make Dex feel strangely comforted. "Think it's my heart that's the problem?"

"I do. He stomped all over it, and you've not done much to get over that fact. Now's the time, man."

"The time for what?" Steph had managed to belly up to the bar without either of them noticing, which said very little for Dex's bartending abilities.

"For Dex to fix his heart," Jonny said, while Dex gave the pub a panicked glance. The rush had stopped just before Jonny got there, but still.

He served a few pints to guys who looked like this maybe should have been last call and kept half an eye on them as he returned to Jonny and Steph, Steph's lager at the ready.

"You definitely need to get off with someone," Steph told him as she grabbed the glass. "I mean, Jonny's right, too. But, like. Return to the joy of meaningless sex for a while. Or something. If nothing else, it'll take the edge off."

Dex laughed. *The Joy of Meaningless Sex* could have been the title of a book about his first year at uni, when he'd thrown himself headfirst into the freedom of being away from home and surrounded by all the best that gay London had to offer. And then he'd met Michael—the tosser—and fell head over fucking heels in love. Michael had been brilliant. Beautiful, bright. As far as Dex was concerned, the sun rose and set with him, but apparently Michael rose and set with more than just Dex. In fact, he turned out to have risen and set with quite a few boys on the side, which Dex would probably have been fine with had he known.

It was the sharp betrayal that had fucked him up so hard. He managed to ace his end-of-year exams out of sheer determination to prove to himself that Michael had mattered just as little to Dex as Dex had to him.

When he'd come out the other side of the year, Dex had found himself facing a long, joyless summer of working and holing up in his room with Corona and Netflix. It was actually so pathetic, he'd got thoroughly sick of himself by the end.

"Maybe," he told Steph.

"Shake up the old routine, I say," she replied.

"Said the girl who makes spreadsheets of her day just to be sure she doesn't forget to eat her two eggs and a coffee for breakfast."

"I am impervious to your remarks." She smiled at them both. "My life is as spontaneous as I need it to be."

"Okay, babe." Jonny patted her shoulder. "You do you."

Dex knew it was impossible to take Jonny's teasing in a negative way. He was like sunshine personified. No wonder he and Steph had clicked from the start. Now she flipped Jonny off with a grin and then fixed Dex with a bit of an unexpected glare. "All I will say is, you have to make more of an effort with people." Her glare became more significant. "Be nice. You can be nice *and* get your heart sorted out."

"Fine. I will be nice. I will be nice all of the time. I will, in fact," he continued as he polished the glasses under the bar, "be *so* nice that you will think I've been replaced by a pod person, and you will miss this grumpy fucking face and wonder, where did it all go wrong? Oh, that's right, that one night at the pub, when we collectively decided that Dex needed a personality transplant and learned the dangers of wishing for things we may someday get."

"Wow," Steph said. "You done, Dexter?"

Dex sagged down. "Yes."

"Good. Pour us another, Jonny here's low."

Dex dutifully poured them another.

Dex was neck deep in Molecular Basis of Diseases reading when his phone went off, Mum's picture lighting up. Crap. He shut his laptop and let his phone go to voice mail. He asked the girl sat a few feet away to please watch his stuff, if she would be so kind. She nodded at him in the vague manner of someone deep in a revising coma, and Dex just had to trust her, despite her looking a bit like the girl from *The Ring*.

The library had a glassed-in corridor in between wings where people congregated to share woes, have snacks, and guzzle coffee away from the glare of the librarians. Dex stood facing the outside world through the dimmed glass as he dialed Mum's number. It went straight to voice mail as she presumably left him a rambling message. He waited, then tried again.

"Hiya Poppet," she greeted. "Did you listen to my message?"

"No, Mum," Dex said patiently. "You just left it. What's up?"

"Oh, you know," she said in a tone of voice Dex knew very well hid something that was probably not going to be good. He felt his stomach clenching up. "Just wanted to say hi to my eldest, didn't I? How's uni?"

Dex watched the cars careening below. Standing in this corridor made him feel like he was in *Star Trek*—the futuristic glass situated high above the ground. London looked nothing like the future, though.

"Uni's fine," he said as he traced the shape of a Victorian building across the street on the glass. "So what's going on?"

He could tell when she realised he was onto her. "Everything is fine," she began. "I've just been a bit concerned about Al."

Dex breathed out. "Why, what's wrong?"

"He's just not been himself lately, since the move, and I can't seem to get him to talk to me."

Dex could well picture this. His mum was the kindest woman in the world, but she could be a steamroller. Subtle she was not. Every time Dex had a problem, she was full-steam ahead with questions and suggestions. He could imagine how spacy, sweet Al was taking this sort of parenting. Probably with a lot of terror.

"Do you want me to ring him?" he asked. "Have a chat, maybe?"

"Would you, love?" She sounded so relieved. Poor Mum. "I just worry, you know, with you gone, and your dad and I working all the time. We do what we can, but with changing schools, too. You know how it can be."

School. Dex had somehow managed to endure a relatively small amount of school-related crap while growing up, largely due to the growth spurt at thirteen that put him head and shoulders above most others before their balls dropped, but it had been enough. Al was small, he was weird, and he was a new kid after his dad's job moved them from Brum to Cheltenham, of all places. Of course he wasn't adjusting well. Dex should have realised.

"'Course I'll talk to him. I could visit over the weekend."

He'd have to rearrange his work shifts and possibly do the bulk of his reading on the trains, but he could do it. If he got back on Sunday, he'd still have a chance to pop by the library for the reserved materials. No, wait, he could do it beforehand. Right.

"No, no, it's all right. It's not quite so dire yet, you know, I don't want to pull you away from your life, love." She sounded sure, and Dex realised he was relieved. He didn't want to miss out on going out with everyone, for one. The guilt crept up, but he tamped it down.

He turned around to face the other side of the corridor and caught a dude blatantly checking him out. He grinned despite himself, then looked up at the ceiling in an attempt to concentrate on Mum. "All right, if you're sure. I'll give him a ring later tonight. See what's up."

"That would be wonderful." She sounded like she was smiling again. "Well, my break's nearly over, I best get back. Send love to Izzy and everyone, will you?"

"Sure thing. Love you, bye."

"Bye, love."

They hung up at the same time. His mum could talk his ear off most days, but she never lingered on good-byes, which he appreciated.

He cast a glance the dude's way, thinking about what all his friends had said about getting his rocks off as part of the whole post-Michael recovery process. The dude looked back and actually raised one eyebrow.

Why the fuck not.

Dex tipped his head towards the stairs, then held up a finger in a universal *back in a mo* gesture and jogged back to grab his stuff. There was a loo on the fourth floor of the library that barely got any use. He might as well get back on the horse.

✛

He phoned Al later that night, making sure to do it once he was completely post-afterglow.

Al picked up on the fourth ring, just as Dex was getting ready to leave him a properly cheerful message. "Hey." Dex's heart sank at the sound of Al's voice. Mum wasn't kidding. He sounded awful.

Dex put on his cheerful voice anyway. "Hey, kiddo, just wanted to see how you were. Haven't talked in a while."

"Mum tell you to call?" Al asked, flat.

"No! Okay, yeah, but look, I was gonna phone you anyway. How are you?"

"Ugh, I'm *fine*, why does everyone keep asking me that?" Al had never sounded less like himself, but also, he was fourteen. Dex remembered himself at that age, with not a little bit of guilt at how horrible he'd been. It was a toss-up, really, if Albert's attitude was down to adjustment difficulties or just being a teenaged tosser.

"Well, I just want to know what's happening in your life. It's been a while."

Al breathed into his phone long enough that Dex zoned out on watching a single GIF of a cat falling off a table for several hundred loops or so. Then Al said, "It's fine. I'm fine. I just want to be left alone."

Dex breathed in. Maybe he *should* go home this weekend, and fuck Nineties Night. He'd already successfully pulled and broken his sexless streak. His friends could get along without him.

A tiny, horrible voice in the back of his head said, *But Nick.* But Nick nothing. This wasn't a thing.

79

"You want Mum and Dad to leave you alone, or?"

"Who else?"

Christ, this kid was not okay. Dex's heart sank in his chest. "Just wondering, mate, don't bite my head off."

"Sorry."

Even worse. "I've been thinking about visiting, what if I—"

"No, we've got plans this weekend."

Dex's heart sank even more. Al had never before refused a chance to see him, not the whole time Dex had been in London. He'd beg him to visit every now and then, take him out, just the two of them. What was happening with this kid?

"Well then, I'll come the following weekend." He tried not to let his worried annoyance come through, but it was hard going.

"Fine." Al sounded resigned.

Dex opened up the British Rail site to start looking at bloody tickets. "Fine."

"Fine."

This was not what his mum had in mind when she asked him to help. He was utterly useless. "Look, let's talk about something else. Have you been drawing much?"

"What are you, Aunt Lottie? *Read any good books lately?* Come off it."

"Jesus Christ, I'm trying to make conversation. That's what people do."

"Well, it's annoying. I haven't got anything to talk about. My life's boring."

"Why is it boring?" Dex went for that opening with a desperate sort of charge.

"It just *is*, fucking hell."

"Whoa, language."

"Are you serious right now?" At least Al sounded a little more alive.

"No, sorry, right, go on. Boring life. Why?"

"Because I'm fucking fourteen and not allowed to do anything fun, why do you think? Was *your* life full-on while you were in school?"

Dex had always done his best not to remember. After he'd come out, things got both better and not. Mostly it had felt like a waiting game. But Dex had also always had his feet planted firmly on the ground. He'd had friends he could trust, and hell, he'd even had a boyfriend for a whole month once. Dex had been all right.

His family had always known Al was different. Dreamier, more fragile. But he'd been such a happy kid. This was breaking Dex's heart. "Well, I suppose," he said.

"Yeah, so," Al grumbled. "Can't all be living it up in London, or whatever. Anyway, Mum's calling for dinner, I've gotta go."

Al was awful at lying. "Wait, Al—"

"What?"

"Look, just. Call me whenever you want. Or, like, text. Or email. Whatever, just keep in touch, all right? I miss you, Palbert."

Al was quiet for a moment. "Yeah, all right. Miss you too, Ambidexter."

"All right, go. Talk to you soon. Love to Mum and Dad."

"'Kay, bye."

Al hung up, and Dex admitted his attempt to reach out to his brother had been largely unsuccessful.

+

Nineties Night was full-on by the time they tottered over from the bar. Dex had vaguely wondered if they'd even find the place. This being Shoreditch, he had half expected to have to take three turns, look for a nondescript fire escape, and pull on a rope just to get through the door, at which point they'd probably end up in someone's living room with a dude in a fedora manning an iPhone, but in the end they found the place no problem. It turned out to be a proper club and everything.

Izzy had taken charge of everything, in fact, including making sure that Nick made it out with them. The guy had exhibited every sign of avoiding this whole business, as far as Dex could tell, but Izzy was Izzy, and so Nick now trailed behind them looking only slightly shell-shocked and already a pint in.

Which was good, because maybe it would relax him. Dex still felt a bit weird, having had to go up to Nick's room and drag him out. Izzy had flung open Nick's tiny wardrobe while Nick looked properly mortified and picked out his outfit for him. To give Izzy credit, it was a nice outfit. Dex's skin had prickled in a way he hadn't liked when Nick, previously decked out in a loose combo of T-shirt and trackie bottoms, emerged from the bathroom wearing skinny jeans and a tight black T-shirt. He really was fucking small, but Dex had sort of zeroed in on his angular shoulders, stark collarbones, and small waist, and, well, then it had been time to get the fuck out of Nick's tiny, weirdly neat room and get some fucking air.

It took a while for them all to file through the club door, and then, like a startled flock of birds, they all dispersed without a single word. Dex managed to hold onto Izzy, who was already making a beeline for the bar across the dance floor. Nick caught up with them both and was busy gazing all around him.

Then it was just—madness. *Blur* was sort of a good soundtrack to this, he thought as they pushed their way to the bar amidst a grinding crowd. Blue, red, and purple lights chased each other all over the walls and the ceilings and the faces all around him, and Dex was relatively out of breath by the time they got in line for a drink. Before he could think about it too much, he twisted around and grabbed Nick's hand to pull him in alongside him and Izzy before the crowd swallowed him up and they had to call out a search party for one lost American.

Nick mouthed something that looked like *thanks* as he teetered into place, and Dex shrugged, releasing his hand.

"No problem," he said when he remembered Steph's dire warnings to be nice. And just like that, he was rewarded with a slow, tentative smile. He was pretty sure it was the first time Nick had smiled at him, personally, and it did things to Dex. Undeserved, uncalled-for things that forced a smile from him right back as he stared at Nick's full mouth and heard filthy thoughts begin to clamor for attention inside his head.

God.

Where was that drink?

He gave Nick a shaky, acknowledging sort of nod and turned away, pretending to be busy getting the bartender's attention. Izzy was obviously already there, leaned full on the bar in between two other girls, her red hair changing colours under the vivid spotlights. She gave Nick his lager, all business, and ushered the three of them out of the way of those still in line. She'd got herself some sort of fruity cocktail, which she only ever did in clubs. She always said she liked that sort of buzz in very specific situations. Most people just went for shots, but Izzy was a woman all onto herself.

"All right!" she yelled when they found a spot along a wall. "I am drinking half of this, and then we're going dancing! Cheers!" She clinked her glass with Dex's bottle, which was already on its way to his mouth and promptly collided with his teeth. "Soz!" She laughed, completely unrepentant.

Dex let his Corona do the soothing. He glanced over at Nick. He wasn't even paying attention to them. Instead, he was taking a long pull of his drink and watching the dance floor in a way Dex couldn't quite figure. In the shifting half-dark he looked even more fey, his long eyelashes fluttering, his throat working to swallow the drink. He was sort of moving, just a little, to the beat. Dex was certain he had no idea he was doing it.

When he looked back at Izzy, she was giving him a side-eye. He raised his eyebrows at her. *What?* She shook her head and shrugged, which was her signal for *nothing yet*, and he leaned down until he could yell, "Go find a boy to pull" in her ear.

She laughed and shoved her cold glass into his free hand, then yelled back, "You too!" before whirling away.

Well, great. Now he was responsible for her drink as well as his. He sucked on her straw and nearly vomited. He washed it down with Corona and decided that Izzy had given up her right to this drink the minute she forced it on him. He set it down, then drank half of his beer. He desperately wanted to be out there, too, but politeness dictated he stay with Nick. Fuck. Did he really have to? This was a cockblock in more than one way.

"You can go, you know!" Nick shouted over the din, still not really quite looking at Dex. "I'm gonna be fine."

Dex gave him a look to make sure he wasn't lying. Maybe Dex wasn't giving him enough credit. Besides, he now had express permission to fuck off politely. He should take advantage of that, right?

He leaned down until his lips were sort of close to Nick's ear and said, "You sure?"

Nick nodded, then glanced up until their eyes met. Even on the edge of things, Dex sweated in the chaos. "Totally. I'll just finish my drink." Nick lifted it as if to illustrate his point, and that was good enough for Dex. It was weird how his flat American accent contrasted with his intricate face.

"Well, thanks, man." Dex pushed away from the wall and gave him one last look, but Nick was already watching the mass of humanity on the floor, so Dex took the chance to escape.

He had to stop this madness anyway. He barely even knew the guy, it was purely physical, and even then probably mostly out of desperation.

He shoved his way into the crowd and lost himself in other bodies for the next several songs.

Nick was sweating profusely. The club was loud and overwhelming, and he found himself mesmerized by it against all odds. It was easy to lose himself in the crowd, easy to become member and witness all at once. He had almost been happy to see everyone disperse, even Izzy and Dex, after they rescued him by the bar. Without anyone watching, he felt his shoulders unwind.

He was at a club and he had no desire at all to leave. It was amazing. He finished off his beer and stood on the edge of the dance floor just bopping to the beat a little, letting the unfamiliar songs take him places. No one was watching him. That was the miracle letting him loose, allowing him to think, *I can do this. I got this.* Zoyka would be so proud when he told her. He swayed more, kept his eyes closed, got into it. Got lost in it.

He had talked himself in and out of coming tonight a thousand times over the course of the week. It was just not him. It wasn't. He didn't do this. The closest he'd ever come was a high school dance, and that had been such torture, he'd been the guy who left first.

He had mulled tonight over again and again, come up with so many scenarios as to what could possibly go wrong that he got sick of himself, shut the process down. He hadn't told his sister about it at all, just so she wouldn't have a chance to talk him into it. But then Izzy's text had come through while he was deep in *The Pickwick Papers,* and before he could think of an adequate way to decline she was banging down his door, Dex in tow.

Dex. Another problem Nick had contemplated numerous times over. He hadn't been sure what to expect from the next time he saw him.

He definitely hadn't been expecting to see him on the other side of his door, looking possibly more uncomfortable than Nick as Izzy filled his room with her presence and threw all of his clothes around like his own psychotic personal stylist. He was beginning to suspect he was in over his head when it came to knowing her, but it comforted him.

If they didn't want him around, would they go to all this trouble?

Nick smiled to himself and pumped the air when "Rhythm Is a Dancer" started up. He'd even known this song before they came to the States. God, he hadn't heard it in years. People around him hollered and whooped, and he joined in, feeling outside of himself for the first time in a while.

It wasn't until he was out of breath and screaming along to "Jump Around" that he felt an arm wrapping around his waist from behind and yelped.

Someone laughed in his ear—a girl—and when he twisted around to look, he came face to grinning face with Natali. Immediately he tensed up, too aware of how clammy and sweaty he was and how ridiculous he must have looked from the outside. This. This was why he hadn't wanted to come. He began to pull away, but Natali slung both arms around his neck and pulled him in.

"I fucking love this fucking song!" she yelled in his ear, and relief, hot as lava, poured through his whole system. Something about the way she clearly hadn't cared that he'd been jumping around like an idiot made it so much easier to yell back, "Me too!" then close his eyes and jump up and down with her. He could do this. He *could.*

So he did.

+

A while later, he had managed to get himself another drink. How, he had no idea. His legs were killing him, he was completely out of breath, he was probably so red in the face that he looked like a cartoon, but somehow he had slunk in between two people at the bar and actually got the bartender's attention, which was a first for him. It was the same dude who'd served Izzy earlier, and when he saw Nick, he jogged over and gave him a grin that took Nick aback. He managed his order and paid like a normal human, and acknowledged in his mind that the look he'd received may have been skirting close to flirty.

He wasn't dealing with that, so he made his way to a relatively empty spot, and the lukewarm beer tasted like manna from heaven. He felt liquid, fuzzy-headed and lovely. He was ridiculously pleased with his current life choices. Pleased that he had successfully danced at a club without anyone pointing at him and laughing, pleased that he'd been able to dance with Natali and not flip out.

"Ohhh my God, I am fucking knackered."

Nick jolted and looked over to where Izzy had sidled up next to him. Her hair was a wild mess around her head, her top falling off one shoulder. Her bra strap looked red, but it might have been the spotlights messing with him. When he looked beyond her, he caught sight of Dex making his way over to them through the throng.

He looked…glowy. It was strange to think that, probably, and maybe everyone looked glowy to Nick just then, but he appeared relaxed and happy and just a little rumpled and sweaty. Not like Nick, who was a soggy mess. Nick tipped his head back against the wall and took a sip of his drink. Dex had great legs, he decided. Slightly bowed, steady, long. Lean. His jeans looked really good on him.

"Having a good time? I thought I saw you dancing with Nat," Izzy said in his ear.

"Yeah, it's been awesome." He made eye contact. "Thanks for getting me."

She looked pleased with herself. "Anytime." She caught Dex by the hand and pulled him into her sweaty embrace.

Now that Nick knew they weren't together, he felt a little...he supposed it was envy, really. He had never felt easy with anyone, not even Lena. Maybe with his sister, but that was different; that was family. They looked so comfortable, Dex sagging against Izzy, dark arm wrapped around her exposed pale shoulder. Nick jumped if you touched him. How must it feel to trust like this? He couldn't imagine. So he just watched them and pushed down anything that could darken his mood. He could feel how a stray thought could pop his temporary joy, and he skated carefully around it, closed his eyes, pretended he was still dancing.

"All right, I'm going back out," Izzy declared. "There was a dark-headed bloke over there somewhere I needed to look at more closely." She went without another word. When Nick turned to Dex, Dex was laughing. He had one hand over his dreads, probably in an attempt to keep them out of his face. It made him look rakish.

He caught Nick's gaze. "Don't expect to see Izzy much if you go to clubs with her. This is her MO."

Nick had absolutely no problem with that, which he felt, just then, the need to acknowledge. "I have no problem with that."

"As long as you know what's in store." Dex settled next to Nick like Nick *didn't* set his teeth on edge. Maybe he was mellowing out.

"Are you mellowing out?" Nick asked and then heard a record scratch in his head. *Oh shit.* When he dared to glance over at Dex, Dex was laughing, head resting against the wall.

"I so deserved that, man," he said. "Look, I've been a dickhead to you, completely inadvertently, and—" Nick's heart beat hard in his chest. "It wasn't you. At all." He pinned Nick with a *look.* A look that shivered through Nick's spine. "Basically, I wanted to apologize for that. I'm going to be less of a dickhead from now on. Promise."

Nick had no idea what to say. All he could think was how Dex's eyelashes were ridiculous and made his eyes look made-up. How Dex's throat glistened with a sheen of sweat. How much he really, really couldn't have been having these thoughts at all because he—couldn't. It wasn't an option.

"It's totally fine," is what he said. "I appreciate it, anyway." Then he nodded toward the writhing dance floor. "I'm just gonna—"

"Yeah, sure, go." Dex nodded and plucked at his own T-shirt, unsticking it from his body in an easy movement.

Nick didn't linger. He ran off.

But Nick couldn't ignore things when it was just him in bed, in the dark. He twisted this way and that, tried to get comfortable and fall asleep, but the swirl of all that had happened chased him. He turned over onto his stomach, pillowed his face on his hands, and looked out into the London night. Maybe if he confronted all the crap instead of running from it, he'd actually be *able* to fall asleep. Maybe it wasn't so bad. Maybe he could fool himself for just a minute.

Embarrassment writhed inside him, though. Now that he was sober, memories popped up in erratic shifts. *Why did I do that?* Why had he danced like an idiot? Why had he gone at all?

He had been rude to Dex, too. He squeezed his eyes shut and felt anxiety pooling in his stomach in a way that nauseated him. Why hadn't he thanked him properly? There was probably something he could have said, but he had no idea what it was, because Nick rarely knew the right thing to do or say.

He groaned and covered himself with the duvet. The close, sweaty air underneath didn't help, but maybe if he stayed there forever, he'd never actually have to deal with any of it. Suffocating on his own humiliation—what an ending.

Dex was a problem. Nick didn't know why Dex being gay flipped Nick's view of him, but it did. Now Dex was—no. Dex was nothing.

Nick was thousands of miles away, but the yoke of all he had to be extended far beyond that.

He wasn't *this*. He wasn't Natali and her confidence in who she was. He wasn't Dex and his grace, his easy pride and acceptance of all that he contained.

Nick was the product of all things unspoken, all things fearful and untold. *Don't tell anyone you're Jewish. It's good, you pass, you don't have the family nose. You have light hair, thank God. Your sister's got the sad Jewish eyes, but you—you took after your dad. You'll be okay.*

Later, he'd begun to say these things to himself. Things like, Don't mention how the sight of your middle school best friend sends your heart fluttering in a way that it never, ever should. You want to be him, that's all. You want to know what it's like to be that good-looking, to have that confidence, to feel your feet planted on the soil they were meant to stay on. That's all it is. That's all it's ever been.

Don't breathe a word of how you cried in the shower every day for a whole summer because you knew you were different and that the door your path led to was forbidden.

Don't say it. Don't even think it.

You aren't that. You can't be. *That* is not for you.

Move thousands of miles away. Accidentally meet people that you've always longed for and wanted to be like. Wonder, every night, why they picked you out of a sea of people who were so much more than you could ever be. You, a mess. You want to be just like them.

But you can't be. Because you have to go back. You will always, always have to go back.

Dex wasn't the problem. It was Nick. It had always, always been Nick.

Dex was lulled watching the stations pass him by. It was off-peak, a rainy Saturday morning slog of a train ride. The train was half full of poshos off to the Cotswolds for the weekend, or so Dex imagined. Ostensibly, he was slogging through piles of research on his laptop. In reality, however, he'd stopped paying attention once they'd passed Reading. He was thinking about the first time he had visited his parents at their new home, and he was thinking about Al.

He remembered how when he decided to pick Al up from school, everyone had begun to file out, and he had watched white face after white face, all uniformed and chatting and so very much belonging. Girls walking hand in hand, long, shiny hair playing in the breeze, boys climbing each other in games of macho one-upmanship. And there, slinking out all on his own, had been Al. One of maybe three black faces that Dex could see. One of a handful of dark faces in all the school, probably.

Small, awkward—an alien in a sea of sameness. Dex's heart had clenched, and he felt almost sick at the sight of it.

His mum hadn't mentioned this part. He should have known, should have thought, but he'd been so busy up his own arse, he hadn't actually realised.

Al had come up to him, and his face said it all. Dex had cuffed him on the shoulder, wrapped his arm around his neck, and they trudged home together, Dex learning the route for the first time. His own family, in the Cotswolds. *Unsettling* didn't begin to describe it.

If he had seen the looks sent his way in just those twenty minutes of waiting, he couldn't imagine what it was like for Al. Day in and day out, consistently the black kid, the weird kid, the small kid who had yet to hit a growth spurt.

Now Dex thought about what would greet him at home. *Home.* It didn't feel like home. Nothing about it felt like home, not even the familiar worn furniture inside his parents' small but modern house. The kitchen was state-of-the-art, incongruous with all of their things. It was hard to believe his dad had landed the *financier to the spies* job he had now, but there it was.

Guilt about wanting to be back on familiar London ground pushed firmly to the back of his mind, he focused on the article he had in front of him and did his best not to think about what he looked like to the crowd of commuters around him. The only black guy heading towards the same destination.

Mum had gone all out with the fry-up. As soon as he was through the door, Dex smelled hot buttered toast, fried eggs, mushrooms, beans, all of his favourites.

"Hiya," he greeted, dropping his bag carefully in the foyer.

"Dexter!" Dad's voice boomed out from the kitchen. Mum was at the hob, looking exhausted but cheerful as she spooned out beans onto toast. Dad looked well, his nose half in his phone, tablet off to the side. Dex wondered how he didn't spill coffee onto any of his electronics day in and day out. Al was nowhere to be found.

Dex sank into a chair. He'd had to get up at arse o'clock to make his train, and one cup of terrible train coffee did not make up for that. "Smells amazing," he told Mum as soon as she slid a plate in front of him. "Got any coffee?"

"The kettle's just boiled, hasn't it?" She leaned down and kissed him on the forehead, ran her hands over his locs. She probably thought she was being subtle, but he always knew what that tiny wrinkle of her nose meant. *When will you get rid of these and get yourself a proper cut?* He shook his head and began shoveling food into his mouth.

Dad put down his phone and pushed his glasses off his face as he watched Dex eat. Dad. He looked distinguished with his grey temples, but it was always a shock to see it. Every time Dex saw his parents now, they looked smaller somehow. Just a bit more worn, just a little more tired. Was it possible that they changed so much in the few months and weeks, or was he being weird and imagining it? They were in their late forties, and Dex had heard somewhere that that wasn't old at all. But it was close to fifty.

"Well, here you are, love." A miraculous cup of coffee appeared next to Dex's plate. "Can I get you anything else? Do you want a bit of a kip after breakfast?"

Dex wanted nothing more than to sleep, but that hadn't been the plan for this weekend. "I'm all right. Sit, relax."

She waved him off, but then sat down with her cup of tea anyway. Now he had both of them staring at him indulgently as he ate. He swallowed a bit of egg and laughed. "All right, what?"

"Oh, it's just good to see you, isn't it?" Mum laughed. "You look good. Maybe a bit thin."

That was crap, obviously, but she always said that. "How are you? When did you get off your shift?"

She squinted at the clock on the microwave. "Just about two hours past, I suppose."

Dex winced. She'd always had a mental schedule and would appear at home at all hours of the day long enough to make sure everyone was clothed and fed and properly looked after and then disappear for a double shift at the hospital. Sometimes, Dex had come home to find her slumped over on the sofa, book open in her lap, dead to the world. She was the queen of the twenty-minute kip. It was starting to take its toll, though, he could see. The skin under her eyes was darker, thinner; the short hairs at her temples had begun to salt-and-pepper like Dad's. "When do you go back in again?"

"Oh, not till tonight, got plenty of time," she said, waving him away. "Now, more importantly—have you got a new boyfriend yet?"

"Muuuum."

Dad just laughed at them both, pulled his glasses back down onto his nose, and went back to checking his phone and iPad all at once.

+

Al didn't emerge until nearly noon. By that time, Dex's mum had already gone into her bedroom for a nap, Dex had had a throw-down with Izzy over text on how it had not been his turn to do the washing up, thank you very much, and Dad had gone into his office—also known as the room where Dex now slept—for some unexpected conference call.

"Oh hey," Al said with little inflection.

"Hey yourself." Dex gave him a few minutes before following him to the kitchen. He parked his hip on the counter, watching Al struggle with his breakfast. It was like he had all of his limbs in the right places, but making a cuppa at a normal speed was beyond him. Dex sort of wanted to grab the kettle away from him for his own safety, but didn't, knowing how easily it could enrage him. Al, for his part, ignored him until he had his tea and toast.

"Do you want me to make you a fry-up?" Dex asked cautiously, and did a double-take when he saw the Waitrose label on the bread. He lifted the loaf in silent question to Al, who just shrugged and shoved a piece of toast in his mouth.

Mum had always gone to Morrisons, or Sainsbury's. For a while when Dex was about ten, it had been Asda. This was new.

Dex flopped down on the chair across from Al. Al was starting to fill out more, and it was possible he'd grown an inch or so. Dex honestly couldn't tell anymore. It was like time and distance was warping his awareness of what he knew his family to be, starting with the unfamiliar house down to how many wrinkles mum had at the corners of her eyes. Disorienting. It was like someone had come in while they'd all been away and rearranged everything in ways you couldn't pinpoint but knew were all wrong.

Dex waited until Al's cup was half-empty. "Want to do something today?"

Al shrugged without looking at him. Dex hated this gulf between them. He had no idea how to navigate it. But if Al was going to be all teenage ambivalence towards him, Dex would just have to push it.

"We're doing something today, and you get to pick whether it's you showing me around town—"

"It's raining."

"—or it's me holing up with you in your room and playing Nintendo. Loudly. By myself."

His tone must have worked, because Al froze with his toast halfway to his mouth and gave him a panicked look. Then he swallowed the toast, bunged the rest of it on his plate, and said, "Fine. We're going out."

"Good."

+

Al used to be a pretty chatty little kid. Half the time, Dex had no idea what he was saying, but then, he also hadn't always been listening. His ears were perked up now, but Al was silent. They trudged down High Street with nary a word said between them, apart from Dex asking Al if he'd been to this place or that.

When would I? or *Why would I?* Dex was beginning to wonder if Al hadn't been replaced by a pod person. He was also vaguely approaching the end of his rope, so he turned up the collar of his jacket, slipped his knotted hands into his pockets, and let the silence stretch out. At least Al had come out with him.

Cheltenham was, as anticipated, exceptionally posh. It was also exceptionally white. Beautiful Regency-era buildings housed all sorts of shops catering to, Dex imagined, all sorts of yummy mummies and their moneymaking husbands. Cafes and restaurants lined each street, with historic buildings and museums announcing just how cultured and one of a kind this place was. Dex couldn't deny it its beauty, but he wasn't precisely enjoying it.

He pictured his mum running errands in between work shifts, wondered what it felt like. He'd got so used to London and its relative diversity. Hell, Birmingham hadn't been bad, either. This felt like a wake-up call he hadn't asked for. And this was where Al was growing up now, the weird kid on the outskirts.

Dex watched him trudging along next to him, looking like Mum, where Dex was all his dad. They barely appeared related, but Dex felt like a wolf protecting his cub whenever a passerby gave them a look of any kind. Was he being paranoid? Or did the two of them really stand out like sore thumbs? Another thing he'd lost perspective on. You never forgot, precisely, but sometimes the sharpness of difference got eroded, just a little, on familiar ground.

This wasn't familiar in any way.

His phone buzzed in his pocket.

How's the Cotswolds you big posho?

Izzy. Dex rolled his eyes before responding. *Stunning, what do u think*

Al led them around the corner until they passed a big shopping centre, but didn't go in. They kept walking.

I think it's probs crap and u need to come home we miss u <3

It was awful that his spirits lifted at that. It had only been a few hours, but he felt so out of his depth here. Guilt at wanting to be back in his own flat with his own friends encroached once again, and once again he pushed it back.

It's been like 6 hours u ok?

"Look, it's raining and I don't feel like being stalked in shops today, so can we just go home now?"

Oh. Dex tried to catch Al's eye, but Al was scowling, looking straight ahead. Dex deflated. Cheltenham. Of course they'd be followed around each shop if they went inside.

"Yeah, sod it. Let's just have a cuppa and see what's on the telly."

They went.

+

By the time he got out of the tube on Sunday, it was freezing and the sun had already set. He felt the drizzle all at once, London welcoming him back into its cold, grey arms. Not even the rain could ruin this return, though.

Al had relaxed a little bit around him, or maybe just got used to him in twenty-four hours, but Dex never got much more than a shrug out of him anyway. They'd stayed up late watching crap telly and drinking Yorkshire tea with digestives, and Dex had got a text off of Izzy with a picture of everyone at the Arms making sad faces at the camera. *We miss uuuuuuu [heartbreak emoji]*, it had said. He'd sent a picture of his tea and Al. Later, he had tossed and turned on the study sofa and looked at Nick's face turned obligingly sad towards the camera. He didn't stop until he fell asleep.

Dex heaved his bag more firmly over his shoulder and trudged back to the flat, knowing that he had failed to help Mum and Dad out with Al and also got approximately zero work done.

He was so happy to be back home that he didn't even care that Jonny had, once again, left beer bottles on the coffee table and was nowhere to be seen. Dex dropped his stuff in his room, then went in search of Izzy, but when he knocked on her door there was no answer. He looked at the time—was it too late or too early for them all to be out? And without him.

He frowned, trudged back down to the kitchen, and flicked the kettle on. Maybe this weekend was anxious mood, tea, and crap telly, and that was fine, because tomorrow was a brand new day or whatever. It was cool. He was fine with that.

His phone buzzed in his pocket.

Emergency mtg at Arms, u back?

Dex frowned at his phone. What could possibly be considered an emergency on a Sunday evening, especially one that would have to be discussed at the pub?

Wtf is happening?

He was already halfway out the door when Izzy's reply came.

Jonny's dads ill, has to go home.

Shit. Shit, double-shit.

It wasn't a secret Jonny didn't get on with his parents, and it definitely was sort of a known thing that his dad was a right bastard. Dex could only imagine what was going through the poor guy's head at the moment. No wonder he'd needed the pub.

Jonny, like Dex, Izzy, and Nat, had spent the past summer in London, but unlike the rest of them, he hadn't really had a choice in the matter. It also hadn't been his first. His parents, backwards as they were, couldn't face the fact that Jonny now lived as Jonny full-time, thriving as the man he'd always known he was.

What shocked Dex was that Jonny's parents had told him about his dad's illness at all. Were they expecting him, or was he going there against their wishes? It must be serious for them to have deigned to communicate with their son.

Dex reached the pub soon enough, shucking his jacket halfway and throwing Tosh a wave where he stood behind the bar.

"Corona?" Tosh mouthed.

Dex threw him a thumbs up in answer.

Beer in hand, he found them, Nick included, in the back. Dex received a round of cheers like he was a conquering hero being welcomed back home. He slipped in to sit next to Izzy, slightly embarrassed, and turned his gaze to Jonny.

"Mate, you all right? What's happened?" he asked.

Jonny looked rumpled. He was usually on par with Steph for most relaxed person to be around, but he looked pale and visibly agitated. Dex noted his glass was nearly empty.

"Dad's got to have heart surgery. It was a bit of an emergency, I guess. I wouldn't have found out, but Sophie phoned, told me." His cousin. The only one in his family who wasn't utterly made of stone. "Said Mum's pretty frightened. I've got to go, haven't I?"

By the looks on everyone's faces, Dex guessed this wasn't the first time this question was being asked, nor the first time it was answered.

"Mate, it's your call," Alex said. "I'm telling you, there's no wrong choice here."

"There *is* though. If I go, Mum might go mental, and who knows what it would do my dad. I mean, what if his heart actually gives out?"

"But what if you don't?" Steph's quiet voice cut in.

It continued in this vein. Dex looked around at everyone and noticed their unhappy faces.

No one, however, not even *Jonny*, looked as pale as Nick.

Dex felt a shock go through him. He barely noticed that Nick had apparently got a haircut sometime between now and the last time Dex had seen him, because Nick looked like a ghost. His glasses hid his eyes a bit, but his hand was rigid around his barely started beer, jaw set in a way that made him look much less delicate than normal. Dex followed Natali's gaze and saw that she'd noticed, too. They exchanged a look.

"Babe, I'm getting you another," Natali said to Jonny. "You too, Iz. Dex, help?"

Dex felt awkward leaving the table a second after he got there, but he knew a signal when he heard one.

"Okay, something's up with Nick," Nat said as soon as Tosh took their orders. "He was with Izzy when Jonny texted, I guess, and she gathered everyone and brought him along, but he's been so quiet, and he looks—"

"Like shit," Dex supplied, even though that wasn't precisely what he'd been thinking. In fact, if not for his dead-eyed expression and rigidity, Nick would look like a queer fucking wet dream right about now. His haircut was of the short-back-and-sides variety, with curly fringe in the front. A complete change from the crazy Beethoven hair he'd been sporting. Suddenly, his face took on a distinctive shape, and he looked different. Strong. *Hot.* It brought his cheekbones into stark relief. It also showed his ears, which turned out to be just this side of Dumbo-sized. Dex found them enchanting.

"Yeah," Nat nodded, leaning her elbows on the bar. "D'you think it's because Izzy told him Jonny's trans?"

Unpleasant thought. Dex frowned, thought about it. "God, I hope not, that'd be shit. When did Iz tell him?"

"I mean, I'm guessing when Jonny texted her to tell her what happened. Nick was at ours, Iz had just cut his hair. I wasn't there, mind, I'm just extrapolating."

"Where was Jonny?" Jonny was openly out as trans, and sometimes Dex forgot there were people who didn't realise.

Maybe people who didn't like it. God, he hoped to God Nick wasn't one of them. How would Izzy have said it?

"With Lance, I think?"

Dex boggled, to which Nat shrugged eloquently. "Why isn't Lance here, then?" *If Lance really was such a good friend to Jonny*, he added in his mind.

This time, Nat gave him an *are you fucking kidding me?* look. It squirmed through Dex. Right. Because he didn't exactly make it easy on Lance whenever he was around. Nor Jonny, for that matter. Maybe he needed to stop being an arsehole to Lance now. *Eurgh.*

"All right, message received. But it would be such shit if Nick was having trans panic or whatever." Who knew, really, if Nick was all right with their collective queerness?

"I know." Natali cast a glance back at their table. "Who knows. Maybe it's daddy issues."

"*That* would be better?"

Nat grinned. "Well, more socially acceptable to our kind."

"Yes, our kind adores some daddy issues."

"Here you go, guys." Tosh sent their glasses sliding across the bar surface.

"Cheers." Nat threw down some bank notes, and Dex followed her back to the table with no better plan than to do his best to talk Jonny through whatever decision he was going to make and possibly to suss out just what the fuck was bothering Nick.

Dex found himself seated next to Nick. He hadn't been this close to him since the club. Somehow, in all the time Nick had spent with them, Dex had managed to avoid just this situation. Now he knew why it had been a good idea to do so, and hated himself for it. He wasn't here to beat himself up about how good Nick smelled this close up, or too feel a tiny stab of disappointment when Nick subtly moved his thigh so it was no longer touching Dex's. Or to be so keenly aware of just how still Nick was next to him that he missed the conversation entirely.

Dex was here for Jonny.

"Look, all I'm saying is," Steph said, "you may have some really shitty times when going back home, but if something dreadful happens, which it won't, but *if*." She trailed off. Jonny looked like misery itself. And to think, Dex had been moping about his own perfectly normal family visit.

Christ.

"You've got to take care of yourself, too, though," Izzy put in. "What would be worse for you, you know?"

Jonny nodded glumly, took a deep breath. "Not going. Not going would be worse," he finally said, voice quiet and resigned. "If I catch the early train tomorrow, I could be there before they take him to surgery, I think."

"Will you be able to get to the hospital?"

"Soph would get me, she said. She's got a car now."

"Can you stay with her?"

Jonny nodded. A silence descended. When Dex dared to tilt his head Nick's way, his locs caught and rustled against Nick's shoulder. Nick jumped. Dex leaned in, whispered, "Mate. You all right?"

Nick turned his face and looked Dex in the eye. This close up, Dex could see that Nick's eyes were redder than normal.

"I'm sorry, I should go," Nick said, quiet as a dormouse, making no move to leave. "I'm not." He cleared his throat and swept his gaze across the table before returning to face him. Dex didn't think anyone was watching them. "It's nothing, I promise, but I just—"

"What?"

"It's just—well, the thing is—" Nick's voice all but disappeared. Against his better judgment, Dex leaned in until he felt Nick's breath on his ear, hoping it was encouragement enough to finally spill whatever the hell was happening inside him. "Ugh, look. My dad died. It was a heart attack. I guess I'm not over it."

The words had been barely a whisper, but they rocked through Dex. Fucking hell. Daddy issues, indeed. Dex couldn't have stopped himself from reacting if he'd tried.

"Shit. Nick, I'm sorry." He did, at least, keep his voice quiet. Even with that, he could tell someone was watching them. He tried to look Nick in the eye, but Nick had trained his gaze on the table. A muscle in his jaw was jumping.

Dex glanced over at Jonny, saw that he was being comforted by Steph and Alex. "D'you need to get out of here?"

Nick nodded, then shook his head. "I can't, that's so…I mean, this isn't my—" He broke off, clearly frustrated.

"It's not rude, man, you're a second away from a panic attack," Dex said, maybe a bit more sharply than he'd meant to. "You could use a bit of fresh air."

He had no idea why he was so insistent. He only knew that Nick was rigid with fright and God knew what else, and Dex could maybe help. And Nick had confided in him. That had to count for something.

Nick finally nodded, a single jerky move.

Dex slipped from the booth to let Nick out. Nick got up laboriously, as if his limbs weren't obeying him. Dex exchanged another glance with Nat, saw the question on her face, shook his head.

"Nick's not feeling well, so I'm actually gonna walk him home." A stupid decision, but a decision. "Jonny, mate." Jonny glanced at him, looking positively exhausted. Ugh. "I'll see you at home, yeah? Pillow talk?" Jonny nodded, gave a tiny smile. "Pillow talk" was what they perversely called their late-night chat sessions on the sofa in front of the muted telly. Dex had no idea which of them had started it, but the name had stuck. He waved good-bye to everyone else, avoided Izzy's questioning gaze, and caught Nick's.

"C'mon," he said. "I could use some air, too." They walked out together.

Nick all but burst out of the pub and then, much to his humiliation, doubled over, dry heaving. God, this hadn't happened in years. His face burned, but he couldn't catch his breath, couldn't stop it. His heart was going to rip straight through his ribcage and bleed out onto the rainy street. Fuck, fuck, fuck.

"Breathe."

A steady hand on his back, a voice in his ear. Nick's throat dry-clicked. He shook his head, *I can't, I can't breathe.*

"C'mon, you can do it."

Nick was vaguely aware of Dex crouching down next to him, his hand moving up and down on his back. He hated it and needed it at the same time. Hated that he needed it. Needed it like air.

Slowly, painfully slowly, his breathing evened out, and he no longer felt like he was going to vomit. His heart pitter-pattered inside his chest still, fluttering like a hummingbird. He felt his pulse in his ears, in his fingers, in the bottoms of his feet. When he swallowed again, he could do it without a cobwebby feel in his throat. He straightened up slowly and closed his eyes. Dex's hand still soothed his back, and Nick had no idea how to make him stop. He was aware of trembling.

If the ground could open up and swallow him whole, he'd have welcomed it.

"Fuck." He breathed through the last of it. His face, when he touched it, was clammy and warm. His shirt stuck to his back under his jacket, and he shook the jacket off, let it drop, felt the cold rain on his arms. He took off his glasses and buried his face in his hands. Street noises filtered in. Dex was no longer touching his back. He was quiet next to Nick, but present. Too present.

Nick didn't know how long they stood there like that. If it had been up to him, he'd have stood there long enough to turn to stone and for Dex to walk away, but in reality, he couldn't just slump like an idiot forever. Maybe everyone else was about to file out, and he'd humiliated himself enough for one night. It writhed in his belly, replacing the panic. At least he hadn't actually vomited. Small favors.

"I'm okay," he lied, letting his hands drop to his sides. Without his glasses, Dex was a little blurry beside him, but Nick could still tell he looked concerned.

"Okay." Dex's voice was careful, quiet.

Nick shivered, the cold finally seeping through, and bent to pick up his jacket, only to notice it hanging from Dex's arms. "Oh. Th-thank you."

"Not a problem. D'you want to walk?"

Nick slipped his rain-spattered glasses back on, put on his jacket, and nodded. They trudged together under the street lamps. Nick attempted not to think by counting numbers and letters on the passing cars' license plates, slipping into the old habit like a comfortable bed.

He had to apologize. To everyone, but especially to Jonny, and to Dex, too. What they must think of him, derailing a night about their friend. Dex had barely even been there ten minutes when he had to go and babysit Nick.

He swallowed and made himself talk. "I'm sorry." His voice was almost steady. He set his jaw. "I haven't...This hasn't happened in a while. I wasn't expecting it, and you really didn't have to—"

"It's okay," Dex said. "Really, promise."

Nick nodded, not believing him for a second but trying to appreciate the lie. "I can probably make it back by myself." He was aware that his attempt at a smile most likely looked wrong, but it was the best he could do.

"Don't mind a walk. It's nice."

It was drizzling and freezing, but Nick shut up. They crossed two intersections before Dex pointed to a darkened park nearby. "Want to?"

Nick squinted, made out a weird sort of sculpture garden. He realized with desperation that he didn't want to go back to his dorm. "Okay."

"Cool."

Dex led the way. The street lamps didn't quite reach inside the park, the trees protecting it from view. The sculptures turned out to be a set of oddly shaped colorful benches, smooth like water-weathered stone. When Nick sat down on a blue one, it propelled him backward and he yelped, just managing to hang on.

"You okay?" Dex turned around. "Oh, is that one of them spring things?"

Nick righted himself, his humiliation complete. "Apparently."

Nick didn't miss his grin. He ducked his head and sighed.

"It's okay, you know," Dex said a moment later. He, Nick noticed, didn't fall ass over elbow when he sat down on his own rocking bench. The thought must have shown on his face, because Dex said, "You tested it for me."

"You're welcome." Gingerly, Nick pushed one foot off the ground, and the bench swayed beneath him. Now that he was expecting it, it was sort of soothing. Like a swing, or a rocking chair. The rain didn't reach them under the cover of trees, and his glasses slowly dried as he sat there, rocking.

The back of his head was cold. Izzy's haircut left him virtually shorn in places he wasn't used to being exposed. He still had no idea why he'd let her, but he was actually pretty pleased with the result. And it had been free. And then Izzy got the text from Natali, and Izzy had dragged him along, and...

He looked down. His shoes were wet, small blades of grass sticking to the tips. It wasn't that he never thought about his dad. He thought about him all the time. But he'd relegated him to the back of his mind, a place it was safe for his memory to inhabit without rendering Nick a complete and utter mess. Because when the mess came out, it came out in a vicious wave of *this*.

"Do you want to tell me about it?" Dex's voice cut into his thoughts, and Nick looked up. Dex didn't look like he was humoring him, but the offer still made Nick feel strange. "I mean, you don't have to," Dex added. "But maybe it'd help?"

Nick was aware of two things. One was that he very much never wanted to talk about this with anyone ever again, and the second was that he probably owed Dex an explanation at the very least. Dex had been deliberately kind, which Nick couldn't bring himself to push away, no matter the extent to which he had no idea how to deal with it.

He cleared his throat, squeezed his eyes shut for a minute, and said, "I haven't reacted like this in a while, like...with a panic attack, I guess."

"How long has it been?"

"Five years," Nick supplied automatically, then looked up. "Sorry, that's—since he died. And I guess about a year or so since I've done this."

He'd just turned fifteen. It had been a muggy sort of summer day, no breeze. He was working at a Dairy Queen at the time. He had been just about to go on his break, brooding about something stupid, when Zoyka walked through the door, the bell clanging to announce her presence. He had never seen her like that before. Not once since. Her eyes, always heavy-lidded and big—she had beautiful eyes—were red and shadowed underneath. Her hair was all over the place. Nick still remembered the way one stray curl fluttered with the force of the AC blowing in through the vent over her head. That's what he was looking at when she told him that something had happened with Dad. Nick hadn't even taken off his apron. He'd been thinking about his best friend. Thinking about how he hadn't seen Josh for a week now that Josh had a girlfriend.

"I'm sorry." Dex's voice was quiet.

Nick nodded, taking in a shaky breath. "Yeah, I guess talk of dads and hearts and...You know."

"Yeah. I mean...yeah."

When Nick glanced up, Dex gave him a small dimpled smile. He returned it, but it felt brittle on his face, a trepidation of muscles that felt unused. Even in semidarkness, he saw the questions Dex wanted to ask. He was grateful Dex wasn't asking them at the same time as answers clamored to spill out, words he hadn't said in years. Maybe the darkness made it easy. Only his mom and Zoyka knew it all. Lena, too. She'd been there. Before they became anything else, they'd been friends. Two immigrant kids, clinging to each other, united by language and misery.

"He'd been working in his lab, and his heart just...gave out." Nick's voice was rusty. He swallowed. "The ambulance got there too late, and I guess they couldn't have done anything even if they'd been there a second after, he—" Died. Between one second and the next, his dad was gone. Massive coronary. Nick hadn't known at the time that his dad hadn't seen a doctor since coming to the States. They'd all had a check-up or two when they first immigrated. Got their shots just in case, had their first dental cleanings. After that, his parents were religious about Nick and Zoya's physicals. But no one had looked after Dad. And then it was way too late.

"Christ, Nick."

Nick looked up, and their gazes caught. He felt the tears pricking at his eyes, hot and unbearable. He attempted a smile, realized his nails were digging into his palms. "Is this too much information? Sorry, I shouldn't—"

"Of course you should, it's fine." Dex stood up and walked over to him. He dropped down to his haunches. The sight of him so close, looking up at Nick with a soft expression, made a light-headed sensation go all through Nick. He told himself to snap out of it. "What happened is...I can't even imagine." Nick couldn't make himself look away. Dex's face was mesmerizing. "God, you must have been Albert's age." He paused. "Sorry, my baby brother. He's fourteen."

"I was fifteen." His shoulders lifted in a self-conscious shrug, then froze somewhere around his ears. "You have a brother?"

"Al, yeah. Good kid, but a pain in my arse at the moment."

"I have a sister, but she's older. Four years."

"What's she called?"

"Zoya." It was always strange to say her name out loud in his American accent. There shouldn't really have been a difference in how he pronounced it language to language, but it permeated his tongue anyway. Made everything Russian sound just a little bit alien. "She didn't want to change her name either."

"She shouldn't, it's pretty." Dex smiled.

Nick fell silent. He'd never considered if Zoyka's name was pretty. It was just her name.

"I'm sorry you had to go through that," Dex said after a while, shifting a little. Nick wondered just how he was managing to stay crouched like that without going numb. It was probably painful. "With your dad, and tonight, too. That looked...bad. I mean, hard."

Nick squirmed. "It's stupid, though."

"You clearly hadn't meant to." Nick sucked in a tiny breath when Dex laid one cool, dry hand over his. "Don't beat yourself up over something you can't control. Anyway, they'll understand, if you wanna tell them?"

Nick looked up at the bit of a starless sky he could make out through the trees. Breathed in. "I should, right?" He didn't know how. Forcing the words out to Dex back at the pub had been punishing enough. "Or I'll just look like a crazy person. Or a real dick." Dex looked like he wanted to laugh but was holding back. Nick, emboldened, nudged him with his foot. "Like a dick, right? It's cool, you can tell me."

"Nah, man." He did laugh, though. It sounded warm, not mean at all. "Maybe just a tiny bit of a dick."

Nick grimaced.

"Seriously, you didn't do anything wrong." Dex caught his gaze, looking serious again. "Anyway, if you want, I guess I could tell them. Short story. Just the reason."

Nick knew it would be an easy out. Well, he'd always been the Cowardly Lion anyway. "Maybe. If you wouldn't mind."

Dex finally unfolded himself, not quite as steadily as Nick would have expected. Well, he'd been down there for a while. Nick didn't want to look any smaller than he already did in comparison and stood up, too. Dex hadn't stepped away yet, and just like that they were mere inches apart, Nick's eyes level with the hollow of Dex's throat. When he looked up, Dex's expression was unreadable in the dark. Nick had nowhere to go because the bench was at his back, and it felt like a small eternity before Dex took a backward step and did a twisty turn in silent indication for them to get back onto the street. Like nothing had ever happened.

Nick followed, his heart sounding hollow as a drum in his ears.

You can't, he told himself. He pictured his mom's face. *Not for you.*

+

121

Dex must have done his part, because Nick had a text from Izzy when he left class the next day.

Hope you're okay babe. Sorry about last night. Here if you want to talk x

Usually Izzy's texts were written with so many shortcuts, Nick sometimes couldn't tell on the first read if they were English. This was—different. Sweet. He wasn't sure how to respond, because he wasn't okay. She had nothing to be sorry for. And he didn't want to talk.

Thank you & I'm sorry x was his final response.

Class had taken every brain cell he had just to sit through it, and he wasn't even sure why. He found the British university system challenging, for sure, but not impossible. His advisor back home had warned him that it would be a lot more independent study and self-discipline, and so far Nick was just fine with that. Being a gigantic nerd had its advantages. The only time he felt like a real idiot was when he was told to show up to a tutor session at *half two* and showed up at one-thirty, twiddling his thumbs for an hour.

But yesterday had been so surreal, he couldn't concentrate on his professor's droning even a little. It was like words immediately escaped his brain before he could grasp their meaning. He heard everything and could recall nothing. He would look down at his notes and see spirals and boxes filling the margins of the page. He was just glad he hadn't been called on to respond to some assertion or other. It was just not the day to perform any sort of mental tasks.

All day, he had a headache, like a panic hangover, and no amount of caffeine he applied to it did a damn thing.

He decided to skip his last tutorial and disconnect from the world via napping, but sleep wouldn't come. He found himself running his hand over the short hair on his nape and going through the previous day in his mind. He tortured himself over and over by remembering everything he said to Dex, every moment where he could have stopped himself.

He could have begged off coming with Izzy, he could have not told Dex the truth, he could have controlled himself and not fallen apart in front of his friends, he could have literally done anything but what he did, and now he was curled up under his blanket, digging his nails into his palms. Dex had to think he was an idiot, or at least pathetic. Izzy was so sweet, but she had to wonder why she'd become friends with him, didn't she? He just wasn't normal. He wasn't okay.

And Dex. Fuck. *Fuck.*

How honest could you get with yourself? He'd often asked himself this question when skating a little too close to unapproachable things. *Not very* was his usual response. Don't think it, and it won't come true. Don't let yourself, and you won't have to.

When he had sat on Lena's bed, running his hands over the familiar pattern of her flowered comforter, and forced himself to tell her that he didn't think a long-distance relationship between them would work, he'd almost believed himself that it was the long-distance part that wouldn't work. When he missed her in the days after the breakup, he believed that he was missing all of her. Her voice, her confidence, her smile. Her scent, her small breasts that fit so neatly into the palms of his hands. It was getting harder and harder to believe these days.

He was nearly four thousand miles away, and he still felt all of his fears like ghosts over his shoulder.

How honest could you get with yourself?

Not very, he thought, pushing away the memory of how Dex's hand had felt on top of his. *Not very honest at all.*

Nick spent the next week wondering how Jonny was doing and simultaneously avoiding any human contact that he could. He went to classes. He went to the library. He watched

Netflix on his laptop, propped up on his thin pillow and eating digestives from a packet. It was strange how they reminded him of his childhood, something about the taste and texture instantly bringing him back to the pecheniya his parents always had for tea.

Luckily, he did have an essay that was due the following week on the Tudors, which he happily used as an excuse to get out of making plans. It was a big enough campus. He didn't run into anyone, and the longest conversation he had was with a guy whose room was across from his and who Nick found putting a sign on the shared fridge that said, IF YOU ARE STEALING ALL MY CHEESE I WILL CATCH YOU AND I WILL END YOU, with a frowny face and a knife drawn on the bottom of it.

And then on Saturday night, as he was leaving the library, his essay triumphantly finished a full twenty-four hours before it was due, he found Izzy chilling on the library stairs, smoking a cigarette.

"Hiya!" she said, with absolutely zero surprise at seeing him.

Nick looked around, just to see if maybe she was waiting for someone else, but she laughed and extended her hand. "C'mere, stranger. Been a while."

Nick took the last few steps and sank down next to her. "Hey." How had she found him? Now that she was here, he felt stupid and guilty. He hugged his bag to his chest. "Sorry I've been…you know…"

"It's cool, I get it. Just thought you might want some company. Alex mentioned he saw you in the reading room a few hours back, so I took a chance. Since you never respond to your texts anymore."

Nick felt his face flushing and fumbled for his phone. He had two texts from Izzy and a missed call from his mom. Jesus, he'd forgotten his phone even existed. "Fuck, I'm sorry. I wanted to finish this paper. Guess I got distracted."

Izzy took a drag of her cigarette and blew the smoke away from his face. She held the cigarette in her right hand, and Nick knew she was a lefty like him. He thought about how her exuberance sometimes overshadowed the small ways in which she showed her kindness. "Want to get a drink? It doesn't have to be everybody. It can just be us."

Nick shivered with the wind and zipped up his jacket all the way up to his chin. "I do," he said. Surprised himself by finding that he'd missed her.

"Cool." She smiled and threw her cigarette to the ground, stomped her booted heel over it.

He was aware of how close she was. He recalled watching her in the mirror as she cut his hair the week before. All concentration, accentuated by the precise metallic snipping of her scissors and the toneless buzz of the clippers. *You need a cut, babe*, she'd said, and he'd laughed and said, *I know. But money.*

I'll do you for free had been her response, and that was that.

"Dex is working, so let's go say hi," she said now as she heaved herself up, then extended her hand to him. Nick took it.

10

Dex was well used to seeing his mates walking through the pub door, but it was still a bit of a shock when he looked up from mixing a vodka cranberry for a purple-haired girl to see Izzy stride in with Nick in tow. He was wearing those glasses that made it both easier and harder to look at him, because they hid his pretty eyes from Dex's view a bit, but also they just looked good on him. Dex was past denying anything.

Last Sunday had been a long fucking day for him, and a longer night. After they left the park, they'd walked back to Nick's building in silence. Dex was fairly certain he had never been more obvious in his life. He might as well have got a plane to write WILL YOU LET ME KISS IT ALL BETTER in the sky for him. As if that would have helped anything, especially a confused kid who'd lost his dad at fifteen. And after he'd dropped Nick off, he and Jonny had stayed up way too late talking. Necessary, but Dex had felt like milk gone off the whole next day.

The bar was pretty full, but Izzy was Izzy, which meant that she managed to squeeze in between two dudes with very little effort. She had once joked that it paid to be a bigger girl, but it wasn't that, Dex knew. Izzy would have been a whirlwind at a size negative zero. Surely she had to see how she turned everyone's heads just by being so very, very Izzy.

He'd singed off his eyebrows at the sight of her, and he didn't even swing that way.

Dex finished ringing up the purple-haired cran vodka girl, then took two more orders and made four more drinks before he could reasonably say hello and bring Izzy and Nick their beers.

"Hey babe." Izzy leaned up until she could land a kiss on Dex's cheek. Nick smiled at him, looking a bit shy. Dex could relate. He waved Nick off when Nick made to put down a tenner.

"On the house, mate." He made a mental note to remember to put some money in the till before closing out. "So what's happening?"

"Nick here has spent the whole day writing a paper, if you can believe that, so he needs to be celebrated."

"On a Saturday? Mate, you're worse than me." Dex smiled, pleasure blooming in his belly.

"It's the nerd life," he said, scratching the back of his neck. "It's the first big assignment for this class. I just didn't know what to expect."

"Whatever, I bet it's amazing," Izzy said with a wave of her hand. "Oh, D, you missed this—Nick called his mum on the way over here, and I have now heard him speaking Russian. Brilliant."

"Oh yeah, my brilliant Russian." Nick made air quotes around *brilliant*. "Half the conversation was my mom correcting me."

"Well, it's better than mine," Izzy laughed.

"So d'you speak it at home, then?"

"Yeah, my mom would disown us if we didn't. She and my dad were always all about preserving our language and all of that."

"Do you think in it?" Dex asked curiously.

Nick shook his head and propped his chin on his hand. "Not anymore. It's weird, I actually can't remember when that happened. But it's mostly English now."

"Huh."

"Uh, mate, hello? Are you on or what?"

Dex sighed and went to an irritated guy seeking attention. Fair enough—Dex's job wasn't to moon over guys he was unlikely ever to get, but to make money. He went about it pretty consistently for the next while, catching glimpses of Nick and Izzy now and again as they managed to actually grab two seats at the bar. From what Dex could tell, it was largely Izzy talking and Nick listening, but both looked pretty happy about it.

When he had a moment to breathe, he sidled over to them and used the excuse of throwing glasses in the dishwasher to eavesdrop.

"It wasn't until Nat's uncle got us a deal on the flat that we even considered it, though, isn't that right, Dexter?"

Dex looked up. "What's that?"

"Us moving into a real-people place instead of halls. Nick was just telling me about some of the people on his floor. Don't miss it, to be honest."

"You do remember I was one of those people, right?"

"Yeah, but you're all right, aren't you? Shit bartender, though, where's my next one?"

Dex grabbed her empty glass and pulled her another Stella. "Here you go, princess."

"I don't rate a new glass?" She raised an eyebrow. "Good thing you don't work for tips."

Dex flipped her off, then noticed Nick's glass was nearly empty, too. "Another?"

Nick smiled and nodded, extending his glass. "Please."

Dex did as asked, glancing at him out of the corner of his eye. He managed to tip the glass too forward when he noticed Nick watching him and wound up with half a pint of foam. Great. Wordlessly he tipped it out. "Here, sorry about that."

"Yeah," Izzy said, taking a sip. "Nobody wants *too* much head, am I right, boys?"

Nick visibly choked on his beer while Dex glared at her. "Must you always go for the obvious?"

"Only when it's staring me right in the face." She indicated Nick with a glance. Subtle she was not. Dex attempted to glare.

"Uh." Nick wiped some foam from his mouth, which had the unfortunate side effect of pulling Dex's attention directly to that part of his face. God, his lips were pretty. Dex had to get a hold of himself, it wasn't *that* long since last he'd pulled. "I wanted to, uh, I wanted to ask, how is Jonny?"

Dex sagged down onto the bar. He had to tread carefully here. "He's all right, I guess." He grabbed a towel and wiped away the mess he'd made with Nick's beer. "Went home, got back yesterday. His dad's not bad. The surgery went well. So he'll make it."

"Good." Nick sounded...normal. Good.

Dex smiled at him despite himself. "Yeah. It is."

"What about his mom?"

Izzy made a noise of disgust. "She's a cunt, that's what she is."

"Iz."

"What, am I wrong? No, I am not."

Dex caught Nick watching them like he couldn't figure out where the trouble was.

"She's still refusing to talk to him," Izzy went on, turning to Nick. "He missed all his lectures, has so much shit to make up, and she couldn't even be bothered to speak to him like a human being."

"That really sucks."

"It fucking does," Izzy said viciously. "Anyway, he got to stay with his cousin, who's pretty cool. She drove him to and from the hospital, that kind of thing."

"He doesn't have any siblings?"

"Only child. So, you know. Guess they took it extra hard when he came out."

"Whatever. He's still their kid."

"That he is," Dex agreed. "Anyway, guess he's with Tweedle Dum and Tweedle Dee tonight—sorry, that's what I call Niall and Lance," he added. "I shouldn't. I know. They're just sort of idiots."

"Well, Niall's not a complete idiot," Izzy laughed. "Anyway, Lance has got his heart in the right place. He's just a bit much."

"Is he the Marxist?" Nick asked, and Dex burst out laughing.

"If only, man—he thinks he gets it, but he really doesn't." Even as Dex said it, he felt guilty. Jonny actually did appear to like the guy, which had to say something about Lance, right?

Nick cracked a sardonic smile. "No, probably not."

"Does it—sorry, this is probably a stupid question, but did he offend you?" Izzy asked. "I mean, I know Russia's not been Communist in a while, but—"

Dex leaned in closer. It was odd, having a real-life person who could have an actual, like, informed opinion on this right there in front of them. He wished Lance were here to listen. It was tedious hearing him spew his revolutionary bullshit from his middle-class white boy mouth.

"I mean," Nick said. "I don't know that I can be offended. It's a bit simplistic, I guess. My parents lived through Communism. I didn't."

"What was it like, d'you know?"

"Well...My mom used to talk about the food shortages, or like...sometimes there wouldn't be toilet paper available. Like. In the town where they lived."

"What, are you serious?" Izzy's eyes widened. "Sorry, that was well rude, wasn't it?"

Nick laughed and shook his head. "It's pretty crazy even to me at this point. But yeah, like…I guess relatives would come visiting from another city and bring toilet paper with them. Or if there was a meat shortage, we'd bring it from our city. That kind of stuff."

"But it wasn't like that when you were growing up?" Dex asked, quickly scanning the bar for patrons. Bah. "Wait, hang on, I wanna hear this—" He trailed off, taking orders from five separate people, mixing cocktails, pulling pints, all the while straining to hear what Nick and Izzy were talking about. He was curious. He'd never been anywhere apart from, like, France and Portugal for hols with his parents and Al. Russia always felt so forbidding to him, so mysterious. Brutal, in some ways. When he looked at Nick, the word *brutal* seemed the farthest thing from his mind.

+

Izzy twisted in her seat to make sure Nick was out of earshot as he went to the loos. "Right. You are *into* this boy!"

Dex quickly scrolled through the ways he could dispute this but found none. Eurgh. "I hate that you know me so well."

Izzy gave him a look that could only be described as *pitying*. "Babe. You're not being very subtle."

Oh God. "How not subtle?"

"Weeeeell. You've done a full-on one-eighty on him, for one. You also get this look on your face, like…" She pulled a face that was presumably a close imitation of Dex's besotted expression. It was excruciating.

"No, God, Iz, please tell me you're exaggerating. D'you think he knows?"

Izzy laughed. "No, babe, you're totally safe. If anything, he'd be the last person to figure out you fancy him."

Dex beseeched her with a look to be honest.

"I swear to God!" She raised her hands. "Seriously, can you see Nick, of all people, sitting there, thinking, golly-gee-whiz, I think that gorgeous, confident Dexter quite fancies me?"

When put like that, she had a point. "All right. Fine. But oh God, I have *got* to get past this. It's insane. It won't go anywhere."

"Whatever. Anyway, you working till close tonight?"

"You know how it is. Bills, bills, bills."

"That a yes?"

He took an order, began pulling yet another pint. "Yes, Isabel."

"All right, Christ, don't bite me head off. I think we should—" She twisted around, looked in the direction of the loos, then turned back towards him, leaning in. "We should take Nick back to ours after this, if he's up for it. What'd you think?"

Dex shrugged, taking the Stella guy's money. "If you think he'd be into it, I suppose?"

He was saved from having to listen to her by a pink-haired girl who sidled up to the other end of the bar. He went to do his job.

Nick blinked. He was feeling good. Really, really good. He was curled up in a chair in Dex and Izzy's living room with a beer, watching them going back and forth on whether or not Dex was being too hard on his brother. At some point, Jonny had come back and joined them, all three housemates scrunched up next to each other on the couch.

"I'm not saying he's a *total* pain in the arse," Dex was saying. "Just that he is *currently* a pain in my arse."

"He's having trouble *adjusting*, Dexter," Izzy countered. She wasn't entirely sober, so *adjusting* came out sounding slurred. It was pretty cute. Nick took another sip, then told himself to chill out with that. He was riding a good sort of buzz he didn't want to tip over into messy drunk territory. He had to watch it.

Jonny was currently eyeballing his housemates with typical Jonny-like amusement. He seemed to be doing a bit better, Nick thought. Nick was glad he was back, anyway. He wanted to catch him at some point to apologize for real, but he couldn't decide if it would just make all the crap float back up to the surface. He was chewing the thought over when Izzy called out his name.

"Hmmm?"

Izzy giggled. "You're all dreamy over there. I was saying, don't you think Dex is being unfair with Al? He's just having a difficult time, and this one here believes that if he doesn't talk about his shit, he won't get his problems solved. But, like. Al's a bloody fourteen-year-old."

Nick took a moment to come up with a careful response. He still had difficulty navigating what people expected him to say and what was the best thing to say and would he stick his foot in his mouth if he opened it? *Probably* was always a safe bet. "What is he adjusting to?"

Dex opened his mouth, but Izzy was already on it. "Dex's parents just moved to a posh new place where it's basically all white people, and poor Al is basically all moody and mute teenager coz he's one of, like, three people like him in the whole school." She paused. "Do I have that right?"

Dex rolled his eyes and nodded. He addressed the next bit to Nick. "Essentially. The problem for me is that I can't help him if he doesn't fucking *talk* to me. He used to talk to me all the time. I couldn't get him to shut up."

Nick nodded. His beer was sitting heavily in his belly, thrumming through his veins. He'd forgotten to eat, and his tongue had loosened. "That's hard. Adjusting to a new school can be hard."

"Oh shit. I'm such an idiot. Of course you'd know."

"I mean, everyone starts a new school at some point, don't they?"

"Well, yeah, but like...You had it extra special, I guess?"

"Still does," Jonny piped up. Everyone turned to look at him. "He's in a different country again, Iz. Duh."

Nick gave him a smile. He couldn't begin to describe how different this was to ten years ago.

"Well, he's all right now, isn't he?" Izzy said. "Right, Nick?"

He nodded, then caught Dex's watchful gaze. A jolt shot through his belly. It wasn't nerves, but it *felt* like nerves. A fluttering hot wave, there and gone. "Yeah. It's better."

"What was it like, then?" Dex asked. He had this way of talking that felt like he was whispering directly into Nick's ear—something Nick really, really wished he had never experienced, because it still made his toes curl to remember. He'd been barely aware of it at the time, but the sense memory had stayed.

"What was what like?" he asked.

"You know..." Dex waved his Corona-holding arm in an expansive sort of gesture. "Adjusting to an American school, new country, all that."

He never knew how to answer this question, because the option of answering honestly seemed nonexistent. Nobody wanted to hear that shit. He gave his usual. "It sucked, I guess. But it got better."

Dex narrowed his eyes at him. Izzy said, "Well, that's detailed." Then smiled, as if to cover up the remark. "So, what helped? Looking for advice, here, you understand. Since Dex won't ask."

Nick's family had been his salvation. He would sit in his last period, look out the window, and watch the school buses line up one by one with a sort of desperation that felt like grasping onto a lifeline. He would picture the front door of their apartment, his mom and Zoyka already waiting on the other side of it. A place where he could speak and be understood. A place where he didn't feel ridiculous just for existing. "I guess my situation was different." He paused. "We were all of us in it together. Does that make sense?" An island of four plopped down in the middle of a sea of hostile forces. "But my sister helped the most. We stuck together."

He'd never actually said that much to anyone, before. He and Zoyka had been pretty close growing up, even with him being the annoying little brother. But it wasn't until they had no one else that they became Kol'ka i Zoyka, a two-headed unit. Their first place in the States, they'd shared a bedroom and had bunk beds. Nick had the top bunk, and late at night, after their parents had already gone to bed, they'd talk in the dark. Zoyka would extend her hand against the wall, and he would grab it. Another lifeline.

"Hmmm." Izzy made a meaningful face at Dex, who tugged at her until she was curled up with one arm wrapped up around his middle. Jonny twisted until his feet were planted under her butt. Talk about a multiheaded unit. Nick had never had that kind of physical closeness with anyone, not even Lena. And the idea of draping himself over Dex's body like a blanket seemed laughable. He had barely held himself together when Dex touched his hand.

"Look, I get it. It's just hard to do when I'm here. And he's there. And Mum and Dad work so much. I just can't be that much help through a phone, you know?"

"Just check in with him," Nick said before he could stop himself. "And listen, if he talks. Don't offer advice. Just listen, you know?"

His palms felt on fire for no good reason at all, but his reward was Dex giving him a smile—a small but still blinding sort of smile that dimpled his cheeks—and saying, "Cheers, mate. I'm gonna try."

Nick smiled shyly back and took another sip of his drink.

The familiar buzzing of a phone broke the silence, and Jonny extricated his phone from under his butt. His frown turned to a hint of a smile, all warmth and light.

"What's up?" Izzy asked.

Jonny looked up and shook his head, quickly slipping his phone back. "Nothing, just a text."

Nick could tell Izzy was on the verge of prying, but stopped herself.

✝

Nick woke up with a hammering heart to a completely unfamiliar scene. He was...well, he was in a room. He knew he was in a room, but whose room? Bits and pieces of the night before began slotting into his foggy brain. Izzy falling asleep on top of Dex. Nick swaying on his feet as he tried and failed to put on his shoes. Jonny putting a warm hand on his arm to steady him and saying, *Mate, why don't you just stay here?* Nick being led up the stairs, still drunkenly protesting that it was too much of an imposition. Nick being gently deposited onto a bed—whose bed, he had no idea— then. Well, then he probably passed out.

He screwed his eyes shut, then opened them again. Something was digging into his hip, and a cursory pat of his hand revealed it to be the phone in his pocket. He moved his legs. Yep, still wearing jeans. He shifted, and his body groaned in response. Great. He hadn't meant to drink that much, but Jonny had kept them well supplied until the wee hours of the morning. Nick was pretty sure he remembered Jonny pouring wine. A lot of wine.

He sat up and winced. Okay, so not too bad. Just a bit of a pounding in his left temple. Probably nothing a glass of water or two couldn't fix. Then he looked around himself. The small room was pretty sparse, furniture-wise. A dresser on the left, a desk to the right of it. The bed was big, though, and soft, covered in so many pillows Nick was surprised he hadn't suffocated in the night. Giant swaths of gauzy purple fabric hung across the ceiling with Christmas lights lining the edges. It all looked very dreamy.

He grabbed his glasses, ecstatic to discover them on the nightstand, and squinted at a poster over the desk. PJ Harvey. Then his gaze caught on a few small pictures tacked to the wall next to the bed, and he looked closer. Natali and Izzy. Natali, Izzy, Dex, and Jonny. Natali and a girl Nick had never met before. Possibly a girlfriend. Natali and an older woman who looked just like her, wearing a sari.

Looked like Nick had been deposited in Natali's room.

God, what time was it? His phone was almost dead at 5 percent, but it did manage to tell him it was ten-fifteen in the morning and that he had an email from his mom and a series of texts from Zoyka waiting for him. He shoved it back into his pocket and swung his legs over the edge of the bed. It really was a very nice room, and he wouldn't have minded sleeping there a little longer, but he had a monumental need to pee and an even bigger need to sneak out before anybody noticed.

Jesus, how much of an idiot had he made of himself last night? He couldn't remember. He took his glasses off to rub at his eyes. Fuck. *Fuck.*

He grabbed his shoes from the floor and slowly opened the door, waiting for it to creak. When it didn't, he did a tiny fist pump and closed it just as quietly behind him. The staircase was brighter than the room had been. He strained to listen and heard quiet voices downstairs. Crap. He would have to be really quiet.

One step, two, three, until he was down to the last stair, which creaked, because he was living out a farce. He winced. The smell of coffee wafted up the stairs.

"Oh, I think he's up!"

Jonny. Nick slapped his forehead and very seriously considered running out even now, but then Dex's voice behind him followed up with, "Oh, hey, morning, Nick—want some coffee?" and he turned around.

Dex's head was the only thing Nick could see over the doorway. He was smiling, and one purple dread stood up in excitement over his head. Nick braced himself on the bannister with one hand, realizing that he was clutching his shoes to his chest with the other. He had never done a walk of shame before, but this was possibly close to what it might feel like.

"You all right?" Dex asked. He stepped out of the kitchen, and Nick's throat went a little dry at the trying view of Dex shirtless, wearing only low-slung basketball shorts. That was a lot of skin. A lot of smooth, dark skin over muscle.

He opened his mouth. "I really have to pee." *Fuck*.

Dex pushed his tongue under his lower lip, clearly trying to stifle a laugh while Nick just stood there, trying not to die. "Well, go for it, man, don't let me stop you."

Nick's feet finally moved, and he darted behind Dex to the bathroom. He definitely avoided catching his reflection in the mirror as he washed his hands.

When he finally emerged, Dex had gone back to the kitchen, and Nick had very little choice but to follow. Both stools were occupied, but as soon as Nick took two steps inside, Dex jumped up and wordlessly indicated for Nick to sit down. Nick shook his head. His nod to dignity in the bathroom had been to put his shoes back on, but now he had nothing to hide behind. He was probably making too big a deal out of this. He usually did. It still didn't feel too great.

"How are you, mate?" Jonny asked cheerfully while Dex danced around the stool in Nick's peripheral vision. Great, now his awkwardness was spreading.

"All right. Fine."

"Yeah? Sleep well?" Jonny took a loud slurp of his coffee. He was clearly amused at Nick's discomfort, but it was Jonny, so it wasn't mean. Nick felt some tension unwind in his shoulders, in his belly.

"Yeah. Natali's got a nice bed."

Dex said, "Yeah, it'll be our little secret." Nick saw that Dex had already sat back on the stool. Good. He realized he was smiling. No idea why, but maybe just because Dex looked so comfortable and *nice*, first thing in the morning. Nick was doing his best not to look below his neck, but it wasn't exactly easy, ignoring the tight curls of his chest hair and treasure trail dipping below his shorts.

"Would she mind? I'm sorry, I shouldn't have—"

"You didn't, man, it was our idea," Jonny cut him off. "Anyway, not like it's the first time this has happened, and Nat's cool." He paused. "Mostly."

"Anyway, relax, have some coffee," Dex offered, and Nick, raised by a rather militantly polite mother, had no choice but to accept his kind offer. He felt their eyes on him as he stumbled around, figuring out where the milk and sugar lived, doing his best not to overturn the French press. Would there ever be a time where he didn't consistently feel like an awkward mess?

He stood at the counter and drank his admittedly delicious coffee, listening to Dex and Jonny chatting companionably until Dex's phone buzzed on the table.

He grabbed it, fingered it open, and without a word he extended it toward them both. Curious, Nick leaned in.

Mum's driving me bonkers again tell her I'm fine

"Well, that's reassuring," Jonny noted, one eyebrow up.

Nick gave Dex a sympathetic look. "At least he's talking to you?"

"There's that," Dex agreed, looking down at his phone again. "All right, what the fuck do I say to that that isn't 'Clearly you're not, so stop being a git'?"

"'Get your fourteen-year-old head out of your arse'?" Jonny suggested, then swiftly moved out of the way of Dex's slapping hand. "'Tell your mum yourself, since you're occupying the same space, presumably'?"

Nick racked his brain for some sort of a real suggestion. He wanted to help. He wanted to say something that would make up for having been an awkward uninvited overnight guest, at the very least. He wanted to please Dex in some small way. "How about, 'Sure, but what's going on?' That way you're leaving the door open."

When he looked at Dex, Dex was already typing into his phone, nodding along. He looked up at Nick like he was waiting for more. The curves of his strong arms were distracting. Nick coughed.

"Um, that's probably good to start. See if he takes it as a cue or whatever." He thought about all the ways in which Zoya would try to shake him out of it when he'd been thirteen and hating everything. Hating the shame of being different, still, after what felt like a lifetime in America. Hating the concerned looks his parents would send his way, hating that they would retreat whenever he lashed out. She'd just wait for him to come to her, and more often than not, he'd capitulate and do it.

Dex nodded, prodded at his phone once more, and laid it flat on the table. Then he flashed Nick a grin. "Thanks, mate. I'm just sort of…unequipped. I dunno. I guess I feel—" He ran his hand over his dreads. His fingers shaped the bumps and grooves easily, like the running of water over stone. "I feel bad, you know? He's stuck there in that posh cesspool, and I'm here—"

"You feel guilty, man. It's fine," Jonny said in a quiet voice. "But it's not your fault, and…I'm not saying this to be an arsehole, but it's not entirely your responsibility either, you know?"

"No, I know that. It's just—" Dex broke off with a frustrated sort of sigh. "I'm just a bit helpless. I should go visit them more. Like, maybe next weekend or whatever."

Jonny rolled his eyes. "You just went twice, and you've got a shitload of work to do. Go next month."

Nick was out of his depth on this one. Apart from one semester in college, he'd lived with his mom until he came here. He had no idea what it was like to bear the burden of far-away family that wasn't prohibitively far away. Like, on a different continent far away. Like, will most likely never see them again sort of far away.

"Maybe. Anyway, sorry, I know this is boring shit. What are you up to today?"

Nick refocused, because Dex was asking *him*. What *was* he up to today? "Uh, Skyping with my mom, probably." Cool plan, Nick. Excellent. "And I finished my big assignment, so I've got some free time. Maybe I'll...walk around or something." What a gripping life, indeed.

"Coffeeeee."

Izzy. Nick hadn't heard her creaking down the stairs, but there she was, walking through the kitchen in the most disarray he'd ever seen her in. Her hair was wild and appeared to be ten times bigger than normal, standing in a red halo around her head. A ratty T-shirt barely covered her underwear, a fact that Nick had glimpsed and immediately looked away from. He was probably flushed now. She was really cute. She also appeared completely unconcerned about this state of affairs, which made Nick feel a little better. She was comfortable, which had to be a good sign, right? He moved out of the way of her zombie walk toward the French press.

"Morning," Jonny laughed, scooting his stool over and beckoning Nick to stand beside him. "Had enough sleep?"

"Mrhhhh. Mugs?"

"Cupboard?"

"Right." She flung open two cabinets at a time, nearly braining herself on the doors. All three of them moved as one to prevent tragedy, but Izzy barely noticed, grabbing a mug with a picture of a cartoon butt on it and shutting the cupboards with a bang. "Right."

All three of them watched, Nick with increasing horror, as she drained the French press of its contents, then splashed an inordinate amount of milk and three heaping spoonfuls of sugar into her cup and swirled it all together with a chopstick. She didn't turn around until she'd sucked down half the cup.

"Oh, hey, Nick!" She smiled wide once she spotted him. "You're still here, yay!"

Nick cleared his throat. "Yeah. Sorry I got, you know." He swallowed. "Pretty wasted."

Izzy made a dismissive 'pfft' sound with an expressive gesture that apparently was meant to convey her current state. "Please. Anyway, our casa es su casa, et cetera, et cetera, and anyway, Nat's not been home for, like, three nights or something. She's called Lotty, apparently," she added, looking at Dex.

"Noted."

"Anyway, what was that about a walk?" she asked, beaming at Nick and catching him completely by surprise.

"Oh, uh, I was thinking about going somewhere, to, like, explore," he said.

"Ohhh, where were you thinking?"

He hadn't. He'd just planned on looking at a map and pointing to a random location. He shrugged.

"Have you been to Primrose Hill yet?" she asked, her earlier sleepiness all but gone from her features. Nick shook his head. "Ooh, would you want to? We could go together. It's really pretty, and there's Regent's Park, and—sorry, would that be all right? I just invited myself, didn't I?"

Nick wondered what his face looked like. Somehow, it hadn't occurred to him that he could see London with actual Londoners. He'd definitely have to go home and shower first. But it sounded nice. "Yeah. Totally." He hoped he looked enthusiastic and not like a deer caught in headlights. "I should probably, like, let you get ready and go back to the dorm." He plucked at his rumpled shirt. "Maybe we could meet up in a bit?"

"Brilliant!" It occurred to Nick that he rarely saw Izzy without makeup on. The freckles dotting her nose and cheeks looked like sunbursts. She really was beautiful. She just wasn't...Well. She wasn't.

Nick smiled in response.

+

"Privet, milyi!"

His mom greeted Nick over Skype with a grainy, pixelated smile. He laughed, hearing Zoyka in the background yelling about not starting without her.

"How are things?" he asked. It surprised him, how quickly Russian could recede from his tongue if left unused. He picked his words out carefully, rolled them around his brain before letting them roll off his tongue. They felt jagged in his mouth, scarily unfamiliar. He hated that feeling. It had only been a couple months.

"Everything is good with us, of course," his mom responded immediately with a shrug, as Zoyka popped up next to her and waved. Their nearly identical faces watched him happily, and for a moment he wished he could reach through and hug them, bury his nose in the familiar scents of his mom's perfume, of Zoyka's citrus shampoo. "How are things with *you*?"

"Everything is good. Classes are good, London's good." Better than good. He felt it wrapped all around him, a trembling quiver of possibility. He couldn't wait to let Izzy show him more places.

"Look at him, he's smiling!" Zoyka laughed, and he stuck out his tongue at her. Mom rolled her eyes, of course.

"Stop that, the pair of you. We want details, Kolechka. Davai." She sat back, waiting.

Zoyka tipped her chin at him. "How are those friends of yours?"

"They're good," he said, chewing on his lower lip. "I'm going to Primrose Hill with someone in a bit."

"Ohhh, who?"

"Izzy."

"Izzy? What sort of name is Izzy?" Mom.

"I think it's short for Isabel."

"Strange. Okay, and what is *Izzy* like?"

Oh, he knew that tone. He rolled his eyes, shrugging off his mounting irritation. "Izzy is nice, Ma. She cut my hair." Zoyka's eyebrows shot up, but she didn't say anything, and Nick didn't encourage her. "Then there's Natali." *She's gay.* How would his mom react to that? "Also Jonny." *He's trans.* How would she react to *that*? "And Alex." *He's black.* "And Steph." She'd probably be fine with Steph. "And Dex." *He's black. He's gay. He's beautiful.*

Nick rubbed his palms on his pants. Even through the denim he could feel the wet heat of them. He scratched the back of his head. He hoped the Internet connection was shitty enough that they wouldn't see his flushed cheeks.

"Well, I'm glad you have friends, that's good."

"Yeah, hope they're feeding you."

"Zoyka, otstan' ot nego. He's been feeding himself for a while now, haven't you?"

"I don't know, still looks skinny to me." Zoya said it kinder than he was used to from her, though, so he just rolled his eyes.

"Nu lando, hvatit." His mom cut them off. "Chto eschio slyhat', malysh?"

Nick shrugged as nonchalantly as he could manage. It was strange. *Not much* was the real answer, and yet it was no answer at all. He longed to end the call before words tumbled out that he could never actually speak. The screen boxed him in, their gazes pinned him in that box. "Nothing, really. All's good."

"Well, that's good." Mom smiled. "It's nice to see you, honey. I'm still not used to the haircut."

Nick wrinkled his nose and ran his hand over the back of his head. "It was nice of her to do for free."

"Well, she's your friend, isn't she? Why wouldn't she?"

Nick shrugged. "Zoyka, how's Jake?"

"He's fine. He's being quiet, but he's here."

"Hey, Nick!" Jake's voice piped up in the background. "Is that girl hot? You should get on that, being a free man and all!"

Nick flushed probably all the way down to his toes and ignored his mom's penetrative stare. He hated that Jake had learned enough Russian to figure out what they'd been talking about. "She's seeing someone," he lied. "Anyway, she's not my type." And how. He hated the relief that switching to English brought on.

"Shame. Have a good one, man!"

"Thanks, J." He waved, then felt stupid. Zoyka was smiling, looking to the left of the screen. They were grossly adorable together. Nick made a point of rolling his eyes at her when she looked back at him. "Dork," he told her in English.

"Kol', davai po Russki," Mom said. "You'll forget it all by the time you get back."

"I won't, don't worry," he said, switching at once and feeling anything but certain.

"All right, all right. Well, we should go. Jake is taking us out for brunch." She looked so pleased. For his mom, a creature of habit, it was rare enough to go out to eat: he couldn't believe that she'd been moved to go to brunch, of all things, with Zoya and her boyfriend. Zoya's face clearly broadcast smug self-satisfaction at him.

"That sounds nice," he said, feeling yet more guilt at the relief flowing through him of knowing the call was coming to an end.

"Yes, yes. You take care of yourself, okay?" Mom was all business again. "Well, schastlivo, Kolen'ka."

"I vam schastlivo!" he said, and then the screen blinked and went black. Nick slumped back against the chair and closed his eyes. Sometimes he wished he had ended up somewhere with no Internet.

12

zzy didn't realise she'd rested her head on Nick's shoulder until about the fifth Tube station, but he didn't seem to mind, so she didn't move. She was still feeling the ill effects of last night, just a wee bit delicate. She dozed, too, until they had to switch at Tottenham Court Road, at which point she felt the caffeine kick in. She should have got a coffee to go, but they could do that once they got off the Tube. They stood, swaying against each other, all the way to Chalk Farm.

Izzy had been to Primrose Hill enough times that she felt confident enough in where they were going and made a slight diversion to the twenty-four-hour Quik Stop. Nick trailed her, looking a bit lost, while Izzy procured them bottles of water and chocolate bars to go with her coffee.

"Adventure supplies!" she announced while putting in her PIN at the till. Nick bit his lip at that, which was obviously precious and adorable, but didn't say anything.

Then, they strode down Adelaide Road.

"This isn't the pretty part," Izzy told him as she chucked an Aero at him. Nick tore into it immediately. "This is just a means to an end. I kind of like it, though. It's quiet, you know? Peaceful."

She watched him munching his Aero and picking bits of chocolate from his enormous scarf. When he'd thrown one small bit over his shoulder, she asked, "So, why England?"

He looked at her surprised, eyes wide behind his glasses, a touch wary. "Well. It's sort of—" He paused and visibly girded himself. Nat had told her that watching him come out with it could be painful, he was so uncertain, but Izzy liked that about him. He was genuine. Whatever he said was probably true, even if it was couched in so many layers of uncertainty you knew he could hide behind even the truth. "I've always loved England."

Still incredulous over this, she asked, "Why?" She bit into her Snickers.

He laughed and played with his hair. It looked so much better now she'd taken her shears and razor to him. He'd been cute and all, but now he was looking sharper.

"I guess I can't really explain it. Like…you know when you just are really, really into something, and everything about that thing makes you want to know more? And it takes on a …mythical quality, I guess, where you almost can't believe it's real, but it *is*, and you can *go* there, if only you had the means, and I suppose I found the means." He paused, visibly startled at himself.

Izzy was positively giddy at this outpouring.

"I do, I think." It was true. "I mean, I've never thought about it that way, but yeah, I have things like that." She shook out her scarf and stuffed her half-eaten chocolate bar into the pocket of her jacket. "I have that with film, but that's different from a place, innit? Can't really go there, I guess. And it's never the same as it is on screen, behind the scenes, either."

"Is that what you're studying?"

"Is that wanky?" She laughed. "It's cool, you can say it. Nat always does."

"No! I think that's really cool, actually."

"Well, that's sweet of you." They grinned at each other. "Yeah, I've just always loved films." Every time her mum took her to the cinema, like…before, and then whenever she'd gone by herself afterwards, she felt glued to her seat just watching the production logos at the beginning of the film. Everything about films dazzled her. So many people came together to work on films. Not just actors and directors and writers, but somebody had to have designed that logo, and others had to make the set look like a real street instead of a back lot somewhere. "Okay, wank alert again, but you know how I said that it's not the same behind the scenes? I guess that's the best part of it for me. Like..." She paused, knowing she was about to drop some serious wankery but comfortable enough to continue anyway. "Have you ever had this feeling like...something is made more special when it's seen through a lens? Like...I'm not saying it right, but like...when I see something in a film, even if it's a street corner I see every day, you know—nothing, like, spectacular, but just something that's highlighted through someone else's gaze, I guess—it makes it...special. Not even only films necessarily, but even a photograph or something. Is that stupid? That's stupid, isn't it?"

"Not at all!" Nick said. He smiled at her. God, he had a pretty smile. If Dex didn't make a move on him, she might need to, seriously. "That's exactly what I was saying, I think. Except for me it's not just a lens, it's anything. Books. History."

"And all of it about England?"

"Largely," he laughed. "But I don't know why. I've always loved All Things European, but England more than anything else."

"Soggy Ol' Britain, huh?" She bumped his shoulder. "Well, I'm glad you're here."

Nick smiled. "Thanks. Me too."

"Do you want to be an actress?"

They were now in Primrose Hill proper—home to those pretty pastel row houses where all the posh-edgy celebrities lived. Izzy had once actually seen actual Daisy bloody Lowe walking her dog and thought she was going to piss herself.

"God, no," Izzy spat. "They wouldn't want me, anyway."

"Really? Why?"

This boy, seriously. "Not exactly movie star material, am I?" Nick looked genuinely blank-faced, so she did a sweep with her arm over her very non-bog-standard Hollywood body. "Not a size bloody zero, see?"

"Right. Sorry." Nick blushed. She felt a little bad.

"Nah, it's not your fault. And whatever, I've never wanted to be. Size zero *or* an actress. Their lives seem shit. I mean, honestly, if I can't have pain au chocolat and whatnot in the morning, there's no point to living."

She'd read enough Hollywood exposés on body crap to last her a lifetime. No thank you very much.

"Nah, I want to direct. Or write. Or both? Both." She did her best to never actually make a decision or she would doubt it to death. She was sort of low-key hating this conversation, but she didn't wish to be rude. "You'd think being in my last year at uni I'd know, but whatever."

"Do you think you'll get to do it? Direct and write?"

She shrugged, feeling sort of itchy all over. It was one thing to declare, *I'm going to do films!* at nineteen, it was another to be in your last year of uni, still not knowing what the fuck you were even doing. "Who knows. I'll try. Start from the bottom and all that. Everyone knows being a woman in the film industry is shit, but what have I got to lose?"

"This is why I chose this place." They made their way to the summit of Primrose Hill. It wasn't, she admitted, the prettiest it could be at the moment. The grass was dead from winter. Dried into hay from the cold snap they'd recently experienced. When she'd dragged Nat and Steph out in the summer, the grass had been half green, half dead already—and it was too sunny. Which, like, of course. It was Britain. It either pissed down all the time or was so bloody hot even the grass didn't know what to do about it.

Nick seemed excited as he stood next to her at the top of the hill. They watched the families playing in the park below them, and as she looked at all of London sprawled out beneath them. You couldn't beat the view.

"Awesome, right?"

Nick was smiling. She gazed out and tried to see London as he was seeing it. He had never been here, which struck her as particularly brave, just dropping everything and flying to an unknown destination. Now he was here, and she hoped it wasn't a disappointment. She wanted Nick to love London the way he had expected to, wanted him to love it the way she loved it.

She looked for the spires of the BT Tower, the Shard, the Eye, which she could never *not* say in her head in Cate Blanchett voice. *One who has seen...THE EYE!!!!* That one was Mum's fault. She was such a Tolkien geek.

Izzy really did love London. Felixstowe, where she'd grown up, was so close to the sea you could smell it. Izzy had loved the water, but she'd always felt just a little suffocated by the solitude of it, or the sameness of the town, the people. She had never managed to feel inspired there, for all the nature was beautiful. While it was *home*, it wasn't where she'd wanted to settle. She'd actually been born in London, because her parents had split up when she was barely a week old and Mum had taken her away from her shithead of a father, so Izzy really did wonder if it had always called back to her. She couldn't imagine leaving it now.

"We come here for picnics sometimes," she told Nick. "On special occasions." She stamped her feet. Standing around had got cold, and she crouched down to sit on the pavement. She patted the spot beside her, and Nick dropped down, too. She'd forgotten to get that coffee, so now they huddled and shivered together in silence, taking in the view and the sunshine and the chatter of the people behind them. It felt nice. Easy. Nick didn't seem as uptight. He looked positively giddy. Izzy remembered she still had a whole Dairy Milk in her bag. They polished it off in quick order.

"So, what did you say you were doing later today?" Izzy asked as they descended the hill. He hadn't actually told her, but she had a goal.

Nick looked over at her. "Nothing much."

"Well, Dex doesn't have to go into work for once, so we were gonna do a whole proper roast later, with all the proper trimmings, the ways of our people. What'd you reckon, wanna come over? I'd put you to work, mind."

Nick's response was immediate. "Yeah." A smile. "I'd love to."

Izzy actually clapped and said, "Yaaaaay!"

When Nick got to the house, the kitchen was a bustle of activity. Natali was back, and Nick skirted
around her carefully until he realized that she either didn't
know he'd spent the previous night in her bed or didn't care.
He relaxed.

"Nick! Good, you're here. Okay, I need you to peel these
potatoes."

Oh crap. Zoyka was right—he was a lost cause at peeling—
but he'd promised to help, so he took the bag of potatoes
and the peeler from Izzy without a word. He found a spot by
the sink and set to work. His mom could peel a potato all in
one go, with a knife, without looking at what she was doing
once. She could also cut them in her hand without slicing her
own fingers off in less than ten seconds. When Zoyka made
a comment about it once, his mom had just shrugged. She'd
learned early and done it often, was the implication.

Nick was just hoping no one was watching his struggles.

When he chanced a glance at the others, he saw Izzy and
Steph readying a hunk of beef for the oven, while Dex was
busy doing some magic to broccoli and carrots. *He* didn't
look like he was having trouble with vegetable prep.

Natali was, by the looks of it, just stealing everyone's
ingredients and chowing down with zero compunction. He'd
only just realized her hair had three blue streaks in the back.

"How's it going with the potatoes?" Dex asked. Nick fumbled and nearly let a slippery potato escape from his already tenuous grasp. He shouldn't have been staring.

"Fine!" He fixed his glasses with the back of his wrist.

"Cool." Dex was, thankfully, no longer in the state of undress he'd been in that morning, but Nick remained hyperaware of him just two paces away. He looked laser-focused on his task, which seemed to be cutting the skin off of broccoli. Nick had never seen anyone do that. Had, in fact, no idea anyone did it at all. He craned his neck and tried to work out the point of the exercise, and when he looked up, Natali was watching him with a crooked grin.

"Dex is a weirdo." She shrugged and took another bite of her pilfered carrot. Out of the corner of his eye, Nick saw Dex look up from his task. "He's got a mate who works for a Chinese place. Apparently, if you peel them, they soak up the oils better or whatever."

"Oh. That's cool."

Dex shrugged, but unlike with Nick's mom, it looked self-conscious, which struck Nick as unbearably sweet. "It works really well for a roast," Dex said and threw another finished piece into a bowl. "Anyway, if you don't mind cutting those up once you're done peeling and getting them ready to roast, that'd be great. Have you roasted potatoes before?"

He could feel heat in his cheeks and his neck and in the tips of his ears. He shook his head.

"That's cool, mate," Dex said as he picked up another broccoli floret. "You just cut up into quarters, toss them in oil, salt and pepper, that's all."

"Sounds good." Nick cleared his throat. "Thanks."

"Hey, at least you're doing it," Izzy said, smile in her voice. "D'you see Nat helping in any way? No. Her mum makes the most incredible food, and she's never made us as much as an omelette, the lazy cow."

"Oi!" A carrot sailed past Nick's head. "I'm not lazy, I'm just no good. I've tried cooking, and it's turned out like shit. Why bother, am I right?" The last part was addressed to Nick.

"I guess. I was never taught. Or learned. It's—" Stupid, now he thought about it. "My mom never wanted us to help, she just wanted us out of the way. She taught my sister the basics, though."

"But not you?" Dex didn't sound accusatory, just curious.

"Zoya's a girl. My mom said she should know how to." He wrinkled his nose. "It's a Russian thing."

"Did your dad never cook?" Natali asked.

"Nat—"

"What? Oh, sorry, Nick."

Nick shook his head. He wasn't a delicate fucking flower. "No, it's fine. He didn't cook, and Zoyka actually used to give him grief over it." He found himself smiling.

"So why did your mum want you out of the way?" Dex again.

"When we were growing up, it was pretty tight quarters, so there was never any room for us to be underfoot." He traced the pattern of the peel as he twisted the potato in his hands. "And she had no time to teach us. She just needed to cook food for the week and go do other stuff. And that sort of didn't change when we moved to the States."

"I could…" Dex paused, and when Nick looked up at him, Dex looked down. "I could teach you the basics, if you wanted. I love to cook."

Nick swallowed and nearly dropped his knife. Before he could reply, Izzy said, "Do it. Maybe he'll actually eat." She winked. "You're skinny, babe. We've got to get some mass on you."

Nick flushed—again—and picked up the last potato from his stash. He pictured Dex taking him through the paces of cutting, frying, stewing. What else was there? Nick couldn't picture the details, but he could envision the mechanics of it. Dex's attention laser-focused on him. His own attention wandering. To Dex. He should come up with some excuse. Not enough time, no interest. He didn't care. Anything.

Instead, he snagged the skin and began to peel it, one long pinkish, papery strand, and said, "Sure, that'd be awesome." He looked up and met Dex's startled gaze. "Thank you."

+

"We're here!" Jonny's voice rang out just as Izzy poured the sweaty, triumphant cooking crew some wine.

Nick caught her wrinkling her nose. "Tweedle Dee," she whispered, then put on her stunning Izzy smile as Jonny and—yep, Lance—walked through the door.

"Smells good in here," Jonny said. He had a covered tray. "Yorkshire puddings, as promised." Lance leaned against the doorway with his dreamy expression.

When he caught sight of Nick, he smiled and lifted his hand. "Hiya, comrade!"

Nick didn't roll his eyes for Jonny's sake. "Hey." He took a sip of his wine. It was sweet and went down easy. When he looked at Dex, who was covering his mouth with his hand. His eyes looked bright, and so warm, Nick thought it would take being the Ice Queen not to smile just looking at them. He wasn't an Ice Queen. Nowhere near. So he grinned and looked away.

"You're a culinary genius," Izzy told Jonny, kissing him on the cheek. "Thanks for letting him use your oven, Lance."

It smelled amazing now, with the meat and the veggies all doing their thing in the oven. Izzy had already explained how growing up, her mom used to just boil everything, which she had found revolting, and it wasn't until Steph and uni that she figured out a roast meant a *fucking roast, d'you know what I mean? We roast it all now.*

Nick, no stranger to boiled everything, did know.

166

When they ate, they did it in the living room. Izzy apparently had a dream of having a real dining table they could all sit around for hours, but until such a time, draping themselves over available furniture was the best they could do. Nick took himself to a corner where he could sit cross-legged and not look like an idiot stuffing his face. For a few minutes, all that was heard in the living room was the sound of eating and an occasional satisfied moan.

Whatever Izzy and Steph had done to the meat made it melt in Nick's mouth, and even his slightly undersalted potatoes weren't half bad. He looked to see if the others were eating them. Lance had already put his away, which warmed Nick to him ever so slightly. Natali had gone in on a double helping, as she wasn't eating the meat. Okay. So maybe he could do more than sandwiches, cereal, and soup from a can.

Dex could definitely cook. His broccoli and carrots were amazing—right amount of seasoning, crunchy, a little salty, a little sweet. Nick felt anticipation build in his belly. If Dex really meant it about teaching him, would it just be the two of them? Or would others be there, as well? Nick didn't want an audience, but he and Dex hadn't spent time alone together since he had his fucking panic attack. What would it be like?

"Ooof," Lance groaned and set his plate aside. "Of all the fucked-up British institutions, the roast is a proper good time."

Nick stuffed half a Yorkshire pudding in his mouth.

"Word," Jonny replied and leaned against Lance's side. "Bang up job, us, well done."

"More wine?" Natali asked.

Impeded by the bread in his mouth, Nick gave her his glass to refill wordlessly as she beamed at him. Nick couldn't figure her out, but at least she no longer filled him with terror. That was a good step.

Later on, Dex went around collecting empty plates, and Nick staggered to his feet before Dex could grab his. He was a guest.

"I got it," he said, and awkwardly followed Dex into the kitchen. They moved around each other by the sink. Dex dumped his dishes first, then took Nick's plate carefully and did the same with it. Natali was refilling Nick's glass, so he took it off her and gulped a mouthful down. He was full, but the wine felt good, cool in his throat.

"Good, right? That's my dad's elderberry. Makes it himself," she told him. "What's that face? No one's forcing you to drink it, *Dexter*."

"Elderberry is gross."

"I like it," Nick told her. "It's nice. Sweet."

"Exactly."

Dex grabbed a beer from the fridge. "Whatever, I'm gonna go and see if I can't be called a fascist by Lance or something."

"Tell him the Socialist Workers are ineffectual, that'll get his hackles up!" Natali called out after him, then turned to Nick. "Let's see what happens."

+

"Oh, you will *not* ask him that, for fuck's sake—" Dex's voice streamed through the hallway as Nick made his way back from the bathroom. He'd killed off two glasses of wine, and he was mellow and happy. He paused outside the doorway, curious.

"Look, you lot keep badgering me to look at it from all angles, and this is prime research material. First-rate source! *Primary* source!"

"He's not a bloody book, man, what if he doesn't want to?"

"Good lord, can I digest in peace, please?"

Nick walked through the door, and everyone stopped talking. Nick leaned against the wall and laughed at their expressions. "Lance, you wanna ask me stuff?"

"Yeah, if you don't mind!" Lance lit up. He was sort of adorable, in a slightly crazy way. Saying no to him felt like kicking a puppy.

"Go for it. But, I mean, I may not know everything. I was just ten when we left."

"No problem, man." Lance settled in against Jonny, and Nick couldn't fail to miss the easy way Jonny moved to accommodate him, the way Lance had leaned into him without looking. "Your parents lived during Communism, right?"

Nick nodded.

"What was that like, they ever tell you? Like, was it cool, knowing everybody was equal and whatnot?"

Nick wanted to laugh. As a kid, he had actually gone through a Lance phase of his own, reading vague Soviet propaganda novels because some of that stuff was historically riveting, moving, but so completely removed from reality it might as well have been shelved in the Fantasy section. "You probably won't like what I tell you, though."

Lance shrugged. "I just believe power should be with the people, not the oligarchical few and whatnot, so the idea's solid."

"I mean, sure," Nick said, looking him in the eye. "But it wasn't like that in execution. It was the opposite."

"What was it like, then?"

Nick slid down until he was sitting on the floor, hugging his knees. "I mean, the first election wasn't even held until ninety-one. And my parents said that Gorbachev was a decent enough guy, but that that was pretty rare. Most of them were ineffectual, at best." At worst, they were Stalin.

"At least it wasn't capitalism and monopolizing and privatizing and all that bullshit," Lance countered. "Not like with Thatcher and whatnot."

"Look, I'm not defending capitalism. I think it's fucked up, on so many levels." Nick struggled to find the words here. It was too confusing, it was too much to explain. He barely understood all of it himself, but he remembered his parents' stories. They'd stayed with him like the black-and-white pictures of their youth, Pioneer scarves tied around their necks, stars pinned to their uniforms, serious expressions in grainy print. "There was just no chance for improving your life at all back then. It was a grind. And people had no power at all." He swallowed. "You know?"

Lance still looked riveted. "So is that why you left? 'Cause it was hard? Isn't that giving in, man?"

"Lance…" Jonny laid a hand over Lance's knee, a bit of a warning in his eyes. Everyone seemed to still.

"I mean, I didn't *mean* it like that. What about the power of the people's voice? Revolution?"

For a split second, Nick was torn between wanting to pummel Lance and legging it out of the house altogether. It felt like if he opened his mouth, bile would pour out. He swallowed. "Look, most people didn't really have a voice. Especially Jews. My parents—" He felt his voice stuttering. Paused. Tried again. "My parents had to get their college degrees in Siberia because Moscow State wouldn't take random Jewish kids off the street, no matter how smart they were. Both my mom and my dad had gold medals when they graduated high school, which is, like, the equivalent of a 4.0 GPA or—" He groped for the British equivalent, trying to remember if they had one. "You know, basically, all A's. But nobody would look at them, because they were nobodies, and they were Jewish, to boot." He paused to take in a deep breath. "It was corrupt as fuck. It still is, Communism or not."

And that wasn't just a Communism problem. His parents left fourteen years after the Soviet Union fell. Fourteen years of anticipating that maybe, somehow, things would begin to improve now. Fourteen years of slowly coming to realize that nothing would ever change, and if it did, it would be for the worse. Zoya would come home in tears because no matter how hard she tried, her Lit teacher refused to give her an A. Fourteen years of still being frightened to utter the word "Jewish" outside the company of other Jews because for all that the nineties saw a certain breath of freedom, a shift in views, several lifetimes of oppression were impossible to erase.

Despite it all, though, Nick had loved his childhood. That was the hardest thing of all to explain, so he didn't even try.

He felt someone's gaze on him and turned despite himself. Dex. A warm wave rushed through him. "Basically, we mostly left because of the Jewish thing."

"Nick, I didn't know you were Jewish," Steph said. "You don't actually talk about it, huh?"

He gave her a quick smile. "Yeah, we were able to get a refugee visa." Eventually. "Anyway, all I'm saying is, Lance, Communism is a nice enough idea on paper, but it really doesn't actually fucking work in reality because people in power tend to want to stay in power."

Lance threw up his hands. "All right, man, surrender. Thanks for letting me go all Grand Inquisitor on you, I get that this is heavy shit. Sorry I offended you."

"It's all right. I don't mind." Not entirely true, but on the other hand, maybe now Lance would stop calling him a comrade every time he saw him. He seemed a decent enough guy underneath the bluster and misguided idealism. Nick smiled. "Thanks for listening."

A collective sort of breath whooshed out of everybody else. "All right, we good now? Who wants dessert?" Izzy asked brightly.

Hola, lover!"

Kat caught up with Izzy in two strides of her long, denim-clad legs and grabbed her shoulder like they were acting out a scene from a wacky eighties comedy. Izzy allowed herself to be steered towards the classroom. Her bag was caught awkwardly between them, forcing her bra strap to dig into her shoulder. She had worn a cute new bra—it was purple with pink edging, and the straps had flowers appliquéd on them—and she was quickly realising that, attractive as it was, it was not up to the strain of supporting her massive tits all day long.

"How are you, my lovely, lively Gingersnap?"

"You're killing me, Smalls." Izzy shifted until they were no longer plastered up against each other like they were trying to win the three-legged race. This was her last tutor session of the day, and she couldn't wait to leg it home and throw off this frilly cage of oppression.

"Soz." Kat grinned, unrepentant. "Anyway, we're going for Lady Dancing, Take Two—wanna join us?"

She'd had a great time on Nineties Night, but nobody else wanted to go out dancing as much as she did, and it might be nice to just go where there was absolutely zero pressure to pull. Not that there was all that much pressure, but she always felt some weird obligation to let her freak flag fly. Going out with lesbians sounded like a lovely alternative.

"When's that, then?"

"Tomorrow night, same place, in Vauxhall. It's a tenner to get in, and the first hour the drinks are half off."

"In."

"Yesssssss! Get in! All right, I'll meet you at the Tube, we can go together. Ladies' night is the best. Maybe we'll even convert you."

"Ha. Nice one."

Kat propped herself against the doorframe like a swooning hero. "Your loss."

When she got home later that night, she called out, but the house really was empty. Dex must have been at the library, which she could never understand, because libraries were so much fucking pressure. She couldn't get any work down what with trying to be totally quiet and getting glares every time she got up for a wee. No, thank you. Cafes were much more preferable if she was tired of her room.

Wasn't Jonny meant to be home, though? Although he'd definitely been spending a lot of time hanging out with Tweedle Dum and Tweedle Dee, so he was probably out with them. What about Nat? Izzy frowned and dropped her bag before making her way into the kitchen and putting the kettle on. She should probably work on her lit reading, but her brain was full. Maybe she'd just have a cuppa and watch some telly before jumping into it. A brain break. Those were meant to be good, right?

She was half an hour into *Gogglebox* when she heard the familiar rattle of keys in the lock and sat up, perking her ears to try and figure out who it was.

"Anybody home?"

Jonny! Oh, yay, she'd been hoping it would be him. "Hiya! Just in the living room."

Thump of the door being shut, and Jonny peeked his head in and smiled. He looked a bit peaky, which had become too much of a familiar sight.

"Want a cuppa?" she asked. "I was about to get up and make myself another one. D'you have a lot of work to do, or can you hang out? What did you have today, anyway?"

Jonny took a bit to respond, which—

"Oh, right, soz, you just walked through the door. I'm doing the thing again, aren't I?" She felt a bit like a puppy, but being in the house by herself always unnerved her. She lived with three other people. Surely being alone under those circumstances was unnatural.

"S'okay. Just lemme drop my bag and whatnot, and I'll make us tea. I don't feel like working."

In a few minutes, he did in fact join her on the couch, with two cups steaming in his hands. "What's on?" he asked, squinting at the telly.

"*Gogglebox*," she told him. "Haven't seen this episode before, but it's a bit boring, to be honest."

"I think I've seen it. It *is* boring."

She muted the telly and turned so she could look at him properly. "How was your day?"

Jonny did his best to look nonchalant, but he was pretty transparent most of the time. "All right, I guess."

"Mate, you don't look all right, if I'm honest."

He shrugged again, but this time it looked less nonchalant and more resigned.

"Is it your dad?" she asked carefully.

He took a sip of tea, then nodded. "He's recovering, but I haven't talked to either him or Mum since I've been back. I think they're starting to catch on that Soph is telling me everything that's happening, so she's had to stop asking as much."

Izzy made a disgusted noise. "Fuck them."

"Iz."

She pulled herself together. "Right. Sorry. I'm sorry. You just look so unhappy." She set down her cup onto the coffee table and drew up her knees, facing him fully. He was avoiding eye contact.

Another shrug. "I know. I guess I'm not all unhappy. I mean, I really am sort of fine."

Izzy fought her desire to help people along if they were struggling for words—something Dex has told her in the past could seem condescending or even infuriating—and waited for Jonny to continue. He scratched underneath his collar, and she saw a bruise that could only be a hickey.

"Hey, man, is that a love bite?" She hadn't meant to say that out loud, but too late.

Jonny instantly colored and pulled his shirt tight around his throat. "What? No. What?"

"Oh my God, it so is!" She shot forward, about to pull the shirt back to see the whole thing—frankly, it looked impressive—but Jonny caught her wrist as he squealed and tried to bat her away with his free hand.

"Hey, hey, no touching! My love bite, not yours!"

"Definitely not mine, but who's the lucky person bestowing hickeys on you? You've got to spill!"

Jonny looked positively shifty. "D'you mind if I don't? It's, like, really new, you know?" He sighed. "That all right?"

"You're killing me!" *Bah.* "But yes, obviously. I am dying of curiosity here, but." She raised her hands. "It's your business."

"*Thank* you."

Izzy rocked back and forth a bit, literally biting her tongue. "But you do understand I'm dying to know and you are killing me, don't you?"

Jonny did a full-on evil cackle. "That's half the fun of being me."

"*Tchuh*! You berk."

"I do try."

He never did, though. That was the thing of it—Jonny was just so fucking good. "Is it nice, though?" she asked.

He echoed her smile. Lovely Jonny. "Yeah."

"Good."

Izzy could feel her cheeks splitting with a grin. It was nice to see him smile like that. She'd get it out of him eventually, so she could wait for a bit. "Oh, guess what!"

"What?" he asked dutifully.

"I'm going out with my mate Kat tomorrow night, for a ladies' dancing type of night."

"Sounds awesome. What ladies?"

She shrugged. "All sorts, I think?"

"Is it gay ladies, Isabel?"

She shook her head slowly. "Well, yeah, but like, not *just* gay ladies. I don't think Kat would have invited me if it was solely gay ladies, would she?"

Jonny made a *how would I know?* face.

"I guess we'll see. You don't suppose Steph would wanna go, do you?"

"Steph? Go dancing? More than once a year?"

"Oh, right."

"Anyway, you don't need us, right? You like Kat, don't you?"

"I *always* need you," she said with her hand over heart. "But yes, I'll probs be fine." She suddenly got a weird image of standing by the wall by herself while other girls danced all around her. "Right? But what if I'm awkward?"

"Are you serious?"

"What?"

"Iz, you're, like, the person I think about when I think of people who can walk into any room and make ten friends from the word *go*."

"What? No way!" She squirmed a bit in place. "Really?"

Jonny cracked up. "Oh my God, yes. You just go out there and you show those ladies how to have a good time, all right?"

"Yes, sir!" She took up her cup of tea lifted it in a salute. "Roger and all that."

"Don't know about the rogering—ladies only, right?"

It definitely look her a second. Then she mock-gasped. "Rude!"

Jonny giggled into his tea.

Izzy had never met any of Kat's other friends—they'd never really socialised outside of coursework. But they all seemed friendly and nice enough, even if they abandoned Kat and Izzy outside the club because Kat was stalling. Then, a few moments later, a blue-haired little pixie appeared out of nowhere, and Izzy felt her eyes go wide. "Beth! What're you doing here?"

Beth grinned and shrugged. "Kat asked me."

Kat, in the meantime, had already sidled up to Beth and smacked her a kiss on the cheek. "Hiya, my little fairy." Izzy watched as Beth flushed and gave her a flirty, slightly flustered look. All righty, then. *That* was an interesting development.

Beth turned her attention back to Izzy. "Anyway, I didn't know you were into ladies."

"'Mnot, just came out to dance, didn't I?"

"Gonna drive all the girls mad with desire and leave them unsatisfied?" Her giggle undercut any meanness to the comment, but Izzy's excitement drooped a bit anyway.

"Do you think that's gonna happen? I didn't—"

"Iz, I'm fucking with you. They don't exactly check your queer ID at the door, I was just being an arse."

Izzy felt her face flaming under ten pounds of foundation. "Okay."

Kat groaned. "God, you're adorable even when you're embarrassed, which I never actually thought happened to you. C'mon, let's get inside already."

Beth gave Izzy an apologetic look and then seemed to forget about everything but Kat's arm around her. Izzy braced herself for feeling like a total outsider, because if this actually did turn out to be, for all that Beth had protested, a Queer Ladies' Night, as the flyer outside the club clearly stated—God, what the fuck was she doing here? What did Dex call straight people crashing queer events? Infiltrating? Something like that. Maybe not infiltrating, but she still didn't feel too easy as she handed the bored-looking woman at the front of the queue a sweaty tenner and allowed her to stamp her hand.

Inside was utter chaos, and she immediately lost Kat and Beth. The bass of whatever song was playing pounded through her ribcage, which relaxed her. She could do this. She was here with mates, and she was here to dance.

First, though, she needed a drink.

The woman behind the bar was gorgeous, like the platonic ideal of a queer bartender. She had a butch type of haircut, a dirty blond quiff on top and short sides, tapering to shaved at the bottom of her skull. She looked older, maybe late thirties, and wore a ribbed vest, which served to accentuate her small chest, defined shoulders and arms, and the myriad tattoos wrapped around her skin. She had Nat's build, a slim body that Izzy had always secretly envied even as she did her damn fucking best to love the build her mother had passed on to her.

The bartender nodded her chin in Izzy's direction, and Izzy leaned and shouted her order. Whilst the drink was being prepared, she looked around, attempting to adjust to the dimness of the club. It wasn't as full as she'd first thought, and it was wall-to-wall women. She realised it comforted her, and she began to relax, especially after getting her shot and downing it immediately. She shook out her hair, straightened her dress, and hit the dance floor.

+

Her feet ached in the best way imaginable. The DJ was incredible, playing jam after jam. Izzy was two cocktails in, and the sugar levels were off the chain. Cider sure never packed a punch like this. She felt a little fuzzy, but so fully *alive*. She never allowed herself to get plastered when out, anyway. She could count on her mates and everything, but what if they got separated, or her phone died, or something? She never ever wanted to be *that girl*. That girl never caught a break.

No, she wasn't drunk. She was happy. She'd needed this. She did feel unbalanced. Not right. Something was niggling at her, but she couldn't catch it.

Maybe it had been that stupid fight with Dex.

Maybe it had been the talk with Nick about her course.

Maybe she was just overthinking everything, which never ended well, and anyway, she never dwelled on the bad shit. Why was she doing it now?

Maybe that was why, when she was taking a quick rest against the wall, catching her breath, and saw a girl appear in front of her and beckon her for a dance with a tilt of her chin, Izzy went.

"What's your name?" the girl shouted in her ear once they were bouncing up and down on the dance floor. Her breath was hot against Izzy's skin and smelled beery.

"Izzy!"

"What?"

"Izzy! Like Isabel but, uh, shorter?"

The girl laughed and pulled back enough to catch Izzy's eye. "I heard you the first time, love, just having a laugh."

It *should* have annoyed her, and maybe it would have had a guy done it. But somehow it only made Izzy laugh. Flush and laugh, but she was probably pink all over from the dancing, so at least it wouldn't be noticeable.

"What about you, then?" she shouted.

"I'm Ruby!"

Izzy thought that if they hadn't been shouting, Ruby's voice would have been husky. It had that edge to it. *She* had that edge to her, anyway. She was shorter than Izzy, just enough to probably be of a height when Izzy wasn't wearing heels. With heels on, Izzy brushed the other side of six foot, which she loved more than most people, probably. She'd once cried on her mum's shoulder that she felt like an elephant compared to all the other girls (and, what was worse, boys) in her class, and her mum had petted her head, then said, *Isabel? Great Danes don't produce chihuahuas.* It had been so absurd, it had actually comforted.

She liked the way she towered over Ruby, because it didn't feel as if she should be able to. Ruby was tall and lanky but had a presence about her. She felt bigger than her build. She, too, had tattoos. Was this a queer lady thing? Izzy would have to ask Nat later, because Nat had also already started on an arm sleeve, but Izzy had thought it was more of a Nat thing, not a lesbian thing. Ruby's left arm was covered shoulder to midway through her forearm. Vines and sea monsters and things. It was cool. She had a lip piercing, an eyebrow piercing, and short black hair in a chunky haircut with fringe that periodically fell over her dark-lined eyes. In this light, it was impossible to tell what color they were, but regardless she was easily the coolest girl Izzy'd ever met.

That she had taken Izzy's hand and led her to the dance floor felt heady to her, like it made her special by association. The way she was looking at Izzy. That was also nice. Beth's dire warnings still rang in her ears, but Izzy was having too nice a time now to turn back. Anyway, Ruby didn't seem like the sort of girl to cry over having wasted a dance or two on a straight girl. Ruby would be just fine.

"D'you want another drink?" Ruby asked as the song seamlessly bled into the next one, but Izzy shook her head *no*. No, she was riding an amazing, bubbly sort of buzz, and all she knew was that she wasn't ready to leave the dance floor, nor did she want Ruby to leave her. Not yet.

Ruby stayed. The push and pull of the people around them forced them into each other's proximity, causing Izzy's breasts to brush against Ruby's. She must have been wearing a sports bra because they barely moved when she danced, Izzy noticed, but they were, well. Very, very real breasts brushing her own, in a way that felt different to giving her girlfriends hugs. Ruby shifted, looked at Izzy from under her eyelashes, and wrapped her hands around Izzy's waist.

Izzy caught her breath but let it happen. For a moment, she wasn't sure whether the right thing to do would be to extricate herself and send a clear message or not. Do that.

Izzy did move, but not away. Instead, she used the push from behind her of other bodies as pretence to get closer, and it was like a series of snapshots she was looking at from the outside. One moment she could see Ruby's face, the strobe lights glinting off her piercings; the next moment their legs tangled. Ruby's face disappeared because they were too close to see each other. Izzy saw, more than felt, herself sliding her hands down until they were past Ruby's narrow waist, until her fingers were brushing the slope of Ruby's arse. She felt it flexing against her hands as they moved. Felt the sweat gathered between the places they touched.

Ruby shifted again, and her thigh moved against Izzy's cunt.

Izzy rocked into it and gasped. She had been slowly getting turned on the whole time they'd been dancing, but avoiding thinking about it. Now it was impossible to avoid anything, as the ache between her legs grew, became a pulsating thing, that delicious, overwhelming prelude to sex.

Fuck. *Fuck*. What was she doing? What the fuck did she think she was playing at?

And then Ruby pulled back, caught Izzy's gaze, and slowly leaned in.

Izzy let it happen as if she were watching a film. Watching it through a fog of want. This couldn't be her, touching her lips to Ruby's and allowing them to open? Surely it wasn't Izzy allowing their breath to mix, sugar and hops mingling?

Then it became a blur. A blur of hot, overwhelming kissing and grinding. Dirty fucking grinding, and Izzy had never realised that two girls could grind as well as a guy and a girl. No cock, but Ruby knew what she was doing, and Izzy was losing her fucking mind. She was so turned on. She was *so turned on*. Ruby was steady and unrelenting. Izzy was aware of them rocking to the beat, but only peripherally, because most of her awareness had transferred downward. Ruby kept her close, so close Izzy was almost on her toes, hands like claws on Ruby's arse. They were barely even kissing anymore, because Izzy couldn't focus.

Christ, she was gonna come. She was gonna come whilst grinding on a girl on a dance floor in Vauxhall. What the actual bleeding fuck.

She was so close, too. God, she was. She couldn't think.

She barely heard herself panting against Ruby's open mouth, faster and faster, now totally lost to need, all of her brain cells scattered in the beat of the music. She needed Ruby to keep grinding them together, she needed to come so badly. All the blood rushed south, her cunt pulsating. She felt it expanding, that feeling of power as she got closer and closer. Without really understanding, she let her head drop forward and bit Ruby's neck. It tasted of salt, of skin. She felt Ruby shudder against her.

"Fuck yeah," Ruby whispered, somehow still able to make words. "God, you're so fucking hot. You close?"

Izzy moaned. She was seconds away, and she chased it, that feeling of letting go. She shut her eyes and focused only on sensation. And then, on another thrust, she caught up with it. Maybe it caught up with her. She came, almost keening, as she shuddered and shook against Ruby. She spasmed against Ruby's thigh, and she wanted *more* even as she didn't think she could handle it. She wanted something inside her, something to come on. A sudden image of Ruby's fingers in her cunt flashed in her mind. Izzy sucked on Ruby's neck as she came and came and came and shut her mind from any further thought.

+

Her thighs burned. Her calves were killing her. Her knickers were an utter mess. But she barely felt any of it, because Ruby hadn't given her any room for thought. Usually, postorgasm, Izzy was either focusing on her partner (which, in this case, she wasn't sure how to do) or feeling vaguely uneasy about the type of porn that had got her off and hiding away the evidence.

This was a bit of an unknown, and she didn't know *what* to feel. The sense of unease was there, sure, but so was Ruby, and Ruby was taking control yet again. Izzy had always enjoyed that with guys. She was pliable after coming, fizzy with endorphins, so when Ruby grabbed her hand and led her off the dance floor, weaving in between moving bodies and wafts of body smells, Izzy let her. She then let herself be steered towards a dark corner of the club, pushed against the wall, and kissed.

Kissed so, so fucking hard.

Izzy loved it. Loved the slow way in which Ruby kissed, like all she wanted in the world was to keep kissing Izzy.

Loved how tough she looked, propped up with both hands on the wall on either side of Izzy's face. Loved the feel of her tongue, tentative and barely there at first, then growing heavier, lovely and expert. Izzy found herself grabbing the edge of Ruby's worn checked shirt and pulling her closer. Then she wrapped one of her thighs around Ruby's hips. She was lanky, yeah, but she had hips. Izzy could feel them, pressed up against her thigh, the side of her knee. She definitely didn't hate it. It wasn't jarring, felt more like a revelation. Ruby's breasts brushing her own as they kissed felt good, too.

Everything was feeling good. More than good. Izzy sweated against the wall as she rethought everything she'd ever known about her sexuality.

Got off with a girl on the dance floor: new discovery.

Continued to kiss said girl off the dance floor post–getting off: another new discovery.

Wanted to rip said girl's clothes off and sink her fingers into her: utterly new development.

Whoa. That had been a thought and a half, but after a dissonant moment in her mind, Izzy felt settled into it. The truth of it. She *did.* She did want to do that. She bit Ruby's lip, brought them closer together, and, as nonchalantly as she could manage, ran her hand over Ruby's breasts. Deliberately touched another woman's breasts in a sexual manner. Ruby breathed out and made a small, needy noise. Izzy's cunt throbbed, an echo of previous dealings.

Well.

Add yet another new discovery: the feel of a girl's nipple hardening against her palm was, apparently, divine.

She had more of an understanding, now, of boys' ridiculous obsession with her breasts. Not that she didn't enjoy a fondle or two or three, but some of them really had gone at them something ferocious as soon as she'd got her kit off.

187

Ruby broke off with an unexpected kiss to Izzy's cheek. They rested there like that, Ruby's thin, muscled arms still bracketing Izzy in, their cheeks against each other's, bosoms literally heaving. This was unreal. Izzy was so turned on she could have come again with a single touch.

"God, you're lovely," Ruby murmured in Izzy's ear. Izzy's eyes shut of their own accord. Her head thumped against the wall.

"Fuck," was about all she could manage.

Ruby leaned down and kissed the crook of Izzy's neck. Izzy shivered, tilted her head to give her better access. Everything between them pulsed.

"Do you wanna go back to mine?"

This was her choice, then. End this madness now or see how far down the sexuality rabbit hole she actually went.

Well, that was an easy one.

"Where do you live, and are you a serial killer?"

Ruby laughed. Away from the throng of people, her voice was easier to pick out. Her laugh was throaty, deep. "Three streets down, and no. I'm a serial puller, though."

Izzy pushed her back and gave her a look. Like. Seriously?

Ruby cracked up. "Too much? God, you're adorable. I promise not to kill you, not literally. Can't say we'll avoid *la petite mort.*"

"Fuck, you're ridiculous."

Another laugh. "There's a reason it's feminine, though," Ruby breathed.

Izzy shivered again; cleared her throat. "Lead on, then."

+

The outside was cold, which had the unfortunate side effect of sobering Izzy right up. Which made her wonder if she should be fucking off home instead of heading into Ruby's

Den of Pulling to make another notch on her Lesbian Sex Bedpost or whatever.

Ruby must have sensed this, because she twisted them around until they were almost toppling off the kerb and kissed Izzy senseless. Then she slid one hand in between them, right over where Izzy's dress clung to her hips and thighs and—

All right, all right, she was *not* about to change her mind. She attempted to communicate this to Ruby with her mouth and hands, but then they were just outright snogging on the asphalt and giggly voices were calling out, "Oy, get a bloody room, you two, honestly!"

That was when she remembered she had come here with a friend and had promptly lost her in the shuffle.

"Fuck, hang on."

She pushed Ruby gently away and then shook her head at Ruby's questioning gaze. Out here in the street light, she saw that Ruby's skin was quite a bit darker than hers, and her eyes were a light golden brown. She was gorgeous. "Got to tell my mate I'm leaving or she'll worry. You know, girl code."

"I live on Randall Row, and my full name is Ruby Lee Weston. You know. Just in case." She leered. Somehow, it did *not* look stupid on her.

Izzy laughed as she fished out her phone from her bra and wiped as much of the sweat from it as she could before attempting to text. Then she shoved it back against her left boob, patted the right one for her keys and money—all accounted for—and said, "All right. Take me to your lair."

Ruby grabbed her hand.

✛

"My flatmates aren't home," Ruby told her as she grabbed her keys from her pockets. Her trousers had a billion of them—she must have shopped in the men's section. They looked good on her. Izzy could never have pulled that off in a million years. "So you can be loud." Ruby threw her a look over her shoulder, and Izzy shivered. Actually bloody shivered, because she was about to shag a girl and probably be completely fucking destroyed by her. Ruby had that look about her. *I have satisfied countless women, and you are about to be added to my list of victories.* Unlike with some of the guys she'd shagged, Izzy didn't feel dirty at being on the receiving end of such a look. Maybe not *dirty*, but lessened, somehow. With Ruby, it felt the opposite.

They fell through the door. The flat was dark, and Izzy just heard the dull clanging of keys hitting the floor before Ruby was grabbing her by the back of her hips and leading her into further darkness. She felt something brush against her calf and yelped.

"Oh, sorry, that's my cat. He's probably pissed off we woke him up."

Her voice really *was* husky. Izzy got lost in her head imagining what Ruby would sound like when coming.

Ruby changed trajectories and led her through a doorway. She switched on a lamp, and Izzy fought the desperate desire to run into the bathroom and check to see what she actually looked like, since it was probably terrifying. She only ever used waterproof eyeliner and mascara to go out dancing—a girl had to be smart about these things—but that didn't mean they always survived the night. She cast a quick glance over at Ruby to see what she really looked like.

She wasn't wearing makeup, for one. She had pink cheeks and was dusky all over. Her hair was messy, but it was *meant* to be messy. Her black cargo trousers sat low enough on her hips that when she turned towards Izzy and ripped her shirt off right over her head, Izzy saw two inches of underwear. And yeah, that had been a sports bra. Her tattoos weren't just on her arm. She had a vine snaking around her torso, a thick line with leaves and tendrils and things. It was beautiful, and it moved every time Ruby took a breath.

Izzy stood there, rooted to the floor, as Ruby strode over to her in two seconds and said, "C'mere, gorgeous."

Izzy hated how self-conscious she felt all of a sudden and decided, *fuck that.* Ruby had called her gorgeous, and anyway, Izzy knew she looked good. Apart from whatever was happening on her face, she had never had any complaints. And if she had, the complainers had quickly been booted out the door, because she had no time for that nonsense.

Her heart fluttered as Ruby kissed her, and her stomach churned. It was just—it was real. And so *physical.* Kissing a girl, a girl with her shirt off no less, if she'd ever imagined such a thing, she couldn't have imagined actually going through with it.

Also, she had no idea what she was doing. It was one thing to picture it happening *in media res*, it was another to have to work at getting there.

But Ruby, it seemed, was a pro. She pushed Izzy back a few steps until she hit the bed and then gently pushed her down. Izzy wound up sat with her legs apart and Ruby in between them. The smell of sex grew sharp, and Izzy forced herself not to squirm. When she looked at Ruby, Ruby's eyes were ten shades darker. Holding her gaze, Ruby dropped down to her knees.

Izzy leaned in and kissed her, because that part had been going well enough, and she had no idea what to do next.

They snogged for about five seconds, then Ruby pulled away. She ran her hands up Izzy's legs. Izzy was wearing tights and boots, but she went utterly still as Ruby's wandering hands found her thighs and sneaked underneath the hem of her dress.

"Can we get you out of these?" Ruby's voice was low, God, so low.

Izzy swallowed and nodded. She felt the texture of Ruby's duvet under hands, didn't know if she should be helping or what. Ruby gave her a crooked smile, then deliberately lifted Izzy's right leg. She unzipped her boot. "If only it was warmer," Ruby said like it was no big deal, "I'd be able to just hike up your dress."

Izzy breathed in sharply, barely felt it when Ruby slid her boots off. Her feet throbbed. A good sort of throb. She flexed her toes.

"But these are in the way," Ruby murmured. She ran her hands up the sides of Izzy's legs. "I think you'd best do this part."

Oh God. Izzy hadn't been planning on pulling, but she *had* wanted to look good, so she'd worn her tightest pair of tights, and getting out of them was a nightmare at any point, much less when you were attempting to be sexy about it.

"You should probably turn around," she said. "It's not a pretty sight."

"Yeah it is." Ruby watched her. The whole time.

Izzy bore it. At first, as her hands went up underneath her dress and she had to roll the whole business down over her belly, she couldn't make herself look at Ruby. All she could focus her energies on was getting the damn tights off past her arse and hips. What was Ruby seeing?

God, probably everything.

Izzy rolled the tights down, and then it got easier midthigh and she was about to roll them all the way off when Ruby grabbed her wrist and said, "Wait. Leave them like that."

What the ever-loving fuck?

"I'm not being funny, I promise, it's just super hot."

Unconvinced, Izzy went still, until Ruby cracked up and pulled her back in. Izzy's arse hit the bed. Thank God she'd worn cute knickers and had actually cleaned up her bikini line, she thought crazily. Her legs—still connected by the fucking tights, no less—were dangling from Ruby's bed.

Ruby, having moved in between her legs, was licking up her thigh.

Izzy groaned.

Her dress was sweltering, she wanted it off, but she was not in control of this situation. She was, in fact, very much unable to do anything but watch as Ruby held herself up on her arms. It was hot, and her shoulder muscles shifted in the light. A trail of heat was making its way to the top of Izzy's inner thigh.

Fuuuuuuck, fuck, fuck, fuck. She'd thought: maybe fingers. Even a dildo? She hadn't been expecting this.

"Fuck, you smell good."

God, that low *voice*. Izzy hid her face in her hands. The heat between them was unbearable. She was so wet.

"Lift up," Ruby commanded, and Izzy, with zero input from her brain, did. "Love the frills," Ruby murmured. She slid Izzy's panties right off her hips. Izzy couldn't watch. She felt exposed. Not in a bad way. Just in that way where she was going to explode from the intensity of it all.

Ruby slipped her powder-blue knickers down until they hit her tights. Twice trapped, now. Izzy longed to raise her knees so she could at least feel like she was about to get fucked. This was such an awkward, strange position to be in, but when she finally found the courage to look, Ruby was staring at her like she'd never seen anything better in her whole life.

"Fuck, you're so fucking beautiful." She rucked the hem of Izzy's dress up, and now her whole belly was on display, too. Her bra was digging in everywhere and she wanted it off, desperately, wanted *everything* off. "Gorgeous fucking ginger." Ruby whispered.

Izzy actually whimpered. "I can't. The tights, please."

Ruby was quick about it. She grabbed the tights and panties in a single handful and tugged until Izzy's heel was stuck, then tugged harder, and Izzy was free. Legs akimbo, sweating onto Ruby's duvet, throbbing, with a beautiful woman in between her legs, ready to blow her mind.

Izzy grinned. She grabbed Ruby's hips with both legs and pulled her in until they were face to face. This courage was new, and she was fairly certain it wasn't courage as much as it was lust flowing like lava through her veins, but whatever it was, it was working. Ruby kissed her, open-mouthed, tongue first. Izzy moaned into it while mad thoughts like *Maybe I'm a full-on lesbian now* and *Wonder who will wind up on top* swirled in her brain.

"Gonna eat you out so good," Ruby murmured, and all thought broke off. She leaned down, and Izzy could only watch as Ruby licked her way into her cleavage. Her eyelashes were dark and full, leaving pretty shadows on her flushed cheeks. She looked so *intent*, so into it. Izzy brought her hands up and ran her fingers through Ruby's messy hair, hoping that was something she was into. Like a cat, she leaned into the touch.

All right. That was good.

Spurred on, Izzy slipped her hands farther down until she was pushing Ruby in the right trajectory by her shoulders. She felt Ruby laugh against her skin. Her dress wasn't exactly modest, but still, she wanted it completely off. Wanted everything. Wanted to keep her bra on so Ruby could admire her cleavage, wanted it off so Ruby could play with her tits. She felt powerful now, powerful and so fucking sexy. She basked in this place of utter goodness.

"Help me get my dress off if you're going to be a tease about it."

Ruby broke off, and when their gazes met, her eyes looked completely blown. God, that was so hot. Together, they managed to wiggle Izzy out of her dress, and it barely hit the floor before Ruby was attempting to rid her of her bra, too.

Izzy grabbed her hands and pushed them away. They'd be here forever if she didn't just do this part herself, or at least that had always been the case with boys. Of course, Ruby probably had quite a bit of expertise in this department, but Izzy made her watch as she unhooked the clasp herself. As she tugged the straps off her shoulders, her tits spilt immediately to the sides, as they always did, the buggers.

Ruby said, "Oh, fucking hell, those are glorious." Izzy gathered them up for her, her face aflame, and Ruby bit the undersides, one by one, then licked a trail all the way up. Izzy was so busy with how good that felt that she hadn't registered Ruby's shifting positions, not until she felt two fingers slip against her cunt and find the seam, and then gasped just as Ruby slipped both fingers inside her. "God, you are so fucking wet," Ruby murmured. Izzy wanted to clasp her knees together and keep Ruby's fingers inside her, but Ruby was in between them. She humped her hand, shuddering. Good God, she was going to come again, just like that.

She turned her face away from Ruby's, too far gone, and moaned. Ruby slid down. Her hand slipped out, and Izzy gasped, desperate, going mad missing Ruby's fingers. She was sort of fluttery and also completely on fire and she bit her hand—she hadn't even realised she'd shoved it against her mouth—as Ruby spread her legs more and licked her.

Fuck fuck fuck, *fuck*. Izzy cried out, bore down. She wanted—she *wanted*. She wanted to trap Ruby's face with her thighs, she wanted to hump her face, she wanted to come so, so badly. Ruby made a noise and it reverberated through Izzy, a shudder down to her bones. She grabbed the duvet with both hands and groaned. "God. *God*."

Ruby was relentless, finding Izzy's clit effortlessly. God, she knew what she was doing. Most of the time if Izzy came from oral, it was because she'd been so worked up before that it was sort of inevitable. She could tell that Ruby could get her there at any time. If Ruby were to suddenly turn up in Script Writing, crawl under a desk in front of everyone, and go down on Izzy, she'd have her coming within moments. *Fuck.* Fuck fuck *fuck.*

She actually cried out when Ruby slipped three fingers inside her and pressed up. Izzy got embarrassingly loud and everything swelled, was slick and felt so *good*. She came the next moment, so hard she nearly whited out, and Ruby *God bless her* didn't stop. Izzy's orgasm rolled through her as she shuddered around Ruby's fingers and rocked against her tongue, her skin sparking like a live wire, until she was hoarse from crying.

Ruby gave her one last lick after the last of the spasms subsided and slipped her fingers out. Her chin and mouth when she lifted up were wet, and her expression was smug as fuck. Izzy looked at her for a second, then fell back against the duvet and laughed. Her head was spinning. She throbbed, sore in the best way.

"Good, yeah?" Ruby was definitely smug. Izzy pawed until she found her bra strap and made a weak attempt at pulling her up. She had only the smallest of hesitations the moment before they kissed. Most guys she'd been with had, like, wiped their mouths after oral, but it was as if Ruby didn't care. She seemed to revel in it, and it turned out Izzy liked it. Loved it, in fact. Her own taste on Ruby's tongue. She hummed. Kissing after coming was always a sloppy affair for her. She was still not in total control.

Then Ruby pulled away, sat up, and slipped her bra off over her head. Izzy stared at her hard, dark nipples, the way they made her small boobs perky and sensual. Unapologetically sexy. Truthfully, Izzy had always admired boobs—she had just always thought it had been mere aesthetics. A friend of hers back in school had once referred to them as *useless flesh bags*, and Izzy had thought, *What an odd way to refer to something so beautiful.*

Ruby slipped off the bed and tugged down her trousers. She was wearing men's boxer briefs, red with white trim around the waist and legs. Izzy swallowed, looked her fill. Light hair dusted Ruby's thighs, becoming darker past her knees. Izzy decided she liked it.

She reached for Ruby. Ruby came easily.

When she woke up in the morning, the sun was just barely making itself known through the crooked blinds. Her head pounded, and her mouth was filled with cobwebs. Then she felt someone shift behind her and froze.

Right. Ruby. A girl. The girl she'd had sex with. A girl who was now totally naked, spooned up behind her.

Through the fog of her brain, Izzy attempted feeling appalled. Or at least displeased.

She couldn't. Instead of condemnations, her brain was sending her image after image from the night before. The one she remembered best was looking at Ruby's face as she reached down between Ruby's legs and found the wetness inside. It had felt both familiar and not, and it had been strange, but Ruby had gasped and let her head fall back, and Izzy had felt a surge of power so overwhelming her head had spun. It was like touching hot, slick silk.

Ruby had been gorgeous when she'd finally come. Flushed down to her breasts, hair matted, eyes blown, nipples dark and pointed. They'd fit so well in Izzy's mouth.

They'd sort of done the hook-up-fall-asleep-wake-up-do-it-again-fall-asleep, rinse, repeat thing for hours. She was sore absolutely everywhere. She was pretty sure her tits were going to be covered in bruises.

What now? Did Ruby expect her to slip out or stay for brekkie and conversation? Either choice felt odd and uncomfortable.

She felt odd and uncomfortable. Not bad, not *really*. Just like she needed a long soak in a bath and about a thousand hours to think things through.

Actually, she needed to talk to Dex. Maybe to Nat, too. Definitely to Nat. Probably.

Maybe.

Oh, crap. She remembered they were all meeting at the café for breakfast in—she squinted at Ruby's bedside clock—an hour and a half.

She lay there, utterly still, waiting for Ruby to wake up, and tried her best not to think.

15

They were sat in a cafe near campus when Izzy staggered in looking wrecked. Sunglasses on, jacket askew, tiny dress in vague disarray around her. Dex narrowed his eyes. She plopped down next to Nick and just sat there.

"Isabel, what the fuck happened to you?" he asked, then exchanged a look with Nat.

He was about to ask if she was just hungover or if it was something actually serious when Izzy said, "I think I'm not entirely straight?" The whole table—him, Nick, Nat, Jonny, Lance, Alex, Steph—froze.

The first person to break the silence was Natali. "What."

Dex shot her another look, but she only had eyes for Izzy, watching her with an unreadable expression. Izzy, from what Dex could tell, was looking somewhere beyond all of them under her sunnies.

"I—" Izzy said. "I went out last night with my mate Kat, right, to a club in Vauxhall somewhere, can't remember the address, anyway, doesn't matter, so there was this girl." Dex would have bet a million pounds Izzy had no idea she was running her hand over her mouth as she sat there. "She was a bit older, I think. My height. She was wearing one of them checked shirts and these baggy trousers with loads of pockets, and she started to dance with me." She cleared her throat. "She kissed me." Izzy paused. "We kissed."

Everyone's coffees and breakfasts sat forgotten. When Dex glanced around the table, he could see all eyes trained on Izzy. Lance's looked to be close to popping out.

"And?" Alex asked loudly enough that a woman at the table next to theirs glanced up irritably from her Kindle.

"And," Izzy said slowly. "It was really nice." She nicked Dex's coffee right from under his nose and drank about half of it in one go. "It was *really nice.* I feel like I need to reexamine my whole existence now."

"Crikey," Dex said, just as Jonny grinned and said, "Blimey." Dex saw him and Lance exchange an almost conspiratorial look. Dex wasn't sure how Lance wound up joining them for breakfast, but at least he wasn't making things awkward for once.

The table erupted in excited talk, everyone tripping over themselves to ask Izzy questions and make rude comments. A moment later, all was brought to a halt by Natali spitting out over everyone's voices, "I'm sorry, what the fuck. Do you expect us to wave a little flag for you now?"

Silence. Dex looked at her just to make sure he'd heard right. "Nat, what the—"

"No, no. I'm sorry," Natali went on. Her whole face was like a storm brewing. She was staring right daggers at Izzy. Dex felt himself going cold. "Right, you have one kiss with some girl whilst pissed at a club, let's bring out the parade? Is that what you're saying?"

Izzy's mouth hung open, and when she looked to Dex for help, all he could do was stare and shake his head helplessly. "Nat," she croaked. "Nat, that's bollocks, that isn't what—I'm not saying that at all, I'm telling—"

"Yeah, fuck that. *Reexamining your whole existence* my arse. One kiss doesn't mean fuck-all, so please don't try to join the queer club. It's pathetic."

Dex was rooted to the spot. He'd seen Nat angry before, but he'd never seen her this vicious, or this—this mean. This *wrong*. This was *Izzy*. "Nat—"

She cut him off. "Fuck this, I'm late anyway." Natali's chair squeaked as she shot up out of it and grabbed her bag before anyone could say another word. "Here's a tenner."

Dex could only watch along with the rest of them as she shoved her way past the chairs and the tables until the bell over the door jingled her dramatic exit.

Izzy slumped and finally pushed her sunnies up off her face. They sat crookedly on top of her ginger mane. Her eyes were puffy and a touch red. "What the fuck?"

Dex shook his head. "Don't—don't mind that right now."

"I don't...I don't understand." She looked suddenly small. Her voice was hoarse, but he didn't think it was because of being out late drinking. "What the fuck?" she repeated.

Dex exchanged an uneasy glance with Alex. "I'm not sure, babe. But you look proper wrecked." A thought occurred to him. "Iz, did you—you didn't come home last night." One look at Izzy's face gave him the answer. He produced a low whistle. "Shit, mate, you move fast."

Izzy coloured but met his gaze straight on. "I'm an adult. I can fucking do whatever the fuck I feel like."

Dex reached out, going for her hand, but she slipped it into her lap at the last minute. His hand landed awkwardly on the table. "I'm not saying a word," he said carefully. "If you need a chat or anything—"

Izzy pushed his coffee cup back towards him and stood up, her chair scraping the floor in an echo of Natali's. "I've gotta go," she croaked and ran out of the cafe before they could do much more than call out her name.

"Shit." Dex slumped down.

"What—why was Natali so upset?" It was the first thing Nick had said since Izzy's dramatic entrance. He was pink in the face, his eyebrows furrowed. His neck and shoulders were all but lost inside his giant scarf. He looked like a nerdy hipster with his glasses.

"I'm fairly sure I know what happened," he hedged. "But I'd have to talk to Nat first, I think." Nick cast down his gaze and nodded, and Dex thought, *fuck it.* "Look, Nat's had a bit of a thing for Izzy for ages."

"Yeah, it's been sort of an unspoken thing, but we all know," Steph chimed in quietly. "I guess this sort of fucked her up." She was quiet for a second. "Which sucks."

"Oh." Nick's eyes were wide, but it wasn't shock, Dex didn't think. It was his way of taking in information. Dex wondered how much of their inner circle crap Nick sensed.

"Shit. Who wants to take who?" Jonny asked, and they all looked at each other before Dex raised his hand and offered to take Izzy. "All right. Alex, you've got Nat. You okay with that?"

Alex looked like he wanted to argue, but then just nodded. "Yeah, all right."

Dex felt his gut churning uneasily. They'd all rowed before, obviously, but this felt bigger—terrible, if he was honest. He reached for his phone and shot off a quick text to Iz, just a few hearts to let her know he loved her.

"Will they be all right?"

Dex looked up, but Lance wasn't asking all of them, just looking at Jonny.

Jonny shrugged, uncertain. "I mean, I fucking hope so? That sort of came out of nowhere, though." He caught Dex's eye. "Did *you* suspect?"

"What, that Izzy had been harbouring secret Sapphic tendencies?" He made a face, largely at himself. Jonny made the same face back at him. Right. "Sorry. Nah, mate. I'd no idea."

"Poor Iz," Steph sighed. She scraped her fork around her leftover runny eggs. "I'll try to talk to her later, too."

After that, the conversation petered out. When Dex glanced over at Nick, Nick was watching his half-empty coffee cup like he was trying to beam it into space. Dex couldn't begin to guess what was going on inside his head.

+

Dex knocked softly but for once didn't wait for an answer. "You decent?" He peered in through the narrow crack in the doorway.

Izzy was sat on her bed with her computer on her lap but was clearly not even paying attention to it. She wore only a ratty T-shirt and pants, and when she looked up her eyes were puffy and red. "Define decent," she rasped.

Dex slipped in and shut the door. "Babe."

She shut her laptop and shoved it to the foot of the bed. He plopped down next to her and opened one arm. Izzy slumped against him immediately.

"She won't fucking talk to me," she sniffed. "Like, friends for two bloody years, and she won't even respond to a fucking text, what the fuck is that?"

Dex ran his hand over her arm and rested his cheek on her head. "She probably needs time to take it in or something," he offered, not really sure he believed it himself.

"You know who fucking needs time to take it in?" she asked in a rising voice. "*Me. I* need bloody time to take this in, it's not like." She dislodged him as she sat up. Her lip trembled. "This isn't a fucking lark, I'm not a bloody arsehole, I never knew. I mean, how stupid is that? How could I not have known?"

Dex shrugged. "People don't realise a lot of things about themselves."

"*You* did," she said.

"Well, yeah, I'm not bloody bisexual, am I?" Dex smiled. "I'm a full-on card-carrying homo, Iz. It's a bit different, because I was only ever attracted to boys."

"But you believe me?" she asked softly. "That it was a real thing, not an experiment or some bullshit attention-seeking crap?"

"Oh my God, of course I believe you." He pulled her back towards him, and she came. "When have you ever done anything just for attention?"

"Well, I dunno. Nat's called me a show-off a bunch." Dex felt his heart breaking along with her voice.

"Nat's got a lot of anger, we know this," he said softly. "She'll come around." She had to. But they all knew how fucking hard she'd fought to carve out her own identity in the face of her parents' disapproval, their disappointment. Nothing had ever come easily to Natali. Not like Izzy. "She says things she doesn't always mean."

"She meant this," Izzy whispered after a long pause. "But so did I." She fidgeted against him. Dex kept still and silent. "I can't fucking tell you how that girl turned me on," she finally said. It was so quiet, he had to strain to hear her over the street noise filtering in through the window. "How had I never known I could be turned on by girls? Is it like a button that suddenly gets activated?"

She seemed to be waiting for him to respond, so Dex said, "Honestly, I don't know. We're all so different, you know?"

"I know. It's just weird," she mused. "All this time, I just thought I appreciated girls aesthetically. Like, oh wow, that dress looks great on her. Or, those jeans were made for her arse. But I had proper sex with a girl last night, and I have zero regrets or bad feelings about it."

"That's good, though. Isn't it? No regrets?"

"Yeah, but now it's all—do I come out to my mum? Does it matter? She doesn't know about half the guys I've slept with, so why should she know about this?" She paused, took a breath. "But what if I actually get into a relationship with a girl? I'll have to tell her then, and who knows how she'll take it. And what about my aunt and cousins? God, Dex. Apparently I'm bisexual, and I've only just figured it out!"

She'd sat up again and was looking at him with wide eyes, her cheeks splotchy pink, almost overpowering the freckles.

"Babe," he said. "Take it one thing at a time, yeah?"

Shakily, she nodded.

"You jumped out of a closet you'd never even realised you'd been in ten seconds ago." He thought about the best way to word it. "It's okay to be confused. And it's okay to not want to come out to your family. That shit is scary. Nobody's rushing you. Right?"

She nodded again.

"So, it's all good."

"But Nat—"

"Well, apart from that, but give it time. You know her, she needs space when she's stroppy, and this is—" He stopped before he said anything he'd regret. "This is a weird one."

"*Why*, though? Why?"

Dex wondered how she could have missed it, but even so, he didn't actually believe this was all due to Natali's unrequited crush. This was bigger. More complicated. Scarier.

"I'm sure eventually we'll get it," he said. "Just give her space to figure it out. Work through it."

Izzy slumped, but nodded. "Fine."

They sat in silence for a full minute before Izzy gave him a look, which was the only warning he got before the attack. "So, you teaching Nick to cook, huh?"

"Oh God." Dex felt his entire face flaming hot and buried it in his hands. "Please don't remind me."

"That was *incredible*, mate. Do you have any idea how hard it was to keep a straight face in front of everyone? What's next, skywriting? Taking out an advert in *the Times*?"

"It's not the 1990s."

"What*ever*, this is amazing. Will you seriously go through with it?"

"No!"

"Bullshit, you can't back out now. He looked excited!"

Dex finally lifted his head and glared at her. "Why are we talking about me, anyway, I'm not the one who just discovered he loves ladies."

"We're *talking* about you because we never actually had this conversation, and it's pretty huge. Do you really like him, babe?"

He slumped against the wall. Her Bikini Kill poster was threatening to fall down again. "Honestly? Yeah."

Izzy was doing her best to hide the *awww* expression on her face. She failed. He scowled.

"Oh, stop," she laughed. She still sounded sort of clogged up and snotty, which made it harder to be stroppy with her. "It's just unusual for you. He's not, you know."

"My type? Don't remind me."

She shrugged. "But we did just learn that human beings contain multitudes."

He laughed despite himself. "True. Skinny white boys are the new, *Oops, I'm bisexual*?"

"We're off-topic again. Would you consider actually going anywhere with it, or will you just pine like a hangdog until he leaves for America?"

Dex stared at her.

"What? This is a legit question!"

"No, it bloody isn't!" Dex exploded. "Have you met him? In what universe do you think that this boy could ever be persuaded to—he's like—*Iz*."

"What!"

"He's the very definition of emotionally unavailable," he burst out. "And I don't even know if he swings that way at all."

Izzy snorted.

"Neither do you," he said, really pretty patiently, all things considered.

"You honestly don't think he's even bi?"

Dex just spread his arms out in answer.

Izzy rolled her eyes. "So I don't know what the fuck is the matter with your eyesight, but he is clearly *into you*."

"What." He stared at her. She stared back. "Isabel."

"Yes, Dexter."

"You've gone off your rocker," he said, going for a light tone while everything in him wanted to scream out, *What do you mean, how do you know, tell me everything.* He was clearly losing it.

"I have done no such thing," she said. "He looks at you with stars in his eyes, he just never does it long enough for you to fucking notice, apparently."

Dex swallowed. Despite it being cold out, Izzy's room felt like a sauna. No wonder she was hanging out in her knickers. "You do tend to see things that aren't there a lot of the time."

Her answer was immediate, like she was waiting for it. "Not just me. Steph's noticed."

"Bollocks."

They squared off. Dex threw up his hands. "Fine. *What* has Steph noticed, then?"

He felt his stomach fluttering a bit. It was ridiculous. He was ridiculous.

"One," she began, ticking off the first finger. "Whenever you talk, you can practically see his ears prick up like a bunny. Two, he watches you. All the time. And then looks away. And *blushes*." Dex attempted to recollect this apparently obvious history. "Have you seriously never noticed?"

"Well no, I bloody haven't noticed, and I look at him a lot!" Shit. That hadn't been what he'd been going to say.

Mercifully, she went on like she hadn't heard that last part. "Dex, I swear to God, he fancies you, but…" She trailed off.

Somehow, in the course of their conversation, Dex went from wanting it to end to the word *but* hitting him straight in the gut. He didn't want a *but*. "But what?"

"But you're not wrong. He is complicated, isn't he? Not in a bad way, mind, I like him lots, but I'm not the one with a crush."

"No," Dex agreed. "And he's leaving."

"Not till June. That's ages."

"Still, though."

A minute passed in silence. Then Izzy said, sounding careful. "So long-term crush, not just wanting a shag?"

Dex should have expected it, but somehow the question caught him by surprise. He hadn't even articulated this to himself, but suddenly, he knew. "Yeah," he croaked, then cleared his throat. "Shit. I guess so."

She made a sympathetic face and grabbed his hand. "Babe. Don't take this the wrong way, but I think that may not be an altogether terrible thing."

"What part of this isn't terrible?"

"The part where you're wanting someone again," she said kindly. "The part that's clearly over Michael the Tosser."

"Oh." Dex swallowed. "Well. I dunno. I suppose that's good."

"Blimey, you're *really* into him, aren't you?"

"Iiiiiz. Don't. Don't say it like that." *If you say it like that, it'll make it more real.*

"Deeeeeex. What are you gonna do? He's part of the group now. You'll have to see him all the time. You *have* had. Is your plan just to moon over him in silence, or what?"

"No," he lied. "My plan is to get over this weird obsession with yet another emotionally unavailable boy and find someone I can realistically date. Maybe I'll just fuck around a lot. That could be fun, too. Dating's fucking boring anyway."

"You're difficult to know," she said, finally.

"Likewise."

She stuck out her tongue at him, but the next moment her face crumpled. "What if Nat doesn't stop being in a strop with me?"

Dex gathered her up and kissed the top of her head. "She will. Just give her time."

"D'you think she'll respond to my texts tomorrow, maybe?"

"I think so." Dex really, really hoped she would.

zzy was, much to Dex's annoyance, right. He was in a bit of a pickle. A sticky wicket, if you will. A somewhat unpleasant state of affairs.

Dex was fucked. Because no matter how hard he insisted that if Nick's emotional unavailability wasn't going to solve his whole crush situation, Nick's inevitable decampment from the country would, anytime Dex saw him, he just couldn't stop watching him. Or being aware of him in a way so intensely physical it was weirding him out. Had it really been so long since he'd liked someone that he'd forgotten what it felt like?

They arranged the cooking night over text, because Dex simply didn't have the balls to do it in person. He also didn't want any witnesses to what could potentially become an excruciatingly embarrassing scene, so he suggested going over to Nick's.

Mistake, as it turned out.

When he got to Nick's room, he couldn't help thinking back to the one other time he'd been there, when they'd all gone out dancing and he'd watched Nick jumping up and down from a distance, wondering how someone so fucking shy could have let it all out when dropped in the middle of a club scene.

It looked like Nick had acquired a few knickknacks and oddities since that night. He'd pasted a few typical postcards of London to his board, and Dex was sort of amused to note the miniature TARDIS sat on his desk. Nick himself was only marginally more relaxed than when he'd experienced Hurricane Isabel tearing through his room.

Dex, not wanting to spook him too much, dropped his bag of shopping on the floor and hovered by the door while Nick got ready. He wondered if Nick always wore skinny jeans when hanging out in his room or if he'd dressed up special. Dex looked at Nick's bony feet and felt as out of place as he had ever experienced. It was too intimate. The room was too small. It was too full of Nick, even just in the spare way he inhabited it.

"Ready?"

Too soon, he found himself in Nick's halls kitchen with a knife and cutting board in hand, Nick hovering nervously by his side while Dex surreptitiously examined him for the smallest signs that Izzy had been right about something else—that Nick liked him back.

He had decided on spag bol from scratch. The kitchen didn't feel altogether unfamiliar, but only in the way that all halls kitchens felt the same. The crusted-over toastie maker sat in the corner sent him back to first year of uni.

"This looks like a lot," said Nick, glass of wine in hand. It was possible Dex had gone overboard. He just hadn't known what Nick would and wouldn't have, and if he was going to do this, he was going to do it properly.

"Well, I thought this would help with the basics." He indicated the onions, the garlic, the tomatoes (tinned and otherwise), the olive oil, the rosemary and basil, the mince. He cleared his throat. "This was the first meal I learnt how to make, so I reckoned it might be a good start?"

The impish corners of Nick's mouth deepened, and Dex took a deep breath. It was quite a bit of pressure, teaching someone to cook, it turned out. He lined up the recipe in his head and focused.

"Normally I'd be frying up bacon, but you don't eat pork, right?"

"What do you mean?" Nick asked.

Dex stared at him. "Oh. Sorry, I just thought. You don't keep kosher?"

"Oh." Nick's eyelashes looked long and vulnerable. He was pink-cheeked just like that. "We didn't. W—we weren't religious," he said, looking back up and taking a sip of wine. "Being Jewish in Russia was sort of a…a problem. Plus, there was no religion during Communism. So."

"Wait, hang on." Dex picked his knife back up just to have something to do. "If you weren't religious, how were you—"

"Jewish?"

"Well, yeah."

"It's weird, I know, but for us, Jew was an ethnicity, not a religion."

"How is that?"

Nick made a noise that sounded frustrated, but Dex didn't think it was at him. "Basically, my whole family is Jewish. Going back to the eighteen hundreds, maybe earlier. And they probably *were* religious, but not the recent generations. For me, for us, it said *Jew* in our passports. We weren't considered Russian."

"What?"

Nick shrugged. "All the better to fuck with us."

In the fluorescent lights, Nick's eyes looked a pale, stormy grey. Dex swallowed, then glanced back down at the cutting board. He had yet to start dicing. "What about in America, you never picked it up?"

Nick shifted beside him, and Dex felt his every move. It was as if his body was attuned to Nick. "I think my parents tried, but it didn't really take, I guess?"

"Why not?"

"They're hardcore scientists, through and through. My dad mostly enjoyed it as fables more than faith."

Dex smiled. "I guess I get that."

"You know, they're chemists. Did I ever tell you that?"

"Seriously?" Dex returned the grin Nick gave him. It was impossible not to. Nick had uneven teeth. They gave his open-mouthed smile a silly look, really. If he normally looked like an oil painting, the illusion shattered every time he spoke or smiled just like this. It freed him. He wasn't perfect, not like a painting. He had a spot on his cheek, for one.

"Yep. That's how they met, at university. Chemistry students."

Dex watched him, caught up for a moment, before remembering why they were here in the first place. "Well, we'll add bacon another time, then." He offered Nick the knife. "Do you want to try your hand at dicing the onion?"

Nick shook his head immediately. "Uh, no. You go ahead, I'll watch for now."

Dex laughed but agreed. When he was halfway through, his eyes began to sting. "Crap. You might want to back up a bit." Nick nodded, his hand already slapped over his face.

"Ah, shit, my contacts." He hunched over. The ridges of his spine looked prominent up close—one, two, three. "Sorry, sorry, hang on."

Dex wiped his eyes with the back of a wrist. "Sorry, mate, I did try, but these are pretty vicious."

Nick waved a hand as he ran to the other side of the kitchen.

It went smoother after that.

Dex diced and then sautéed his veg. Nick looked into the saucepan curiously.

"You know," he said after Dex threw in his rosemary and narrated his *aromatics are the key to every good sauce* bit, "Cooking has always seemed like magic."

"Magic?" His own approach had always been on the side of culinary science. "Magic in what way?"

Nick shrugged again. "I could never quite figure out how all these disparate ingredients could make up a whole like this. I guess it's stupid."

Dex watched him and waited. After a long moment, Nick continued.

"It's just that I was never part of the process, you know?" A brief glance up at Dex, then down again. "And my mom is a really good cook. So it just never made sense to me how someone, I don't know, even makes a broth or a stock or whatever, even though she does it all the time."

Dex reached for the mince slowly. "I think I get it." Trust dreamy historian Nick to believe there was magic in a simple Bolognese. Dex felt as if his bones were dissolving on the spot and had to brace himself on the counter for a moment. The mixture of rosemary and basil wafted up between them in a slow sensory takeover. "Cooking has always calmed me," he said quietly. "It's so methodical, and it makes sense, but it's not just that, I guess." Nick was watching Dex almost without blinking. His messy eyebrows were drawn together. Preternaturally serious. Dex swallowed. "It's soothing, and maybe there is a bit of magic in that."

The room was so quiet that Dex nearly jumped when the door creaked open and a stocky white boy walked in.

Nick moved away from Dex as fast as if he'd been burnt. "Oh hey, Jack." He sounded breathless. Dex felt it in his toes.

"'Sup." Jack made a beeline directly for the fridge. Dex willed his heart to calm back down and waited until Jack the Interloper had gone before he showed Nick the next step.

Nick consented to give stirring the mince a go. Dex felt an absurd relief at that. Something about it made the distinction between a cooking lesson and Dex cooking for Nick, which had too much of a date whiff about it.

His earlier reticence notwithstanding, Nick looked comfortable enough at the hob. Despite his every misgiving, Dex felt his pulse flutter every time Nick swayed into his orbit, smelling like aftershave and just a bit of sweat. He'd missed a spot shaving at the dip of his jaw. Steam wet Nick's curly fringe, and Dex had to beat a hasty retreat, nominally to start the process of boiling the pasta.

Truly, he had never sweated as much over spag bol, not even the first time he'd made it at fourteen years old.

He narrated the rest of the recipe, all talk of magic versus science left off for the time being. He added the tinned tomatoes, some stock, the rest of the herbs. When asked, Nick would pass him what he needed, but apart from those acknowledgements, they neither one of them looked at each other again.

They should have done this at Dex's, witnesses and all. The kitchen was beginning to smell like heaven, but Dex could not imagine choking down a single bite around his constricted throat, feeling like this. He needed Izzy, or Jonny, or fuck, give him bloody Niall and Lance, he didn't care, anything to break up the tension. They danced around each other as the sauce simmered and the pasta boiled and Dex just ran his mouth on the best way to strain spaghetti and how adding parm and red wine gave a piquant, sharp note to the meal like he was Nigella bloody Lawson. Nick polished off his wine and bustled around as he set the table with bowls and forks and spoons.

Finally, it was done and they were sat across from each other, both staring into their bowls of pasta like they held all the answers in the universe.

"Tuck in," Dex said, attempting to follow his own orders. Luckily, after the first couple of bites, it wasn't a hardship. It was just right, not too spicy but full of flavour and texture. Their grins were slightly obscured by the steam rising from the bowls. "Good?" Dex asked, feeling well satisfied with his own efforts.

"*Really* good," Nick confirmed and wiped the corner of his mouth.

"Think you could recreate it?" He didn't mean to sound cocky or challenging, but Nick sat back and tilted his head.

"I could chance it."

Dex wanted to draw him out until he had him pinned against a wall and see what Dex could chance. Before he could think about it, he said, "It's a date, then. Spag Bol: The Reckoning." Then his own words caught up with him, and he quickly looked back down at the ball of spaghetti rolled around his fork.

Nick cleared his throat. "Sounds good." His voice sounded distant through the pounding in Dex's ears. "Just name the date and time."

It felt like nothing less than a challenge to a duel. Dex had no idea how things had slipped out of his control this fast.

Dex's phone buzzed as they were washing up. Nick had insisted that he be the one to do it, and now it was Dex's turn to hover awkwardly nearby with an occasion swipe at a dish with a towel.

He was set on ignoring his phone, but it wouldn't stop, so he sighed and fished it out. His heart jumped in his chest. "It's Al," he said, answering Nick's curious face. "I'm so sorry, d'you mind? He never phones."

Was it Mum, or Dad? What happened? He was already swiping at his phone as Nick said, "Of course."

"Al? What's wrong?"

Al was slow to respond. "Uh, nothing. Just felt like a chat?"

Relief flooded every single muscle in his body, swiftly followed by rather unwarranted annoyance at having his night interrupted. But then it hit him. Al wanted to *chat*. He gave Nick an incredulous look even as he said, "A chat? Sure, I'm here." He mouthed *sorry* and turned around, planting himself in a corner as Nick continued washing up. He thought he could trust Nick to understand.

"This place is shit, Ambidexter."

"Oh, Al." He sank down onto the nearest chair. "What's happened? Or is it just general shittiness?"

"It's just shit, all right?" God, he was stroppy. "I don't know anyone, and like, I had Ralph back home, but he's all busy and he's got a *girlfriend* now, so we never talk, and I hate this fucking school. It's crap."

Dex had no idea what to say. What was it Nick had told him? Just let him talk and listen? "I'm sorry, Palbert. Is everyone a total idiot?"

He thought he heard Al sniffing. His poor Al. Christ. "I guess not everyone, but—" Dex waited even as he hated doing it. *Just be patient.* He watched Nick finishing up the final pot like he was trying to make the task last, to give Dex space. Hunched over the sink, Nick looked a bit like a dark question mark in the dingy white kitchen.

"It's like. The teachers are fine, but I'm…Dunno. I guess it's boring and stupid and I hate it and have no friends. There."

Well, at least it was concise.

"Pal, I'm sorry. School can be such shit."

"*You* didn't have a shit time," Al said, an accusatory edge to his tone.

"Mate, I was gay. It was shit enough." A stray thought caught him. "You're not telling me—"

"No! Christ," Al interrupted, then said, voice lowered, "Sorry. Guess I didn't think about that."

Well, he was definitely the most fourteen he could be. "Don't worry about it. But I do remember how that went." Of course, his school had not been Posh Hell Central. At least there'd been that.

"I'm well sick of it. And Mum is constantly on my case and can't leave well enough alone."

"She cares, mate. Mum will be Mum."

"Whatever, I'm not a kid."

"But you're *her* kid, and you're clearly unhappy," Dex snapped. "I mean...I only mean, she worries about you. She doesn't want to see you miserable."

"Well, her asking me about school and all that every time I see her isn't helping. Whatever."

Dex breathed in and out. He heard the water shut off and twisted around to see Nick drying that one last pot. He really had to wrap it up.

"I know," he said. Mollifying. "I'll talk to her. If you want." Oh God.

"*Please.* Just tell her to get off my case."

Christ almighty, he was happy to no longer be a teenager. "All right, but you have to do your part, too."

"What?"

"Don't be a proper dickhead to her. She'll worry less." Straight talk sometimes worked, didn't it? Dex was sure he'd heard it work on telly from time to time.

"Fine. Anyway, what's up with you?"

Dex almost pulled the phone away in shock. He couldn't remember the last time Al had asked him anything about himself. "Not much, I guess."

"What're you doing right now?"

"Having dinner with someone," he said carefully.

"A boy someone? Are you on a *date*?" Al went on, sounding gleeful. "What are you doing answering your phone on a date for, you plonker? You're the worst!"

"Oh my God, shut the fuck up. I answered because you called, you fucker, so thanks for that."

"Oh." A pause. "All right. Well, thanks, I guess." Another shocker. Talking to Al these days was very like riding a bloody seesaw.

"No problem. Look, phone me anytime, all right?"

"All right. Thanks. Bye."

The call was dead before Dex could say another word, and he stared at his phone in bewilderment for a full five seconds before looking up and catching Nick staring at him.

"Sorry," Nick said. "I was about to give you space."

"Oh no, no, please." Dex got up and shoved his phone back in his pocket. "I'm sorry about that, it's just, he never rings."

"Sure." Nick gave him a small smile. "Do you want— If you have other plans, you don't have to, but there's still that other bottle of wine."

"I'd love some." Whoa, slow down, Cowboy. In truth, he had wanted an excuse both to stay longer and to leg it out of there, and it was good to have the choice taken out of his hands. "If that's all right."

Dex felt rooted to the spot in the dingy kitchen.

"We can go back to my room?"

God. Could they, though? Dex pictured them scrunched up on Nick's single bed, breathing the close air of his tiny room. Dex indicated the door. "'Course."

Two bottles consumed between two guys over the course of a couple of hours was not exactly a recipe for drunken debauchery, but Dex still felt the buzz of it in his bones. Low instrumental music played over Nick's computer. Sorting themselves out on Nick's bed had taken some pains, but Dex had finally settled at the foot of the bed, knees drawn up, shoulder propped against the wall. Nick had settled by the pillow, mirroring Dex in position, and they faced each other as they downed the wine.

It was a red, because Dex had thought it'd go best with the meal, but now he was conscious of potentially having purple teeth even as Nick's turned a shade of maroon. Absurd, but it didn't stop Dex from wanting him. All it really did was make him want to kiss the traces of wine from his lips, lick it from his teeth, share it with his tongue.

Dex had just finished telling him about Al and his troubles and was wondering what the fuck to say next when Nick asked, "How is Izzy? I haven't heard from her in a while."

Dex smiled despite himself and settled more comfortably against the wall. It wasn't comfortable at all, in fact, but he was scared to upset the equilibrium. "She's all right, I guess. Confused as all fuck, but she's Izzy, you know? She'll pull through."

"Good. I hope. Is Natali—"

"I think she's coming around. It's hard to explain, but she just needs time to get past—" He sighed and scratched the back of his head. "Her own stuff, I guess."

"Is it that she likes Izzy?" His tongue sounded like it wasn't quite catching up with the words, and you could hear the traces of an accent. Could tell that English wasn't the first language his tongue had learnt. Dex wanted to hear even more.

"Yes and no. I mean, you have to sort of know where she's coming from." Nick was too distracting. He focused on the few books Nick had lined up on his shelf. A couple were definitely not in English. Dex squinted. Or any alphabet he knew. "She had a really hard time coming out, so she sort of believes that if you haven't sweated blood out of it—" He was making Nat sound like an arsehole. He may not have agreed with her anger, but it wasn't his anger to agree with. "It's just hard on her. This came out of nowhere."

"It makes sense." Dex waited to see if Nick would offer anything else more personal, but of course, this was Nick. Nick, who only shared when the information was pried out of him with blood and gore. Dex had none of Izzy's gift of insistence, so he was left to wonder if Nick had a story of his own and if one day he would share a part of it.

Like a padlocked gate, this boy was.

"I hope she comes around."

"You and me both, mate. Living with the both of them right now is a bit like trying your hand at being Switzerland."

Nick's uneven teeth glinted wine-purple in the light. "Sounds rough."

"You've got an accent when pissed, did you know that?"

Nick clamped a hand over his mouth. He mumbled something, but Dex couldn't make out a single word. He was across the bed before he could think about it and grabbed Nick's wrist to pull his hand away from his mouth. He felt them both stop breathing for a moment.

"Sorry." His throat felt like he had gorged himself on wine-flavoured candy floss. Their pulses thrummed in counter-rhythm. Nick's wordless music saved them from having to hear only their own hard breathing. "What were you saying?"

"You weren't supposed to notice." Nick said. It was too quiet in the narrow space between them. Dex became aware of where his knees were digging into Nick's hard shin, of how small Nick looked this close up.

Dex dropped his wrist and shoved himself backwards. "Well, I did," he said in a pathetic attempt to restore some balance between them. "It's not a bad thing, though, is it?" God, he was so obvious. Nick *had* to know.

"I don't know." Nick's shrug looked like a stilted thing. "I guess I like that I pass. Most of the time." He picked at the frayed bottoms of his jeans.

"Why?" He wasn't drunk, but he didn't feel entirely in control of himself either. *Get a fucking grip, Dexter, he's just a boy you sort of like.* His heart beat hard.

"I don't like—" He huffed out a frustrated breath. "This will sound worse than I mean it, okay, but I just don't like talking—"

"I'm sorry—"

"No." A fraction of a smile. "I didn't mean with you. I just mean in general. It's always a *thing* if you have an accent.

People are always asking my mom where she's from, even if she's buying groceries. My sister, too. It gets…exhausting."

"Are people arseholes about it?" Of all things to float to the front of his mind, his dad's face wasn't what he had anticipated. He pictured their old Sainsbury's, the one around the corner from his school.

Nick shook his head slowly, like he was really thinking about it. "No, not usually. You know how there's one thing about you that people focus on all the time, but it's not the only thing about you, but nobody ever gets past it? That's sort of what being an immigrant feels like. Except, I mean. It *is* important. It's a *huge* part of me, but it's not the *only* part."

"I do," he said. He pointed to his own face. "Black."

They watched each other for a long moment. Nick said quietly, "Yeah. Except I can pass."

"Do you think that I might want to?" His heart felt hollow inside his ribcage.

"No! God, that's not…that's not what I'm saying, shit, I'm sorry. I just always *do*. I always *want* to pass. I wish I didn't, but I do. And I can, because I was young enough when we moved that I lost my accent. God, I'm saying it all wrong, I'm sorry. You probably think I'm such an asshole."

"Nick, Christ, slow down, mate, I don't think anything." Before he could think better of it, he grabbed Nick's hand. Nick was looking at him almost desperately. "It's okay. I get it. I'm sorry that it has to be that way." He let go of Nick's hand carefully.

"I look like my dad," Nick said abruptly, and Dex stopped breathing. "I mean, I look mostly like my dad, except just different enough that I never—this will sound awful, but just hear me out—I never *looked* Jewish. Not like the rest of my family does." Dex watched his throat move. Nick was so thin, his neck was all fragile definition. "My mom and sister, they're the most obvious. My sister was walking home once and got threatened on the staircase of our apartment building."

"Jesus," Dex breathed. "Was she okay?"

Nick nodded. "I mean, she was upset, but they didn't physically hurt her or anything. But she was only thirteen at the time. They looked at her face and knew."

"How?" Dex asked, despite himself.

"Long nose, big hooded eyes. Curly dark hair. She looked like a Jew, so she was treated like one."

"God, Nick. I'm sorry."

"Well, don't be, honestly. It's done. It's different in the States. But I just got used to being invisible, and coming to the States and not speaking English made me visible, and I hate that."

Dex could not begin to wade through all the layers of fucked-up-ness Nick had just spilled between them. He was just near enough a question he thought he could get away with when Nick said, "Anyway, sorry. Guess I'm drunk."

"No, it's okay."

"What about you?"

Door shut again. Dex could have laughed. "What about me?"

Nick sucked in his lower lip, ran his teeth over it. Christ, his mouth. "I don't know, tell me about you." It could have been a trick of the light, but Nick's cheeks looked flushed now.

Lightness stole over Dex. Like bubbles fizzing through his system. "But *what* about me?"

"Anything. Doesn't feel fair that I've said all this crap, and you've listened, but you—"

"It's not crap. Honestly, I like hearing you talk. I mean, if you don't mind," he added, the lightness quickly replaced by panic. Stop talking, stop talking, *stop talking.* "You're interesting." *Fuck.*

Nick, shrinking even more inside himself, smiled. Dex was all tension waiting to be released. "Thanks. You're—you're interesting, too."

"I'm so not, man," Dex laughed and scooted back, propping himself up on the wall again. He felt like a thread between them snapped as he did so. Tension seeped out. He could breathe again, but he found he didn't want to, after all. Too late.

"Okay. Well, why were you so grumpy when we first met?" Even as the question left his mouth, Dex could see Nick panic. His own panic hit him full-on in tingling fingers and his stomach dropping to his toes.

"Um—"

"Sorry, that was stupid—"

"No. It was just—" He couldn't. How could he begin to explain or to attempt to defend himself? "It wasn't you. To be honest, I was just grumpy in general then. I was—getting over someone."

"Oh. Shit, I'm sorry. I shouldn't have—"

"I'm over it, mate." He found it was true. "Honest. It's good to talk about it, actually. Now, I mean."

"What happened? If it's okay—"

"Yeah, it's okay. He cheated on me. For a while, apparently. I didn't know. Broke my heart, really."

It was hard to read Nick in that moment. Harder than normal, that is. "I'm sorry. That's really fucking shitty."

"It is, isn't it? Oh, well. At least I found out eventually, I suppose. Reckon I'm better off now."

"Yes." They both laughed, sounding so bloody self-conscious.

Dex grabbed his glass from the floor again and took another sip. He was in danger of sobering up, and it was the last thing he wanted. Feeling reckless, he said, "What about you? Anyone back home?"

As soon as it was out of his mouth, it occurred to him he didn't want to know. What possible answer could Nick give that would satisfy him? What if he did have someone? What then? What *sort* of someone would it be? And what business was it of Dex's, anyway, from where Nick stood? God, maybe he needed to sober up, after all.

Nick took ages to respond. "No. No one."

He had more questions than answers now, but he knew when to leave well enough alone.

"I should probably get going," he said. It was way past time. He had to get out. He needed air. He needed his own room. He needed to clear his fucking head.

"Oh, okay." Did Nick sound disappointed?

"Yeah, I've got loads of work to do tomorrow." It was only half a lie.

He got up, barely swaying on his feet, and reached for his jacket. Nick was still sat on the bed, and Dex quashed another reckless impulse. They'd never hugged before. What made him almost do it now? Nick's posture did not look encouraging of hugs. A thought about how Nick might feel with his defenses down flitted through Dex's head. Impossible.

He really had to get the fuck home.

"Thank you." Nick was smiling. "This was nice."

Dex smiled helplessly in response. "It was. Next time, you cook for me?" It was out before he could stop it.

"Deal."

"Well, have a good night, man."

He blinked in the too-bright corridor for a full minute, stood against the door, rooted to the spot. It wasn't until he finally started walking that he heard the lock clicking shut.

It had been over a week since Izzy had told everyone about her night with Ruby, and it felt like most people had accepted and moved on, thank Christ on a bike.

Most people save Nat. Nat was doing her fucking best to pretend like Izzy was just part of the flat furniture.

"Good morning!"

"Hey."

"What're you up to today?"

"School."

Done. Those were their conversations now. Nat avoided Izzy's room like it was bloody Chernobyl. Was that rude to say, now that she knew Nick?

One night, Izzy waited up for Nat to come home only to fall asleep in front of the telly and wake up at two with a crick in her neck. Nat never emerged from her room the following morning, so she'd probably not come home.

Izzy only talked to Dex about his own crap. Jonny had tried to engage her in an awkward conversation about *it* once or twice, but Izzy immediately felt herself recoiling. Wasn't she always the one who told everyone talking about stuff helped? She didn't want to talk about it. Ever. Not with her friends. They all seemed to understand her anger better than Izzy could.

She felt utterly shut out.

Which led to her avoiding them all the more.

Which made her feel wretched and lonely.

It was all so fucked up.

She had considered talking to Kat once, but Kat was still not past her delighted shock at Izzy's Surprise Night of Sapphic Romance (was what Kat had called it, because of course she had) and avoided the topic by flirting aggressively. As Izzy did not wish to cause any more strife with her friends, however peripheral, she began avoiding Kat, too.

She began judging her conversations with people. Did it pass the Isabel Is Tired of This Bullshit Test? If the conversation included the words *you* and *Nat*, it did not.

"Babe, you have got to snap out of it," Dex said.

Izzy growled at him as she switched the channel.

Dex did not pick up on her signal and flopped down next to her. Nat was out—obviously—and Jonny had disappeared to wherever it was Jonny had begun disappearing to and coming back with hickeys hidden under clothes. *Good on him.* It was an excellent way of avoiding the house, too.

"Leave me alone."

"Not a chance."

She moved away from him.

Dex sidled closer. Tosser.

"Stop being so bloody annoying!"

"Shan't."

He wrestled the remote from her hands and turned off the telly.

"Oh my God! What the fuck d'you think you're doing?"

"We are not going to talk about Natali."

"Liar."

"I swear to God."

"I don't actually believe you. What are we going to talk about, then?"

"You."

"And?"

"Well, we could talk about me, too, but only afterwards, if you're good. How's your screenplay project coming along?"

Low fucking blow.

"I didn't mean to upset you, I promise, but you just haven't talked about it in a while. I've been sort of worried."

He should have been. Hell, *she* should have been. It was pathetic, really, that she'd let whatever the fuck it was with Nat block her from writing, but every time she opened up the doc it would just blink at her until she found she'd spent two hours in a fugue state of backreading film blogs or down a makeup tutorial YouTube spiral. She hadn't been able to bring herself to talk to her advisor, either, because it was so embarrassing. Like, what the fuck, pull your shit together, woman. They'll say you're too emotional to work in film.

"I know."

"She—"

Dex broke off at her furious gaze.

"This will work out eventually," he continued in a tone that was clearly meant to placate her. Because it was Dex's soothing voice, though it actually was working. "But you've got to—"

"What."

"Take care of yourself."

God, she fucking hated the feeling of inevitability right before having a cry. She felt her chin drawing up, lip trembling.

"Iz…"

There she went. Hot tears leaking from her eyes onto her cheeks. *God.* It was the worst. She wiped at her face, but the tears kept coming, and then she was soaking Dex's T-shirt with them as he gathered her up against his chest and let her get tears and snot all over him.

"It's all right, babe. I've got you."

It was both humiliating and so fucking comforting to have him on her side. The only other person who made her feel all right about herself was her mum.

Well. Nat did, too. Had. Before.

But now it was Mum and Dex.

Her friends loved her. She knew that. But it was different with Dex. A best mate meant you got to blubber on their chest and they made you feel like your mum was holding you. She trembled—crying always made her have the shakes, which she hated—and tried to think again, not just about She Who Shall Not Be Named, but for herself.

The weekend stretched ahead of her, and she thought, fuck it. Fuck everything.

"I think I'm gonna visit my mum." Her voice hitched on its way out of her constricted throat. Another reason to hate crying, this wretched inability to talk like a normal person.

"Yeah?"

Yeah. She nodded, resolved. "Need to get away, I think."

"D'you want company?"

Going on a seaside adventure with Dex. That sounded lovely. But mum would be easier with no witnesses.

"Thank you, but I think I've got to do this on my own."

Dex kissed the top of her head again. She loved that he was so outwardly grumpy but such a bloody marshmallow on the inside. "Thanks for putting up with me."

"Well, same to you."

"God, we're a wretched pair, aren't we?"

"Eh." She felt him shrug against her. "I like us well enough. I even like your snot."

She sniggered. "You do not."

"I do, actually. It's comforting."

"God, you weirdo. Let's see if maybe *Friends* is on."

"All right, Snotface."

"Shut up."

✛

Alex handed over the keys to his beat-up Peugeot without question. "Take care, all right?" He peered at her in a way that meant he wasn't talking about the car. Alex. She loved Alex.

"Thanks, mate. I'll return it with not a scratch on, promise."

He pulled her into a hug. Alex had always been closer to Nat, so Izzy appreciated him not taking sides.

It was odd that despite them both being basically the only straight people in their entire friend group, nothing had ever happened between them. Alex was too gorgeous for Izzy, and she was probably too Izzy for Alex. It had historically been the reason why she was dumped—*You're just, you know. A lot.* So it was probably for the best. But the hug was lovely.

Oh God, how she'd missed driving. It wasn't until she was out of the London gridlock and on the A12 that she felt the freedom of it, and when it hit, it was so bloody good. She'd forgotten the feel of it, how the car would roar underneath her, horsepower and mechanics and *zoom, zoom, zoom.* She passed the slow drivers, lowered the windows, felt her hair fluttering about.

Her and Alex were the only ones who could drive, and she didn't know what had made him decide to get his licence, but for Izzy it had been her mum's stuff that made her realise she needed to take some control. She was so glad of it now.

Countryside. It really did feel like coming home. That surprised her every time. She loved the rolling hills, and it felt both like a homecoming and a hard pressure over her chest, all at once.

Ironically enough, she had to use the SatNav the closer she got, since the last time she'd driven had been years back, but she switched it off rather violently once she was three streets away from Mum's place. Chip shops, a rundown Boots, a Nando's—that was new. But still.

This, she remembered.

✝

"Isabel? Rocco, *sit. SIT.* Isabel, is that you?"

"Yes, Mum, who else are you expecting?" Izzy threw her keys in the bowl under the mirror, unwound her scarf, undid her coat, and dropped it on the bench, all the while adjusting to the gloom.

Mum came forward like a ghost figure, but once she fully materialized in front of Izzy, she looked just like she always did these days. Too thin, too pale, but still so beautiful. Her hair was a touch grayer, maybe. It was hard to tell. Rocco's nails *click-click-clicked* as he followed immediately behind.

"Mum."

"Izzy, what's happened?"

She breathed in her mum's scent: Boots shampoo, coffee, smell of home. Since she never left the house, Mum smell was always home smell. "Coffee? I'll tell you everything, it's fine, just needed a weekend away." Mum pulled back and looked her in the eye. For, like. A really long time. "Mum, I'm not dying, I just wanted to see you."

"That's what I'm worried about." She looked out the front window. "Did you *drive*?"

"Yeah." Izzy leaned down to scratch Rocco's head. He panted in her face. Doggy breath. "Alex let me borrow his."

Mum looked like she wanted to ask more questions, but let it go.

They made their way into the kitchen, Rocco jumping up and down and wagging his old tail. Izzy stole a biscuit from the jar and fed him underneath the table.

"You know I can see you both, right?"

Izzy shrugged and let Rocco lap at her fingers until the biscuit taste was gone. He curled up at her feet and looked at her like, *Biscuit? What biscuit? I've never had a biscuit before in my life. Feed me a biscuit?*

She fed him another biscuit.

"All right, all right, that's enough." Mum walked over to the table and sat opposite Izzy. "He's a right spoiled old beast as it is."

Mum looked older in this light. Izzy supposed that's what staying indoors did for you, but still, it hurt. It hurt like it had hurt every time she would ask her mum to walk the dog with her and Mum would refuse, find an excuse. And then she'd dropped the pretence. *Don't like the outside, love. Best stay in, I think.*

The neighbours walked Rocco whenever Izzy wasn't around.

"At least open the windows."

"It's November. The wind is something else."

"It's sea air, it's good for you."

She used to yell and shout about why they should even live by the sea if Mum never went out, but she'd had to stop for her own sanity. Now she walked over to the kitchen window, the sill cluttered with knickknacks and heavy with dust, and cranked it open. The faded paper crane she'd made back at school fluttered immediately to the floor. Izzy picked it up. She settled it on the table next to the biscuit jar.

"How's Aunt Claire?" she asked as Mum watched her silently.

"Same as always, I s'pose. Well enough."

The kettle boiled and clicked over. Izzy rose before Mum could, fixed them two cups of coffee. The fridge was in a right state, but at least the milk smelled fresh when Izzy sniffed it.

"Honestly, d'you think they wouldn't deliver fresh milk out here?"

Mum sounded cross and worried, so Izzy decided milk would not be the hill she would die on. "Sorry, habit," she lied. "Jonny's forever letting the milk go bad, and I'm forever forgetting to get fresh."

Back at the table, they sipped their coffees.

"You look good," Mum said after a minute. "Bit tired, maybe."

Izzy sighed. "It's all the uni stuff. Getting to me. Been knackered."

"Is that why you're here?"

"Mmhmm." She didn't look at Mum as she said it.

"All right." Yeah, she wasn't buying it. Oh, well. They had all weekend, anyway. "Well, since you're here, we might as well have coffee on the sofa."

Rocco jumped up immediately. He always knew his treats. Izzy laughed and realised it had been a while since anyone was that excited to be around her. She'd take it.

Mum had the sofa buried under a thousand ratty blankets, and Izzy curled up on one end of it, with Rocco immediately attempting to climb into her lap until she forced him down onto her feet. "Warm those," she told him. He huffed. She rewarded him with a scratch to his ear while Mum settled herself opposite.

"Want anything to eat?" she asked. "Should have asked earlier, shouldn't I?"

Izzy shook her head. She hadn't actually felt hungry in a while, she realised. Weird, that.

"How have you been?" she asked.

Mum took a sip of coffee and muted the telly. She did look all right, nothing to really worry over. Mum was Mum. But when you had only the one parent who wouldn't go outside, you couldn't help but worry. "I'm well, love. I promise. Don't look at me like that, haven't I been fine always?"

Well, not always, but they never really spoke of the Year from Hell, aka 2007, aka when Izzy had almost been taken away because Mum couldn't get out of bed.

"You opening your mail?"

"Isabel. I'm an adult, stop treating me like I'm infirm. Yes, I'm opening the mail."

And she was, actually. Izzy could see it scattered on the sideboard by the telly.

"Sorry."

They sipped their coffees. That, too, tasted like home. Douwe Egberts instant, farm milk, and sugar. She could use the car to do a proper big shop for Mum, she realised. She could maybe go and get Mum something from Asda, a new cardi or even pyjamas or socks or something. Fresh flowers for the kitchen. Stock up on food for Rocco.

Maybe. Maybe she could take Mum out for a drive to the coast.

"It's fine," Mum sighed.

+

Later, Izzy took her holdall into her room. She flung aside the curtains, slid open the window. Thank fuck, fresh air. Turned around, hands on hips, and surveyed her old domain. The wallpaper was a bit yellow around the edges, and lighter where her posters had been—nothing new there. Ikea dresser she had got to replace the battered one, her bed. Her duvet. Chair and desk, everything in its rightful place. It made her uneasy. It wasn't as if her room was terrible; it wasn't. It was small, but it was cosy, homey. Still, she didn't want to linger, so she changed into comfier clothes and went back downstairs.

Mum was watching telly again, but she looked up as soon as Izzy walked in. "Oh, it's good to see you, love." Her smile was the part of home that Izzy missed. She plopped down and wormed her way under Mum's arm, wrapping her own arm around Mum's middle. She mumbled *missed you* right into Mum's jumper.

"So," Mum said, carding her fingers through Izzy's hair. "Tell me about your life. It's not the same over the phone."

Izzy tensed again. It wasn't as if she was going to keep it from Mum. She just didn't want to get into it now, not when she'd just arrived. "It's fine, I guess. Just, you know. Stupidly busy. Last year and all that."

"I remember that," Mum said. "Well, you're my doer. You'll be all right."

It was weird to think of Mum the way she had been before she'd had Izzy. Mums sort of weren't really supposed to exist on their own, were they? They were your mum. They were put on this earth to care for you and love you and maybe be a bit barmy. It was all tremendous bullshit forced on women by the patriarchy, society measuring a woman's worth by her uterus and femininity instead of doings and brains, but it was still impossible for Izzy to picture her mum at uni. Outside, out in the world. Laughing with her friends, revising for exams, meeting men. Men like James. Izzy never called him "dad" or even "my father." He'd never done anything to earn that title.

"Yeah. I know."

"Any plans for after, love?"

"*Mum.*"

"Sorry, sorry, I know I'm not supposed to ask that. All them off the telly are forever saying that."

Izzy snorted. "Who off the telly? Why would you be listening to them talking crap?"

"Well, you never call, you never write. Who else am I meant to talk to?"

"*Mum.*"

"Sorry, sorry."

"You're the worst, oh my God."

"But I'm the only one you've got."

And that was true enough.

✝

She had to get out of the house, so Izzy took the Peugeot for a spin. She drove out to Harwich and spent nearly two hours at Asda, wandering from aisle to aisle, not really knowing what to get Mum that would be useful. In the end, she returned with six bags filled with all sorts, from frozen curries to sad-looking avocados and even a pint of currants. She'd used her own card, painfully aware of the money she'd just spent, but she couldn't really regret it. Mum's disability benefits only got her so far; the rest they eked out between them from the money Nan had left. It wasn't insubstantial. It was just not enough to feel all that comfortable spending it willy-nilly.

"What is *this*?"

Izzy grunted as she hefted the bags through the door and dropped them down at her feet. Rocco immediately nosed into the one with his food in it. "Shopping."

"Yeah, for who, an *army*? You do realise I'm just one person?"

"I'm here, too!" Izzy made an offended face as she scooped up three of the six bags and dragged them into the kitchen.

"Until tomorrow, and then what do I do with all of this?" Despite her protests, she began peering into the bags with curiosity. "Currants!"

Izzy grinned. Mum's favourite. "Obviously."

"All right, you can stay." Mum squinted at her. Izzy mostly did take after Mum, but apparently she had James's eyes, which was a pity. Mum had glorious eyes—bright green, large, a colleen's eyes. Izzy's were a boring brown.

She busied herself with putting away the shopping while Mum ordered her about, telling her where to stash what. Rocco kept tripping her until she yelled at him to get off her arse and, chastened, he whimpered and lay down at Mum's feet.

With the last prepared curry put away, Izzy straightened and turned around.

"It's beautiful outside, by the way."

"Mmm."

"I was just thinking of driving down to the pier, you know, take in a bit of fresh air."

Mum was studying the back of the Muesli box.

"Want to join me? It's just a short drive down. We can even sit in the car, if you like."

Mum dropped the pretence but still didn't look at her. The doorbell rang.

"Oh," Mum said. "That'll be the Dawdles to take Rocco out. I forgot to ring them and tell them you were home."

Izzy was already striding to the door, putting on her best smile and fixing her hair simultaneously.

She opened the door. "Oh, hi, Mr and Mrs Dawdle!"

"Izzy, well!"

They were both grey-haired but fit-looking, the sort of middle-aged people she had once thought her mum should have been like. They probably jogged regularly, made Sunday roasts that were proper roasts, and watched the Bake-Off together.

"Hiya! I popped down for the weekend, Mum didn't get a chance to tell you."

They were wearing matching tracksuits. They were unbearably sweet. "We did wonder about the car. You look well, love." Mrs Dawdle had always wanted Izzy to date their son, but Izzy could barely spend five minutes with the guy before wanting to spork her eyes out. He was a complete and utter bore.

"Thank you." She smiled.

Then the three of them stood there for a moment.

"Well, would you like us to—"

"So, I think I'll take him out—"

"I mean, maybe give you a break—"

"Sorry!"

"Oh no, sorry!"

They proceeded to laugh awkwardly, as English manners required. Then Izzy took a breath and said, "Thank you both. I can take him out, no worries. I'm leaving tomorrow early evening, so maybe?"

"We'll come back tomorrow night, then." Mrs Dawdle sounded relieved. "It was nice to see you, dear. If you get a chance, do pop in for a cuppa, won't you?"

"I will, thank you," she said, door already halfway closed. Mr. Dawdle waved wordlessly, and they were gone.

Izzy sagged against the door.

The Dawdles had always liked Mum, and the next-door neighbour was a close friend. Maybe Izzy wasn't giving Mum enough credit. Maybe things were better here than she always imagined.

"Did you tell them to come back tomorrow evening?" Mum asked once Izzy was back in the kitchen.

"Yeah. Mum, let's go to the sea."

This time, Mum met her gaze, and there it was, the anguish. Izzy was so familiar with that look, and still it took her breath away every time. She had to stop pushing, she knew she did. Why would she be able to help her over doctors, over therapists, over all the social workers who had been through this with her? Pushing Mum had only ever upset them both. But it was so hard to stop. Hard to stop hoping.

"I'm sorry." She sagged down. "You don't have to."

"Darling."

"No, really. I'm sorry." She came to sit beside Mum at the kitchen table. "It's unfair of me."

"It's not you. I want to go to the sea with you. I want to see where you live. But every time I have to take a single step outside the house—"

"I know, Mum."

"I can't breathe. And a person's got to breathe to live, don't they?"

They sat there in silence with Rocco restlessly threading in between their feet.

+

It was late at night, the telly showing Graham Norton on half mute, when Izzy did it. She had longed to do it on the wall by the sea, with the wind whipping in their faces and sunlight reflecting off of the water, but Mum wasn't making it to the sea anytime soon.

So Izzy poured them both a generous helping of wine. "Mum, I've got to tell you something."

Mum looked at her like she'd only been waiting for it.

"You knew."

"Of course I knew. You don't just show up out of nowhere unannounced, love. What's happened? Is it school? Friends? A boy?"

Ha. She was just trying to find the words. For all she imagined telling her mum, she hadn't actually lined up the way to do it.

"So." She paused. "I found something out. About myself." She fiddled with the stem of her glass for a bit. "All right, so apparently, I'm not entirely straight. It turns out."

Mum's face was worth it. Surprise, confusion, relief. She really put my Mum through it on this one. "Oh, darling. Is that what's got you all upset?"

"Well."

"So, you like girls now?"

Izzy took a deep breath and let it out. "I had no idea."

"And you think it's a bad thing?"

"God, no! It isn't—" Words got stuck in her throat.

"C'mere, love."

Izzy set her wine glass down on the coffee table and shooed Rocco out of her way before stretching out into her mum's arms. Her lip wobbled. Oh God, no. "Mum," she said, and her voice cracked.

"Love, there's nothing wrong with that. Were you worried to tell me?"

"I guess I was."

"Did you want to tell me by the water so you could throw yourself in if it went badly?"

"Maybe."

She felt Mum chuckle. "You muppet. Don't you know I love you always?"

First tear, and then it was a steady leakage from her eyes. She sniffled as quietly as she could manage, but Mum always knew.

"You're my pride and joy, aren't you?" she went on. "Don't cry now, Isabel. It's all right. Have you got a girlfriend, then?"

Izzy shook her head and attempted to stop the tears to the best of her ability. "Nah. There was a girl. A one-off. She was great."

Mum searched her face. "Did she not want it to continue?"

"It wasn't that. It *isn't* that. It's not the main issue right now, I guess." Izzy swallowed, thick mucus building up in her windpipe. "It's...I told my friends, and they were cool, obviously, you know, but...Nat."

She was quiet for so long that Mum finally asked, "What about Natali?"

"She's not speaking to me."

"What, because you're gay now?"

"Mum, it's called bisexual."

"Whatever it is, what's got in her bonnet? Not talking to you? What nonsense is this?"

"She—" And that was the thing. Izzy just didn't know. After weeks, Izzy didn't know, only she kept hearing Nat's voice in her mind, telling her over and over that sexuality wasn't defined by a single kiss. *Do you want a parade?* "I dunno. I think she thinks I'm trying it on, you know. Like an experiment."

"And are you?"

"No!"

"I didn't think you were, love. Then why does she think that? Have you spoken to her?"

"I've tried, but she's avoiding me, like. Hardcore."

"Not even a single conversation?"

"Not for *days*. She's not *talking* to me. *Hi, bye*, that's it. It's like she's determined not to *hear* me, and I don't know what to *do*. And things are so bloody awkward with everyone now, and fucking hell, we're housemates, she can't avoid me forever, but she's definitely doing her best. Dex is telling me to be patient and whatnot, and everybody's looking at me like…with this…this *pity*, and I don't want pity. I want my mate back. She's being the stroppiest cow you've ever met, and I just can't handle it. Mum, I can't *write*."

"Oh, love. That sounds like a right nightmare."

The look Mum gave her *was* pitying, but somehow it was all right coming from her. It was all right to spill her guts all over the sofa because Mum would always care and clean it up in the end. It felt safe to do here on this ratty old sofa that Mum kept covered up with blankets. When Izzy had been younger, Mum had told her that the blankets were there to protect the sofa. It was only later that she realised the sofa wasn't some precious antique left over from her mother's grandmother, but a secondhand bit of tat that was the only thing they could afford at the time. The blankets were protecting them from the sofa, it turned out. But even after Nan died and left them money, Mum kept it, because it was theirs. Izzy bloody loved this sofa.

"She's not being fair to you," Mum finally said.

"Mum."

"No, listen. I know what it's like to get swept up in something and let it take over your life, but you're not me, and you've got goals, all right?"

Oh God. Izzy couldn't look at Mum when she was being this earnest. She stared at the ceiling instead, watching the single cobweb in the corner shift in the telly light.

"I know, but you just told me you can't write, and Isabel, this is not a reason to get blocked."

"That isn't how it works, Mum," she said, exasperated.

"Well, I wouldn't know, I was never a writer, but remember I told you about that one guy, Matthew?"

"Yeah?" Vaguely. He'd been the one before James.

"I was mad for him, and stopped revising. I nearly failed two classes because of him, and let me tell you, he wasn't worth it."

This wasn't helping. Still, Mum so rarely talked about her past, Izzy couldn't really interrupt her.

"I know your life is different, I know you aren't in love with Natali or anything, but you owe it to yourself not to get caught up in this."

Was that how she thought of what happened to her with Matthew? Or James? Or after Izzy was born? That she got caught up and never escaped? "I don't know what to do."

"I know." Mum gave her a smile and said, "It hurts. You haven't done anything wrong, and she's shut you out."

Izzy sniffed. God, that felt good to hear. *You haven't done anything wrong.*

When Dex had come to her the night after she told everyone, she got this feeling as if he was maybe even siding with Nat. Not in a mean way, just that he understood things better than Izzy. That his queerness made him understand Nat better. But wasn't Izzy queer, too, apparently? Mum was right. She *hadn't* done anything wrong.

259

She hadn't led Ruby on. She'd loved their night together. She wasn't in love with Ruby, but she had her number *just in case*. She had told her friends.

Whatever was going on with Nat, it wasn't Izzy who was the main problem. It couldn't be. She *hadn't done anything wrong*. It felt like a boulder had been lifted from her chest.

Fuck it. She was done with this pity party.

She hoped.

She let Mum talk her into remembering she was the girl who was going for her film degree. She was going to be an award-winning writer-director, and she didn't have time for this bullshit. Surely, this would be behind her soon enough.

"Yeah. Fuck that. Sorry. Sod it, I won't let her make me feel bad."

A new emotion surfaced, spread through her blood. She was angry. She was, now she thought about it, properly cheesed off.

She didn't need Nat. She had other friends. She wasn't going to let this crap get in her way. So she was bisexual. So what. It just opened up a whole world of possibilities for her. Girls! Who knew! Girls were wonderful. Girls were *lovely*. And Izzy was coming for them. As soon as she caught up on her writing.

18

Nick couldn't sleep. It had started worsening a few weeks back, and he had no idea what to do about it. His mom once told him that even as a baby, he wouldn't go down easy, but this was getting ridiculous.

He blinked and tried to focus in on the digital numbers glowing around the vicinity of his desk. He thought he could make out a three. Nothing good ever happened at three AM.

When they'd first moved to Ann Arbor and he and Zoyka were still sharing a room, she would talk him through it. She'd made it sound so reasonable. *What are you worried about right now? Okay. Think about the worst that could happen. It probably won't, right? Can you deal with it in the morning? Good. What's next?*

He kicked off his covers and attempted to breathe in deeply a few times. His heart was beating hard. His throat was dry. He needed water. His pillow was thin. He needed another one. He could solve one problem by padding into the bathroom and drinking from the faucet.

The cold water on his face woke him up further.

Irritated, he climbed back into bed and pulled the covers over his head. The air was too warm and smelled too much like him.

What are you worried about right now?

I think it's true.

What's true?

Even to the Zoyka in his head, he could not say it. She'd always been the one he told things to. She'd always kept his secrets.

But she wasn't actually here. Not now. It was just him under his duvet, and this room, at least, knew. It had witnessed it, been part of it.

What if I am?

What. Just say it. Why are you so fucking scared?

What if I'm gay.

He ripped the duvet away and sat up, attempting to dislodge every thought with a shake of his head. If only it were that easy. He breathed. It was no good, his heart was too fucking fast. The cycle fed itself, his heart sped up his breathing, his breathing forced his pulse to flutter like a trapped moth. His gut churned.

When he closed his eyes, he pictured his mom. His aunt. His uncle. Zoyka, Jake. His grandparents.

Dad.

You're what? Mom would say. *What are you talking about? You're Russian. Ty-zhe nash. Don't talk nonsense.*

She had a trembling crease between her eyebrows when she was really upset. In the last few years, she had developed a slight tic in her mouth that preceded her laying out the worst thing he and Zoyka could ever hear. *What would your dad have to say about this?* She didn't trot it out too often.

She would trot it out for this.

He told himself firmly he had to go to sleep. He had class at nine o'clock. He was always a zombie if he got less than seven hours' sleep, and it was much, much less than that now.

If you go to sleep in the next twenty minutes, you'll have just over four hours.

Time continued to drain, and he fell asleep with the sky slowly washing out to gray behind the half-closed blinds, his pillow jammed beneath his neck, his hands clammy and hot.

There were times when Zoyka was wrong. Nick didn't feel better about his worries in the morning. At three, his anxiety had been a shapeless thing, with weight and texture, but part of dreams. A sort of terrifying unreality he had to breathe through.

At eight, as his alarm shrieked at him to wake up, the shapeless, textured thing coalesced into something more terrifying than the nightly ghosts.

He wanted men. He hadn't really wanted Lena in all the years they'd been together. He hadn't really wanted Ashley during sophomore year when they'd kissed in the art classroom, her hair tickling his palms where his hands had trembled on her shoulders. Fruitless humping in her sunroom, sweaty and shaky and half hard.

He wanted *Dex*. Of all people, of all the people he had met, he wanted *him* so much his hands ached with it. Nick was past denial. Truth frightened more than denial.

He brushed his teeth, and past the bags under his eyes and morning stubble he saw Dad's young face looking back at him in the mirror.

He went to class. He looked at the other students, watched them respond to the tutor's comments, give theories, write notes, and he wondered, *What must it be like*? What must it be like to know yourself and to like what you know? To take up space the way they did and not feel strange or ragged around the edges? To know that you belonged somewhere, inside and out?

He'd watch Dex sometimes and marvel. He seemed to have no fears. At least none that Nick could see. He moved in a way that assured the world had room for him, and it did. He had family he didn't seem to hide things from. Alex had once made an offhand comment that Dex had gone through hoards of boys his first few months at college, and Nick had thought about it ever since.

It seemed so impossible—sex that satisfied, sex that felt the way others made it sound. He couldn't, and yet he couldn't stop trying to picture Dex with all those faceless, joyful boys. He had no idea what it would even look like. Physically, he couldn't picture it. Maybe if he couldn't picture it, that meant he could never do it. Did it work like that? If you wanted something badly but could not shape it with your mind, did it exist at all?

He'd started asking himself *why* so long ago, it felt like a part of him. At thirteen, he had been just as desperate to have the answer as he was now, at twenty. *Why me? Why couldn't I be normal*?

He'd run four thousand miles from home, but all he'd done was get closer to the question. Why had he thought England would be neutral ground? If anything, it was like a conductor, and Nick was standing on it, entirely exposed.

Four thousand miles, and nothing was getting easier.

It was getting worse.

Once again, Nick used a big paper as an excuse to hermit himself back into his one-man existence, but when Izzy texted him and asked for the second time if he was up for a coffee, he couldn't find it in him to say no.

He told himself it was because Izzy needed a friend despite the fact that she had better, more helpful friends than Nick, told himself it was because he wanted to know how she was, told himself it would have been plainly rude to refuse.

It was all of those things. But it had also been five days since Dex had come over for the cooking lesson. Five days since Nick had stupidly, thoughtlessly, and in a fit of delirium said *yes* to another one—and exactly as many days since he'd heard from Dex at all.

He and Izzy had agreed to meet up at the same greasy spoon where Izzy had dropped her bombshell on everyone, and when she came in this time it looked like she was still feeling the effects of it. She smiled as wide as always, but Nick could see the shadows beneath her eyes. He kicked himself for not seeing her the first time she'd asked.

"Hi, babe." She plonked down her bag on a chair across from his. "Back in a tic."

Nick sipped his giant coffee, looking around. The place was hopping, noisy with the sound of cutlery and conversation, orders being called out, shit getting dropped. It wasn't exactly conducive to conversation, but Nick relied on Izzy being her usual exuberant self.

"So, how have you been?"

"I feel like I should be asking you that."

She made a face. "I guess I'm all right. You know."

Nick waited.

"Just sort of thinking about shit. A lot of thinking."

"About what?"

"How weird are humans, you know? What the fuck? I thought I knew myself."

"Yeah?"

"Yeah. I've not exactly been hiding secret thoughts and desires." It took a lot of Nick's strength to nod nonchalantly. "But at the same time—so you're kissing a person you really like, and they're not a terrible kisser, so it feels nice, *really* nice." She cleared her throat. Nick liked kissing. Kissing *was* nice. To this much, he could relate. "It feels natural. Good, you know?" She paused, and Nick looked up. "Sorry, is this TMI? Should I stop?"

"No, no, it's fine."

She gave him a tiny smile and focused on something beyond the window. It was a grey day, which made her hair look just a tad muted. "Well, then. Basically, when Ruby and I—kissed, it felt just as good as kissing a guy. I don't know, it just surprised me, I suppose. I'm still—I just can't believe I never knew." She cleared her throat again. "And then I thought, well, kissing is kissing. Kissing is—almost safe, you know? 'Cause there's the other, uh, stuff. And—oh God, am I completely embarrassing myself?"

"Not at all." She eyed him with suspicion. "I promise." He reached out in a fit of bravery and grabbed her finger. "Pinky swear."

She squeezed back. "Well, if it's a pinky swear. Everything else *also* felt natural, it turned out. But that's not even the part that I've been obsessing over, not really."

"Natali?"

She sighed. "Yeah. Like, sexuality is fucking weird, and I'm still getting used to the idea that I like women apparently the same as I like men, that I'm *bi*, but I think—what if it cost me a friend? Was it worth it, to find out?"

When their gazes met, Nick saw that the tip of her nose and her cheeks had grown pink. Nick panicked. Would Izzy cry? *Did* Izzy cry? "Has she talked to you?" he asked carefully.

"No. Well, I mean. She says *morning* and *Can you pass me the sugar*, but she barely spends time at home anymore. Even Jonny and Dex seemed surprised."

"I'm sorry." It was so inadequate, but he didn't know what to say. It sounded awful. *Was it worth it to find out?* What a good question.

"It's been two weeks, and she's still shutting me out, and I don't know *why*. Why? Shit, I even went home and cried to my mum."

Nick startled at that. Had she told her mom—everything? He had no idea what that would even be like. And she'd gone home? Where was home for Izzy? She hadn't told him, and he hadn't asked.

"It's such shit. At first, I'd text her, try to get her to talk to me. I tried in person, everything. Fuck, I almost asked Beth, one of her baby dykes, to help me out, but I'm pissed off now.

If she won't talk to me, I've got to stop chasing her. It's shit. It feels like shit." She sniffed. "I did nothing *wrong.*"

"Yeah." He was out of his depth. "I mean, you didn't. Nothing wrong."

"I miss her." Izzy went on as if he hadn't spoken. "She's one of my closest mates. And she's shut me out."

The next minute was spent in silence as they both sipped their drinks. Nick briefly pictured what the two of them must look like. The saddest date in existence, probably.

"God, sorting out your own crap is annoying, isn't it?" Izzy mused after a while. "I dunno. Sex is such a fundamental part of the world, why do we have so much bullshit associated with it?"

Nick managed a nod.

"So you're gay or straight or bi or what have you, why's that so bloody fucking important? Have you ever thought about that, really thought about it?"

He was shocked to hear his voice come out even when he said, "Not really."

He was an awful liar. Izzy could tell. He couldn't move a muscle. "Really? But I thought—" She stopped.

Nick was caught in the moment. He had no idea how to stop or reverse it.

"Sorry, that was so fucking rude of me. Nick, I'm so sorry if I made you uncomfortable, that was—shit. *Shit.* I'm *so* sorry."

Nick barely managed to unstick his tongue from the roof of his mouth. "No, it's—it's fine. You didn't." Had he just inadvertently come out? Or could he make her believe she'd thought wrong? His heart hammered.

If Izzy could tell, who else could? Every single interaction he'd ever had with a human being flickered through his mind. All but with his family. It would never have even occurred to them. Lena, though? What about everyone here? Steph, Alex, Natali, *Dex.*

Fuck.

Dex.

"Nick, babe. Nick. *Breathe.*" When she reached out and touched his hand with her fingers, he jumped. She retreated. "Christ. You okay?"

Nick had no idea. Thoughts jumbled in his mind, bouncing against one another like marbles. So much clatter, so much noise. "Izzy," he choked out. "Izzy, please don't say anything."

She was looking at him with so much concern. He was close to breaking down.

He made himself continue. "Please, don't tell. Promise."

"I promise, I swear to God." She hooked her pinky over his. "Pinky swear, all right?"

He kept hold of her pinky. For a long moment, he did his best to breathe.

"So you're not out then?" She sounded so careful. Nick shook his head. Words would probably be good, but he had none. He felt numb. His head was filled utter stillness. It wasn't calm. It was just *there.* "I'm so sorry I put my stupid foot in it. Do you need to get some air, maybe? What can I do?"

Nick managed to breathe. "I don't know." He put his hands over his flaming cheeks, shut his eyes. The smell of grease and coffee clinging to his hands made his stomach recoil. He dropped his arms on the table, then his head. "Fuck."

"Look at me, I just word-vommed all over you about this stuff, and I'm...dunno. I'm lucky. I took it in stride. You know. For the most part."

Nick wondered which part she meant.

"Do you want to talk about it?"

Did he? He no longer had any idea what he wanted.

"You don't have to. It might help. Just to. Share or whatever. You got pretty upset. This seems big."

Nick nodded.

"C'mon." She patted his elbow, all business. "For once, it's not pissing down, so let's go find a bit of green to sit in and air out. D'you have anywhere you have to be?"

Nick didn't.

"Good. Let's go."

+

They wound up in the sculpture garden where he'd poured his heart out to Dex. Why was he only here post–panic attack? And why did he keep having those in front of people?

Izzy was silent as they walked up to it. Last time, the trees had leaves on them, and it had been dark. Nick was surprised to see the park so sparse now. So much less mysterious in the gray light of day, with weak sunlight streaming through the bare November branches. He'd barely even noticed there was some sort of building at the end of it all—a typical brown London brick with bright blue railings on the steps and the walkway.

When he gingerly lowered himself onto the rocker, he didn't fall. Izzy followed suit, and together they swayed for a bit, quiet amid the city traffic noise.

He was with Izzy, so the quiet didn't last for long. "So, you're gay, then?"

What a question to lead with. "Honestly? I don't know. But I think I might be. I mean. Probably."

"You've never been with a bloke?"

Nick shook his head. His feet were cold. He probably needed to invest in something other than Chucks, now that he thought about it. He'd left his winter boots back home.

"What about a girl?"

Nick finally looked up at where she was watching him, bouncing slowly up and down on her own weirdo bench. "Yeah."

She nodded like that explained it, even though it explained absolutely nothing to Nick. "And you just didn't...sorry. This is so completely none of my business."

"It's okay. Honestly, I don't know." He looked up at the sky, the sunlight was diffused by low-hanging clouds. He'd forgotten his scarf, and now he shivered in the chill. "I can't. Not with my family."

"Would they be very angry?"

"I don't know how to explain. It's never been an option. Not how I grew up."

"Why?"

"It's how they grew up, too. Back there, it was not talked about. If it was, it wasn't good." How to truly describe the insular circle of friends his parents had surrounded themselves with? Jewish intelligentsia who feared much and talked largely of high art, or science, and only sometimes of politics—in hushed voices and in vetted company. Their kitchen table was always crowded with makeshift dinners and discussions of how cultural standards had fallen along with the government and taken intellectual thought with them. Queerness would never even enter into such conversation. Once, Nick remembered someone mentioning a particularly flamboyant pop star. Mom had wrinkled her nose. *Distasteful.* In her reality, being gay was like being a wizard. Outside her realm.

And then, America. A fleeting sense of freedom quickly replaced by the sharp edge of incongruence.

"I literally can't imagine telling them. They'll never understand. It's like when my sister decided to be vegetarian for two years and every time my mom made dinner, she kept forgetting, because why would anyone be vegetarian? Does that make sense?"

"But America isn't Russia, right?"

"My mom isn't very American." Ten years on, she surrounded herself with Russian friends, Russian books,

Russian movies. "It was hard on my parents, leaving, and with my dad...I can't imagine doing that to her."

Izzy was quiet for a long time.

"Please don't tell anyone else."

Dex. He meant, don't tell Dex. For some reason, the idea of Dex finding out, or figuring it out, or even knowing already but also aware that Nick was scared, made him feel panicked and sick. It fed on itself and dizzied him.

"I won't, babe. I promised. I'm sorry it's this hard, but I'm really glad you told me."

Nick breathed in and out. "Yeah. I'm glad I did, too." He was, he thought. Somewhere beneath the panic and the embarrassment, the banal tragedy of it all, he felt a sense of gratitude to no longer be the only person in the world to know that he was so far from a perfect son.

Back in his room, Nick waited for the walls to crash down around him. It was a shock that things looked exactly the same. His room was just as he'd left it to meet Izzy. Socks balled up at the foot of his bed, duvet sliding off, his glasses resting on the windowsill. Perpetually warm, the radiator blasting heat into stuffy air.

Everything was the same except his own perception. It would have been much easier if he felt a lightness in his shoulders, but he didn't. Izzy was wonderful, but Izzy wasn't his sister. She wasn't his mother. She wasn't the one he was scared to glimpse over his shoulder in case they guessed the truth. Izzy existed in a world where difference was only that—a difference. It wasn't moral failing, grotesque disappointment. Difference wasn't danger.

In his unchanged room, for just a moment, he wondered what it would be like. To stop being afraid. To accept the truth.

To look his mom in the eye and say it.

He plopped down onto his bed and mindlessly counted up the number of letters in all the words printed across his postcards. He knew they didn't, but every time he hoped that all the letters would divide into three. He needed a word with five letters in it to make it work. He was still looking for one.

Impossible, that's what it was. Literally. He couldn't picture telling his family.

He could sooner tell them he was dropping out of school and becoming a construction worker.

You know. It's 2014. Your mum might surprise you.

No, Nick knew better. The only Melnikov who could surprise anyone was him.

It was strange how time worked. One minute, Nick felt like he'd only been in London for a week at most, and the next, early December was knocking on his door and he was swept up in end-of-term mania along with everybody else.

Dex texted.

Haven't forgotten about the cooking test :) got caught up in projects & fam stuff but mb next week sometime?

Nick had waited for it, despite himself. He barely had a moment to see anyone either, but every time his phone vibrated or lit up, he looked for Dex's name. Every time it was someone else, he told himself that the churning in his gut was relief.

Nick shoved his phone under a pile of papers. Then he pulled it out again to look at the message. To see Dex's name addressing itself to Nick. It wasn't a mistake, either, no matter how hard it was to believe.

He pushed the phone away again, but his mind wouldn't settle back into his reading. His eyes scanned the same paragraph about the War of the Roses again and again, the repetition of it droning in the back of his mind. The memory of Dex's hand hot on his wrist intruded in the forefront.

Dex's hand on his wrist, Dex's body looming over his. His beautiful face with its wide brown eyes intent on Nick. If it wasn't the most ridiculous idea in the world, Nick would have believed Dex had gotten close to him on purpose.

If Dex had a league, Nick would have been disqualified before even entering the competition. But he'd had to curl his knees up just to hide that he'd gone half hard at what had been perfectly regular, friendly sort of touching, and it had been humiliating. It had been electric.

He'd told Izzy he didn't know for sure, and he hadn't really lied. It was a real possibility that if, in some other universe, he got to kiss a boy, he wouldn't feel a thing. But that possibility was harder to believe after Dex had crossed the few feet of bed between them and woke Nick's body up in a shower of sparks.

Nick *was* busy. The coursework seemed almost overwhelming at times, and he was going to be damned if he fucked up in a way that didn't land him the grades he wanted. He should have been telling Dex he didn't have time for another lesson.

But he didn't. *I'm free Sunday the 13th.* He hit send before he could change his mind.

A week and a half from now. Nick licked his lips and tried not to think about how that date was six days before he was due to fly back home for Christmas break. It barely seemed possible. He didn't feel *ready*.

Dex was sick of the same four walls of his room but too lazy to get his arse to the library. Plus, he was starving. He shut his laptop and allowed himself a luxurious hour break with a promise of enjoying it if he got right back to his desk for more data sifting. Right now, his eyes were fucking crossing.

He went searching for some sort of sustenance that wasn't caffeine in a jar and found Jonny rooting around the cupboards in the kitchen like a rabid fox.

"Hey, mate. We have nothing but biscuits and insta-noodles in here. This is highly unsatisfactory."

"Maybe we should suck it up and get a Tesco order. This is pretty dire." He peered inside the fridge. Pickle, cheese, brown sauce, and something that had probably at one point been some delightful leftover roast chicken, which looked like Dex should toss it into a hazardous waste bin and wear a protective suit in the process. He shut the door. "Takeaway?"

"Please."

They ate their curries on the sofa with the telly, as always, on half mute. To the drone of the BBC, Dex filled himself on poppadoms and green curry and washed it all down with beer. "So, what's up with you?"

"Dunno. A shitload of essays. You?"

"A shitload of experimental data. Bloody well sick of it, to be honest. I can't believe it's basically end of term."

Jonny nodded and took a long sip of his own beer. He was looking at the television like it actually had something good on.

"Y'alright, man?"

"What? Oh yeah, 'course."

They'd been missing each other due to everyone's mad last dash of term, but now he could see the restless way in which Jonny shifted on the sofa, like he couldn't get comfortable.

"You are so lying."

"What? I'm fine! What the fuck are you on about?"

"You look bloody knackered and cagey and weird. Is it your parents? Has something happened?"

Jonny's expression melted into something Dex did not expect—an impish sort of pleasure. Not his parents, then. Dex narrowed his eyes.

"All right. But you can't tell anyone, all right?" Jonny set his beer down onto the coffee table. "*All right*?"

"All right, all right! Spill it, and leave no detail untouched."

"So, I've been seeing someone? Dating. Proper dating."

Dex grinned. The penny had dropped about two seconds before Jonny said it, but now the shadows under his baby blues made sense. Dex missed those sorts of sleepless nights. The closest he'd come recently was losing his shit on Nick's bed and running out like an idiot. "Thought so. And who's the lucky—" Another penny dropped. "Oh blimey, fucking hell, it is *not*—"

"Dexter." Dex shut up. "Look at my face. I am happy. Do *not* fucking ruin this for me."

Dex took a deep breath. "It seems like you and Lance are, in fact, quite happy together." Just because Dex thought Lance was a bloody idiot didn't mean the dude didn't have excellent taste in the people he chose to date. By the looks of things, he was making Jonny properly happy. *Well.*

Jonny beamed like someone had turned a torch on inside him. "It's brilliant. He's so lovely. I know he can be a lot sometimes, but he isn't always like that, all right? He's so kind, and he really is super clever."

Jonny looked down at his beer, and his face broke into the sort of smile that felt almost too private for Dex to be witnessing. A pang shot through him. Jonny deserved no less than someone who was kind to him, and if nothing else, Lance had always seemed to appreciate him.

"And the sex is. I can't. I can't even tell you. It's off the charts amazing."

Dex was trying to be nice, but he wasn't a saint. "Really? *Lance*?"

"Yes! Lance! He's, like. Yeah." Jonny's cheeks flushed red under his lowered pale lashes. "Like...really. *Yeah*. Wow."

It was impossible not to smile back when Jonny grinned. "That's great, mate. I'm so happy for you." And he was, too. If he was also wistful, that was all right. Dex bit adieu to referring to Lance as Tweedle Dee, even in his head. "So, is it serious?"

"It is for me. I'm pretty sure it is for Lance, too. He actually— He invited me back to his family's for Christmas."

"Whoa. That is pretty serious. Are you going to go, d'you think?"

Jonny sighed. It appeared that only the thought of home could dim his light right about now. "I dunno. I want to, a lot, but there's my mum and dad."

"Have they said anything?"

"Well, no. It's assumed I'll be there. I really don't want to see them, though," he said quietly.

"It was pretty bad last time, wasn't it?"

"It was shite. Before Lance asked, I had considered staying here for hols."

"But?"

"But it's selfish to take him up on the offer, innit?"

"Is it? Or is it protecting yourself from crap you don't deserve?"

"I guess." He didn't sound convinced at all, but at least he did appear to be considering other options. That was a good step, probably.

"I'm sorry," Dex offered. It felt wholly inadequate.

"Not your fault. Thanks for not being a dickhead about Lance and me."

"I may be a sort of dickhead, but I'm not *that* much of a dickhead," Dex protested. "*You're* a dickhead."

"I have never been a dickhead in all my life," Jonny protested, and to be fair, he was absolutely right. How they wound up with Jonny in their lives was unclear, but Dex was not about to look a gift horse in the mouth.

Izzy had decided that they needed a group study session. It was a strange thing to arrange. They all studied completely different topics apart from him and Alex, and at best they'd all be sat in a room going bonkers simultaneously. But Izzy had sounded so off her rocker when she'd suggested it, Dex had acquiesced just to keep her from rolling off a cliff.

Now—as Dex had predicted—they were all squashed into their living room, every piece of furniture and available floor surface taken up by humans, books, and laptops.

Nat, for the first time in a couple of weeks, joined them. Dex did his best to suppress both his surprise and his pleasure, lest he spook her. Alex had pulled him aside and told him that Nat had been feeling horrifically guilty for blowing up but was still fucked up over the whole thing, so this was her own small step back to normal. Alex had had to drag her there a bit, but she did come, which seemed to be a good sign.

Nat had brought her laptop along with a pile of marked-up papers, and she settled in to working on her thesis two feet away from Izzy, whose hopeful face said it all. Dex wanted to hug her. He hoped Nat being there was a good thing and not an awful distraction for her.

So between those two and Jonny and Lance on the sofa completely unaware of anybody else in the world, Dex was having a hard time concentrating. And this was before you threw Nick in the mix.

Dex had managed not to see him since the night in Nick's room. He hadn't been avoiding him, he had been genuinely busy. He'd gone home one weekend to see Al and his parents, and every other day he was either revising or working, working or revising. His only nod to civility had been to send Nick a text and arrange for another cooking date. *Not* a date-date, just a cooking *thing*, but even so, when Izzy opened the front door and Nick walked through, Dex's heart kicked up like he was being chased.

Nick had smiled politely at everyone, giving Dex the barest of glances, and then settled in close to Izzy's side and buried himself in his laptop. It was a strange feeling, this slight resentment towards Izzy.

They'd had a *moment*. Dex knew it had been a moment. He couldn't quite put his finger on what sort of moment it had been. Had it been just him? He didn't think so. He'd locked Izzy's assumption that Nick fancied him inside his brain, and every now and then he would pull it out and consider it. Like a kid, he had memorised her every word and repeated it to himself.

He watches you. All the time.

Not today, he wasn't. Nick kept his nose either in his laptop or in one of a thousand printouts he had brought with him. Every now and then, he would say something to Izzy.

Dex shook his head to clear it. This was stupid. If nothing else, he had a shitload of revising to do. He clicked his laptop back to life and concentrated.

+

"I can't bloody think anymore. Like, the word *zeitgeist* no longer looks like a word. I need a break."

Having made this pronouncement, Natali unfolded herself from the floor and began an odd stretching routine. Dex noticed Izzy watching her.

"A break sounds good," he said and stretched his arms over his head. When he looked around, everyone else appeared to unfreeze, as if Natali's words released some sort of spell. An awakening of the zombified.

"Should we get food or something?" Izzy asked.

Dex's stomach growled. "Chinese?"

"Pizza," Jonny said without looking up from his phone. Dex scowled at him but gave in. Pizza was cheapest anyway.

"Fine. Pizza. Everyone good with that?"

It took a while to work out what to order. Between the veggies and Steph, who was coeliac, three different orders had to be placed. Once accomplished, though, he could finally escape for a slash.

He ran into Nick on the way back from the bathroom.

"How's the Peterloo stuff going, mate?" he asked. Nick pushed his glasses back up his nose before responding, and Dex tamped down the ridiculous desire to kiss the dip in his lower lip.

"Pretty good." His gaze was slightly unfocused, like he was a thousand miles away in his head. "Though another week to finish it all up would be nice."

"Tell me about it." Dex had stood apart from Nick, for his own safety or Nick's he wasn't sure, but now he wished he had engineered a close-body situation. Which was obviously stupid, because if you had to engineer it, it wasn't going to happen either way.

He wanted Nick to acknowledge it. To acknowledge *him*. To acknowledge this *thing* between them. He wanted Nick to strip that wall he'd built around himself and to show Dex that he maybe mattered in a different way from everybody else. If Izzy was right, of course.

Izzy wasn't always right.

Maybe Dex was making a fool of himself for no reason at all. Maybe Nick really was straight. *Maybe he's gay and just not into you*. What a bugger of a deflating thought.

He let Nick pass him without another word.

"Sit with me, Dexter, and tell me I'm pretty," Izzy commanded as soon as he walked back into the living room. "Well?" she demanded.

"You're very pretty," Dex intoned dutifully.

"And?"

He should never have shown her *Firefly*. "And," he went on, "were I not gay, I would take you in a manly fashion."

"Good," she grinned and pecked him on the cheek. Across from them, Nat was frowning down at her phone. He felt Izzy sigh next to him.

Nick surprised himself by getting ahead in two out of his four classes. It felt like one moment he was sore and hunched over on Izzy's floor, typing random nonsense just to try to grab hold of any idea, and the next he had finished drafts of two final papers on his laptop in need of revision. He supposed this was where his increasing insomnia came in handy. His brain worked overtime to make up for all the things edging into his consciousness, attempting to distract him with fear and panic.

At least he had something to show for it.

Izzy texted him silly, inconsequential things that made him smile. She was checking in with him post–freak out. He hadn't particularly wanted to go to their study group, but it would have felt like poor repayment for her kindness to skip it.

And it was probably good to see Dex again. Dex had been north and Nick a compass needle. When Dex had moved or spoken, Nick felt the pull of him. The hardest thing he'd ever had to do was fight the urge to watch him. Nick watched people. He often zoned out on it, not even thinking about whoever he was staring at as a live human but more as a painting to be studied, a book to be read.

But Dex was fully alive to him. Human, real, intricately beautiful. It was the little things, and the way they came together to form the full picture. His large hands, veins prominent under his dark skin as he typed, or pushing his dreads off of his forehead as he read. His lower lip jutting out in concentration. He'd looked like that when he stood over Nick's stove and filled Nick's kitchen with the aroma of tomatoes, basil, and parm. Secure and powerful, like a manifestation of steadiness. Dex was everything Nick wasn't, and everything he longed for.

He thought about telling Izzy, then changed his mind. If there was anybody closer to Dex himself, he couldn't think of who. But he'd opened up Pandora's Box, and it took an unbearable effort to seal it shut again.

It was a wonder he had gotten any work done. He'd had a slice of pizza and legged it out of there.

Tomorrow night, he was going right back into that lion's den. Why had he ever agreed to that? He couldn't remember the first thing Dex had done in his kitchen, but Nick wanted to do something in return, even if it wound up being a humiliating, tortuous mess.

So he found himself in Sainsbury's on a late Sunday afternoon. It was a strange realization that he was both familiar with the store's layout and completely baffled by it. He hadn't ever really searched for the things the recipe told him to search for, and now he wandered up and down each aisle, dodging little kids and their harried parents, tuning his radar to canned tomatoes and ground beef.

His eyes nearly crossed at the total, but he told himself it was worth it. He just couldn't believe how much Dex had spent to make him a single dinner. Nick had managed to go through the entire semester on two meals a day, stretching teabags of Earl Grey to three separate cups and having a single spoonful of Nutella for dessert as a form of luxury. The most he ever spent at once was in pubs and on occasional takeouts. As he stared down a total that represented what he would probably pay for a week's worth of food, he wondered if he was man enough to attempt to get a job that could pay him under the table next semester.

Probably not.

At least he would get more loan money beginning of next term.

With plastic handles digging into his cold fingers and his heart beating hard inside his chest, Nick rang the doorbell and waited.

Dex opened the door wearing a Christmas-themed apron. Nick was so shocked, it took him a minute to get that Dex was beckoning him in.

"Thanks for grabbing the shopping," Dex said as he took the bags off Nick into the kitchen. Nick followed him. He wondered if anyone else was home, but apart from the soft music streaming from the kitchen it was quiet.

Dex was barefoot, wearing only jeans and a soft-looking gray T-shirt with a stretched-out collar. Nick's body thrummed with the idea of catching the edge of it and pulling down to reveal more smooth, dark skin. What a crazy fucking thought.

"So! How would you feel about giving it a go straight off? Or do you want me to start?"

Dex was heading toward the counter, where he had clearly already prepped. A cutting board, two different knives, three colorful bowls, and a bottle of Pinot with two glasses sat on top of the white surface. Two pots graced the stovetop.

"Wow," Nick said. "You're all prepared." His palms were sweaty. He was eyeing the bottle of wine.

Dex must have caught him at it, because he laughed and moved to open it.

"Liquid courage?" Dex said as he offered Nick the filled glass. Their eyes met, and Nick felt a molten heat go through him. Thank God he was flying back home next week. He needed the distance so badly. "You'll be fine," Dex added.

"Thanks." He looked over at the prepped counter. "I think I can figure it out."

Nick unloaded all the ingredients. He felt like he was attempting to pass some sort of test. This was a terrible idea.

He had remembered that Dex mentioned bacon last time, so he slid the knife through the taut plastic of the package and asked, "How should I cut this?"

Dex poured himself wine, his every movement sending an electric awareness down Nick's side. "Just, like, small chunks. Cut into strips, then crosswise, if that makes sense."

Nick nodded. The bacon was slippery and kept catching on the knife. He wanted Dex to stop watching him, or at least back up enough that the body heat between them wasn't as excruciating.

Nick wondered what it would be like to have Dex like him as much as he liked Dex.

What would Nick even do with such information? What *could* he do? Lena had told him many times that he was *pretty*, but all he saw when looking in the mirror was his father's face. Talk about a face only his mother could love. If given free rein, Nick was no longer sure he wouldn't give in, even with the sensation of his family hovering just over his shoulder, reminding him of everything he couldn't be.

He kept butchering the bacon until it was in bits, then realized he didn't have the first clue what to do with it.

Dex was pouring olive oil into a pot. Nick realized they hadn't said a word to each other.

"Oh, yeah…thanks."

"No problem, man. Do you remember the next step?"

Nick reached for the onion. "You probably want to back up for this," he said, joking.

The sting of it was unbearable. Once again, he was wearing contacts, and once again, he thought he would have to rip his eyeballs out, except this time he couldn't just run clear across the room. He had to stop crying and finish slicing the demon onion through foggy, pricking eyes. He tried to hold his breath, but it did nothing to help the stinging. He could barely see through the tears. Christ, this was going just magnificently. He dropped the knife and covered his eyes with one arm, the moisture seeping into the sleeve of his sweater. He heard himself gasping.

"Fuck." He tried to breathe without breathing in, which obviously never worked. Half blinded, he groped for the knife again and attempted to slice through the onion without looking. He felt the pain in his finger a moment before he flung the knife away. He hissed.

"Did you just cut yourself?" Dex was on him the next moment, grabbing Nick's hand. Nick's breath caught again. "S'not too bad." He relinquished Nick's hand. "Wash it under the tap while I grab a plaster."

Funny, Nick thought as he turned the water on and stuck his stinging finger underneath it. Maybe that's where the Russian 'plastyr' came from.

Instead of giving him the Band-Aid and retreating, Dex took gentle hold of his hand as he studied it. "Just nicked it, but it's better to cover it all the same. Hygienic and all that." Nick watched, rendered entirely silent save for the incessant beating of his heart, as Dex wrapped the Band-Aid securely around the cut. "There."

Nick looked up. They were impossibly close. Dex was still holding his hand. He was looking into Nick's eyes. He was *looking* at him. Their hands felt damp together, and something like a distant alarm blared at Nick the next moment, forcing him to extract his hand from Dex's. He managed to smile, hoping it was a smile that communicated friendship instead of the crazy, overwhelming need swamping his whole being.

"Thanks!" He sounded like an idiot. "Guess I'm not ready for the advanced onion-cutting lessons." His voice sounded like he couldn't get enough of a breath in.

He thought he heard Dex breathe out, but he looked normal. He didn't look the way Nick felt. "Onions are a massive pain in the arse to chop, so you're just earning your stripes," he told Nick.

"How many stripes to finish it off?"

He turned back to the onion with a new determination to conquer it. He put knife to onion again and almost sliced through its pearlescent surface when Dex stepped up to him and laid a hand over his, stilling it.

The only sound he could hear over his heartbeat was the tinny music coming from Dex's phone. It was a familiar song, but Nick couldn't place it.

When he could no longer bear it, he looked up at Dex in his personal space.

"Nick," Dex said. Nick realized how rarely he had heard his name in Dex's voice. If Dex called him anything, it was *mate* or *man*, something he used with everyone. Nick's name felt remarkable. It was a pull on his bones, an invitation that he could not have refused if his life depended on it.

The air around them shifted. His reality changed. He knew this heady feeling before something happened. He wasn't sure if he could handle it. Still, he could not stop himself from turning to face Dex and getting so close there was barely air between them. He swallowed. Dex pulled gently, fingers slipping among Nick's and coming to rest between them.

"Am I wrong to think—" Dex broke off, and Nick wanted to help, but he couldn't. All he could do was stand rooted to the spot, caught up in the tension, incapable of believing his own eyes and ears, his muscles and bones.

He looked into Dex's eyes, willing him to understand.

Dex made a frustrated noise and dropped Nick's hand. Cupped both hands around Nick's jaw.

He met Nick's eyes, asking for permission, and then he leaned in, and then he kissed him.

The moment stretched. Nick did not breathe. Dex's lips were full and gentle. *This is happening* was replaced with need Nick tried and failed to contain. He moaned. He opened his mouth and touched Dex's tongue. His knees threatened to give. The taste of a true, hard, overwhelming kiss was going to undo him.

Nick felt himself splintering in two, a painful tearing of past and future. Before he knew and after. The truth of it laid him bare and nestled inside him. He knew, now. He *knew*.

Dex took a step forward and pinned Nick against the counter. His tongue was velvet against Nick's, and his body. *God.* Hard, warm, so present and alive. Nick shook, grateful that he had nowhere to go, since Dex had him trapped. Things slotted into place, and they unspooled him from the inside out.

He felt something nudge his hip and with a jolt realized it was Dex's erection. The shocking intimacy of it was too much. It shredded him.

Nick tore his mouth away, ready to end it here and now, when Dex leaned in and kissed the joining of his neck and shoulder while his hands grabbed hold of Nick's waist. Nick clutched the counter in desperation. All the hair on his arms and legs stood up. He barely believed the noise that tore from his throat.

"God, Nick." Nick was pretty sure he would walk through fire just to hear his name spoken like that for the rest of his life, but the smell of hot oil and burning bacon slammed him back into reality.

He couldn't.

He could not.

Knowing and acting were two different beasts.

He had control over one of them.

With shaky, numb hands he pushed at Dex's chest until he had room to breathe, and, not daring to spare him even the smallest of glances or apologies, grabbed his bag and jacket and ran out into the hallway, pretended not to hear Dex calling him back, and tore through the door before Dex could catch up.

The house was three blocks behind him before he realized that he'd been running and his chest hurt and his eyes stung, and he doubled over and dry heaved for long enough to draw concerned looks from passersby.

His heart slammed.

Oh, Jesus fuck.

It really had only been a matter of time before he ruined everything.

He didn't remember the rest of the walk back to his dorm.

21

Three...two...one...Happy New Year!"

Dex's feeble *yaaaaaay* must not have satisfied Izzy, because she blew her bright red air horn right in his ear and threw him the V-sign.

He threw one right back at her.

"Cheer up, mate, it's a new year!"

People stumbled all around, drunks attempting to kiss other drunks and sing off-key at the same time. He and Izzy probably didn't look much different, what with Izzy climbing into his lap planting wet kisses all over his face.

"*Geroff!* God!" His attempts to push her away only resulted in further barnacling by Izzy. Dex was only mildly pissed and doing his level best to shake off his shitty mood.

"You know, it could be worse," Izzy shouted into his ear over the din of the horns and the merry crowd. Her sparkly purple fedora was digging into his forehead.

"How?"

"You could be all alone at home with Al and your parents, alternating between cringy fireworks banter and Jools' Hootenanny whilst crying into your lager."

"I would not be *crying.*"

"Have you looked in the mirror lately, babe? You look like someone's stolen all your collectibles."

This time he did push her off him, and she giggled as she tipped over onto the bench. "I'm just letting you know that you're back to Grumpy Dex and I'm essentially being an angel, stuck here with your scowling face in the arse-end of nowhere instead of bonking someone hot that I'll never see again and whose last name I probably won't know in a Camden loo somewhere."

Dex gave her the side-eye she properly deserved. He wasn't the only one here who was avoiding shit. "Deflection," he said, "is your middle name."

"You shut up now," she slurred.

"Iz, let's just face facts, all right? We're both properly pathetic right now."

She laid her head against his shoulder and slurped the rest of her drink in one go until all that was left was a blue tinge underneath the ice cubes. "I *hate* being pathetic."

Dex nodded in sympathy. "There, there. It'll pass." Get a load of him, sounding wise and accepting. He had not even checked his phone in the last hour. That was a vast improvement over the past two weeks.

"It fucking better. Fuck this, let's get another round. Start as we mean to go on."

"Pissed as shite," Dex agreed, and went to procure them more alcohol.

+

"I just hate that she still won't bloody act normal towards me."

She was wailing loudly enough to draw concerned looks from the other drunks staggering down High Street, which was not an entirely enviable position to be in. He held onto her a bit harder and did his level best not to steer them both into a pole.

290

"She's just a bit confused," he slurred in what he hoped was a soothing manner. He closed one eye, then switched over to the other. He was *fairly* certain he knew where they were going. Nearly. Essentially. "She'll come 'round."

"You've been saying that since *November*," she moaned. "It's January bloody first now, it's a *new year*, and still!" She shook her phone at him. "Nothing! I wished her a happy new year with a *heart emoji* and got fuck-all in return. I ask you!"

"Shhhh." He patted her on the head. She'd dropped her purple fedora a few streets back and had looked at it balefully before sighing and letting him know they must both move on if they were to continue on this earthly realm. "It's only, like, two am. It'll be okay."

"When?"

Dex shrugged. "Soon," he told her, then belched. "Oh, fuck, Iz."

"What. What. Are you gonna vom? Fuck, should have kept the fedora. Are you vomming? Do you need me to hold your hair?"

"No." He didn't think. "Don't touch the hair. No, not vomming."

They were jostled on both sides by a laddy group of staggering celebrants Dex hoped would take no notice of them. "What is it, Dexter-Baxter?"

He tried to remember what he was sad about. Oh, right. "He ran out on me," he said. "Kissed me so bloody good and then ran off."

Izzy made a sad face in return. "Aw. I know, babe. We've talked about it. He zhust needsh, you know…time. And shit."

"But how *much* time?"

"Should we just fucking get a fucking cab?"

Dex looked around the busy street. "In Cheltenham? On New Year's?"

"Ugh."

"Let's just…keep walking," he suggested and pulled her along. She clutched at him and staggered half a step behind.

"Don't toss us into a ditch."

"Are there ditches on High Street?"

"How the fuck should I fucking know, I'm not the one who lives here."

"I don't fucking live here, either, you cow."

"Tosser. Ha! Tosser. Toss into a ditch. *Toss toss toss.* I'm hilarious."

"You are, babe. You're the most hilarious."

"Tosser."

"Shut up now."

"All right."

✛

Dex's mum was the best mum. She had sneaked into the room just after ten sometime and left a pot of tea with two cups, a packet of paracetamol, and two glasses of water on his dad's desk. He had been vaguely aware of this happening and only realised its full import after Izzy kicked him awake in her sleep and rolled over, snoring.

He dislodged his body from hers and nearly brained himself in an attempt to untangle his limbs from the sheets. The room had been surprisingly stuffy for winter, and they'd managed to shove the duvet off at some point in the night. He had a wedgie all the way up to his taint, but it all paled in comparison to the headache currently pounding through his temples.

He sat up gingerly to test the waters. Murky. He buried his face in his hands. Luckily, his father's study was small enough that getting to the paracetamol and water was a matter of extending an arm and being able to form a grip.

He shouldn't have thought of waters, or at least should have taken the pill dry.

Oh God, he needed a wee.

He did not think he could make it down the stairs, though. He also did not think he could face his parents or Al just yet. His options, however, appeared slim. He could either wee out the window onto his mother's flower beds, go into his glass of water, or gather up what was left of his dignity and do his best at using an actual toilet.

"If you don't stop shifting around I'm going to murder you where you sleep."

"Oh, look who's bloody awake now."

"I hate myself," Izzy croaked. She didn't move. "I hate you. I hate tequila. I *really* hate Nat."

Dex shifted just enough that he could poke her in the arse. "Your phone went off at some point in the night. Don't you use Do Not Disturb?"

She almost nailed him in the balls in her scramble to get out of bed. "Don't do that again," he pleaded feebly.

"Holy fuck," Izzy breathed.

Dex popped one eye open and tried to focus on her. She was hunched over her phone on the floor in her bra and pants and mad hair, grinning like a lunatic.

"What? Don't make me come over there. Because I can't move."

"She's only gone and texted me back! Look!"

She thrust her phone in his direction and when he didn't respond quickly enough shoved it up to his nose.

Happy new year. See u soon, babe xo

"Whoa. That's basically a love letter right there."

"It is! Oh, God, I think maybe she'll actually act normal at some point. Like, we'll be able to have a proper conversation? Don't you think?"

"I do," he assured her, covering his eyes with an arm. "I really do."

"Unless…God, it was bloody half three in the morning. She must have been fucking paralytic. Oh God, do I respond or what? What if she regrets it? What if she doesn't mean it? Dex, help, oh God, what does it mean?"

"Babe," he whispered.

"What?"

"Shhh."

"Oh. Right." The futon dipped around his feet. "Want me to check yours?"

"Who cares. It'll just be a bunch of offers off Pizza Hut or some shit. Maybe Alex or Jonny will have texted."

Dex heard rummaging around where he'd dropped his jeans and jumper on the floor before crawling into bed and passing out. "Got it."

"Well?" he asked. "Out with it. *You have zero messages.*"

"Well, not zero," she said. "You've got a text off Jonny, that's nice. Oh, and a picture!"

"Please tell me it isn't him and Lance snogging, I couldn't bear it first thing in the morning."

"You are such an arsehole," she laughed. "No, but it *is* him and Lance and Alex and, oh! Nat! In a pub. They all look proper shitfaced, too, blimey."

"Get in," he mumbled.

"Anyway, he says, 'We miss you both come back soooooooon not the same without you,' with like ten heart emojis. Aw. That's nice."

"That's it?"

"Sorry."

He shrugged again and finally made himself move. He sat up. Swallowed through the dizziness. "Need a wee," he sighed, and did as both nature and society demanded of him.

It wasn't just that Dex had gone through the past few weeks pining and sad, but Dex had gone through the past few weeks pining and sad with a side order of ticked-off and confused.

When Nick had given him a boner and then ran off before they even made the fucking sauce, Dex hadn't quite known how to feel. Izzy had found him in the living room watching Antiques Roadshow and drinking the dregs of the wine, finishing off a packet of crisps and half a pack of digestives. If she hadn't known his plans for the evening, she probably wouldn't have worried, but she had, and she'd taken one look at his face and said, "What's happened?"

Dex still didn't really know. Well, he sort of did. But that didn't mean he couldn't resent the fuck out of it.

"Why?" he asked Izzy for the millionth time after they'd finally had his mum's fry-up for a very late breakfast and lazed in his parents' living room whilst his dad was having a kip, Mum had gone to work, and Al was busy doing Al things in his own room. "Why do I always fall for emotionally unavailable guys? What is wrong with me?"

"You're exaggerating. Didn't you have a nice boyfriend at school?"

"Yeah, at sixteen, for about a month. And then we got bored of each other."

"Of each other or you of him?"

"A bit of both. Anyway, that's hardly relevant. Michael was the *real* first relationship."

"Your schoolboy is feeling very sad and neglected. Wasn't he your first, like, shag?"

"Point taken. But we're talking relationship here, not just sex. I liked Jamal, but Michael was, you know. Love, I think."

"I know. But he's in the past, and Nick is now, and it's different."

Dex swallowed the Jaffa Cake as it transformed into a lump in his throat. "I am guessing he is also in the past, Iz." Finished before it had started.

The thing was, Dex could tell Nick had been into him. It took him a while to get there, but he wasn't a complete idiot. And if he hadn't known before that kiss, he sure as shit knew afterwards. Sadly, the afterwards had also included Nick shoving him away and running out like the house had been on fire, and then not contacting anyone and buggering off to America for the holidays.

Despite better judgment, Dex had texted him a few times. He'd received zero response.

"Maybe just give him time," Izzy said. Dex had attempted to get more out of her, because he had the distinct feeling that she knew something, but his every attempt at wheedling it out of her was met with assurance that it was none of her business nor his. Which was crap.

"Well, I don't fucking want to give him time. He doesn't need time, he needs to sort himself out, and I'm not going to wait around, it'll probably take a million years."

"That's bollocks, and you bloody well know it. If you fancy him, you can wait. And I think you do."

Dex switched the channel on telly a little bit more viciously than he had intended to.

"Ignore me all you want, but you know I'm right." There was an *Eastenders* omnibus on. He could ignore her forever if he wanted.

He did fancy Nick. He didn't particularly want to, all things being equal, but he did. He hadn't been able to stop thinking about that kiss in his kitchen. In one moment, a world of possibilities unfurled in his mind's eye. The things he would have done for Nick if only Nick had asked him. Had let him. It had been a while since Dex felt like that. Not just horny and happy to get off, but excited. Really excited about someone and the feel of their skin, the way they sounded when he made them feel good.

He had made Nick feel good. Nick had *liked* it. Liked Dex. Which was salt in the wound when he'd run off and disappeared without a trace.

"You're being melodramatic. He'll be back eventually. We'll probably see him before term even starts."

Dex highly doubted that last bit, even as the thought made his stomach fizz with sick anticipation. Dex knew Nick was good at making himself scarce. *I don't like being visible*, he'd told Dex once.

"Iz, he's just so fucking complicated. I don't know what to do. I don't know how to start anything."

"Babe. Just give him time. He may come around. It's not about you."

Dex didn't know if that made it better or worse. Maybe if it had been about Dex, he would have felt like he'd mattered. But what Nick had made him feel, first and foremost, was rejection.

"I think that makes it worse," he told her, and she petted him wordlessly and shoved a biscuit in his mouth.

Nick must have dozed off sometime after midnight, because he woke up on the couch covered by a blanket, and all the lights save for the tree had been turned off.

He blinked and focused on the glowing display of the cable box.

3:30

Eight-thirty in London already. He watched his mom's small tree, lit up in all colors, the garland winking with the lights, and zoned out. It was a miniature of the sort of tree they used to have when he was a kid. It had been years since his mom had bothered with anything bigger than this fake little one she kept in her closet the rest of the year.

New Year's had always been their big family holiday, but the last few years Zoyka had abandoned them to spend it drinking with friends, in true American spirit, while Nick stayed behind with his mom and Lena and toasted to the New Year over his mom's usual feast of Salat Olivier, kholodetz, gefilte fish, and all manner of cold cuts. And, of course, the main course of roasted chicken and potatoes, the sort that had always been Nick's favorite. They got so crisp and perfect, he would stand over the emptied baking pan and pick up the bits that the spatula had left behind.

This year, Zoya had stayed, and so had Jake, because of Nick. No Lena, of course. Nick hadn't heard from her. When he thought of her now, all he felt was overwhelming guilt for not feeling much at all.

When he thought of his mom, he also felt overwhelming guilt.

When he thought of Zoyka, and even Jake, too.

His Aunt Sveta, his grandparents.

Dex.

Nick turned over onto his back and shut his eyes.

Coming home had been so strange. Of course it had already snowed in Michigan, and after Zoyka squealed at seeing him and wrapped him up in a bear hug, the drive home had been tense. Dirty slush on the roads and, everywhere around them, the sort of snow-muffled silence that Nick had loved as a kid but now set his teeth on edge. Another strange realization—he hadn't been in a car in months. He'd ridden in a cab once, when they had all gone dancing. He wondered if he would even dare to drive now. The snow made it harder to recall the physical intricacies of controlling a car.

His mom had been so happy to see him, he'd felt a stab of vicious guilt when he realized that he hadn't quite been prepared to face her. He hugged her back tighter than he would have otherwise.

She'd fed him all his favorite foods, stared at him with her chin propped up on her hand as he sucked up three meals' worth of pelmeni. She had run her hand over his hair, twisted the curls of his bangs between thumb and forefinger, and said, "Synok. Did you fall in love over there or something?"

He kicked at the blanket now until it fell away from him. It was suffocatingly hot. He unzipped his hoodie, flopped around until he managed to free his arms, then shivered the next moment.

He'd said, "Ma!" as irritably as possible while his heart jumped into throat, and then he'd shoved more pelmeni in his mouth.

"What, *ma*? You have a look about you."

"Maybe with London."

He wasn't in love, though. It couldn't be love.

Whatever it was wasn't love, because love was supposed to make you feel good, and all he felt was desperation clawing at his throat. It was as if with one kiss, Dex had crawled inside him and laid a trap. *Got you. You won't escape easily from this one.* There was only so far he could run with its hook lodged in his chest.

It had been with relief that Nick switched out his British SIM card for his normal one once he got home. His number was back to a 734, and any messages from London remained inert on his other card. He relegated all social media to a folder buried deep inside his phone, just in case.

But the trap had been set, and whenever he shut his eyes at the end of each day, he relived that moment. Not even the kiss itself—although that stayed fresh in his mind in a way that terrified—but the moment when he had pushed Dex aside and run away like the biggest jackass on the planet.

What did Dex think of him now? Nick rotated on the couch like a pig on a spit. Get up and go to bed. Just do *something*. Brush your teeth. Take off your jeans.

He lay there, alternating crawling back under the blanket and shoving it to the floor, and listened to his mind whispering to him over and over and over again just what a mess he had made of everything.

Not the most auspicious start to the year.

✛

"I meant to get this for her by New Year's but didn't get to it. So it can be a present from you," Zoyka told him as they pulled into the mall parking lot.

"So what am I getting her?" Nick clambered out of the frozen car. It was so strange being back home. It felt tilted. Not quite right. The roads were too wide, the sidewalks too narrow with the piles of snow already accumulated from the first storm. The buildings were too squat, too sparse. Too much glass, not enough brick. The sky was perpetually blue once the storm had passed.

"Tupperware. I'm done with her saving Chinese containers." She rolled her eyes. "You give her the Tupperware, distract her, and I'll pack them all up and take them to the dump. Well, to recycling. Loving the planet, blah blah blah."

"She'll know it was your idea."

"It can be both of us. Saving her from herself. Reusing all that plastic can't be good for you."

They found a set with red lids at Target on post-Christmas sale. Zoyka made Nick trail after her through the clothing section, stopping in front of a clearance rack that made his eyes cross.

"Do you need anything? Socks or anything? My treat."

Nick really didn't. He started to say so, then stalled out as a figure walked around the jewelry corner and froze, something sparkly dangling from one hand.

They stared at each other for what felt like an eternity. Nick tracked every small change in Lena's appearance. Haircut, different color. Hardly any makeup at all. She still looked small underneath her bulky winter coat and sweater. She still wore her flowered Docs and jeans.

Nick raised his chin at her. Such a futile greeting. Her response was no less awkward. They might have sufficed with that, nodded at each other as if they hadn't been each other's firsts, hadn't held each other under her blankets hundreds of times, each lost in their own thoughts, as if they didn't know every secret about each other.

Well. Not every secret.

It might have ended with their nods, except Zoyka saw Lena, too. Nick saw the moment their eyes met because Lena's snapped alert. She shook her bangs out of her eyes and said, "Privet, Zoy."

"*O*, Lenka, privet! We were just—" She waved toward the cart with the Tupperware set inside it. "For our mom. Nick's home for the holidays."

"I figured. Well, my mom's waiting for me over there somewhere. Poka!"

She didn't look at him once as she turned on her heel and sped off to parts unknown. His lungs burned. His cheeks burned. He hadn't been prepared. How stupid was that? Of course they would have run into each other sooner or later. Their mothers were friends. How had he not expected this?

"You okay? Sorry I was awkward there, I just didn't know what to say."

"At least you said something. I just stood there like an idiot."

She eyed him. "Hey, so there's a new place Jake and I tried close to campus. They have awesome mixed drinks and funky appetizers and stuff, very froufrou. How about I treat you like you're an adult and take you there?"

"Uh, I'm underage." It was weird to realize that having crossed the ocean again, he had regressed.

"They don't always card. And anyway, you can get a virgin something, and we'll share the apps."

"Sure, why not." They hadn't gone out, just the two of them, in nearly half a year. Secretly, he always felt a little thrill when she would offer to take him out. Didn't matter how old he was and what he'd done, she was always the cool older sister.

"All right! You stroll, I pay. And then I'm throwing every shitty piece of plastic in mom's kitchen straight down the chute."

+

The froufrou place was called Yedi's. It was painfully hipster— fake tea lights in Mason jars on reclaimed wood

305

tables, mismatched chairs, and waitstaff all dressed in different patterns of plaid. The effect was marred only by the fact that everyone's booths and chairs were covered in bulky Carhartts and Lands' End jackets. It was hard to be cool in Michigan.

It wasn't even that packed—likely due to the bulk of the students still being off for winter vacation—and they were seated in a nook with Christmas lights strung above them.

"I know. It's hilarious. But the drinks and stuff really are good."

The waiter did not, in fact, ask for their IDs. Nick ordered his drink with as much self-assurance as he was capable of, and it was only after the guy disappeared that Zoyka looked up at him with huge eyes. "Check you out! You're all grown up!"

"Shut up."

The thing was, she kept him comfortable with chitchat until he was two-thirds of the way through his drink, which consisted of God only knew what but tasted amazing, then looked him in the eye, and said, "Tak. Bratishka."

"Hmm? Chego?"

"Chto s toboy proiskhodit?"

"What do you mean?" He gripped the glass, then wondered if that was a giveaway.

"I mean, something's going on with you, and I'm wondering what it is."

"Nothing's going on with me."

"Lenka. What happened there?"

Nick's heart was beating against his ribcage. *Thump-thump-thump.* She'd asked him this before, and he'd evaded her. For so long, he had evaded her. He planned on evading her now, except that when he opened his mouth, his tongue went on without him, and what he wound up blurting out was, "I can't tell you."

Shit.

"Kol'ka. You're so unhappy. Did you know that? What can't you tell me?"

He had always sought her attention, in the smallest of ways. Discarding it felt impossible even now.

"Look. I've noticed, *mama's* noticed."

"What has she noticed?"

She narrowed her green eyes at him. Nobody else in the family had green eyes. It was the strangest thing. *She looked at pine trees, so the pine trees stayed in her eyes,* his dad used to say about the time when he had taken her on a monthlong trip to Puschino while Nick had been sick enough that they had to be separated. That's how she'd come back. Green-eyed, at six. "That something's clearly happened. That you're unhappy in London, maybe, but I don't think that's it."

Nick shook his head.

"I think you love it there. So what's going on?" It occurred to Nick how weird it was that Zoyka wasn't considered the sensitive one of the Melnikov kids. To everyone else, she was the doer and Nick the dreamer. But not to him.

She was so *familiar*. Svoya. He'd forgotten what it was like to be with someone you really *knew*, from the inside out. Nick remembered how she had believed it was Jacek's friendship Nick had been mourning when their Polish neighbors moved back to Warsaw, how she kept telling him, *You can still email each other, or Skype. Friendship doesn't have to end here* as he slunk around the house at thirteen, knowing full well that Skype could never make up the loss. And—it *had* only been friendship. Just not for Nick. For Nick, it had been the worst secret he had ever had to keep.

"Kol'," she said quietly. "You're scaring me. You know that, right?"

He hated crying. He hated how little he could control it. He had to leave, at least run for the bathroom, but she held hard onto his hand, and they hadn't even gotten their check yet. He squeezed her hand.

"Zoy...Zoykin, I can't," he managed. "Can you pay? I gotta go. I'll be outside." He needed air. So much air.

She'd seen this enough times to know what was happening. After a hard squeeze, she let go of his hand, and Nick almost overturned the table as he shot up out of his seat.

The cold air hit him at once, and God, it felt so good.

When Zoya found him, Nick was more in control, but he was shaking all over. Without saying a word, she extended his coat and scarf toward him. She waited until he shoved them on, then took his hand and set off at a calm pace down the street, away from the car. The silence and the walk really did feel good. The rhythm of it steadied him, as did Zoyka's hand.

There was another parking lot down the street, and the cars sat separated from the street by a low brick wall. Whoever owned it must have had scruples—it was free of snow, and it was a matter of a hop for both of them to park their butts on it. It wasn't late, but the dark and the relative quiet of the street made it feel like one in the morning. Most people were in bars, restaurants, their homes, or simply out of town.

"Mom'd be pissed at you for sitting on the wall," Nick said as he looked at a darkened coffee place across the street. *Dozy's Donutz.*

"I know. I'll never have children if I freeze my ovaries off."

Despite everything, he snickered. Their mom lived and died by the old-world rules. Zoyka bumped his shoulder, and Nick stilled. He felt it, the change in the atmosphere. Here it came. She didn't make him wait too long.

"Kolechka, what's the matter?" she asked. She sounded like she had when they'd been kids. She always wheedled it out of him when he cried, even when she was only ten and he six.

Chto ty plachesh? Chto sluchilos'? Rasskazhi, malysh.

She'd always loved him. Since day one.

Nick took a deep breath. It escaped him in a puff of cold air, evaporating under his nose the next moment. The tinsel around the Christmas trees at Dozy's Donutz shivered, as if inside the darkness someone had opened a door and let cold air in. It sparkled off the streetlights.

He bent over double until he was a pretzel on that brick wall, and he thought, frantic and somehow certain, that this was it. He had to tell her. And he would just have to live with what came next.

Her hand on his back was sudden but still weirdly expected. She rubbed it up and down. He barely felt the motion of it through the parka. "Do you need more time?"

He shook his head. "I think." He frowned, then shook his head. "No, I know. Zoy, I'm gay."

He was intensely aware of her hand on his back. He didn't move for fear of it disappearing. He felt his heart beating, a rushing in his ears.

"I sort of thought maybe," she said. Nick looked at her and saw she was smiling. He startled when Zoya reached out and pushed a stray curl off his forehead. "You've been so freaked out recently, I couldn't imagine what you'd have to be so scared of, and then I thought...the breakup with Lena." She shrugged and dropped her hand. "Did you think I'd be mad?" she asked.

He nodded, then shook his head. Relief. That's what he thought it was, anyway. A hot crashing wave of *something* flooded his body. "I had no clue."

He fumbled for the words to describe what it had felt like, carrying this secret. Carrying it for so long, it became a lead balloon inside his chest propelling him backwards with every step.

"It's not because I thought you'd be freaked out," he finally managed. "It's just that I had—" *No words. No expectations. No way to even say it.* "We're not this."

She was frowning, but not like she was upset. She was thinking. "I know. But *you* are. You're ours. Do you think mom will stop loving you if you tell her?"

The very idea threw him into a panic. "You can't. Zoy, please. Don't tell her."

"Shush, stop! Of course I won't tell her, glupyi. Who do you take me for?"

"Okay." He was still breathing hard. "I'm not ready."

"I know. So you've got someone, then? A boy?"

His head felt so light, like he could faint. The up and down of tonight had him nearly limp with exhaustion, and now here it was again, another up and down. "Sort of," he managed. "No."

She raised an eyebrow. "All right, there's a story there."

"I *like* someone."

"A boy."

"Right." God, this was weird. It felt weird. Why did it feel weirder than telling her about Lena all those years ago? But it wasn't weird enough for him to stop now that he'd started. "We...I mean, he. I don't know. I think I fucked it up."

"Does he like you back?" she asked, like it was simple. "Have you. Have you guys—"

"We kissed," he said quickly. "And then I ran away. And we haven't talked since then."

"Oh, boy," she said, and he could hear the smile in it. Weird how it brought him more comfort than he could have imagined possible. "When was that? What's his name, by the way?"

"December thirteenth. Dex."

"You remember the date? That's serious."

"Don't."

"I'm sorry." And she meant it, he could tell. "Why did you run away?"

Because he was an idiot. Because he was a coward. Because Dex had wrung him from the inside out and undone him in the span of two minutes.

"But you still like him?"

"I do." She squeezed his middle in sympathy.

"So, you're really gay, huh?" she asked after a moment. Nick shuddered. "Hey, that's fine. It's okay. You know that, right?"

"But Mom."

"I know. It's gotta be terrifying, but..." Nick waited as he watched her gather her thoughts. "I guess this is really new. You talking about it is new. I feel like you've taken so much on, you know?"

Nick didn't, but he nodded anyway.

"Give yourself a little break. Don't think about Mom or what she might say right now."

He couldn't begin to imagine ever having the guts to tell her, feeling her confusion and disappointment and unhappiness.

"I know." Zoyka grinned. "Worrywart. But seriously. This was a big, brave thing you just did, telling me." She was looking him in the eye as she said it. He was the very opposite of brave, and they both knew it. He couldn't make himself contradict her. It felt too good to be called *brave*.

"Relax for a bit, all right? Feel the weight off those shoulders." She shook him a little, and he couldn't help laughing. "Can you do that?"

Nick nodded. He felt as if some tension really had seeped from his shoulders. Then he wondered if he was just deluding himself. Probably. But for the moment, it was nice to live a different sort of lie.

Now two people knew his secret.

No. Three. Three people knew it, and at least one of them still appeared to love him.

He wondered if Izzy would ever talk to him again after what had happened with Dex. He was under no delusions. Dex would have told her about Nick's kiss-and-run.

Dex. Best-case scenario was Dex was over him by now.

"All right. It's fucking cold out here, and I probably *am* freezing my eggs or whatever off. Let's go home and have some tea and watch *Ironiyu Sud'by*. Sound good?"

Nick breathed in and out. It came out fairly smooth.

Zoyka took them home via the scenic route. They were quiet in her Civic, letting the hush of January slip over them like a blanket. Zoya grabbed his hand, and Nick looked out the window, not pulling away.

Dex stood outside Nick's building and breathed on his hands to warm them against the chill of January wind. He had no idea what he was doing or why he was doing it. He just knew that all the crap that he'd been feeling over the holidays had boiled over into something he could no longer contain.

He had, at least, been able to wait until Friday before his feet took him here seemingly of their own accord.

On Monday, just as he had been blearily pouring coffee into a mug, Izzy sneaked up behind him and delivered the news that Nick was back.

Turned out, Nick hadn't received any of Izzy's messages at all until he got back to London. Something about his SIM card. Dex didn't care. He had yet to receive any response to his texts.

No. Nick was still avoiding him. And it was crap, because Dex had utterly failed to stop thinking about him. Instead, he was genuinely pissed off—something he hated, but also couldn't seem to shake. It was completely unfair, he knew that. Nick owed him nothing. But it had hurt. Hurt in a way he hadn't been prepared for. It had been monumentally stupid to go and start liking a boy before he was properly over Michael. Except, he found, he *was*. Over him. Because Nick.

What was worse, London felt more alive to him now that Nick was back. Even with all his hurt and simmering anger, Dex felt his heart thumping hopefully inside his chest. He'd almost turned around three times on the way here, but even as he considered and reconsidered the entire venture he knew he would go through with it. Now all that stood between him and Nick was a door, a staircase, and his own unwillingness to see what would happen on the other side.

Just talk to him babe

Izzy's text alert sat on his screen.

Easy enough for her to say. Even if she was right. He just had no idea where to start.

He took the stairs two a time, just to get it over with.

Hey, was just passing by, thought I'd say hi, by the way, why did you run out on me when things were going so well?

No.

Fourth floor.

Oh hey, Nick, how about we try that snog again?

Ha. Definitely not.

Sorry I accosted you with my mouth and hands and stuff. Truce?

Ugh.

He pictured himself walking through the door and throwing himself at Nick. Embarrassing. Or Nick opening the door and Dex turning right back around and running off in mortification. What he couldn't picture was Nick's face. What he might look like when he opened his door and found Dex on the other side of it.

His heart was going overtime by the time he found himself in front of Nick's door. He leaned in to listen, just on the off chance that maybe Nick wasn't alone. Or maybe was asleep. Oh God, what if he was asleep? What if he was in the bathroom? Fuck, fuck.

Just talk to him babe

Not helpful, Isabel. She hadn't been helping or had any pointers on how to start the conversation, and Dex was completely at sea.

He lifted his hand and rapped on the door.

It didn't take long. The room was tiny, after all. It couldn't have been more than five steps for Nick to cross it and open the door.

When he did, Dex had to force himself to breathe. Nick looked so pretty. Dex had nearly forgotten. He was barefoot, wearing a worn T-shirt and trackies. Behind Nick's glasses was an expression of such genuine shock that Dex found himself simply saying, "We should talk."

Nick swallowed visibly and stepped away from the door without a word. He seemed uncertain, but when Dex looked at him, Nick didn't look away.

"Nick," Dex breathed, and felt his muscles draining of tension. Something about seeing Nick's face, seeing him here, right in front of Dex, felt so good, he couldn't even hold onto his anger. "I'm sorry."

"Why? No, *I'm* sorry. I didn't..." He petered out, and Dex's lungs burned with anticipation.

"You didn't what?" Something about the muted light of Nick's desk lamp and that raw, uncertain expression on his face called for quiet. The only other sounds came from the bathroom pipes and the clanging of the radiator. Dex was beginning to sweat. His skin was too aware of Nick's proximity.

"I didn't think you'd wanna talk to me, actually." He sounded sad.

"Oh." Dex swallowed. "Why?"

Nick shook his head like he was dislodging thoughts and made the three paces towards the bed. Acknowledged Dex with a shift of his shoulders.

Dex shrugged out of his jacket and let it drop to the floor. Then he shucked off his shoes one by one and made his quick way to the bed.

They now faced each other the same as they had the time when he'd cooked for Nick and only *thought* of what kissing him might be like. When Nick had opened up, even just that little bit, and Dex had soaked it in.

The silence between them now weighed on Dex, but he waited a full minute before saying, "So why wouldn't I have talked to you?"

More than anything, he wanted to know that Nick was just as confused as he was, just as muddled. There was another part of him that was frightened, too frightened to admit to himself. The part of him that would hear Nick say, *I hadn't wanted to kiss you, I don't like you, I'm not queer.* Where Nick would look at him and say, *I never wanted you.*

Nick skittered his gaze over Dex, then looked at the wall and drew patterns with a single finger. "Because I was an asshole. And ran away."

Dex felt hunger build in his belly. Maybe it was messy hope. Whatever it was, he drank in the sight of Nick in front of him, all bony knees and elbows, mad hair, beautiful fucking mouth, those fox eyes framed by long eyelashes. He knew the question to ask now. Should have asked it before this whole mess had happened, but he'd been too fucking scared. "Nick," he said. "Are you gay?"

Nick visibly coloured. His throat and cheeks flushed an uneven pink, but when he met Dex's gaze, he didn't look away. "Yeah," he croaked. "I am."

Dex felt as if his very hands were on fire. He asked, "Have you ever been with a guy before?"

"No." His voice was barely a rasp, and Dex swallowed against the tide of regret that threatened to swamp him. *Fuck.*

He'd scared him. Of course he had.

"I'm sorry. I freaked you out."

"You didn't. You did, but...it wasn't all you." Nick was rubbing his face with both hands. He had nice hands. They were well-made and expressive. An artist's hands. Dex remembered holding Nick's hand before they kissed, sticking a plaster on his finger. A shiver went down his spine. He had to calm down. Rushing was what got them into trouble to begin with.

"What do you mean?"

"Oh God. I'm not out. I've—it's—" He broke off, clearly frustrated, and Dex wished he'd thought to bring beers or wine or anything to make this easier. "This is...new. It's hard to talk about."

"All right."

"Just, um. Wait here, okay?" Before Dex could reply, he was left alone in Nick's room.

Well. He was fairly certain that Nick wouldn't have actually run off on him again, if only because he'd have to come back eventually. Nick's room hadn't really changed since the last time Dex had been there. Maybe a few extra of those postcards, which were so banal it was adorable. No sign at all that Nick had been gone—not even a suitcase. Dex wondered where he even kept it. He was about to stretch out to look under the bed when the door opened and Nick walked in.

He was holding two Stellas. Nick grinned as he handed Dex a bottle. Then he plopped back onto the bed and mirrored Dex in leaning against the wall.

Dex accepted that if he wanted to get anything out of Nick, he would have to be the one to start the conversation. "So."

"The first person I told was Izzy. She guessed on her own."

Christ. Izzy had fucking known. He guessed she'd known something, but she never said.

It's none of my business, she'd told him. Fucking hell.

"But that's...that must have been just this past—"

"December."

"And you'd never said anything to anyone before? Not ever?"

Nick shook his head. He looked so small that his skinny, square shoulders were like armour rather than a part of his body. Dex wanted him so much.

"Fuck. How did you—" He shook his head. He had no idea where to start. "Wait, am I the second person to know?"

"I told my sister," he said quietly. "When I went home. Over break, I told her."

"Oh." Dex swallowed. "Uh, how did she...?"

"She was good. It went...she was great, actually."

Dex breathed out. "What about your—"

Nick shook his head. "Just Zoya."

Dex nodded. Made sense.

What didn't make sense was how Nick could have stood that. How he could have lived for twenty years and not breathed a single fucking word about being queer to anyone.

Dex could not have done it. And all those times they'd all just taken for granted that being queer was part of life and talked as if it was no bigger deal than anything else. All those talks about Nat, after Izzy had figured out she wasn't straight, all those times when Nick had just sat there, accepted it all, and kept fucking mum about everything having to do with himself. Never shared, not *once*.

How? How was that even fucking *possible*? Where did all of him fit inside that thin, rigid body? What else was he hiding? How was he managing it?

Dex felt filled to the brim with questions, questions bubbling up around other thoughts, thoughts like, *I know nothing about him,* and *What if that's how he wants it?* and *Told you, Izzy, emotionally unavailable. It would never work.*

"How? How did you—how could you live like that?"

Nick frowned.

Fuck.

"I guess—" Nick frowned, and his gaze was turned inward. Dex forced himself to relax his own shoulders, to breathe, to attempt to make this better without really knowing how.

"Wait. I'm sorry. You don't have to explain. You're—" *Different.* And he was. Dex was being an utter bellend. "You told me once that you felt like you passed. Being Jewish, that is, that you didn't look it. Has being gay been like that?"

Nick genuinely flinched. "It's been worse."

Dex felt a dark shiver down his spine. "Why?"

Nick took a long pull of his beer, which drew shadows across his throat. "Because I'm not supposed to exist."

"Nick—"

"No, really." Nick pushed on, and Dex forced himself to shut up. Nick was talking. He was *talking.* "I've never known another Russian gay person. I'm sure they exist, I mean, duh, of course they do. I know that. Now. But when I was a kid, I had never met one. I didn't know anyone. I didn't know any gay people."

Dex was frozen.

"I don't—I was alone. My parents never talked about anything like that, not ever. At least, not when I was a kid. And then they talked about it like it was something Americans did. Some Western thing. Not necessarily awful, just not for us. Not *ours.* So I couldn't be…that. I couldn't. I could be Jewish, I could be an immigrant, but I couldn't be gay."

Dex took a deep breath. His parents hadn't been thrilled when he'd told them, but they got past it. And he *could* tell them. He knew of kids who couldn't. Natali was still fighting her battles. God, being black and queer hadn't been a fucking lark. He tamped down the memories, tried to bury them as they threatened to float up to the surface. Looking through gay magazines and seeing white guy after white guy, turning to porn and seeing only white guys or, worse, black guys without faces.

But he didn't know anyone who'd flat-out never said a fucking word.

"Fuck. That's—harsh, man. That's really hard."

When he looked at Nick, Nick simply shrugged it off, like he always did. Dex felt an overwhelming urge for Nick to admit everything he wasn't willing to admit so he would see for once that he didn't have to bear it all in silence.

"Nick, for fuck's sake. You just admitted it was horrible, why are you always shrugging shit off?"

What was he doing? *Making it even worse*, a small voice reminded him, but he was too gone to listen to it.

"Do you know that you never fucking talk about yourself?"

"That's not true!" Nick rose up on his knees so they faced each other. It wasn't exactly an easy position to maintain, knees digging into the soft mattress in a lack of balance.

"It is! You give the barest of facts, you just throw shit out there like it's nothing, even though it's clearly *not* fucking nothing, and then you swallow it back down, like you're not supposed to talk about it, but you get you're no longer a kid, right? You get that you can, and you *should* fucking tell people this shit, and you don't have to live like that?"

The sound of Nick slamming his hand on the wall brought him up short. Nick looked furious. Terrified. It seemed impossible that the two should coexist, but Dex saw it, all of it.

He was breathing fast, waiting for Nick to give him more. Vaguely aware that this wasn't at all what he'd come looking for when he'd come here tonight, Dex couldn't stop this ball rolling if he wanted to. He didn't want to.

"I talk! Nobody fucking wants to hear this shit, all right? It's boring, nobody needs it! What the fuck would talking about it do, anyway?"

"It's not *boring*, Jesus, do you not listen when people ask you things? They want to *know*!" Dex threw the last vestiges of being cool to the fucking wind. "*I* want to know! I've told you I find it—"

"Okay, but for how long? How long do you think you would listen for?" Nick yelled over him. "Because if I start, I'll never stop, okay? If I start, I'll never *stop*."

His voice was shaking along with the rest of him, and Dex was paralysed. He hadn't—he hadn't meant for this. He had never meant for this.

Dex didn't think. He unfroze, reached out, tugged Nick's arm away from the wall, and then he pulled him in. Nick went like he had no other choice, and the next moment Dex had him in his arms. Nick's beer had spilled between them, soaking the duvet and their knees.

"I'm sorry," he whispered. "I'm so sorry," he repeated, again and again.

Nick wasn't hugging him back, just allowing himself to be held. Dex swallowed. Nick's glasses were digging into his collarbone. They were both trembling now, like Dex had taken on Nick's fear, and maybe that was good. Maybe that was what Nick needed. Had always needed. Dex took it, and he let himself be a spot for Nick to rage against.

Dex realised that Nick's rage wasn't like other people's rage. It was contained heartbreak, the kind that didn't know where to go. Nick's hands found Dex's shirt and grabbed on like pincers. Even as he quivered in Dex's arms, Dex wanted him frantically. Desperately.

He sagged down. Nick was light, and he didn't put up a fight. It was easy for Dex to nudge him away just long enough to slide the glasses off. Dex set them down on the bedside table. He splayed his knees to allow Nick to settle in between, and Nick did. Dex wished he could see his face.

But Nick buried it against Dex's neck, and they sat there in a deafening silence. Dex didn't know if his pulse ever would slow. God.

Kissing the top of Nick's head felt so natural, he did it once, then twice. He lingered there, just holding him. He heard Nick's breath hitch, felt it against his own chest, but neither of them spoke.

It felt like a long time, and also like no time at all. Dex was cold when Nick pushed himself away. He held his breath.

"Sorry. That wasn't. Sorry, I was stupid, and you—"

"I was stupid, too," Dex interrupted, and he thought about what he'd said. "I mean…I was stupid. You weren't. I'm so sorry I yelled. That was a dick move." He didn't know what else to say. It all felt too big for words.

"You were right. I don't know what to do." He stayed where he was, still halfway between Dex's knees.

"What if we just talked?"

"Yeah?"

"Yeah. And you can say anything. I want to hear it all."

Nick's face was a picture of skepticism.

"Or, you can not tell me a thing. But I'd like to stay with you for a bit. If that's all right."

It felt like an age before Nick nodded and finally looked at him. Nick seemed done in, but Dex felt his chest lifting. "Yeah. I just have to…first." He indicated the bathroom and slowly got up.

It wasn't until the door lock clicked that Dex assessed the situation. Nick's duvet was ruined and smelly with beer. He got up and left the door open as he ran to the kitchen and poked his head in the fridge. He found two more Stellas, hoped they were Nick's, grabbed them, ran back. Nick was still in the bathroom, so Dex popped them open with his key ring, left them on the desk, then set to work on the duvet situation.

He dragged it off the bed, flipped it soiled-side down, and made a sort of nest on the floor.

There was hardly any floor left when he was done. He grabbed the two Stellas off the desk and just managed to get his arse onto the duvet when the bathroom door snicked open and Nick walked out.

He looked exhausted. He'd tried to tame his hair with some water to zero success, and wet ringlets hung down his forehead. His cheeks were splotchy pink, eyes swollen and glassy. Dex extended a beer towards him. His reward was a tiny crack of a smile—lopsided, uncertain, but a smile.

Nick made his careful way around Dex so he could settle down across from him, back against his bedside table. "Look, I really am—sorry," he said.

"You don't have to be sorry."

Nick shook his head. "I am, though."

Dex waited.

"I should have said something. Texted you. Or...*something*, but I couldn't. I'm sorry."

Dex thought about it all, remembered running after him. "You were scared, I get it."

"I was terrified." Nick's voice had never sounded more firm. "But I hate that, okay? I hate being terrified. I'm done with being terrified."

He *looked* terrified, but stubborn, too. Determined. His cheekbones stood out as he set his jaw and looked at Dex. Dex's fingers twitched around his beer. "All right."

Nick shifted and moved one leg until the tips of his toes were touching Dex's ankles. Dex held his breath.

"I like you," Nick said quietly. Dex clenched his jaw. "And I want you to know that. Now."

"Good." *Crap.* "I like you, too." Might as well, right? "A *lot*. Glad we've got that sorted, then."

Nick laughed. He looked at Nick's uneven teeth, imperfect in his gorgeous mouth. He looked lit up from the inside. Maybe it was that his eyes were no longer spooked.

Dex pressed his advantage. "So, tell me things, then."

"What kinds of things?"

He shifted until Nick's toes slipped under his ankle. "Things that you've not let yourself say out loud before."

Nick took in a deep breath—so deep, his chest filled out before collapsing in on itself again. "I'm always scared that my mom can see what I'm doing. Or hear what I'm thinking."

"Wha—?"

"When I was a kid, I saw this movie. It was some...fantasy, I don't even remember what it was called. It was in Russia. Anyway, the main character had this magic ball of some sort, like a fortune-teller's, and all she had to do was ask it to show her a person, and it would. It would show her what they were doing at the time. It left an impression. And I really wanted one, too. I guess I internalized the possibility. That sounds dumb."

"It doesn't." It made a bizarre sort of sense.

"Well, ever since then, I've imagined my parents having one and knowing everything about me. It really does sound dumb out loud, Jesus."

"No. I think I get it."

"When you and I...When we kissed." It was the first time either of them had actually said the words to each other. "In the back of my mind, I thought my mom could see. After I ran away, I thought I was gonna throw up."

Dex shut his eyes. Not exactly the reaction he had been hoping for, but this wasn't about him. He felt a warm touch to his hand. He looked up. Nick was watching him, and when Dex moved his hand, their fingers caught.

"I fucked up so much. I felt like I couldn't stop fucking up."

"You didn't."

Nick squeezed his fingers and then slowly let go. "I did, though. And I guess it's okay, because you're still here."

"I am."

A pause. Wondrous. "Thank you."

With anyone else, he wouldn't hesitate to close the distance, kiss them, take control. But not with Nick. Tender and fragile, that's how Dex felt around him. Clumsy and skirting disaster from too much feeling. So he waited.

It took barely any time at all, in the end. Nick, eyebrows drawn in concentration, rose up a little on his knees. Dex was aware of his every move. Aware of how much closer Nick suddenly was, and how hard the bed frame dug into his shoulder because he'd tensed in anticipation. Every tiny moment of Nick shifting closer sparked off Dex's skin, electrified him into disbelief.

Nick leaned in, and their gazes met in a deliberate question. Dex looked at Nick's lips.

Dex leaned in. So did Nick.

Their first kiss had seemed so natural, and had ended in such utter disaster, Dex hadn't been sure this would even happen.

Nick kissed him. His lips touched Dex's and lingered. It felt so all-encompassing it was painful. It became impossible to wait, and so Dex slotted their lips together on a gasp. He closed his eyes and he simply held on.

He felt their kiss in his whole being. Felt the way Nick leaned into him—their bodies barely touching, connected at their lips and nowhere else. The close warmth of his presence was making Dex's head spin. Nick was letting himself kiss and be kissed, and it was making Dex's head spin.

Nick opened his mouth, and Dex found the courage to touch his jaw, and then it was as if a thread had snapped and they went frantic. Tongues and breath, too much of everything, and not enough. Dex went by feel and instinct, forgot all about technique and playing it cool and anything that wasn't Nick clinging to him, devouring him whole, and then Nick was climbing into Dex's lap, wrapping his slender arms around Dex's neck.

Dex couldn't breathe. He was all synapses and nerves, fingers that sought and clutched at Nick's back, his waist, against his ribs under his T-shirt. Dex felt the weight of him, his thighs and knees digging into Dex's hips, his hands roaming Dex's back, and he had to hold himself back not to rip Nick's shirt straight off of him, to grind up against him and get him off, make him lose his mind.

Dex was losing *his* mind.

He wanted to get closer, feel even more, get to Nick's skin, *fuck*, get underneath it. His fingers found Nick's hair all on their own, and he grasped it, felt the silky-coarse texture. His mind raced ahead of him, images of Nick naked beneath him, a sea of possibilities of Nicks—smooth and hairless chest, or maybe a sparse dusting of hair all down his stomach, or maybe it was tight curls, like Dex's. His mouth was flooding with want, his dick with blood, his veins with heat. It didn't matter what Nick looked like beneath his flimsy shirt and trackies, Dex was fucking desperate for him.

When Nick broke off, Dex fought back panic that he'd retreat and halt the moment. He held his breath. When he pulled back and looked at him, Nick's lips—God, those fucking lips, now shiny and flushed—smiled.

Dex caught his breath and unclawed his fingers, allowed them to settle at his nape. "All right?"

Nick leaned in until their foreheads touched. The heat between them rose close to unbearable. "Yeah. Yeah. I'm all right."

When Dex leaned up again, his breath ghosting just over Nick's mouth, Nick met him halfway to the kiss. He didn't hesitate.

24

Nick wasn't all right. He felt frenzied and wild, a river gushing past a crumpled dam. It rolled through him, and for the first time ever, he allowed it.

Dex's arms around him were the only grounding thing about this room, the whole world, maybe. His ears still rang with all the things he'd never said before, and now that he was saying them he felt nearly empty, hollow in spaces that had been too crowded for too long.

He was so hard. He squirmed in place not to give himself away too soon, but the more they kissed, the harder he got, the less he could stop himself from sidling even closer.

He wondered if he was crushing Dex, but Dex was holding him so tight, Nick couldn't escape if he wanted to. Not that he would want to. What he did want, or what he could pick out of his myriad wants, was to get more. He wanted more of Dex's mouth and his tongue and his breath and his skin.

Dex broke them apart. Dex wasn't pushing him away. Instead, his hands moved until he was caressing Nick's cheeks, which already felt too hot to bear, and looking at him. Dex's look, usually warm and attentive, was enflaming.

"Nick." If Nick had felt undone by the way Dex said his name back in his kitchen that December Sunday, it was nothing compared to now. The consonants sounded so soft on his tongue, the 'k' a gentle click of his throat. Nick barely breathed.

The next moment, when Dex brought his thumb up to Nick's mouth and touched his lower lip, Nick felt his breath stutter back.

Dex's touch. The way his finger slid gently over Nick's lip and his eyes followed the movement, hot, sending shiver after shiver down Nick's back.

"Your mouth." His finger was gone and replaced by his lips. Nick surrendered to the feel of him. He felt it again, that cleaving in two—before and after. With each kiss, the after drew him deeper and deeper in. He hadn't ever felt like this before, and he had never known he could.

His heart beat even harder when Dex placed his palm against it over Nick's shirt. Nick's hands roamed, touch-hungry, over Dex's arms and sides and neck. Their breath was hot and damp, electrifying.

It smelled like a *kiss*.

Nick had always loved kissing. That had been the best part of the physical stuff he and Lena had shared. If everything else made him feel clumsy and awkward, kissing her he could have done for hours. And had.

After a while, it had become a delaying tactic.

With Dex, it was a prelude to everything he could have ever wanted and had no idea how to ask for. But beyond the want and need and the hesitant freedom, Nick couldn't stop thinking about all those boys Dex had been with, all the ones who'd probably known exactly what to do when Nick had no idea where to even start. So Nick kissed him as best he could, and then, between one moment and the next, closed the distance enough that his erection ground against Dex's hip.

"Oh *fuck*." Dex's voice ran through Nick like a knife. He shuddered. It was, all of it, so much. It was too much, and he probably should have been stopping, but the crack in Dex's voice, his breath so hot against Nick's mouth, and the feel of him, even through layers of fabric, was close to sending Nick over the edge. He didn't want to stop. Couldn't.

"Can we—" He didn't know how to ask for it. He didn't know what to ask *for*. He was filled to the brim with too much sensation and not enough thought.

"Yes, God. What do you want, I'll do—whatever."

Nick kissed Dex. Ground so hard that they both gasped in just a little bit of pain, but he didn't know what to say. He felt small and stupid and completely out of control. Dex ran his hands all the way down Nick's back, setting him alight in the wake of his touch, grabbed Nick's ass, and pulled him in.

Nick rocked against him. Dex's hands guided him away, then pulled him back in. Nick squeezed his eyes shut and rocked once more, rolling his hips in a way that felt unbelievably dirty and unbelievably *good*. He let Dex guide him.

Dex's touch was hard, nearly painful, but it felt like purchase and allowed him to lose himself in the rhythm. Dex moved his mouth down Nick's jaw, to the spot that had nearly undone Nick the first time they'd kissed.

Nick gasped. All his bones felt liquefied. Dex sucked. Moved them both faster. Nick tried to stop himself from making noise, tried to contain it, even a little, but then Dex's harsh breath ghosted over his ear and he murmured, "Just like that, baby, yes. God. So fucking good." And Nick couldn't have stopped if his life depended on it.

He rode the wave, rode Dex's hips, let it wash him so far off shore he may as well have been lost to sea. He didn't fucking care. He *was* lost to it, all of it. To Dex, to his truth, to all that had been laid bare in this small, warm room.

He wrapped his arms around Dex's neck, his dreads dry and a little prickly against his skin, pushed himself even closer, lost the rhythm of it but kept going anyway, and then Dex took hold of his hair, pulled him back, and crushed his mouth against Nick's. It wasn't even a kiss. Mouths hungry, tongues seeking and finding filthy contact. Nick's blood rushed south. He tried to stem the tide, to get enough control not to come, but Dex whispered against his mouth, "You're close, aren't you? God, so fucking *hot*." Nick shuddered uncontrollably and came.

A murmuration of starlings, this release, like a vast emptying of thought. He trembled in place, but Dex had hold of him and Nick felt, for the first time, like he could fall apart and not hit the ground on impact.

When he came down, he could tell Dex was still hard—and that was a revelation, the sheer physicality of Dex's want—and Nick tried to give something back. He hid his face in Dex's neck and snaked his hand down in between them until he felt it. Then he ran his palm all the way down Dex's erection, felt Dex shudder against him. In the silence where all he could hear was Dex's breath, Nick worked his palm up and down the hard length.

It felt like—nothing else. If he had allowed himself to think of it before, he would have thought it would be like getting himself off, mechanical and easy. He hadn't expected to feel that longing tug in his belly, or the way in which his own pulse stuttered under his skin. This was *Dex*, and Nick was making him feel good.

Spurred on by the way Dex grabbed onto him and let him do this in silence, Nick fitted his fingers against as much of Dex's dick as he could with denim in the way and worked him faster, pressed against him harder. He licked a stripe up Dex's neck, bit his earlobe. Tasted the salt of his skin again and again. And then Dex tensed, gasped, and shuddered as he came. Nick felt the heat of it against his hand a moment later, and a lightness stole over him, so fizzy and bright he had to hide his grin in the darkness of Dex's neck.

They breathed against each other as Dex came down. Dex stroked Nick's hair and held him. Nick let him.

+

Dex roused them. Kissed the side of Nick's head, forcing a tiny wave of shivers down his skin, then pulled Nick gently away.

"You all right?"

Nick nodded. The situation in his pants wasn't too pleasant, but he would endure it tenfold if it meant staying this close to Dex. "I'm good. I mean...really good."

That was when Dex's dimples appeared. Nick relaxed at the sight of them, breathed out.

"Yeah?" Dex's voice was soft and a touch uncertain.

In a fit of courage, Nick placed both thumbs in his dimples. "I love your dimples."

Dex huffed out a tiny laugh, and Nick watched as he shut his eyes, looking lost in—well, Nick, he supposed. In pleasure. He looked content. He had such pretty eyelashes.

Emboldened, Nick let his hands wander. Touched Dex's cheeks, then slipped lower, felt his jaw, his neck. A rasp of stubble against his skin. He had no idea that something as simple as stubble would do a thing for him, but it did. He spread his hands and then ran them down to Dex's collarbones, letting his thumbs stretch out the collar of his T-shirt, exposing more skin. Even though he'd seen Dex shirtless before, his heart still sped up at the idea of being able to see it again. To be allowed to look his fill. He cupped Dex's shoulders, gave them a bit of a squeeze. Hard but yielding.

He checked that Dex's eyes were still closed, then ran his hands towards the middle, over Dex's chest. Across his heart. The room was still around them.

Dex's breathing changed again. So did his own. He took in air deliberately, followed thought with movement, slipped his hands further down, over the planes of Dex's abs. This time when he looked at his face, Dex was watching him. No trace of a smile now, and his eyes so dark. Nick didn't let himself stop.

He ran his fingers down until he could catch the edge of Dex's shirt and tug it up. Just the smallest bit, exposing a thin strip of skin. He dipped his hands beneath it.

Dex stayed still. Nick felt him tense beneath his touch, but not like he didn't like it. More like he was trying to stay still for Nick.

Dex's skin was smooth and warm. Again, a revelation. Not like he'd never touched other people's skin before, and not like a person's stomach was some great unknown, but his pulse sped up just from this. He never wanted to stop. He swept his thumbs toward the middle and felt a change in texture and springy curls. He leaned in. He had no direction. He knew now that he had started, he never wanted to stop touching Dex, and Dex was letting him.

So he touched his lips to the rounded edge of a collarbone. Dex was breathing fast and shallow. Nick shut his eyes. Kissed the spot again. Dex's fingers twitched where they were planted on his hips—and how could he have forgotten that he was being touched too? But he had.

He moved until he could kiss the dip of his throat. In the stillness, he felt Dex drop his head back to give him room. Nick took it all. He licked his neck, kissed the side, sucked on a spot. The frenzy was returning. Not even five minutes after coming, he was filled with heat.

Nick moved his hips and felt the answering fullness of Dex's cock against his own.

If they were going to do this again, they'd need fewer clothes.

Nick stilled. He wanted Dex naked more than he could remember wanting anything in his whole life, but—that was Dex.

And this was him, in all his gangly, pasty-white, awkward glory.

Dex didn't give him a chance to question it. He was grabbing Nick's hair and pulling him into a kiss. No preamble, it was a full fucking kiss, his tongue melting Nick from the inside out. Now they had started again, they weren't stopping.

Dex plucked at the back of his T-shirt, rucked it up, and Nick broke off the kiss to raise his arms and let Dex do his worst. His T-shirt landed on the other side of the room, but he barely noticed, because Dex touched Nick's back. His skin was coming alive under Dex's fingers. He was trembling.

"Fuck, *Nick*."

Nick could have sobbed with how good that felt. He leaned back enough to grab fruitlessly at Dex's T-shirt, but the angle was wrong. "Can we—"

"God, yes, please. Here."

He grabbed Nick's bare waist with both hands—Nick nearly buckled—and lifted him up enough that he could get his legs underneath him. Then they were somehow up and scrambling to get Dex's T-shirt off him.

Dex reached for Nick's sweatpants and Nick reached for Dex's jeans, and he knew they were both a mess inside their pants but he didn't fucking care.

Dex succeeded first, and Nick stilled with his hands on Dex's zipper, which in itself felt like the most intimate thing he'd ever been permitted to do.

He swallowed hard as Dex nudged him to step out of his sweatpants.

"Oh."

Dex wasn't watching his face. Oh God. Was he not enough? He couldn't figure out Dex's expression. "What?"

"I thought—you're intact."

Nick frowned.

"I mean, you're Jewish," Dex said, smiling. "I thought you'd be cut."

"Oh." Nick grinned despite himself, like he wasn't literally on display in front of the person he wanted most in the whole fucking world. "No religion, remember? No religion, no mohel. No mohel, no bris."

Dex pulled him in and kissed him. "Well. I know just what to do with you."

He was so fucking hard. He wanted so much. He wanted everything.

"C'mon," he whispered and tugged on Dex's zipper. "Now you."

Dex stepped back and took care of his own situation. Nick watched with wide eyes as he stepped out of his jeans and briefs all in one go.

God. Dex was fucking breathtaking. He looked like a picture. He was *everything*. Nick's throat went dry, but he couldn't stop *looking*. Dex's cock was so dark, and so hard.

"Oh, God, is that a tattoo?"

Dex looked unfocused as he glanced down. "Wha— oh, right. Yeah. It's—it's stupid, I know."

It wasn't. It was beautiful. Black ink curving around his upper thigh in the space where the cut of his hip ran into sparsely haired leg. Three lions, it looked like, two lying down, one standing tall behind them.

"Is that—"

"Pride. I know." Dex rolled his eyes. "Corny."

"No, it's beautiful." Without thinking, Nick reached out and grazed a finger across it. Dex hissed. Nick splayed his fingers, marveling at his own bravery, and took the final step that separated them. He looked up and wove his free hand under Dex's dreads, pulled him close. Felt the wetness of their tips licking at their bellies and hips. "You're beautiful," he whispered.

Dex grabbed him around the waist and kissed him. "God. C'mere." Dex sat and pulled Nick down until they both toppled onto his stripped-down bed, and *oh*. There was so much skin touching skin. Nick was drowning in the feel of Dex, so close and warm and alive next to him.

It took a while, but they eventually managed to settle the right way on the bed, and when they did, they couldn't stop kissing. Nick's hands didn't know where to land, so he touched Dex everywhere he could reach. His inexperience became a problem when Dex showed every sign that he wanted to move beyond aimless groping and Nick tore his mouth away from Dex's to try and—he honestly didn't know what.

Dex latched onto his throat with his lips and teeth, forcing a shuddering gasp from Nick's mouth and gooseflesh all down his skin.

"God, you're so—*fuck*," Dex said against him, and Nick was probably in a dream, because this felt too fucking good to be real. "What do you want, baby, what can I do?" Dex talked as he moved, his lips barely touching Nick's skin and still forcing endless shivers from him. Hot breath, hard teeth, soft tongue, and Nick was losing his mind just from the endearment alone.

"I don't—"

He could barely think, much less talk, much less know what to even ask for. With Lena, it had been a sort of done deal every time. Some touching to start off with, but mostly it was just...sex. And then a vast emptiness for a long moment after, filling him up with postorgasmic sadness that felt absolute. Like he was broken inside.

He realized with a belated clarity that he hadn't gotten the same flooding sadness in his chest after coming with Dex. He'd simply felt good.

Dex moved further south, interrupting Nick's thoughts. Dex moved until it was no longer a question of what he was doing. His dreads spilled messily against Nick's belly, and Nick swallowed, watched helplessly as Dex wrapped one hand around Nick's waist and pulled back the foreskin with his free hand and licked the tip of Nick's dick.

Nick's neck arched. It wasn't—he wasn't—*fuck*.

"God, you're so wet." Dex's breath ghosted over the sensitive skin, and Nick squeezed his eyes shut in a panic, tried to think of *anything* that wasn't Dex's mouth a breath away from his cock, because he was liable to come before Dex even got his lips around him. Nothing, absolutely nothing was coming to mind, so he reached down and squeezed the base of his dick in an attempt to stem the tide. His heart was going to burst.

He heard Dex mutter a curse under his breath.

"I'm sorry, I just—" Jesus. He was gonna die of embarrassment.

"Are you fucking kidding me? That is so fucking hot. *Nick.*"

Nick had no words for him, because the next moment, Dex wrapped his lips around him and went down. Nick bit his own wrist. He still had a grip on the base, and so he felt the movement of Dex's jaw against his wrist, the swallow of his throat. His skin came alive where Dex's dreads caressed it, and his spine arched off the bed from trying not to come.

Dex was amazing. Nick had gotten blow jobs before, hell, he'd even gone down on Lena, but it wasn't—it hadn't ever been this ownership. Because that's what it felt like. Dex owned what he was doing, with his whole body and heart, and with that, he owned Nick. For just this moment in time, he had Nick's pleasure in his hands and his mouth, and Nick felt it overwhelming him as he lost himself to sensation. So tight, so wet, so *hot.*

Then Dex pulled away and wrestled Nick's thighs apart enough to settle in between, splaying him, putting Nick on show, and before Nick could do a thing about it, went back down. Nick cried out. He felt so fucking wanton with his thighs spread by Dex's shoulders, completely at his mercy, trying not to thrust up but failing. And Dex wasn't playing around. He wasn't taking his time about it, he was laser-focused and so fucking *good*, Nick could no longer hold back.

He let go of his dick and patted Dex's hair, babbled, "Gonna—gonna come," and finally, Dex pulled up. But it was just enough that when Nick shuddered, tensed, and came, Dex had the head in his mouth and looked at Nick. If Nick could get hard again, he would have in that very moment. Dex owned him, all right. It felt as if he came forever, pulse after shuddering pulse until he was run dry.

Done, he fell back and tried to get control of his breath.

Dex finally let go with a dirty popping noise that made Nick's bones quiver, and Nick felt him drop onto the bed next to him.

Nick drifted somewhere around the ceiling, vaguely groping for the familiar sadness of posteuphoria, but all he found was the awareness of Dex lying beside him. He managed to raise himself up on his elbows, and when he looked down, Dex had his dick in a grip, hand not moving.

"Come here," Nick whispered.

Dex looked tense and beautiful, sprawled naked on Nick's bed, watching Nick like he was all he wanted to watch forever. There was a trace of Nick's come at the corner of his mouth.

Giddiness welled up in Nick's belly. He reached out a hand and said, "Let me."

Dex moved up until they were lying face to face, and Nick kissed him, tonguing that bit of come from Dex's lips. Dex shuddered, opened his mouth. Nick tasted himself on Dex's tongue. He went slow, swallowing Dex's gasps. Dex was so generous with them. Nick drank him in, inhaled him, and it was—everything.

"I can't—yet." Nick fought through embarrassment. "But I want to—"

"Anything. Just touch me, anything, *please*." His breath ghosted against Nick's mouth. Without thinking, Nick kissed him again, bit his chin, reached for his dick.

The next moments were filled with their ragged breathing and the sounds of Nick's hand learning the feel of Dex. Nick wasn't getting hard anytime soon, but he was so turned on, so tuned in. Everywhere he touched Dex felt like a relearning of himself.

Where his fingers gripped Dex, he felt an awakening of every bone and tendon and skin that did it. Dex's cock was like silk to his touch, the thickness of it different from his own, and God, so much *more*. Dex was still, but his shallow breathing was giving him away. His mouth hung open, shiny, hint of pink tongue behind his teeth.

Nick sidled closer, sped up his hand to a rhythm he could control. He didn't want to blink for fear of missing anything. He was rewarded with a ragged moan, a thrust of hips. He wanted Dex to move, to lose control the way Nick had, so he grew bolder. On the upstroke, he cupped his hand around the tip, deliberately slid it down so he exposed the head, spread the moisture he found there, and Dex hissed through his teeth, eyes squeezed shut.

Hand beginning to cramp, Nick went on, just a little faster, a little harder, a little slicker.

"God, yeah, just like that." Dex's voice was grit and sand. Nick hid his face in the crook of Dex's neck, which smelled so good. Smelled like the both of them.

Dex stopped being still.

He thrashed against Nick, hips pumping, belly pressed up hard against Nick's hand. They were so close.

Dex was so close.

Nick squashed the urge to slide down the bed and reciprocate the blow job. His mouth flooded at the thought, but he'd just mess it all up, and Dex was getting closer. The thought wouldn't leave him alone, though, so he did the next best thing he could think of and put his mouth back to work on Dex's neck. Dex made a strangled noise and flopped backward, giving Nick the unexpected freedom to roll over him and continue working him just like that. Dex laid out on his sheets, struggling to breathe, hips pumping, and

Nick with the newfound freedom of pinning him there and watching his face.

It didn't last long after that. They panted together in the silence of the room until Dex's voice broke and he tensed up—so, so hard—then shuddered beneath Nick for a wild moment as he came. Nick worked him through it, couldn't seem to let go, because he felt and looked so *good*, but eventually Dex pushed his hand away. It was gentle, and Nick barely had time to feel stupid because the next moment, Dex tangled their fingers together and pulled until Nick landed on his chest.

"Fuck. That was one hell of a hand job, man." There was laughter in his voice, and Nick hid his smile against Dex's chest. He felt a kiss on top of his head just as Dex squeezed him harder from all sides. "Well worth waiting for."

Nick, still smiling like an idiot, bravely settled his thigh on top of Dex's. "You were waiting for it?"

"Babe, you've no idea."

Despite himself, Nick lifted his head enough to catch Dex's eye. "How long?"

"You really *haven't* got any idea, do you?"

His face grew serious. He ran his fingers through Nick's bangs, pushing the wet curls off his forehead. Nick followed every movement as if from outside of himself. He was both sluggish and completely, utterly aware. The duality of it all was threatening to upend him. He welcomed it.

"So pretty. You've been sort of driving me mad for months now. *Months.* If you don't believe me, just ask Izzy."

"Izzy knows?"

"Mate, Izzy knows everything. Well, most things. Hell, she knew about you, didn't she?"

"Yeah." They reeked. Nick inhaled, reveled in it. Both of them had done this. Made this thing happen between them.

And Nick hadn't chickened out.

His reward was this. Dex, content beneath him. Dex, running a slow hand down Nick's back, soft and electrifying, and like it was something he did every day. Dex, welcoming Nick against him, showing him everything he was made of. So beautiful and open and—and wanting Nick.

Nick smiled and drifted off.

✛

He woke up to a dark room, huddled against the wall. Not where he'd fallen asleep. Startled, he sat up and nearly elbowed Dex, who was awake and lit up by the glowing screen of his phone.

"Hey," Dex said as soon as he saw Nick.

He lay back down, careful, unsure how much of Nick Dex wanted covering him. Dex switched off his phone, threw it aimlessly over the side of the bed, and turned over so they were facing each other. He reached for Nick and Nick reached for him, and then they were kissing.

Nick had beard burn. His chin pricked against Dex's, just the smallest bit of pain in all the pleasure, and his lips felt just a little sore. He was filthy, too, he could tell. A bit crusty, definitely sweaty.

He inhaled through the kiss.

So was Dex.

He smelled so good. No hint of anything but Dex—his skin, his sweat, his come, his breath. They kissed until Dex had Nick pinned beneath him, his cock hardening against the groove of Nick's hip, his hands tunneling through Nick's hair. Nick wrapped his leg around Dex. It felt like a place out of time, this silent darkness around them. Nick never wanted it to end. He ran his hands down Dex's back, learned every shift of muscle, every bump of his spine. Each movement turned him to liquid. He went lower until they were rocking against each other with Nick's fingers digging marks into Dex's ass. God, he was perfect. He *felt* perfect. *Everything* felt perfect.

They came one after the other, mouths open on silent gasps. Nick was pinned by Dex, and Dex was heavy. Solid.

This time, they managed to clean themselves up, Dex sacrificing his shirt to the cause. Dex climbed off the bed and padded to the bathroom. Nick wished the light were still on so he could watch him in motion. Dex didn't close the door, and Nick listened, half amused, half embarrassed, while Dex peed. That, too, felt intimate. Maybe a bit too intimate. Nick squirmed on the bed, pulled the sheet over himself, and waited.

When Dex climbed back into bed, they just lay there, staring at each other in the dark, tiny grins barely visible. This high up, the streetlights didn't really reach, so all the illumination seemed to come from the moving haze of London, like a shifting, glowing sky blanket stretching out from below.

"You couldn't sleep?" Nick whispered.

"I slept a bit. But then my phone went off. Forgot to set it to silent."

Nick wanted to ask if it was anything important but decided it was probably not for him to know.

"And couldn't really sleep after that."

"How come?"

"Thinking."

The dark really did give Nick courage. "About what?"

"You."

"What about me?"

A rustle as Dex reached out and tugged a stray curl away from Nick's forehead. The touch was light, but Nick shivered anyway. "Dunno, just—this."

"This?"

A silence. "Yeah. This. I guess I'm just…happy."

A flutter of wings in Nick's belly. He reached up and touched Dex's hand where it still rested against Nick's hair. He curled his fingers around it, tugged it until he could touch his lips to Dex's palm.

"And I was thinking about what you said earlier."

"Which part?"

"About how you felt like you weren't supposed to exist."

He still couldn't believe he'd blown up like that, but it had felt...good. Like a tiny door inside his chest opened and let some of the pressure out.

"And in a way, I know that feeling."

"Really?"

"Yeah. You never really see queer black kids portrayed much, either."

Nick thought about it. He wasn't sure what it was like in England. He only knew Michigan, really. America. "But...you're so." He didn't know how to end that thought. Confident. Yourself. All the time. "You seem so comfortable."

"I know. Wasn't always like that."

"I can't even imagine that."

"I hadn't really...thought about it for years."

Nick waited as Dex struggled to find words of his own.

"Man, I—maybe—fuck, sorry."

Nick's heart was beating fast, *thump-thump-thump*. In the meantime, Dex dropped Nick's hand and ran his fingers over his dreads. Nick thought he saw them trembling.

"Fuck, I'm tired," Dex whispered. "Okay, so...basically, my family are great, right? I love them. I knew I was gay really fucking early."

"When?" Nick whispered.

"Like...eight, maybe? Nine?"

Nick couldn't begin to imagine that. "How?"

Dex shrugged. "I just did. I can't really explain it. It was part of me. Just like anything else."

Nick couldn't say anything to that, so he just waited.

"And I was fucking scared. 'Cos I didn't know anyone else like that. Growing up, we lived in…well, definitely not where my parents live now. Birmingham was totally different, working-class and all that. There were black families around us, and brown families, and it wasn't easy, but it was, you know. Fine. Good. My parents had good jobs, we were totally fine. Al was just a baby, or toddler, I guess, and it was good."

"And then?"

"Dunno. I was a bit of a loner as a kid, to be honest. A real nerd." Even in the dark, Nick must have been easy to read, because Dex laughed and raised a palm. "Swear to God. Proper *Star Trek*–watching and science geek. Don't believe me, ask Alex, man."

"Did you guys know each other?"

"Nah, we met at uni, but he's seen it all by now. He's quite the nerd himself."

A part of Nick squirmed in not a bit of resentment. He hadn't known that. He didn't know so much about Dex. But, of course, that was how he operated. *Sit back and don't ask questions. Don't make yourself known.* He never learned to be an actual friend.

Dex laced their fingers together as he spoke, and Nick memorized every touch, took in every word. "Anyway, I just—I knew that gay kids got the crap beaten out of them, heard enough queer jokes to last me a fucking lifetime."

"Did anyone ever mess with you?"

"Yeah, a bit. Luckily, my growth spurt came early."

There were some days when Dex seemed invincible to him. He was probably just over six feet, but he felt like a mountain of intimidation to Nick's five eight. He always took up room as if it belonged to him. It was hard to imagine him ever being small.

"And then what?"

"Then I guess it wasn't a good idea to continue calling the big black kid a fucking queer if you didn't want consequences." Dex's voice was a harsh whisper. "Parents sent me to counseling once, though."

"What—why?"

"Well...I came out to them sort of...dramatically."

"How?"

"I came home one day with a gay porn magazine practically sticking out of my bag."

Nick let out a sound like a croak.

"I'd sort of been trying to figure out how to tell them. I mean, I was thirteen, so I felt, you know, like a man. Rawr, my balls have dropped, I'm wanking off left right and center, so I must be brave and all that rot. Can't live a lie, right?"

Nick swallowed.

"But I realized I couldn't actually say it to them in words. So much for being a man. So I let my mum take my homework out of my bag, and dad was there, too. So was Al, by the way—he got an eyeful that day. An earful, too."

"Were they mad?"

"Yeah, I mean—no. They weren't *happy*. They wished I'd used my words, instead, and had at least made sure Al hadn't been in the room." They were palm to palm. Dex drew his hand up, and Nick's followed like it was glued to it. "But in the end, they made their peace with it. Not the Al part, mind you. I got grounded for that stunt. But they pulled through."

"And the therapy?"

"To make sure I was doing all right. I was. I guess. All right. But—" He broke off, made a frustrated sound. "I'm sorry, it's stupid...here I've been all. I dunno. Ragging on Al and wailing on you, but I sort of...forgot, I guess."

"Forgot what?"

The air between them felt thick, charged. He didn't know that was possible when just talking, but...this felt like more than just talking.

"What it felt like to feel so alone. So different. Because my family's…we're different just in who we are, or, like. That's what white people think."

"How?" Nick suppressed the desire to squirm. Was he one of those white people?

It was impossible to tell what Dex was thinking. "Being black is different for everyone. But my dad's family has been here for centuries. Like, genuinely, he can trace them back to the seventeen hundreds, but…he still gets asked where he's from."

Nick's heart pounded in his chest. *Thump. Thump. Thump.* Dex was staring at the ceiling.

"Because people don't believe that we're British, you see. Fuck's sake, he's called Michael Cartwell, it's not like— anyway, a lot of the other families we knew growing up *were* immigrants. From Ghana, from Trinidad, Nigeria…all over. So I guess it's normal I got asked where my parents were from, but it fucking—I hated having to say it each time. *Brum.* Like, where the fuck do you think we're from, the same bloody place as you, innit?"

Thump-thump, thump-thump.

"Nobody thought we were supposed to exist, either. And they saw us, every day, but on telly and everything, you just kept seeing segments on fucking…immigration this and that, and so much of the time, it was mostly dark faces. I know it's all exploitative crap, but it sticks with you, doesn't it? My dad's a fucking accountant in a lucrative firm, my mum's a head nurse, but we're still seen as outsiders, I suppose. Because we don't fit into their little narrative of who we should be."

His voice had risen enough that Nick forced himself to stay still and not flinch, because raised voices always scared him, but Dex never had. Maybe at first. Now there was nothing separating them but air, and the only thing Nick flinched at was what Dex had unspooled before him. He thought back to when they first met. Had he been surprised that Dex was a biochem major? *Yes*, a tiny, vicious voice inside him said. *Yes. You were.*

He knew he had to say something, something to let Dex know that he was listening. Listening with his whole entire being. Nothing came to mind that sounded right, though. *I'm sorry* was pathetic, even he knew better than that. *You're so fucking brave* was even worse. *I wish I had your strength* was equally bad.

In the end, it was Dex who lifted his head off their shared pillow and asked, "You all right? Was that...was that too much?"

Nick screwed up his courage, tried to line up proper words. They refused to marshal themselves into obedience, so what came out was, "I didn't...I didn't know."

Which was the stupidest of all. Dex had said something to him once. He had pointed at himself and let Nick know he knew exactly what it was like to feel different. *Black.* But if difference curdled into fear and humiliation in Nick, it seemed to blossom into confidence and strength in Dex. Nick hadn't known because Dex had never shown it. But here he was, naked in Nick's bed, laying it out in stark works, and all Nick could think was, *How do you do it? I could never—will never—be as brave as you.*

Before Dex could say anything in response, Nick rose up on his elbow. He felt his entire body flush as he said, "I mean, I knew intellectually, obviously, but you're—you never—" He swallowed. "I guess you never show it."

Dex was quiet for some time. Nick became aware of the prickling of shame all down his spine. How quickly could he ruin a beautiful thing? Or for how much longer could he hide the truth of his own cowardice and cluelessness from Dex, and how had he even managed to do it for this long? In fact, how was Dex even here? Nick had had an emotional fucking breakdown and spilled beer down his own duvet, but Dex had held him, and had stayed, and called him pretty. Had kissed him. Was…was telling him things that felt so private, Nick could only hear them in the dark.

"I guess I was just always annoyed," Dex said. "Annoyed and a bit angry. I guess I translated that into not giving a fuck after a while."

"And do you?"

"I do. I give a lot of fucks," Dex said, a flash of white teeth in the dark. His fingers were threaded through Nick's curls, a heavy, comforting weight. "But I only give fucks I'm willing to give, if that makes sense. I know who I am, I've known it all my life, but…it took me a while to be all right with that, so I guess once I did, I managed." He ran his fingers down until they were warming the skin of Nick's nape and treading the dip of his spine. Nick shivered. "I liked how it felt to be me. So I made myself forget how it had been before."

Nick took that in. Could he possibly ever come close to feeling like that? He didn't think so. Nick wasn't Dex. Dex, who took all that life had thrown at him and made himself powerful with it. Nick had let his own troubles pelt him into cringing submission.

He didn't know what to say that wouldn't ruin the moment, so he took the cue from Dex and ran his own hands down Dex's body. He started with the spot over his heartbeat, his hand pale against the expanse of Dex's chest. Then he let his fingers wander over the dips and bumps of Dex's abs, not washboard but hinting at the strength beneath. Dex was rounded, beautiful, warm. When Nick's palm reached the fuzziness below his navel, Dex scooted closer, took in a hissing breath.

Nick felt the heat of Dex's touch progress all the way down to his ass and shuddered. With some force, he willed all his other thoughts away, filed them away for *after, after, after.* Please, let him think about it *after.*

"Yeah," Dex breathed against him. "Fuck talking." Dex grinned and closed the distance between them.

Izzy was rummaging around in the back of the fridge when her phone buzzed in her pocket. Thinking nothing of it, she nearly dropped it when Nat's name came up with "new iMessage" on the screen.

She couldn't remember when she'd swiped her phone open faster.

Hiya. So we should probs talk. Maybe drinks tonight?

Izzy blinked. Then, before she could second-guess herself, she typed out a swift reply.

Yes please. Arms?

The reply dots appeared almost immediately. Disappeared. Appeared again.

How about that bar with the ducks?

Sure. 8?

See u then

Well.

Izzy clutched her phone in her hand and felt her thoughts racing ahead to tonight. What did *we should probs talk* actually mean?

+

By the time eight o'clock came around, Izzy had wound herself up into a frenzy.

We should probs talk, she had decided, now translated to one of three things: *We need to stop being friends because…reasons, I'm sorry for being a stroppy cow will you forgive me*, or, well, Izzy couldn't actually think of a third. That was the one that worried her most, an unidentifiable mass of ectoplasm ready to suck up one of Izzy's most important friendships. If it was even still a friendship. Did it still count as a friendship if you hadn't actually properly spoken in nearly two months whilst still technically living together and hanging out with the same group of people?

A smaller part of her felt mean and petty and ready to lash out because it seemed like Natali was calling the shots. Hadn't Izzy meant to stop caring as much at some point?

She snorted. Good one.

Anyway, Nat had reached out earlier. It was clear she was, at least, trying. Right?

Izzy had pregamed a bit at home, sucking down a glass of wine like it was her job, so by the time she walked through the door—and she couldn't help thinking Nat had picked a neutral ground for some nefarious purpose—she was more or less a tremulous mass of nerves.

Nat was already there. She hadn't noticed Izzy yet, so Izzy took the moment to pause and look at her. She'd got a haircut, and Izzy hadn't even known. Her stomach did a thing. Nat had been using Izzy for her hair-cutting skills since they'd met, and she had gone somewhere else for this one.

Ectoplasm.

Izzy braced herself and walked forward, watching for the moment Nat would notice her.

She felt like she was approaching a tiger, with David Attenborough's voice narrating the moment. *Observe how narrowly she watches the predator, keenly aware that this peaceful moment could result in the bloody end of friendship should she make one wrong move.*

Nat saw her and made a gesture like she was about to stand up but then thought better of it. Her beer was halfway gone already. "Hey."

"Hi. Let me just grab a drink, all right?"

Nat nodded. For a moment, their gazes met. She forced herself to drop her stuff onto the bench before legging it to the bar.

Cider in hand, she made her way back. Nat allowed her to sit down and take a sip before opening her mouth and saying, "Look, I'm sorry."

Izzy nearly choked on her drink. "About…which part?"

Nat rolled her eyes. "For being, you know. Horrid about this stuff to you."

Izzy was rooted to her spot. She hadn't honestly been anticipating this option. She had wanted it, longed for it, but now that it was unfolding before her, she didn't know what to feel. It seemed somehow incomplete.

"Iz, say something."

This, too, felt off. Nat was nervous, Izzy realised. Bizarrely, it never once occurred to her as a possibility that Nat would ever be nervous talking to her.

"Sorry, I just—I'm not really sure what to say, I guess."

"I know. Look." God. Izzy'd missed her. She'd missed her even while she'd hated Nat for abandoning her when Izzy had fucking needed her so much. "I had reasons for being pissed off, but I realise that it wasn't enough to freeze you out, either. Or, maybe it was, but it was still a super shitty thing to do. To you."

Izzy gripped her pint of cider. She had no idea how to even feel, much less what to say. She concentrated on the way Nat's fringe fell over her eye and kept as still as possible. *Ears pricked for the slightest sense of danger*, Sir David supplied helpfully.

"Here's the thing, all right? I was pissed off because." A long pull of her drink. "You're so."

Izzy froze, still watching Nat, but Nat looked away the next moment. *What, what, what am I?*

"You swanned into the place and dropped a bomb on us, and like it was nothing to you. Like, a kiss had—"

"It wasn't just a kiss," she whispered. Had Nat fucked up their friendship because she thought Izzy was an actual fucking idiot? Or just an arsehole? She felt the need to defend herself bubbling up her insides.

"I know." Nat deflated, looking into the depths of her drink. "I know it wasn't. It was just—sudden. All right? You know what it was like for me to come out."

Izzy made herself nod. So Dex had been right, then. This wasn't about Izzy at all. She wasn't sure if that stung more or less.

"I was fucked up over it as a kid, you know? I'd even thought about." Nat stopped again.

Izzy knew this, too. How could she ever forget Nat telling her? Fourteen-year-old Natali had been so desperate, she'd reached for her mum's pills, and she hadn't gone through with it, but...yeah. Izzy knew.

"Anyway, I hated myself, all right? Just for being different, for being gay. And here you came in and were, like, oh, hey, turns out I like ladies, Kanye shrug."

"That isn't—" Izzy cut herself off. "Sorry. I know."

"No, you're right. It wasn't like that, but that's how it felt to me, and I was so bloody angry, Iz. I'm sorry. It wasn't your fault, it wasn't fair, but it was hard, all right?" The look she was giving Izzy was so fraught, Izzy felt like she was falling into it. Her head was spinning. "And I was angry for a while, but it wasn't all on you, and I know that. So. I'm sorry. And then I was embarrassed and didn't want to apologise because I'd been such an arsehole."

Izzy waited for more, but Nat seemed to be done. Or at least waiting for a response, which she now tried to marshal, though it felt like walking through water. Slow, and every movement an effort. "All right. Thank you. I do understand, I think. Or it makes sense."

"Look, that's not the only reason, though." *Oh.* "Like...yeah, being queer and experiments and—I know, I know, you aren't just experimenting, trust me, I've heard all about it from Alex and Dex and anyway, you could have realised you were queer even without the sex bit, so I know. I was an arse. But that isn't the only thing."

She lifted her eyes to Izzy.

Fuck. Door number three.

Nat looked paler, suddenly, maybe it was just her lips. Something about her went a bit grey, and Izzy had just enough time to panic, to imagine a thousand different horrific scenarios—she'd accidentally slept with Nat's ex, Nat had found out she was ill and dying, Nat was leaving London—when Natali said, "It isn't just that you'd discovered you were queer."

Izzy waited. She couldn't feel her feet.

"It's that you hadn't done it with me."

It was like tunnel vision, or a lurch forward, she wasn't sure. There was this one scene in *Fellowship* where Frodo felt the pull of the ring and the trees on his path suddenly looked like they'd shifted, only they had clearly stayed still. It was brilliant camera work, and Izzy had always shivered at that scene.

That was what this moment felt like.

It was a pull of unreality, a sickening feeling growing from the pit of her stomach and into her heart, up to her throat.

She opened her mouth, but nothing came out.

Nat, when Izzy refocused on her, looked miserable, but also defiant, maybe. She jutted out her chin. "I'm sorry, all right? It isn't your fault I've been in love with you since, like, forever. I just never thought it'd be an option."

"You—"

"You never saw me that way. It's fine, obviously. But, like. I feel like a complete arsehole right now, so you don't have to say anything, okay? I just wanted to come clean, I've been—I just wanted you to know. It's not you. Or, it *is* you, but not, like. Not like that. You did nothing wrong."

Izzy swallowed through the dryness in her throat and stared as Natali reached for her messenger bag. "Wha—wait, Nat—"

"I'm going to be a cowardly shit right now and scarper." Natali's voice seemed to be coming from somewhere far away. "But that doesn't mean I'm going to do what I've been doing. I miss you. I want us to be all right. So I'll see you at home later, all right? I just have to go right now."

Izzy somehow nodded through the din of her brain between her ears. All she could do was watch as Natali hesitated, stood up, gave Izzy a look she couldn't quite interpret in the moment, laid a hand on top of Izzy's, squeezed, and walked out of the bar.

Izzy sat in place, her cider forgotten.

She didn't move until her phone buzzed in her bag, making her jump.

Without looking, she reached for it and swiped it open. She forced herself to look down.

Im sorry. Xo

Author's Acknowledgments

This book could only have come into being with the help of the many incredible and generous people in my life. First and foremost, I want to thank my wife, Tracey, for her infinite patience, especially when, in the depths of grad school, I decided to write a book. I am so sorry. Her unceasing, unwavering support throughout this entire nutty process has kept me going. She is my treasure and my rock.

I want to thank Alexis Hall for believing in this book, for bearing with me as I dithered over this and that, and for giving me invaluable guidance. A special thanks, too, for showing me that Izzy needed her own place in the sun, allowing her to blossom.

Thank you to my wonderful agent, Courtney Miller-Callihan, for taking me on, and talking me down when it was desperately needed. You are a treasure.

My deepest thanks to James Loke Hale for their sensitivity read. Incisive, educational, and invaluable.

With my never-ending gratitude to Megan for the gorgeous artwork and being such a kick-ass person to work with all around.

Huge thanks to Mary Ann Rivers and Ruthie Knox for wanting this book, and believing in it, and all the guidance and wonderful support throughout. I am more grateful for getting this chance than I could ever express.

Special thanks to my friends and original readers who got this thing paragraph by rough paragraph, cheerleading me from word one: Katie, Sarah C., Nell, and Julia. You four made this happen, and I cannot tell you how much your faith and support has meant to me. Thank you to Bex, for believing in me, telling me to go for it, and being an utter inspiration.

Thank you also to Roan, Moog, Lal, and Kat, for your endless support, big hearts, and constant validation. Thank you to Judith, a terrifying and fearless woman, for being my strength and determination when I had none of my own.

Thank you to my amazing online writing group for being a constant source of support, love, and comfort. I don't think it is an exaggeration to say that I could not have done this without you.

Special thanks to my best friends (and additional Platonic wives) Sarah and Lea for being there for me this entire time while I have run around flailing. You guys are the best. Always.

Finally, a big, incredible thank you from the bottom of my heart to my whole family, who have been proud and supportive since the moment I finally fessed up that, oh yeah, I wrote a...book? And it's, uh...getting published? A special thanks to my older sister for, well, everything, really, but mostly for reading and believing in me.

There are countless other people who have supported me, either in person or online, and from the bottom of my heart, I say to all of you — спасибо!

About the Author

Liz Jacobs came over with her family from Russia at the age of eleven as a Jewish refugee. All in all, her life has gotten steadily better since that moment. They settled in an ultraliberal haven in the middle of New York State, which sort of helped her with the whole "grappling with her sexuality" business.

She has spent a lot of her time flitting from passion project to passion project, but writing remains her constant. She has flown planes, drawn, made jewelry, had an improbable Internet encounter before it was cool, and successfully wooed the love of her life in a military-style campaign. She has been nominated for the Pushcart Prize for her essay on her family's experience with immigration.

She currently lives with her wife in Massachusetts, splitting her time between her day job, writing, and watching a veritable boatload of British murder mysteries.